Literary
Outtakes

Literary Outtakes

EDITED BY
LARRY DARK

foreword by Harold Bloom

Fawcett Columbine ▪ New York

A Fawcett Columbine Book
Published by Ballantine Books

Library of Congress Catalog Card Number: 89-92582

ISBN: 0-449-90514-4

Cover art: A manuscript page from the notebook of Isaac Bashevis Singer.
Used by permission of the author.
Text designed by Ann Gold
Manufactured in the United States of America

First Edition: September 1990

10 9 8 7 6 5 4 3 2 1

Acknowledgments

In addition to the writers whose contributions have made this book possible, I would like to thank my parents, Bob and Elaine Charny, for their years of support; my wife, Ali, who encouraged this idea from the start; and my editor at Ballantine, Betsy Lerner, who recognized the potential for a book-length collection of outtakes.

Contents

Missing in Action (Chapters, Verses, and Scenes)

Odd Men Out (Uncollected Pieces)

Editors Will Be Editors

Double Takes (Alternate Versions, Titles, and Endings)

Foreword

I *had* thought of beginning this foreword with an illustrious apothegm of Paul Valery, to the effect that no literary work ever is finished, but merely abandoned. Then I thought of an even grander apothegm attributed by James Thurber to one of his aunts in Columbus, Ohio: "God made the morning to punish sinners," a perfect if unintentional crusher with which one could respond to Nietzsche's "Try to live as though it were morning." Mr. Dark's splendid and mad collection shows many of the best of our contemporary writers learning that Thurber's aunt rather than Nietzsche was the true sage of literary composition, if one interprets "the morning" as a trope for starting a poem, novel, or story.

Since Mr. Dark is a superb magpie of "taking out," or the art of ellipsis, his anthology prompts me to my own darkening mode of literary speculation, which centers upon the authentic sorrow of originality and origination, a grief that might be termed the anguish of contamination. For what is it that holds together the scattered *materia poetica* that Dark gleans? Journal entries, abandoned projects, starts that ended, cast-off chunks, lost scenes, uncollectible entities, editors' rejects, and spurned alternates: all together these are unachieved anxieties, abortions of influence, orphans of the agon for literary survival. However high-spirited they may be in stance or tone (and many of Dark's darklings manifest lunatic glee), these outtakes are casualties of what Blake would have called War in Heaven, the desperate battle for canonical continuity.

If literary value could be decided by the rabblement of lemmings who have taken over all academies in the Western world, then Mr. Dark's volume would be of little interest. The School of Resentment (*Feministas*, Lacanians, Foucault-inspired New Historicists, Deconstructionist clones, Marxists, purple-haired semioticians) is held together only by its furious resentment of literature itself, of imagination as value. Gender, race, social class have nothing to do with the reasons or causes for the outtakings that make up this book. Everything that is here would have gotten into or remained within a published work but for the writer's darkest drive, which is to join herself to the most inescapable of the mighty dead. The motive for metaphor, according to Nietzsche, was the desire to be different, the desire to be elsewhere: different from what one is, elsewhere from one's own place. That double difference takes one to what Yeats termed the place of the daemon, which I will translate, simply but accurately, as the state of the canonical. It is because the canonical is everything, and our current rabblement nothing, that Mr. Dark's writers labor so incessantly to winnow and exclude.

If I were to attempt to read through Mr. Dark's volume with the eyes of currently fashionable Resentment, then I would search for motives (societal, political, economic) scarcely to be found here, motives that exclude in the name of group interests. Reading as myself, I discover that some of what Mr. Dark found was taken out precisely because it manifested rather too much sincerity. All bad poetry is sincere, the sublime Oscar Wilde rightly assured us, thus reminding us again of the aesthetic necessity of telling lies. Aesthetic necessity is the hidden god of Dark's volume. But what is that necessity? We know that Shakespeare had *no* literary outtakes whatsoever; Ben Jonson complained bitterly that his friend and rival never had blotted a line. If you are not Shakespeare, then you scarcely can blot too many. Literary values, despite the Professors of Resentment, clearly do exist, and they are governed by the goddess *Ananke,* or the Necessity of origination. What is forgettable will be forgotten, even if endless legions of lemmings proclaim its ideological splendor. We have not canonized William Blake and William Wordsworth because they were male, and denied canonization to Felicia Hemans and Laetitia Landon because they were human females but because their collected poems all ought to have been outtakes. Many if not most of Mr. Dark's outtakes are of more literary interest and value than most of what is now acclaimed by the School of Resentment as politically correct writing, but that is as it should and must be.

Schopenhauer notoriously thought that the sexual drive stemmed from our illusory lust for immortality. Freud outrageously speculated that there was a death drive, and that it came from an organic longing to get back to the inorganic. Poets and storytellers always have mused that they wrote so as to outlast marble and the gilded monuments, sadly inorganic relics. Darkian outtakes ensue from the agonistic lust for overtaking, for getting the satisfactory answers to the three questions that define the Sublime: More? Equal to? Less than?

Canons are achieved anxieties for the very sound reason that great writing is an achieved anxiety. Politically correct writing is an incoherent proto-anxiety. What marks so many of the passages or fragments in this volume is the anxiety of what deserves to be called the third drive, as strong as love or death, the authentic literary drive, anxious to survive every mere fashion; every difference in gender, race, and class; every historicism, old or new. What is here was taken out because of the literary drive toward immortality, or the necessity of an aesthetic supremacy.

Shelley, like Longinus before him, believed that literary value depended upon both reader and writer renouncing easier pleasures for the sake of more difficult pleasures. That would appear to be the underlying pattern of Dark's gathering of outtakes; these writers were questing for what might be judged a poetics of pain. Shakespeare, Jonson averred, refused to revise, but we see now that each major Shakespearean drama revises everything that he had done before. Outtaking is the essence of revisionism. The self corrects the self either by rejecting part of the self, or by insisting that what has been written was a betrayal of the self. Either way, necessity governs.

Emerson, though to me a mortal god, chills me when, in his grim essay "Fate," he urges us to worship the Beautiful Necessity, urges us to build altars to her. Much of what is brought together in this book would be seen by Emerson as so many sacrifices upon that altar. After all, Mr. Dark's authors are nearly all Americans, which means that their authentic faith is in the American Religion, which has nothing to do with Judaism or Christianity. It is a religion that exalts solitude as the only freedom, and that finds in the inmost self a spark or breath that goes back before the Creation. Not all of Mr. Dark's authors admire Emerson (John Updike is an overt instance), but most of them are Emersonian anyway, in that their revisions are attempts to recover the Gnostic spark that became scattered in the Creation-Fall. What they have taken out are obstacles to the spark's survival, or else disguises that concealed what was best and oldest in their authorial selves, companions to the spark.

Literary outtakes remain inescapably *literary*; they testify to what never can be politically correct. Readers who come to this book will find in it a paradoxical affirmation. These outtakes, one way or another, seemed deviations from the quest for aesthetic vitality. But as deviations, they testify to the glory of that vitality.

HAROLD BLOOM

Introduction

This is not a necessary book. Nor is it a book for readers who would prefer to maintain the illusion of effortless creation that is fostered by reading only finished work. For some, the material that writers cut from their work, the ideas they don't pursue, the pieces they start without finishing, or finish without publishing, could easily remain in file cabinets or desk drawers, later to be thrown away or relegated to the back rooms of library collections. Although we are used to looking at the sketchbooks of painters and listening to the unfinished symphonies of great composers, it isn't often that we have a chance to see the stages written work passes through on its way to completion. For those of us who are curious to know more about the writing process, this collection provides an opportunity to see literary work in progress, examples of which should demonstrate that, inspiration and talent aside, most good literature is the product of hard work.

Because of the nature of this book, it shouldn't surprise anyone to find drafts and ideas that have been justifiably cut or abandoned, but readers may be surprised to find work so good that one can only admire the courage of the writer willing to abandon it. In part, the process of revision is about eliminating writing that isn't good, but it is also about cutting what is merely good and coming up with something better. It is an exercise of mature artistic judgment for a writer to realize that every thought is not golden, that every good sentence isn't carved in stone. Nor will every idea lead to the completion of a satisfying artistic work. The accomplished writer must be honest enough to discard clever lines and moving passages that notwithstanding impede the purpose, unity, or flow of the work as a whole, and those who make it their profession to write have to find the discipline and endurance not only to write regularly, but to put aside work that most people would be pleased to accomplish.

For the purposes of this book, an *outtake* is that which has been taken out of or excluded from the entire body of a writer's work. Given such a broad interpretation, the term is best defined through the concrete examples provided, several of which expand the concept in unexpected directions. Nicholson Baker's piece, for instance, consists of a page of "typos and failures of phrasing" generated in writing his novel *Room Temperature*. Thomas Lux contributes several pages of "semiautomatic writing" written "to get a pile of rough material from which [he] could glean lines." Edward Hoagland's "Roadless Regions: A Journal Sampler," collects ideas and observations that haven't yet found their way into an essay or novel. Sharon Sheehe Stark tells of the time that her obsession for revision cost her the publication of a story. W. D. Snodgrass recasts a poem to fit the tune of "The Stripper." And Robert Coover's piece consists of unattributed lines of dialogue cut from his novel *Gerald's Party* and sorted into alphabetical order.

Many contributors provide explanations as to how their work came to be an outtake. In some cases these explanations *are* the outtake, as in Amy Tan's account of how she arrived at the title *The Joy Luck Club* and how this choice shaped the novel. Other explanations identify some of the pitfalls into which a writer can easily fall. Toby Olson, in setting up his outtake from *Dorit in Lesbos*, tells how easy it is to get carried away by details. Jim Harrison relates the story of how a not-so-good idea temporarily took possession of his imagination under strange and trying circumstances. Allan Gurganus tells of the difficulties he encountered in trying to transform an anecdote into story form for use in *Oldest Living Confederate Widow Tells All.*

I have also included outtakes found in the posthumous collections of renowned authors who are the immediate predecessors (and in some cases contemporaries) of the writers contributing to this anthology. My reason for including work from Jane Bowles, E. E. Cummings, F. Scott Fitzgerald, Theodore Roethke, Delmore Schwartz, Anne Sexton, Dylan Thomas, and Thomas Wolfe is to show that though the term *outtakes* may be newly applied, note taking, revision, and self-editing have always been an integral part of the writer's craft.

The pieces in this book are sorted into eight categories that roughly represent the stages a written work goes through in its progression from initial inspiration to finished, published work. "Grist for the Mill" collects notes and journal entries used to generate new work. "The Best-Laid Plans" presents ideas never fully executed. "False Starts" includes the beginnings of unfinished pieces or abandoned starts to finished work. "Cast-Off Lines and Fragments" consists of deleted lines or passages. "Missing in Action" includes cut chapters, verses, and scenes. "Odd Men Out" are finished pieces that have never before been published or collected. "Editors Will Be Editors" consists of work changed or cut partly because of an editor's input. The last of the eight categories, "Double Takes," encompasses alternate versions, alternate titles, and alternate endings. Of course, every writer works differently. Some start with endings and end with beginnings. Others may begin with titles, lines, plots, or structures. Several outtakes could have been classified under more than one category. Still, it strikes me as useful to compare different writers' strategies at similar points in creation. And besides, a book must be put in order.

Though readers may be drawn to *Literary Outtakes* by the prospect of reading outtakes from the works of their favorite authors, I hope this collection will also lead readers to discover writers whose work they are not yet familiar with and, additionally, lead them back to original sources. The false starts to *Killshot*, contributed by Elmore Leonard, differ greatly from the opening he ultimately settled upon. Scott Sommer's original ending for his novel *Still Lives* is entirely different in consequence from the ending he chose to use. Meg Wolitzer's outtake from *This Is Your Life* represents an important character's perspective that was necessarily left out of the novel to preserve a consistent point of view. Though all of the pieces in this book can be read on their own, a deeper understanding of the decisions writers make in cutting or changing work can be gained by examining many of the outtakes in light of their original contexts.

One purpose of *Literary Outtakes* is to provide readers with new insights into the creative process, but I also see this collection as an opportunity for writers to present work that for one reason or another has fallen by the wayside and for which, in the words of poet Rachel Hadas, they retain a certain "residual fondness." No particular tricks of the trade are revealed along the way—this is not, after all, a how-to manual. Nor is it, appearances to the contrary, a how-*not*-to manual. What *Literary Outtakes* is, more than anything, is a glimpse into the writer's workshop, a chance to see concrete examples of the efforts that go into transforming thoughts into words on a page and words on a page into literature.

Grist for the Mill

(Journals and Notes)

Edward Hoagland

ROADLESS REGIONS: A JOURNAL SAMPLER

M.'s father liked to eat food companionably off other people's plates when suppering with his friends or family, and might exchange shoes with a man whose feet were about his size—in token of friendship would go home wearing his.

Moose tracks tilt in deep snow according to which direction the animal was headed in. You can measure with an ax handle which way the tilt lies.

Emil Gillels: the piano's notes like marbles spilling, and then he gathers them in.

What we possibly need is a new variety of the neutron bomb, designed to kill people and leave behind, not empty buildings, but the rest of Creation.

"That's the chair you were nursed in," my mother tells me one day, disconcertingly. Speaking of an old flame of hers, she pumps her dress over her heart with two fingers to show how it had throbbed.

Story about a man's tie to his first wife, who lives not far from his neighborhood and hangs a towel in her window for him to see as he drives by if all is not going well.

Indians of certain tribes wrestled for the available wives before going out for the winter on their separate traplines. Strength superseded wealth in these contests, but the winner was sometimes the smaller man, if he had shaved his head and greased his ears so his opponent had nothing to grab onto.

A story told from the viewpoint of a Galapagos tortoise being carried upside down on the deck of a sailing ship to be eaten later on, and lined in a row with others, equally unable to turn over.

A story about a man who hires a baby-sitter for himself. He is exhausted, drained out, simply wants to be sat with (not prostitution).

3

■

The Greeks pursued by the Persian general Tissaphernes sacrificed a bull, a wolf, a bear, and a ram in order to escape.

A wit who after each clever comment he makes wears the triumphant but tiptoe expression of a percussionist after clashing the cymbals.

By boiling caribou horns for two days and then skimming off the white stuff that congeals on top and salting it to taste, you can make "butter" in the far taiga.

A lynx I saw in late spring crossing the road was shedding its winter fur and so on its legs it appeared to be wearing galoshes.

I've noticed that the best dogs have a taste for vegetation, sampling it often, with much enjoyment, nibbling and chewing it, wagging their tails as if it were a tonic.

My apple trees are blossoming, a week after the chokecherries. Today I went up the east branch of the Nulhegan River to a roadless region. The trees creaked like a fox's bark. Saw coon tracks where there were frogs' jelly-and-eggs or tiny tadpoles in the puddles. Saw a merganser on the river, and a deer and a fisher, both nimbly quartering away from me. The fisher's back looped up into a high curve as it smelled my dog Bimbo's tracks. Saw a little bird picking the eyes out of a bird of the same species to recover its proteins.

Hiked today for five hours up the west branch of the Moose River to its head and watershed near what was once the Rhubarb Logging Camp, between East and Starr mountains. From there, one can go on over to Madison Brook and down that to Paul Stream and turn south along Granby Stream to Granby. Or from Madison Brook one can veer north to South America Pond and on to Notch Pond; then to the Nulhegan and up one of its branches; or, instead, climb West Pond Mountain and go down to Bloomfield. These are all trips I hope to carry out. Saw lady's slippers in the woods. Saw a porcupine sitting in a young poplar tree in an alder swamp, balancing itself with one hand while the other held a leaf to its mouth. Looked like a yellow-backed baboon.

Ephraim Webster, white prototype of Fenimore Cooper's Natty Bumpo, was a pioneer fur trader near what is Syracuse. Married two Indian girls, telling second he would stay married to her as long as she remained sober. But twenty years later a considerable white settle-ment had grown up and he wanted to marry into it and shed his old

Indian squaw. Tried repeatedly to make her drunk, but she avoided his ruses. Finally succumbed to whiskey concealed in milk, and left the next morning, and died brokenhearted.

Beware of a man who wears jockey shorts and uses shoe trees, M. was told, and agrees.

A cat's eyes are ten times as efficient as a man's at night, but a horned owl's are ten times more efficient than a cat's. Mice bound along awkwardly, too light for their legs, which makes them as jerky as butterflies and sometimes saves them.

"I hope it is said when I am dead His sins were scarlet but his books were read."

(Hilaire Belloc)

An Indian family in New England needed an estimated six thousand temperate acres to support itself.

"A plump wife and a big barn
Does no man any harm."

"Mackerel sky,
Not long dry."

"Beware of that man, be he friend or brother,
Whose hair is one color and his beard another."

Pat R.'s mafioso uncle is so generous that he refuses to have his hospitality declined. Pushed the face of a visiting little boy into a bowl of spaghetti the little boy didn't want to eat. The uncle has never been caught for the big things he did, and "doesn't have to carry a gun," only the smaller things, except that he has had to serve seven years for personally beating up cops.

Rifka is built big in the hips with a low center of gravity such that she bounces back from life's blows like one of those bowling-pin punching bags that can't be knocked down.

Went to the fights at the Garden with Vic Ziegel. Saw Walter Seeley outpoint a Korean who at 27 has won 74 fights, lost 25, and drawn 13. "He fought first with rattles," Vic says. Sat next to fighter who retired in 1952 after killing another middleweight (fought three more times to give the purses to the widow). Now is a sales manager for Rheingold. "Punch up!" he keeps yelling to Seeley, meaning a left hook to the belly, which happens to have been his own best punch ("like lifting a garage door," says Vic). But Seeley, as we later learn, broke his left hand in the second round. This man is also a movie adviser and his eyes and features were used as a model by Marlon Brando's makeup men for *On the Waterfront*. Tells stories of itinerant guy who fought Primo Carnera thirty times under nearly that many names around the country, and of "loan job" championships, held just for the interval between two fights. The Korean taps Seeley's back when they clinch, as the ref would do, but is waiting to sucker-punch him if he thinks it's the ref. Paddy Flood comes over to greet Vic, and meets the one man he ever lost to in his own career, who is heaving chicken crates now at Hunt's Point Market in the Bronx—but as the guy keeps saying, "I was too strong for you, right, Paddy? Just too strong." "A nut case," Paddy mutters to us. Another Paddy, under indictment for attempted murder of his landlord with a hammer, strolls up to talk about good old days in the ring with Bobo Olson or Paddy DeMarco, and the groupie girls at the training camps. Paid "nigger" sparring partners $10 a round and then tried to knock their blocks off. DeMarco was a "billygoat" because he butted. Our new Paddy got so angry he tried to hand him a box full of tin cans, as fitting for him to eat, and called him a "fucking guinea" (being Irish).

The Louvre is named for its site, which was originally a wolf breeding ground.

Dog trots along with a smile on his puss and his tongue dangling from the side of his mouth like a piece of red meat that he's grabbed.

Indian kids slid on sleds made from a buffalo's jaws tied to its rib cage.

I find in the woods at the edge of a field among broken car parts, in half of a broken wine bottle, a shrew's nest with many mouse skulls.

Story of a huge flock of ducks that settle on a cold lake, and the lake freezes over during the night, and in the morning the ducks fly away south carrying the whole lake with them.

December's is the Cold Moon, January's is the Wolf Moon, February's is the Hunger Moon. Squaw winter precedes Indian summer.

My sperm, when I was young and strong and masturbating, used to fly up and hit me in the chin. Maybe 30 million sperm cells manufactured a day.

W., the son of a Fifth Avenue dowager, a Yalie who helped my midwestern father successfully penetrate the thickets of New York social life as a young Wall Street lawyer, ended his life dying of gangrene on a Brooklyn side street due to having taken a leg injury to a chiropractor and otherwise not treated it, while buying gas station sites for a local distributor.

"You think when you're dying you'll at least have some original thoughts, but no, your thoughts just go round and round," Shoshana says.

Melville's pleasure at feeding pumpkins to his cow between stints at the "Whale book."

Two types of writers fall short: those who write well about unimportant things, and those who write badly about important things. Then there are the experimenters, who never get their bags unpacked, just try out techniques for when they'll begin.

At the dentist's, how like two monkeys we are: one with his mouth wide open, the other helpfully picking inside.

Archie the bartender moving his sister over in the bed they shared when they were little so it would seem *she* had wet the sheets. His father, to box with him, would put on one glove and smoke a cigar and say knock it out of my mouth.

Women are drawn to a writer for his intensity but will leave him for the same reason, said James T. Farrell.

The very new rich have two first names; the very old rich two last ones.

Two kinds of men: those who in adolescence were good with jalopies, and those who caught fish or turtles.

A nightmare: man stands in a corner vomiting, and when he is finished and turns around it is apparent that he has vomited his face off. It remains on the ground.

The human body uses about as much energy as a 100-watt bulb.

Grave marker on the frontier: a saucepan upright.

Frank Crowther died of pills last night with his plastic gloves on, hands folded on his chest, with notes left to be opened by his bar friends. His whole body was so inflamed with skin ailment that (a bachelor in his late forties) he could no longer take his clothes off in front of a woman, he claimed. On the wall were pictures of him with Cary Grant, the Kennedys, and so on. Always liked to say he moved in many circles, high and low (ours being the low).

■

In the cold north of Europe, life was thought to have originated from the divine cow Audunla's licking of frozen stones.

Saliva is alkali, stomach juice acid.

A hurricane may begin from the wingbeat of a single seagull, suggests Eric Kraus, a meteorologist.

Saw Robert Lowell in Central Park by the Mall looking very eager, alive, rhapsodic, his gangling body moving fast as he tried to see all of the bicycling kids at once—finally slouched on a bench to watch at his leisure. Six months before at same spot had looked muddled, sick, mumbly.

Teaching at Sarah Lawrence or any other women's college is more like being a eunuch than having a harem (as some people think) because no actual sex occurs. Rather, one is acclimating very young women for a future with other men, and you notice that although the female teachers remain as they were, the tenured male teachers become silken and lenient, soft and dreamy, "luxurious," limited.

Oct. 17, rabbit hounds around this notch all day long, and Paul Doyle's bear hounds too, till, about five o'clock, yet more yapping sounded from uphill. I was so riled by then I thought maybe this time I'll knock one of those hounding dogs over. But no, instead, it's thirty geese, up six hundred feet in a wavy checkmark, flying south.

Thoreau's wilderness: "A nature which I cannot put my foot through." Emerson: "We are like travelers using the cinders of a volcano to roast their eggs."

At my last sight of Peter Murray before his stabbing in the bar brawl he looked like Pinocchio in bad company, so innocent, undernourished and flushed, his nose sharp and stark under his guileless grin.

Bon Ton potato chip truck driver gets a blow job for $10 under my window (the price is scrawled on the wall). Tall black girl in green sweater and brown boots fluffs her thick hair as she waves him to curb, climbs partway in on the passenger side, lies on seat and pumps with her mouth for a minute or two, then quickly turns and spits out his jizzim. Gets out with his money in hand, scampering, prancing, very actressy, as if primed with dramatic images of herself—she's the action here on the waterfront—as she goes to hot-dog peddler with pushcart who keeps an open bottle of Coca-Cola for her to rinse her mouth with and hands her a piece of waxed paper to dry her lips on.

■

Molly writes ultimatums and pep talks to guinea pig and leaves them on the floor of its cage.

I see a horned owl's nest hole thirty feet up in a silver maple tree. The hole itself is owl-faced.

Mother Nature created gorillas and God made them into men, Molly says. God made the round world and Mother Nature created dinosaurs and the rest.

To draw bats you throw up a pebble and they swing towards that.

The combination of fife and drum was much more effective than either alone, and was bigger than both: the contrast conveying bravery vs. war, life vs. death.

On the Niger River, men call out from their canoes as they paddle along, and, hearing an echo, will throw a token of food overboard to the spirit there.

David Hippie's wife ate her own afterbirth after her baby was born.

Hot-natured Jersey cows eat best out-of-doors, whereas Holsteins, like the milk machines they have become, eat best standing in the barn.

Kissing my mistress, I missed my wife's scarred neck—not the actual scars of her operation, which I avoided, but the vulnerability they stood for, which touched me deeply. Smoothness seemed unsatisfying and callow.

Faulkner's Snopeses and Trollope's Slopeses.

Professional diver for Moran tugboat company stands duck-footed even without his flippers on and blinks a lot, as if punchy from the bends he has suffered, his big forehead furrowed like a pro wrestler's.

Hernia operation: "I did all the laundry but I don't have a will," I tell M. the night before. Afterward my penis turns black. And the added oddity of having a bottle of gin and a bottle of mustard hanging from two poles, linked to your veins. . . . "Better red than dead," says M. to her dermatologist as he scrapes a skin cancer off her face.

John Lennon after throwing off society's disciplines needed Yoko's.

The fine line for artists between incubation and procrastination. And there are mimickers versus explainers, actors versus intellects.

Writing in the present tense is like playing the harpsichord; no forte possible.

■

Peshka in her oxygen mask snorkeling toward death. Her lungs, when listened to through a stethoscope, sound like a day at the beach. "Am I dying? Maybe I'll make it? Maybe I'll pull through." Told not to talk, she says, "I think quite the opposite. I think I *should* talk." Dreams of drowning, or lying kidnapped with her mouth taped shut, because of the water in her lungs. Tormented by memories of World War I, when German soldiers stole her family's pots and pans to make munitions from and left a note saying "God will pay." Her job during their several flights was to "count the children." So she has awe of but no trust in God. Says, "God needs more staff." Recites a Lermontov poem, "The Runaway."

Calendars are printed now that don't even show when the moon is full.

Leonore's strangely self-indulgent yet generous gesture of clasping a lonely stranger's hand to her breast in an airport limousine, then waving good-bye to him forever.

My father guarded himself fervently against germs and chills but died prematurely of bowel cancer. Dick S.'s father guarded himself against bowel cancer by eating fruits and nuts but died by suicide, shooting himself after his car hit a rock while he was trying to drive it off the Palisades.

A mother in Little Italy puts the names of children who bother her kids in school in the freezer compartment of her refrigerator.

Nancy Miller keeps her third husband's ashes in a Cremora bottle. Dorothy Deane, dying, asked friends to put hers in their window boxes. "Café coronary" was the old name for choking on your food.

Pileated woodpeckers have survived better than ivory-billed woodpeckers; whistling swans better than trumpeters; sandhill cranes better than whooping cranes. In each case, the less complex, extravagant, exuberant birds.

Polygamous warblers have a short song, but in monogamous species the male's song is long because the monogamous female must pick a quality male who will aid her. Short song only helps a female locate a good territory where she will later fend for her young alone. Short song is thus a turf song mainly between males; long song is informative between male and a prospective female.

I see a mink crossing the road at inlet of Crystal Lake with a blackbird nestling in its teeth, a flock of redwings mobbing it, to which it is impervious. Indigo bunting eats a grasshopper, perched on a rock, with quite some difficulty with the legs. A bittern concealed behind two tussocks of grass spots a frog and twists its head back and forth, coordinating the aim of its side-looking eyes before stabbing its beak down. Grabs frog by one leg and lifts it with the frog's other leg kicking, carries it to a mud puddle beside the riverbank and spends two minutes choking it down, with many mouthfuls of water to ease the task. Similarly, a duck will swallow a mouse with a great deal of swizzling it in the water to grease the job, and snakes lather their prey with saliva to get the meal down, lacking teeth too.

In the evening my dog barks at fireflies; also at a skunk, which stamps its feet like a boxer feinting, preparing to spray. I see pine grosbeaks, with sweet william and rose mallow in bloom, and the mock-orange bush behind the tamaracks; raspberries a week away. Yellowthroats are nesting in the berry patch. M.'s father used to make his children smell his wrists when he came home to the apartment after working all day on skunk-fur coats. Joked of the sexual purposes these expensive coats were put to; but told her he wanted to see her getting behind the wheel of a Daimler herself some day, pulling on her "driving gloves."

The vireo and veery: high and low in a tree. Ants distribute a bloodroot's seeds. "Pale Dale," they call the local livestock dealer here, because of his slightly sinister air. "One of those sons."

Story about a heart attack victim coming home, having been told he must abstain from sex. But he must try for a child now, urgently, he feels.

The soft sigh with which a panful of steamer clams open their shells and surrender their souls.

"Life is a warning," says boxer Larry Holmes, when asked if Muhammed Ali's physical decline seems like a warning to him.

John Morley died on the Bataan Death March; Cousin Seymour Mintz won the Distinguished Flying Cross for climbing onto the wing of a Flying Fortress to extinguish a fire, on one of his 40 missions; then died of a heart attack at 35 with five children back in New Jersey. Both of them are unsettling presences in their families.

Grandfather Morley had been paid $5 to read "the whole New Testament, every word," my mother says, when he was a boy. Grandmother Morley hired a woman to wash my mother's hair once a week, it was so long.

■

A good literary memoirist was often a brown-noser in life, a dissembler and hypocrite, a moth-to-power type, to have gathered the material he sells. He hid his opinions and smiled like a villain, pretended a lot.

The primly ripe mouth of a skate.

"What will become of me?" she asks, between fits of coughing. "I'm off to see the Wizard!" Going to see the cancer doctor.

"The hawk almost got me," they say in the Arctic, after a close call.

Eating deer meat: the taste of beechnuts and crab apples. A fox's bark sounds like the snort of a deer. Hunter says feeding a dog a little gunpowder in his meat makes him tough and mean.

Yoga for some is primarily athletic, for some contemplative, for others therapeutic. But light takes only a second to bounce from the moon to here.

In the early '80s poor people ate dog food in New York City, and some jet-setters wore dog collars. Short story about a woman who comes to prefer talking into people's answering machines.

Magicians have categorized five basic types of illusion: Appearance, Disappearance, Levitation, Transformation, and the Divided Woman.

For one's sex life, mine was the ideal generation. We had its mysteries in the 1950s; then got in on the sexual revolution in the 1960s and 1970s, when there was hardly such a thing as age-appropriate behavior, it seemed, and everybody mixed it up; and finally by the mid-1980s "safe sex" became the rage, which was precisely the time when we began to need safe sex because of the advent of impotence, at least situationally.

Prusten (German) is the term for the fluffing sound that tigers produce to talk to each other and, as it used to be, to me.

Crocodiles yawn to cool themselves in hot weather, but coyotes yawn as an agonistic device. Mice yawn from sleepiness, as people do, but we also yawn from boredom, which is to say contempt—agonistic again.

Be true to the dreams of your youth, Melville said. And when I go to the Natural History Museum at Central Park I find that I have. So many of the dioramas in the African and North American halls that awed or delighted and overwhelmed me with yearnings when I came here as a ten-year-old boy depict splendid scenes where I've managed to get since then. From Bigfoot to leopards and elephants, from the Stikine River and Alaska's fjords to Kilimanjaro and Masai land, there are quite a good many majestic intimacies pictured here in this womb-of-the-world that I have shared or achieved.

Maxine Kumin

Notes from my journal, Kyoto, 1984, December

There are 172 members of the Emily Dickinson Society in Japan. Emily is revered by professors of literature; they see her poetry as a forgivably loose kind of haiku. Can an American writer bridge the cultural gap? Can a poet write haikus in English? Tankas? If so, why? These and other issues arise over dinner. I have a wonderful consecutive interpreter, he goes like the wind even though he has never interpreted for a poet before, scribbling notes in Japanese and English on a thick lined pad. I find I have to make notes, too, to remember what I want to say next, when I must pause frequently to let him deal with the material. Afterwards we are full of mutual congratulations. He confesses that he dreaded this assignment, afraid it would be technical, beyond his grasp, but now he says he feels a deep affection for poetry. The supreme compliment!

The temples are as orange as Howard Johnson's. The plastic mockups of meals outside the meanest restaurant are meant to leap the language barrier, but since the foods themselves are unfamiliar, the displays raise more questions than they answer. Can this be pickled sea-worm? How closely these things resemble testicles. The braided hanks are a vegetable. And so on.

It is only 5 days since our Japan Airlines plane blew a tire on takeoff from Bangkok, skidded to a halt on the far end of the runway, and caught fire. . . . I haven't been able to get rid of the sounds the little flight attendants made as they ran ululating up and down the cabin, in terror for their mortal souls. The smoke was not very thick but the danger of an explosion felt real enough; I remember turning to V. and saying, "I'm glad we're together. . . ." And I never want

mother language and its treasure of ~~its~~
idioms. Literature must deal with
the past, not become ~~an~~ an instrument
of pondering the future; its topics ~~are~~ the
individuals, not the masses; ~~believe in~~
~~God and His Providence is its very~~
~~essence~~ It is and will always remain
an art, ~~not~~ never a science. Moreover, belief
in God and His Providence is the very
essence of ~~literature~~ creative. It ~~assumes that~~ actually states
causality is only a ~~mark~~ mask on the face
of destiny. Man is constantly ~~watched~~ watched
by powers that know all his involvements
and complications. He has free choice
~~but he is also~~ being led by a mysterious hand.

    I am glad to ~~say~~ see that the ~~short~~
story is very much alive now. It still is
the greatest challenge to the ~~creative~~ to prose
writer. and its highest achievement is the
~~succeeds~~ in being imaginative and ~~brief and precise~~. Even Yiddish
~~I refuses to be~~ liquidated in the melting pot of
assimilation— an omen to me that this ~~will be the~~ lot ease
of all minorities, their language and culture. I.B.S

to go down a yellow escape chute again. After they finally got one open at our end of the plane, people were very orderly, not at all like sheep crowding to go into the dip they fear. By the time we got to the top of the slide, there were rescuers in huge white (asbestos?) space suits stationed at the bottom. They caught us as we flew down, stood us on our feet, and urged, "Run!" In English. I remember I was struck by that. If you don't get caught by people at the foot of the slide, chances are excellent that you will break both ankles. And then the dreamy sequence of a day spent at Rama Gardens, like an R & R center, sitting by the pool, cruising the splendid buffet, dozing in a suite of rooms, getting up the courage to reembark that same evening. I am cured of international travel.

Isaac Bashevis Singer

A page from the author's notebook

. . . mother language and its treasure of idioms. Literature must deal with the past, not become an instrument pondering of the future; its topic is the individual, not the masses; it is and will always remain an art, never a science. Moreover, belief in God and His Providence is the very essence of creative literature. It actually states that causality is only a mark on the face of destiny. Man is constantly watched by powers that know all his involvements and complications. He has free choice but he is also being led by a mysterious hand.

I am glad to see that the short story is very much alive now. It still is the greatest challenge to the prose writer and the highest achievement if he succeeds in being imaginative and brief. Even Yiddish refuses to be liquidated in the melting pot of assimilation— an omen to me that this will be the lot of all minorities, their language and culture.

Allan Gurganus

An Anecdote from Oldest Living Confederate Widow Tells All *(Alfred A. Knopf, 1989)*

I.

E. M. Forster shows the gap between an anecdote and a story by telling one of each.

Anecdote: "The King died and the Queen died."

Story: "The King died and the Queen died of grief."

Two added words. One of them the merest technocratic preposition. And yet those monosyllables provide motive, history, pathos, and the greatest of subjects: life and its limits, love and its limits. Two words, words that only connect.

"Anecdote" might seem the larval stage of "Story." But, in fact, certain anecdotes cannot be dressed up and taught the forks. With these, the annals of the outtake must abound.

I tried to build my novel, *Oldest Living Confederate Widow Tells All,* only of stories, pure protein, no filler, no cornstarch, no MSG anecdotage anywhere in the book. I figured if Forster could, with two words, transform journalistic fact into narrative motion, motive and emotion, why shouldn't my novel's every fillip and furbelow evoke a larger question, a set of complications worthy of its own short novel?

The work's 719 pages, its forty main characters, fountain forth with stories earned and invented and saved. "Myth," the work's epigraph runs, "is gossip grown old." Lucy Marsden, our hostess and widow in question, repeats with authority her husband's gory lore from the War Betwixt the States (though she herself was not born till 1885). Lucy has, over time and via time, become her missing loved ones' living archives. "Stories," she says, "only happen to people who can tell them." She clearly means herself. She never mentions Anecdote, a subspecies of epic narrative that Lucille fails to respect or even quite notice.

I worked hard at helping the following example pass from its own translucent fetal anecdotage toward some shaggy rangy independent Storyhood. There's a reason it refused: this recorded event is merely and literally true. For me, that constitutes a stubborn limitation. You find that Life has put a lien on certain material, however good. You know how some seashells look exquisite at the shore but fade to lumpen grayness even in the beachfront parking lot. And certain details—too local, too often retold—will just not budge beyond their native turf. The following anecdote, so vivid in my life, hated travel, would not—despite my coaxing, my compliments, my bullying—even pack an overnight bag, never really made it past the porch.

During the Spanish-American War, this incident befell a certain plucky young Private Thomas Alfred Morris, my maternal grandfather. Maybe I felt overattached to the literal truth. Maybe that impeded my noticing or inventing a further metaphoric life, a larger use. Something prevented the premise from evolving a luxuriant middle, then a startling if inevitable end. The literal episode had, during fond family retellings, grown so layered and rich. It concerned a tight-lipped fellow who rarely confessed his own mistakes, a man who—as a civilian husband decades later—never once saw fit to cook again. A yearning toward Mythic meaning is heard, I think, in Lucy's voice at the end of the short passage; this plainly mirrors my own attempt to push a real-life fragment toward some imaginative wholeness that it simply will not bear.

For me, autobiographical fiction often smacks of Forster's flat first example. In seeking to honor literal and gorgeous inherited details, I feel corseted and staid. It's more fun to begin with nothing, or a mood's coloration, some scrap garnered from dreams or skilled eavesdropping; it's more fun to furnish and construct an event from the ground up, chair by wallpaper by drawer pull by facial tic by sidestreet weather. Those writers whose every work of fiction is thinly veiled memoir have both my pity and my respect. For me, the great inward delight and outrushing adrenaline of writing still springs from free-fall invention—"if this is true then that might be, and if that is. . . ." We all know what total license still bobbles in the wake of that grandest phrase, "Once upon a time. . . ." My novel's heroine is Once Upon a Time's options and drawbacks embodied. She could, half-blind, ninety-nine years old, make partial sense of everything, she could make myth of most lived deeds—most all except my literal granddad's literal and endearing wartime mistake.

So, this good-enough passage never survived that crucial transubstantiation. It never "took," the way a transplanted heart must, to live anew in that superior body where two words, "of grief"—award humanity—even to a king and a queen, otherwise unknown and unloved.

Here then is a nugget that remains so literally true it never felt the need to leap beyond being a homebody Anecdote and on toward the motion of emotion, on toward that highly mortal immortality we call Story.

II.

Sometimes we'd get a stubborn batch of State University history majors visiting the house. They'd come to see my old man—the last vet to yet live or breathe on either side of that old moldy war. They wouldn't leave without my husband, bearded and in bed, telling them at least one. At least one war one.

"You ain't concentrating," I'd scold my Willie, sounding stern but just to get his attention, don't you know. "Think back. Maybe do 'The Soldier That Loved His Wife Too Much'? Or 'The Death of the Harpsichord.' Or 'When the Colors Switched.' What's shortest? Look, I know—do your 'Rice' one, darling. Listen up. These people ain't clearing out till you say something. Study my mouth, honey. 'Rice.' I say 'Rrrice.' " Well, he finally whispered the word. A dozen pencils scribbled that down. And for this, folks get Doctor Degrees!

Finally I spied some old mischief flare back of my man's cataracted eyeballs. Captain toyed with bedclothes, he stared at his own ruint hands, he acted shy as a child made to do elocution lessons for company come clear from New York City. Then, slow, out it came in dribs and drabs till it steadied into meaning something.

Was eighteen and sixty four, said he. Seems like the company cook was doling out corn-on-the-cob, saying, "One for you, and one for you, and one . . ." Cook was a large overaverage friendly fellow, he called the troops "my boys," he just loved to see them eat. This same cook falls backward. He looks embarrassed like somebody's complained about his grub, he still clutches the tongs.

—See, poor man'd been shot betwixt the eyes by a sniper and, still in his apron, laying there, mackerel-dead already. Others dodge to cover, quick. They lug that pot of corn—still scalding—to a nearby grove. Somebody brings the tongs. Though feeling sad, soldiers eventually chow down anyway. —People always do. The worse things get, the more your next meal means.

My Willie, a Reb private, he'd not yet gone fourteen. He was made the new chef. That boy knew nothing about cooking except the expert eating of it. Will was a sum total of cowlicks, sunburn, homesickness, excess wrists and ankles. Feeding one hundred men scared him. He recalled his mother's grand dinner parties prepared by expert house slaves who really suffered over company's coming, who endured his mother's fingerbowl fussiness. Young Will now stood off to one side, fretting.

A nice lieutenant stepped over and hinted as how rice might be a good start, plus real easy to do, rice. So, after the others marched out of camp, young Marsden found hisself a twenty-pound sack in the rations wagon. With all that dry rice, he filled a ten-gallon iron pot to its very lip. Willie Marsden then dumped in many a tin cup of water, he lit the fire under its tripod, said, "That's that" (or something like it—his exact words have been blotted out by time, and, frankly, worse things've happened, child). Willie wandered off to gather kindling.

When the boy dragged back, a big group stood being rowdy all round the fire. Wee Willie Marsden pressed forward, arms piled with wood. Supper won't seriously started yet but, off in the woods, he'd begun feeling like he might have some hidden cooking talent. (Imagine someday baking scones for Lee!) It sure hurt a boy's feelings to see other fellows bunch—cackling—at your first night's cookfire.

Great gobs and hunks and pounds of rice were pouring over flames. Behaving like lava nearabout, wet rice nuzzled close to men's boots, this whole tide of it now moved downhill, steaming, pushing along every twig and smallish rock. A tin ladle was borne along upon uncurling white goo. The pot and tripod were so sticky, they hid under the gunk like . . . well, maybe a snowman made of wallpaper paste or something, maybe. This part, I made up just now.

Men laughed, "Some cook, Marsden." Soldiers thanked the Almighty that their last dedicated chef hadn't lived to see this type of mess. At first, Marsden frowned and turned away, arms still heaped with sticks. Then somebody decent clapped him on the back, told my Willie to cheer up—he'd get it right someday.

"Well . . . ," the boy commenced shy grinning. "I didn't know. —How do you people always know stuff?"

One red-haired company clown ran around in front of the advancing mush. He laid down before it—pretending that his hands and feet were hogtied. Squirming like a virgin roped to train tracks, he squealed, "I'll do as you wish, sir. Just please, don't get any ON me!" Everybody considered this as funny as the world ever managed being. When some rice did smudge onto the funny man's hair, when he grew honestly peeved at this, then soldiers really slapped their knees. —All these months of being sure you'd die the next day, next minute—that strain switched so fast into laughing till you cried. Felt just excellent to.

Well, rice jokes became a type of fad. Caught on, they did. Some wag would say, "Just think, pals, the Chinese invented warfare's two wickedest weapons: gunpowder and rice." Then the yuks and hollering'd start.

A few campaigns later, some corporal was chef. But young Private Marsden, pinned down during heavy fire, might hear another Southerner call, "Quick, boy, Mr. Yankee's gaining on us—boil the secret weapon, fast. Rice for everybody. Wash them back to Maryland!" And—from all them holes and ruts where soldiers hid like security-minded rodents, much chuckling rocked toward the safe civilian sky. Over rifle reports, laughing'd lift. Cannon blasts made trees shiver sideways, whole meadows got Swiss-cheesed with craters, but one hundred men in mud stayed busy with low-grade giggles that lasted and lasted. Rice jokes made about as much sense as anything else out there—more.

After Surrender, rice never seemed as funny to my old man. He could only grin over how hard they'd all turned it into something extra, something else and something fine. "Strange," he told me back in the days when he could still remark a story, not just tell it, "That was the best twenty pounds our side ever spent. The goodness we wrung out of that one sack! Sometimes, mistakes are the finest things that'll ever happen to you—you know, Lucy?"

"I sure hope so," says I, casting a thought back over one shoulder at my life, so-called.

And so his tale is done. But students still stand around watching. I hold Cap's hand, I grab it a little harder. My man's glaze-fronted eyes are watering with joy recalled. "Just goes to show you," he says and then—shaking his whole head and whole beard side to side—you can see him slipping back into fog—his usual home and foxhole. I yet clutch his paw but can feel how even his grip . . . loses . . . its . . . way.

"That's all, folks," I tell young history-minded strangers back of me. One boy says he's still hoping to hear a Robert E. Lee one. Claims my husband told the best of his Lee ones to a group flown down from Harvard College not six months back. "The Captain here, he actually saw Lee, or so one hears," this lad thinks to inform me, wife of Mount Rushmore here.

"That's right, darling. —But six month is a while ago for a man my Captain's age and, believe me, he's not holding out on you a-purpose. Rice'll have to do for you today, thank you. This ain't a juke box we got going here. Thanks for coming." Grumbling, out they file, not sure what rice has to do with the winning of a war. Off they wander, mumblish, studying their notes.

"Just goes to show you," my husband had ended. But Captain never explained exactly what them rice jokes showed. —Maybe how what's funny gets people through? Maybe the merciful way what's pathetic sometimes strikes you as nearabout hilarious and saves the day? I don't know yet.

That part, child, I'm still working on.

III.

See? "The King died and the Queen died." So what?
Therefore, cut it.

Thomas Lux

Here some pages of semiautomatic writing I did during a stay at the Mac-Dowell Colony in the summer of 1977. By semiautomatic I mean I wrote the pages in a free-associative manner but wrote them relatively slowly, did some editing in my head. The point of most of it was to get a pile of rough material from which I could glean lines, images, word couplings, titles, notions, etc. Several of the fragments I have used in poems over the years, most in the late seventies, but I'm still picking at the bones of these pages. The little rhyming pieces here and there are exercises: quatrains, clerihews, cinquains, etc. None of these were ever printed or used. I did about eighty pages or so during a six-or-so-week stay. If I had to estimate I'd say about 5 percent of everything I wrote in these pages eventually found its way into poems, published and unpublished. This was a common way in which I worked for several years but the only time I gathered so much material over one brief period. I do very little of this kind of forced-march semiautomatic writing anymore.

JUNE 17, 5:30 P.M.

One bone in a skillet, the tombstones looking like,
from here, neat rows of dice
sitting happily on perfect moss
and the sleepers beneath
sigh with contempt . . .

∎

like a magnet picking up whiskers of iron
like a hardened glove her hands at serving tea
like the last time the moon shrugged
like a man in the forest with only his teeth and hunger
like the comb of the wind primping the common fir tree's hair
like raw milk—still warm—in zinc buckets
like the little blue calf in the furthest pasture
like the railsrolling over low hills: your secret animal stripes
like the lamplight: steady, low-wattage, constant and insipid
like the shocked lump of gold in the sluge-sifter's hand

∎

Beat the wings last night, the wings of *alcools*, —
tonight we're at it again: it and me: the fool. . . .

JUNE 19, 5:35 P.M.

The air crackling with idiocy, the youth lolling by the pond's
edge, farmers merely bored by drought, nearly the full pains
back already: the sleep uneasy, the little inside out shakies,
The swatch of sky—is it the same swatch always?—lunatic
with vast boredom, invented the various
birds as toys and if we hold one in our hand
we can hear its heart pumping: the flying-noise

So often did I drink
Amazing I can think
Still of her blue throat
The dream there, the hope.

∎

Old Ted Roethke
sure could turn 'em,—
the poems: hefty
or small, *learn 'em!*

∎

My Pal Franze Wright's
got this odd sight.
He sees moles, souls
on walls: fear's gnawed rolls . . .

■

he started shakin'/his big heart was breakin': example
of a contemporary lyric . . .

■

the simpering rollcall, tombstones flipping to attention,
a pool of hush . . .

JUNE 22, 4:05 P.M.

"Fraught with meaning."—The N.Y. Times
"Apt."—The Baltimore Sun
"In tune with the Cosmos."—The Phoenix Ledger

■

Strum, and horn, and some stylish *bings,* and we got the
     beginning
to the tune again . . .

■

So it didn't work: blah, blah,
He lost a princess
She lost a rajah—
More, or less and less . . .

■

THE WORLD'S TALLEST MAN
The world's tallest man
Had problems with his glands
and grew sensitive while growing
ceilingward. Lonely, he wrote
verses, and learned insurance:
money and poetry: his final furnace.

■

a pony only a pony because he didn't eat his oats
while still foal and wobbling
on each slim and absurdly beautiful leg . . .

■

The special nouns waving their arms wildly, standing on top of
     each
others heads, snapping their bandanas, saying: I'm *more*
than a person, place, or *fling*—I'm a breather,

or built by breathers, or infested by breathers,
or wrestled by breathers . . . Revolt of
the Nouns! The nouns who go beyond themselves
in the right combinations . . .

■

I'm worried about Mr. Wally Stevens—
I wonder if he's sleeping even—
He sang so incessant and so long
and the best of his are song, pure song.

■

The hymnal open on your lap, the beautiful heavy
but thin pages, gold edges, and bad rhymes by the bevy.

JUNE 24, 4:15 P.M.

Blood-easy, easing down a stairway one foot nosing
ahead of the other, slipping down
in the dark, into the dark
kitchen: there to look out across the frozen
stubble and the earth turned so many times it's nothing
but rubble, the uniform
dullness of moonlight, mountain, field,
apple boughs bent dumbly, a little dope walking out
in a gray sweater across the pastures—liking the hardness
of the earth after a few frosts
before the first snows . . .

■

Running off at the zipper, he professes to lapse,
the magenta as you lift your ankle from the strange waters,
the tent in which the deer hide their fawns
having forgone the natural camouflage provided: if it's dappled
and moves in the opposite direction
of the wind, shoot it.

■

A horse running alone: loping. With a human aboard: galloping.

■

Unperturbed, the napper ignored
his dreams which were half
going on, half going out. Bored,

the couch became a boat   [as if when the wind began the
drifting across the ocean   extra syllable climbed on its back]
of every livingroom in this laughter
known as our lives.

■

INSTRUCTIONS FOR HUNTING FAWN
If it's dappled
and moves opposite
the direction
of the breeze
shoot it.

■

A longing for those dirt roads long covered
A longing for a light that around us hovers

JUNE 26, 5:05 A.M.

There is only one rain that matters: the first one you experienced with
the associations of rain: gloom, sadness, the chill of watching it from
the inside of—not a house exactly, a barn—yourself. All the other
rainfalls, including the one while those who are still alive lower you
to its purest seeping-point, are redundant. Along with the farmers
whose celery depends on it, I call it down, down I desire it to fall, the
rain.

■

Charles Simic, *Charon's Cosmology*: the best book of poems I've read
in this year, 1977. Would that I had the brains to articulate its beauty!

the sentences within sentences, the burrowing getting deeper
and narrower until we are inside (this repeton?) a pinhead
of zeroing in so hard inside (so hard that in comparison
diamond is cream) so hard in its center
that what grows around it is soft
and deceiving . . .

■

Two humans, named Mom and Pop
coming for to visit Tom, a sot.

■

Where the snake has just passed over, where the earth still
bears a little of that mobile slime, where we can go on skating
as long as light consents, where the veils and screens and shields
are their own literal words only, where the dancing bears
rip off their skirts and head back to the Yukon, where the saints
of your ice stain their cassocks to a darker scarlet or
purple of the certain pains, where your sidewalk deceivingly
uphill moves, where your heart attack monitor blips and there
is one scar remaining in a hover above a flesh-colored landscape, and where the loutish run the show and derby, where
the intricate webs of lame loom most present, where the linen
says no don't sleep on me, where the bridge passed over
my students and teachers and I—held there, the million tons
of iron held there by the genius of physics, geometry and
so forth—saving our individual language—drunk, dizzy, and
fire-white (as the riveter lowers his goggles), going
to hell, of passing significance, lives.

∎

One leaf today and you can take away that forearm pressed to my
throat . . .

JUNE 29, 1:20 A.M.

Refuge extended to July 15. New goal of 75 pages of this. Seems to
get a little better. . . .

∎

Just because a poet can be articulate (about one of the abstracts—
love, for example) doesn't mean he knows anything.

Wanting to holler at nearly every poet I hear and say: you do not treat
language with enough humility nor with impudence enough. You do
not seem to love language, your subjects are snore-inducing, your
self-abuse without a glint of humor is tedious, your erudition is simply
an avoiding of the subject, you are the real enemy, etc. Besides that,
you're OK.

∎

I don't have to go looking for it, pain, it has a nose to sniff
me out, bloodhounds hounding after
blood, yowling all night
after someone running . . . Present tense-
ness, singular, masculine ending, iambs on wrong, the little

black wells of imagination just about
haulded dry so I lower myself in the bucket to the bottom,
pile mud in a handkerchief, squeeze and swallow
the drippings, and besides, it's cooler
down here, slime-favored, and the lovely disc of light
like a coin so far above . . .

■

Alone at a banquet celebrating your own joys—acting as
butler and cook, dour man in tuxedo pouring sherry, about
    twenty
assorted and fascinating personalities, etc.—the whole thing
alone: as host, guests, and personnel. And later on your left hand,
the perfect hostess, saying hopefully to the right hand, the butler
(as the last guest departs): O Jarvis, it was just wonderful wasn't
it? But can you imagine Mrs. B not eating her truffles after sniffing
them first! That's the last time I'll . . .

■

Say I'm a liar. Who should be more offended by that fact—others or
myself?

■

Because I won't talk to them they are hurt. Why? Why want even the
smallest part of me? I begin each night ignorant and by dawn the
improvement is so imperceptible one would need an atomic and
optimistic microscope to notice. I dumb I dunno.

JUNE 29, 6:00 P.M.

He puts on his writing suit: purple striped socks, robin's-egg blue
karate pants, red t-shirt with *Hart Crane* stenciled above the heart,
red baseball cap. The poet's clown outfit so's he doesn't lose his sense
of the absurd whilst trying to write about something serious.

■

Last night's dream: rewriting, and rewriting, and rewriting one line
of a poem and not being able to get it right. Took ½ of a yellow valium
to quell that bum REM-run. I mean who wants to dream what in
waking is a main reality?

■

Like those little carts on rails that miners would push deep into the
dark mountain, load up with the sore-got ore, and then push out
again . . .

If you think you're about to be happy
and are worried about it . . .

When you want to leave
the door locked from the outside

When at night the stones big enough to be boulders, yawn
disdainfully, helplessly

When the rain comes on finely
and the smallest shoots of grass
with their mouths open   [Their tongues out Their mouths
                                          open]
When he—his face
smeared with honey—
opened his mouth
as hive
■

A very long loose line at the end of which a delicious sword is dropped

JUNE 30, 3:40 A.M.

Michael R. Ryan
sits in the library tryin'
to get his mind on prosody.
That, and other oddities.   ["Dithyrambic Repetitions"]
■

Lame below, lame above, lame from the long walk away from
noon,
lame on the table lie the loafs of bread, lame the embrace
of light, lame the spavined horse, lame the room
and its lamps, lame the man beating his lonely spoon
on his knee, lame the least trace . . .
■

"The Dunce's Crown"—a sequence of 10 "sonnets"—11(?) lines
each, irregularly rhymed.   ["The Sun On the Other Side of
                                          the Planet"]
Out on the porch past noon a few hours
to him it's morning again although the dew
is long gone the leaves warm so, few
things just alert You could say⌃ runs his clock
backwards that he preferred the shock
of dark to that of light He was not of the lower

animals no it ~~was~~ ^{is} he did odd at night
all night trying to figure the joy
of alphabet ~~memory~~ and metaphor [Amphimacer cretics]
You should see him first in this light
A few hours past noon out on his porch

■

(fast example)

■

Sledding down the slag-heap
one child's dream
and the father every day heading
towards the center
of earth . . . the horses bored
out of their brains
and gnawing their stalls all
one blind and buried
winter . . . pounding their noses
blue against the ice
in the buckets, ignoring the blue
salt licks . . . fighting
the cold, everyone daily going at it
with the cold . . .

■

<u>When the various chips of blue float down</u>
<u>we know an angel is sculpting something</u>

Pamela White Hadas

From notebook for sonnet sequence "Preludes, Etudes, Fugues"

Nightmare: t.v. game show: I've been chosen
at random from a vast desiring sea
of faces keen to perform as I'm not; not I,
who came here only to watch, watch, not join in.
I'm too shy not to comply. But why choose me?
As photogenic foil? for my dumb grin

to pose beside the one they've coached to win?
.........jeopardy.

But first, things first, the prize spills from behind
its curtain: a holiday in Paradise. . . .
Now, even if I had the knack, I would not choose
to answer for this temporary chance
(not one in Hell) of a lifetime
not meant for me alone.

■

Touched by estrangement, framework,
do not disdain the all embracing fragile
chaos, nature's, the *Ding an sich* that makes
King Lear disrobe, play brutal's opposite . . .

an affected act? or affection's—the crazy state
of being more acted upon than acting? or maybe
both acts interfused, as only theater
and so-called self would be?

the freedoms of compulsion do come to bear
their infant seed, the voice unvoiced in the rose,
intrinsic need, as a butterfly goes
to flower, a condescending grace;
silence, a naked noise:
the golds fools grieve for.

■

. . . a mood of no intention, stagnant basin,
stone and shallow, a dish a bird might visit
momentarily, to dip her wing in a residue of rain
or stopped jet, splinter the stillness, use it . . .

how long has the water pooled there, how clear is it,
or unclear, gummed with algae, bugs, debris—
who will scrub this empty—hand or sun? or fill it
once again, more clearly? will this be done?

■

with a buzz and a lisp the world is made quite visibly alive, a humming mud and disappearing flecks
that count to be *exactly* that identity or this
enigma, this weight of gold, that sex,
this added triangle to that precise
and boiling degree of chance
where you pick up sticks
to prophesize
all over
0

■

the *moi* of a threadworm, *toi* of a lark,
spirit's radon, a vaporous ideal,
the mute cacophony of ultrasonic
leaves in a sulk, in a nutshell.

consider the luminous agitated habits
the sky trails from breach to breach as gossip orbits
from mouth to mouth, dribbling the same old plots—
the geometrical bulges of uncertainty
predictably doing just any old number— just one more time,
this rhythm of a mind—   beyond the mind.

■

MEMORY (SONNET?)

fug,
        swat,
                blur,
                        puff,
an artifact,
a sack,
        mud,
                mute,
                        a gift
of elephant
                not quite
in fact
                but thought
                        a certain drift . . .

Dylan Thomas

From The Notebooks of Dylan Thomas *(New Directions, 1967)*

XXIV

if the lady from the casino
will stop the flacillating roof
de paris and many women from my thinking
over the running bannisters
who can tell I may be strong enough
to push the floor away with a great gesture
but for the navels and the chandelebra
mending my coloned head in hands
And are you parallel in thinking good with me
Of us beneath the shepherd's crook
Driving the wolves away
And walking the metallic fields
An inch's time away with every step
Who has no hope
I know him for he lives in me
lady gap
they're there I see them
on railings and on pots of ferns
seeking a sex in me
beneath the nose . . . .
Iif its no beginning in our love
wise woman true for heat
it's no end to us
or even interlude between the abstract
and the side or shell
hindering my knuckles or my knife
our modern formula
of death to sense and dissolution
where there is love there's agony
Ttheres sex where our mad hands rest
. . . .
Of ever watching your light
Come to a point with mine

Your pity left me high and dry
For appetites aren't fed with
can they for ever
stop their navels with their finger tops
or
. . . . . Bbranch off straight to nonsense narrow . . . . .
Hope ah I know it
one naked hand upon the bracket
out of the pages
would I blind in puberty the phrases
grow and here's a castle
Hope I knew him out of Reason
Faith messiah for what death
though they do not speak like that in France;
But while I'm deft and aphrodisiac
To her who her the nought for my loud nerves
Not to the incubator or the brain
A mass of words above the window
Chiming for room
One brings you allonal
Which bells grotesque parade
Of leg on breast
And vomit on a shining cheek
Of masks *two* can't take off
But in its true light devil naturally
And let there be an end to
evil
I have an explanation
And what is more an egg
So with my mind's catastrophe
And white and yellow anna
Three has no message in his sin
And *four* a skull for tympani
Choked up with wit
The *rest* shall wait for not engendering
And I along the skin
Think of my passionate alloy
I cool who's chastity
now nothing yes loud purity
With
bawdy
Eyes and with the nerves' unrest

shatter the french
to let the Old Seduced crowd on
over the hurdle of the belly de
through mercy to paris
I'll in a moment but my version's sane
space is too small
hover along the saxophone
and tread the mandoline a navel's length
the women on the ground are dead
who her dont care for clothes
and I no longer itch at every trouble
16th June. '31

David Ignatow

Like Wallace Stevens, I was raised to become a businessman, a partner in my father's bindery business, but which I abandoned after his death. In the pages I have enclosed I neglect to write of my father's influence in forging my business life and thought, material that I go into in depth in several of my essays, published among my three volumes of prose.

POET IN BUSINESS

This is not meant as a reflection upon the validity of such a course. The situation I am interested in is that of the poet who has inevitably to choose to stay outside and, what is more, enter in an executive capacity that kind of business which is universally execrated. To be sure, such a step could not have been taken without the background to account for it. One does not willfully break with a long, respected tradition. However, that too need not be gone into as the interest at this moment is in the kind of life and thought and writing such a poet adjusts himself to under the circumstance.

Now business, as we understand it in its plain meaning of profit making, of necessity has certain stresses and strains. We say that of all occupations and careers, but in the case of business there are special tensions, which do not show up elsewhere. For one, an executive understands he must use people, not for their own selves but as a means of production and profit. Other businesses may have ameliorations and modifications of that principle, such as is found in charitable institutions, the employment of nurses and social service workers, the entertainment field. Here, above all, people are used with themselves as the value. Here people are compensated above and beyond their immediate use value. They have contributed to socially useful or culturally useful activity. This again emphasizes the isolated and yet universal problem of business in which people employed are not strictly valuable in themselves or give value of themselves.

With this being the condition in which the vast majority of people live, there would seem to be no cause for uneasiness or guilt in an executive working among them. There is none, to be frank about it, the situation being such that these so employed accept and tolerate and even encourage it for private ends that they have been able to establish for themselves.

A poet entering this world takes with him another tradition. To begin with, he has been led, through instruction and a reading of the classics, to associate people with ideals and/or souls valuable in themselves and for themselves. People are to be judged and used primarily as souls or personifications of an ideal. How they deviate from either norm is the measure of their guilt or sin in the eye of their maker. Also, individuals are not to judge or use or abuse one another simply as individuals but with the proper qualification as instruments of good or evil, wherein judgment is in the hands of an almighty, either through the working of character or circumstance, if not through an assumed God.

Of necessity then, a poet thinking along these lines lives in this manner and must write that way. The first task, then, for one who has become an executive is to discard these ideas or at the very least so modify them as to give them relevancy as of the circumstance in which the poet finds himself as an executive, which is to say very little. The question then arises as to what kind of poetry does the poet write? How does it differ from the work, say, of an Auden or a Spender to whom business for profit is a foreign, hostile, divisive element? Such a question can only be answered by entering into the actual nature of business itself: how it is run; who benefits from it, and why.

A moment ago I mentioned the encouragement that workers give their employers to expand and build by the enthusiasm and energy they contribute in aid to him. How has this come about? Why does it establish a new viewpoint of a business for profit? Now every business, regardless of its plan or motive, inevitably belongs in an overall pattern of the economy itself. Whether the business so acts or

not, it must contribute some element of value to the structure of the
economy as a whole. This is the law of society. It may once have been
otherwise, when taxes were not universally mandatory, or when individuals employed in private businesses had no opportunity by
union or other means to protect themselves or to gain the extra
money they needed for their own comfort. All this has changed, even
for the strictest kind of business. People now contribute in one way
or another to the overall prosperity of their group or community.

Let us, for example, take the steel industry. Since the years that
have gone, a change has come about in the direction and tendency
of the industry that would make its founders not believe it the same
industry that they had built. It now has pension plans for its workers
and a kind of profit sharing and a cost-of-living index system agreed
upon between the union and steel executives. We may go directly to
the source of all modern capital, the banks. There too the situation
has developed along similar lines. And so this is conclusive proof that
profit in itself no longer has the frightening aspect it originally had.

And so, what is the position of an executive in such a development? He no longer is bound by his conscience in his manner of
dealing with people, knowing as he does that he has no sharp curbs
upon him. As management, he will but do the work called upon by
his side of the game and let the rules be called by the empire. Under
certain circumstances, he will recognize what is fair play and abide by
it, but he will know, nevertheless, that he has nothing to fear in the
way of opprobrium for being in the position of a profit maker in the
sweat of his workers' brows. In one way or another, they will have
managed to balance his effort for the company, and they will have
taken it into consideration as one way of achieving the end toward
which all now strive, an accumulation of capital and its good, worker
and employer alike. And so the poet finds himself in a society that
has a certain self-exploitive character and yet partakes of a sense of
unity of the whole. He no longer has the divided elements of soul and
matter to struggle with: spiritual values and bodily needs. All have
been conjoined by the majority.

If he would write and live in his society, he must go with it on
its own bases. As an executive, he has squared his conscience with
what he had read and learned in school. He has to break with a style
of writing that now is completely foreign for his purposes. He has
become a servant among servants, with no serious distinction to be
made between his function as executive and that of the worker he
manages from his office. His writing takes on this indefinable character and he has a new problem facing him as poet. Can he write so

as to distinguish himself from those over whom he presides? Can he act as an individual of exclusive judgment and value, that which should reflect itself in his poetry? He is faced with the excruciating problem of finding himself in the welter of sameness of which his society is composed.

Cleopatra Mathis

This bit of prose originally was meant to be a poem, as entries in my journal often evolve into poems or parts of poems. Written just after waking in that early-morning emptiness which lends itself so well to writing, it eventually did lead to several poems, but the experience recorded here seemed always to resist my efforts to transform it into "poetry." I thought finally that I could make a prose poem out of it, much as a parent "decides" what's best for a child, but in these two months of struggling with it, I began to see it almost as a battle of wills. I began to understand that the voices I heard were enough, that they were trying to speak, and it was my job this time as the writer to listen.

WAKING: NOVEMBER 18, 1985

I

Deep in sleep, I drink the real water. I fall to taste its abiding cold, clean and clear after the ambiguity of dreams. Sleep water is old water, childhood's cup, last call for Mama. To keep us safe, the town puts in chlorine; not enough to mask the iron, its journey out of the ground. Smell the copper residue of the pipes, the hint of manure stacked by farmers and washed away in the spring floods, filtered between swamps. . . . But when I wake, tasting, it's Provincetown, and I lie here freezing, the cold pulsing inside me, ice in my veins, and around me the flannel sheet, the down and wool are nothing in fighting it. The comforter's lightness stands away from me, puffed out like an aura, a halo for my cold. Every avenue in my body slows, buzzing with chill, bee-like in the vibrating cells of my center, the negative of warmth and light. This day of my brother's death hovers over me, repeating the little it knows. A day like any other: my mother was sorting pecans, she saw my brother leave without his wallet, without his gun. He said, I'm going out. Be right back. Somebody's pickup met him on the road; the afternoon turned to rain and night. Now he comes back over and over with all the weight of the unburied. He comes like one more ritual. In Louisiana we gather the last roses for the church vestry as late as December, save their petals for pot-pourri scarcely six weeks before the first spring planting. I'll be right back, says the one long season, each month ordinary in its need: fish for luck, bird for beauty, talismans of cloth and hair to keep us stocked with deer. It's November, after all, month of my mother's birth and her deepest grief. Month of the dead and missing, when things most loved disappear, though we've been warned, haven't we? The magic show of leaves ends in days of turning and flying. The great shimmering ground goes flat and silent, while down there, deep in woods, the only charm of a Southern fall has lost its glory: the persimmon tree's gold fruit and leaves gone without a trace. This month, the swamp gives up its green activity to the undivided scum. Some tiny part of it lies over him. We need an ordinary funeral, that's what she says, boiling the water, studying the tea leaves and eggshells. We believe in signs. How much water standing in the yard will tell the month; the same with bird chatter all night, particular as the rotation of stars, or waking to rooms still full of heat and the smell of fried meat. Now I'm waking to another realm, to the salt cold of this house buffeted by the sea's wind and the harbor's lunatic bell. At least once in my sleep, the water laps at the pilings under me, and I marvel at the faith of whoever builds a house with the ocean moving beneath it. Shivering through the sea-lit rooms, I run a bath—where else to go in this cold when my brother goes on dying. Here are the essential oils, musk and rose, to take away the sour of my skin, salts to purify the old names and voices. I lower myself through the steam, savoring the moment my body sinks, the shudder like a bad spirit escaping. I'm hoping for a baptism when I rise, the lines of my body seamless as my mother's faith. I'm hoping to come back and bring him with me—north toward reason, toward the rational winter spring summer fall that govern life here. Then I hear him laugh at that, the way he said, *why leave: you can't leave this.* As simple as those words, I'm talking to him again, justifying, coaxing, as I dress and go about the small automatic chores. Our arguments go back and forth, matter of fact, the way they always have, though now this is the world that claims me. His being shines in my daughter's; one particular smile and a certain way she can push away my hand say everything I need to know about the spirit. It's the physics of this world that matters: the

layout of this room facing the sea, the litter of my girl's toys and
drawings, figures coming to life in the pre-light. If night is one dense
blanket of illusion and fear, images of a lifetime moving, settling, then
daylight means *now*, the endless catalog of details claiming their
places. I make a cup of coffee, lay bread and cheese on the table.
Interested, the black cat springs, proof in the claw on my arm. And
outside, the permanent ocean, contained by its charts and course, the
tides. In the dark it moves toward other meaning: a piece of silk
rippling, a flash of mercury tearing the fabric. Each reality lends itself
to something other, like the flip side of dreams he pulls me back to.
I work best in clear light, anchored by an ever-present set of needs
I use to drift off into work. My friend the sculptor makes little white
boats, ordinary arcs, and white fish to live in plain plaster houses.
She's left one here on my desk and the famous light plays on it,
trickery of white teasing the door, the boat within. What, I wonder,
is it holding? But I'm too restless: my eye moves away, would rather
change the ducks to seals far out in the bay. Jimmy, I say, look at that,
as if this were the exotic life, not our childhood. The truth is, I'm
formed and informed by the ordinary. I drink a few beers, run for my
heart, and three times a week do aerobic dance in a room whose light
comes purely from the open sea just a few feet away. The music's wild
with the exhilaration of bodies. I get it up for aerobics, one hot-pink
T-shirt claims. The women are lovely, so much variety in hair and
shape. And the one man—blond, muscular and proud to do the
hardest steps, his hard ass in tights. This *is* Provincetown, you know.
But Jimmy, you would like Marianne, the thin one who leads us, goads
us; her insistence on balance and breath. Her skin's like buttermilk,
you'd say, your eye on the shallow basket of her ribs. Old hunter, you
always pay attention to bones, to the spaces that allow the bullet's
cleanest entry. I've got your old buckskin jacket, and it fits; this town
is full of leather. The news is full of AIDS, of summits and anticipated
warfare, our latest trespass in Central America, the immense physical-
ity of survival. My hairdresser, Paul, won't last much longer. He's a
big man with your coloring and size, though the disease is eating that
away. Five years now, I've loved him for being a little like you; he's
loved me for my hair, his hands filled with the length and weight of
it—oh his passion for it all: not just snow and blackout in this tiny
town, but ocean on ocean he wanted to travel, and with him half a
world away under blooming cherry trees, the Japanese man. In the
picture both of them are smiling with the strain of sheer hope. Now
Paul's home, but no longer in his shop. He can't bear the hours on
his feet; the pain cuts him across the back. I think about the particular

tilt of his head as he worked, his fingers lifting my chin just so. Our intimacy lay in the washing and cutting of my hair; odd how one body touching another, even in service, is enough permission. He had a way of cradling the back of my head with one palm as he turned my face to his. He had a way of speaking. Tell me, what is sweeter than human need? So when the raunchiest gay outside at two A.M. screams *I want you,* jerking me out of sleep, I know the message is for me. And from far off you speak as I've learned to hear you, your quiet voice keeping me safe, answering me from the other side of this life.

James Tate

What follows are excerpts from a diary I kept in Spain during the years 1976–77, to which I gave the name "The Sun's Pets." I was working on a book of poems, Riven Doggeries, *and did not know what purpose this diary or journal might serve. I just wrote in it instinctively, or compulsively, without particular literary intent. I knew that if it was to be of any value at all it would have to survive the passage of some time, at least ten years. Well, twelve years or more have passed since I made these hasty and reckless entries. I suppose they are "outtakes" in the sense that they formed the context out of which a few good poems came into being. In selecting these passages I strove to follow a few loose threads, cast of characters, namely those related in some way to Federico García Lorca.*

CHRISTMAS, 1976

We had expected Maria and Carlos to come by last night but then they never showed. Instead they came by this afternoon, around two, and we were glad to see them. Lisa had dinner started. She hadn't met Carlos yet. We all got on wonderfully, laughed. Lisa served glugg. Then Carlos and I had one scotch. We asked them to stay for dinner, and they were surprised and pleased. Maria went to their apartment and brought back two bottles of champagne.

The turkey was perfect, sweet potatoes, lingonberries, mashed potatoes, dressing, gravy, 2 bottles of wine, then champagne, and really uncontrollable laughter at the mad stories Carlos was telling of Spanish bureaucracy. He is being pressured to accept the chairmanship of the Department of Physics at Barcelona University. Sounds awful, can't imagine how he would survive it.

We talk also of Teresa's strange linked fate with Pedro Salinas's daughter, both of their husbands in the Spanish History Department at Harvard, lifelong competition with each other. Jorge Guillén now reaping such distinguished acclaim, financial success as well, while Salinas's daughter has been tormented all her life, her husband in a mental institution for years, she herself suffering nervous breakdowns. Also spoke of the Lorcas at length, Francisco's relation with Federico, Federico's death, the war, his sister's mysterious death also in Granada in 1952 just returning for the first time in 14 years to the home she fled after her father and brother had been executed there, her car wreck, nobody else hurt but her neck snapped from the collision on just entering Granada.

But the other hilarious stories, too difficult to capture here now. Then they left at a timely 7:00; Carlos by then slightly loaded I think, at least his stories were now becoming impossible to follow, such as the one that started off with the conversation about the rarity of his name, Angula: "There was a Mandarin in China had a wig under his armpit . . .," and he never got past that, what it had to do with Angula.

Lisa and I sat around the fire together after they left, thinking of the two of them. Carlos is a restless man, erratic, demanding, domineering, without any plan. Plenty of intelligence, but no idea what he will do. Maria moved us both by her situation, no children, this crazy house business about which Carlos hardly seems to care and which is taking up her entire year. She seems fragile, not grown-up in some way, and now, in the present, looking slightly resigned or defeated.

Paca showed up unexpectedly as we were relaxing and talking. She brought sweet potatoes. Lisa served her Spanish candies and ginger cake. Paca talked on at length, telling Lisa about the cakes she would make and bring to her. Then Lisa told her about her gifts, and our turkey, and cards and lottery and Paca as usual takes everything in, calculating costs and figures and conclusions about our financial state as we talk. She doesn't miss anything. Lisa offered her some turkey and Paca watched closely exactly how much Lisa was cutting; when she had what was needed she told Lisa. Then she gave Lisa two kisses and shook my hand.

JANUARY 14

Francisco Giner de Los Rios came by this afternoon and invited us over for dinner this evening. He is the "Lorca" that we had met at Paul and Hannah's the day after New Year's. Now we are happy to go.

The next-door cat is in heat and there are a total of six cats consequently howling and fighting and screwing day and night in our garden and on our patio. It has been going on for more than ten days and I have begun to throw rocks at them when they are howling at their worst; it threatens to become an obsession this afternoon; my ears have had enough of their caterwauling. I hide behind the steel beams, jump out, and chase the horny devils.

The evening was fun. Ajo and Karen from the beach restaurant were there, and then Maria arrived a little later. Francisco was a good bartender and we were all talking, a good fire in the fireplace. Maria Teresa showed us a drawing Federico had made for her in 1934—I must confess I was still in the dark as to who was what to Federico. I had thought Marie Louisa was his sister, but wasn't really sure. And Francisco, he seemed to be in there somewhere, but I didn't know.

Ajo is a gypsy from Nerja, 38 years old, taught himself to read and write. Grew up poor as hell, meat almost never, maybe a *chorizo* once a year and he would go almost crazy with ecstasy at its succulence. He wanted to be a long-distance runner when he was young, so he ran all the time, everywhere he went; he ran to Torre del Mar, he ran the highways outside of Nerja, he ran through the narrow streets of the villages. He did it completely on his own, no support from school or government, and the people of the village thought he was stone crazy. They'd say, "The poor mother of that poor crazy boy who runs everywhere," truly believing that anyone who would choose to run when he could walk is not all there. There were enough idiots in the village anyway from interbreeding, all kinds of albinos and hunchbacks and deformed people of every description.

Ajo did quite well eventually, he was winning some honors and moving up in the national competition when a terrible fate befell him. At a championship meet in Madrid one spring all the athletes were fed a midday meal that included a good big piece of meat. Ajo never ate meat before a race; in fact he almost never ate meat. He still was not able to afford it; his father was mainly a layabout, an unmotivated handyman. So Ajo, not wanting to refuse a chance to eat meat, and also socially pressured not to show that he was not used to eating meat, ate his portion and paid for it terribly later that afternoon halfway into his race. He was taken with such powerful cramps that he finally ran right off the course and to the nearest thicket for a rendezvous with diarrhea. That was it for him; he never ran in a race again.

He has a wonderful genuine spontaneous face, and a string binding his hair across his forehead. Karen was lively too and unleashed great passions in her stories of run-ins with pushy and rude tourist customers at the restaurant. She loves Spain, has no interest in ever moving back to Sweden.

Francisco and Maria Louisa left Spain in 1939 and came back just recently. He worked for twenty years with the UN, ten years in Mexico, which they loved, and then they were moved to Chile, which they also loved. They were close friends with Salvador Allende, also Neruda and Paz, and have fallen out with Nicanor Parra because of his sellout to the current regime in accepting a post as professor of mathematics at the university there. According to them he has fully thrown his hat in with the rightist regime.

Francisco and Maria Louisa would have been 20 and 18 respectively when they left Spain. So many of their friends killed, Lorca most loved, but so many, the family and friends and writers, something to not forget even in forty years. Being with these people one feels as if they might have just escaped the sorrow and havoc, fear, hatred, three months ago.

Perhaps I read into their words, looks, silences, face lines. One can imagine a forty-year flight, suitcases around the world wondering when can we go home. So Francisco and Maria Louisa came as soon as they could; they were anxious to begin the reconstruction, to piece together what they could of the dispersed. Francisco himself has followed closely, all those years, the works of the exiled writers; he has kept files, volumes, everything to make a living history for these writers too, deprived of their chosen audience, their natural readers. F. has given thought to a big project here to see that they are now published in their own country, and their names cleared off censorship lists. F. proudly tells us he owns twenty thousand books, ten thousand still in Mexico, impossible to ship them here, much trouble anyway and $6,000; and then they have 10,000 in their Madrid apartment where they spend most of their time now. Their villa here too has books everywhere. F. is a mysterious old crank of a scholar; but I don't know all his interests.

He is now working on the first edition of Lorca's *Collected Essays*; and recently he completed gathering a *Corona Poética* for Federico, that is, poems from all over the world that are dedicated to or are about Federico. He has also worked on Lorca's longest, greatest play for years, *The Public*, but for some reason the family, meaning mainly Isabel Lorca, will not yet allow it to be published. He has published six volumes of his own poetry, all in Mexico, in limited editions mainly. Now he has offers to publish an *Obras Completas* here in Spain, but he is not ready, he says. He is working on his long autobiographical work and it sounds as though that would take his remaining years.

I have no idea what his poems are like, unfortunately. He is not very well. He has the beginnings of emphysema, and also other ailments that may be equally serious. He fainted last month in Madrid and was out for two hours. While not robust he is warm and life loving and an attentive conversationalist. We talked about Whitman and Emily Dickinson, also Neruda and Lorca, especially *Poet in New York*.

Dinner was served by two young Carabeo kids, all supposed to be very proper with Maria Louisa ringing her bell as signal to the 13 year olds tittering behind the bead curtain. Guacamole mixed with white rice as first course, very good, and hot; then roast beef and brussels sprouts; and dessert, coffee. And then Francisco is eager to pour more whiskey.

At one point Francisco suddenly invited us to join them in their trip to Málaga this coming Monday to see Jorge Guillén and his wife. F. said he knew Jorge would enjoy meeting us, American poet living in his beloved daughter's house in Nerja. We said yes, we would very much like to go. Maria immediately stopped the enthusiasm by saying she wouldn't have room for us because she had to bring a load of tiles back from Málaga. Lisa said we would be happy to take the bus. Francisco said well if you take the bus I'll take the bus too.

JANUARY 15

We go to the beach sometime around 1:30. A gorgeous afternoon, a large gathering at Ajo's. Lisa and I have the cheapest fare on the menu, fried eggs and pomme frites, 50 pesetas. I have a big cafe leche and Lisa a beer.

Then Felix arrives, never one to miss any decent beach day, with Daniel and Nicol. He looks still asleep at first and I tease him when he starts to repeat old themes; I tell him to wake up and say something new, we've heard old records too many times. Later, he does wake up, though we must inevitably return to some of "the old themes." Felix has endearing qualities of honesty and clarity when he's not endorsing the social value of war and other population-reduction measures expedient to clearing the planet of some of its litter.

The atmosphere of the day is so intoxicating we stay later than usual, until five-thirty, before saying good-bye. It's exactly the kind of day that makes living in Nerja so seductive. We need more of those days to balance our months of cold and rain.

Back home Lisa thinks I should take my books over to F. and M. L. as they had expressed real interest last night. I hesitate because I really would like to go to my study but I know that it would be a friendly thing to do. So I go and F. answers in a long black-and-white Chilean serape, looking quite wasted and low-key. Inside the television is on, a Spanish film comedy, silly, but I can understand their mood also. The house has a distinctly day-after enervation and malaise. F. is not feeling well at all, letting this light movie take him out of his problems. I want to leave immediately but it is awkward and then the movie ends after 15 minutes and Maria Louisa is fixing us tea and toast and we are talking some. F. is reading five or six poems from *Ha-Ha* and *Absences* and grunts pleasure saying he likes what he reads.

He and I walk down to their "Pulpit" after tea. Very beautiful view, a quiet little table. F. said he could flirt with Teresa from there when she leaned over her own balcony. But he said he couldn't write there, too windy, not room enough to work; and swimming was now ruined on the beach below, the water spoiled by a village sewage outlet just by their beach.

We talked of the problems of money and integrity in managing Lorca's rights and royalties. M. L. said that everyone in the family seemed obsessed with getting their share, all watchdogging every move to calculate their cut, and that really there was no coherent policy, no one U.S. publisher for instance, no appointed team of translators to share the labors of a complete English edition. F. had applied for a Guggenheim to study the problems of availability of Lorca's works throughout Mexico, South America, and the U.S.A. It was Pedro Salinas who had told him to apply, gave him the application; then later told him he wasn't eligible because he was not a U.S. resident. M. L. said how unlike Lorca it all was, how he just gave everything away to those he loved without thinking of money at all.

F. offers me a whiskey, wants one himself, but I decline vaguely. Then later I accept one and he has one too despite his doctor's advice. He previously smoked four packs of cigarettes a day and obviously drank one hell of a lot. All his pleasures are being taken away from him.

The government here wanted to name a Parador after Federico but Paco, the recently deceased brother, and Isabel refused, obviously still too bitter to let the Francoists make any pretense of glory for the poet they murdered.

JANUARY 17

This is a strange, long day, the day we will visit Jorge Guillén in Málaga with Francisco, Maria Louisa, and Maria Angula. We left Nerja on time at 10:30, all of us dressed for the occasion, and cheerful. It was an adventure in a personal way for all five of us, I suppose. I didn't know what to expect except that I had heard he was a quick and intelligent man for his age, 84 tomorrow!

All this talk of "Federico" and Salinas and the Civil War, it was a bit surrealistic for me: we were constantly speaking of forty years ago as though it were a matter of months. And from the evening of the dinner party at their place in the Lorca compound, I had a very warm and sympathetic feeling for Francisco, I enjoyed listening to him. I doubted that he was a great poet; instead he was something of a shabby fool with a big heart who had fought and suffered long ago for something he believed in. His family, distinguished in politics and government positions, was able to get him out. Yes many, many friends died, famous or poor, and Francisco, with his connections again, secured a flunky office job for the UN, first in Mexico, then Chile, and for 40 years drinks up his sorrow, and also perhaps some guilt, name-drops through the interminable cocktail parties and dinners, with the help of Maria Louisa and her distinguished family as well.

But Francisco has never had the discipline to pursue his proclaimed profession of poet. He writes, he writes on airplanes, he writes sappy love poems to the women he courts away from home, he writes of Federico. And then his scholarly work, well it's something; but the thing about Francisco, for all his important friends and his family and his wife's family, U.N. be damned, he is a shabby weak character, a gentleman tramp.

First we must stop at Velez-Málaga for Maria to consult with a brick magnate. It seems that one cannot be with her in any circumstance without there being an almost immediate connection to The House Problems. Everyone accepts this in her now; I don't know why really. As she's rattling on nonstop with the brick man, Francisco and I stare in astonishment: neither of us could have been so forceful.

Then we drove into the center of the town; very attractive, set 4 kms back from Torre del Mar. I'm always amazed at the difference, palpable, that small distance from the sea can make: here, for instance, you do not see foreigners (such as myself). There is a very large and wonderful city market; Velez is the center to which farmers bring their produce, the center for the area outside Málaga to Almunecar.

There's a very strange church in the main square, different than any I've seen before; it looks more like a mosque. Wonderful African/Arab feeling to the whole village. Maria Louisa buys about 8 chorizos on a reed. Everyone agrees that they are guaranteed to give you some kind of upset stomach, but M. L. and M. dig in like bandits; M. L. eats three, M. three, Lisa doesn't finish half of one, and I finish my one, almost. We eat them in a little antique shop. The proprietor was a rotund, impeccably tailored fascist gentleman, extremely courteous and subservient to M. and M. L. who were noticeably moneyed. They browsed, testing brass antique door knockers, knocking on wooden tables, munching their chorizos. We were then taken a few doors down by the same 350-pound owner and led upstairs through a dozen or more rooms on three floors, all packed with beautiful brass beds with porcelain decorations, lamps and chandeliers and books and many hundreds of paintings, a magnificently stocked warehouse of relics of a gone age. Back downstairs both M. L. and L. bought brass hand and ball door knockers; Maria's, the better of the two, was $30.

Then we were back on our way to Málaga. Maria stopped again to look at some toilet fixtures on the main highway. I joked that she needed one fast after all the chorizos she had eaten.

There was a discussion of possible restaurants for our afternoon meal. Maria said her workers had recommended two where the eating was superb. We decided on the one that was supposed to be less expensive. In fact, it was awful. Lousy clam soup with big chunks of potato and little else, and then *rape a la plancha,* which we hadn't had before and were looking forward to. The food was served cold and it wasn't very good. F. and I knocked back a gin and tonic before lunch and then we all drank wine. We were about the only customers in the place, and the waiter insisted all the vegetables were canned. Maria doesn't complain, as if this is what she had wanted. Francisco insists on paying for all of us; we must go elsewhere for coffee because this place doesn't . . .

The place we find has a poster on the wall describing the ten sizes of coffee that could be ordered there, from an empty glass to a brimming one, a name for all ten fractions. It was a lively downtown place, busy with all manner of demented and deformed variations of local color. We were, in a way, killing time, not due at Guillén's until 5:30 or 6.

Francisco and perhaps M. L. and M. as well, were thinking about Guillén, the circumstances under which they last met, 6 or 7 years ago. F. had told me of the time Isabel Lorca had beseeched him to accompany her when she was to meet Guillén some time after the war, in Mexico City. He seemed to feel ambivalent about seeing him this time. I think he is intimidated by Guillén's great confident gusto. Guillén, almost 25 years F.'s senior, but you would never think so to see them side by side engaged in stories: it is Francisco who is beaten; Jorge is triumphant in his great age.

We walk back to the main boulevard, Paseo del Parque, where M.'s car is. Now she must go see the man about the tiles; Lisa and M. L. choose to go with her while F. and I walk up the Paseo and across to the waterfront for several long blocks, toward Guillén's apartment building, which is on the harbor, looks out to the sea.

Francisco and I talk pleasantly as we walk, talk of his first attempt at writing. He was seventeen and it was a play which attempted to imitate Lorca as best he could. He showed it to Federico in Granada, their families had been friends. Federico was twice his age and immensely famous and popular all over Spain and loved by everyone. Federico read the play and told Francisco right on: "You have no experience in love, no real experience with a woman. Therefore you cannot write. If you want to be a writer you must fall deeply in love with women." Then he invited him to join him in a visit to Sacromonte that night.

It was the cave of a large middle-aged gypsy woman and she, like all the women of the caves, loved Federico, worshiped him, slept with him whenever possible, sang and danced for him as she would for very few others. Federico had a bottle of brandy and they were sharing it. At first the woman wouldn't sing when Federico asked her; she said she wouldn't sing in front of foreigners. Federico quickly explained that Paco, as he called F., was no foreigner but a very close friend and that their families were very close and so on. *Ah* then, that was very different, if they were so close then it would be as her gift to Federico to sing for the two of them. But first she drank a good bit more and they were all very loose by the time she performed, husky and rough but with the real *duende* that Lorca was to define in his essay. There were other gypsy women in the cave as well and the dances were lively and no doubt erotic to the two drunk poets. By the end of the long evening F. was eager to follow the chubby woman to her bed. Finally she consented by again considering it as a gift to her beloved poet Federico, the most vital, vibrant, and virile figure, charismatic in the extreme.

Francisco says he visited her several more times, always bringing her some gift such as a bouquet of flowers, never money, for that would be an insult to her feelings for Federico. Francisco told me of an incident where a poet of the time, no longer of any count, once engaged Federico's wrath by asking him directly if it was true that he was a *maricón*, a fairy. Federico lashed at this man with a fury, told him that he was an idiot to even consider that the writer of such great works of love and celebration of Woman could be such a flimsy one-sided creature as the word suggests.

But it was true that Federico did sleep with men. Apparently he was very discreet, as he would have had to be back then, especially in Granada where any sort of sexual deviance was severely ostracized. There are several men he may have even been in love with for a time, or even over a long period, but he never lived openly (to my knowledge) with another man, nor socially revealed a preference. He lived fully, a passionate artist of integrity, great interest in others, consideration, loyalty and tenderness. Francisco was a young, impressionable youth, and no doubt Federico was an impressive companion to venerate.

Francisco selects a bar next to Guillén's apartment building; F. says he needs to gather strength to face the old man. He is visibly nervous, getting himself tangled up inside talking to me about Federico. He has a Johnny Walker and I a Soberano brandy.

Finally he and I are ready to face Guillén. Why it should be so difficult, I don't know. For Francisco it is a momentous time, still the freshness of being back in a country after 40 years. A figure like Guillén is more than symbolic, but he is also symbolic. He is a survivor, the one who should know it all by now if he can remember.

So here is the great man, my God what a lively old buzzard. But that isn't fair: at 84 he is not yet even an old buzzard. Surely he is as bald as one, not even a couple of baby feathers around the ears or nape of the neck! But no matter, he is electric, powerfully expressive with arms and hands and especially the face, skin slightly dry and papery but elastic and fresh too, not a loud laugh but certainly hearty, throwing himself back against the sofa. The most alert, keen, verbal man I have seen in a long time.

His wife, 30 years younger, a rather short and plain Italian widow that married Jorge 10 years ago, offered us drinks and some soggy little cheese crackers. We all arranged our chairs in a semicircle around Guillén who was so magnetic with his clear and impatient energy. Since his return to accept the Premio Cervantes, he and his wife have been in a frantic whirl through television interviews and radio programs and official dinners, friends and others, traveling; but Guillén shows no signs for the wear. He talks in modulated surges, displaying a phenomenally detailed memory of events fifty and sixty years ago; first meeting with Maria Teresa's father, the famous poetry critic of the day. He then would shift to Francisco and make some almost lewd comment about a 23 year old lady interviewer he met on a television show in Málaga this week, suggesting that there could have been room for action. Francisco claimed he was shocked and told the birthday boy to watch what he was saying as his wife was right there; but Jorge didn't heed and went on with another story.

Most interesting of the day was his declaration that he intended to use the prize politically, as a base from which to speak, to say some things that needed to be said to make the healing of the wounds more complete. He told Francisco of the four months he spent in jail in Seville before he immigrated to the States; Francisco says that Guillén had never talked about this before. The revelation staggers him, it changes everything. And how incredible that Jorge Guillén should choose to keep silent the very fact of his life that would have made him a hero instead of a dubious cold fish all these years.

Now Guillén thinks it is time everything be spoken that has been silent. He has a radiating confidence and vitality that makes the mission seem not only possible but inevitable.

There were intimate jokes about Federico and Alberti, Salinas. Guillén and Federico had been something like best of friends. And I still get strong hints of competition with Salinas, for reasons that are not exactly clear to me, perhaps more personal than professional/ poetic.

Guillén told Lisa and me that we should call him sometime and make a date for a visit when we will all speak English.

Lisa and I had to rush across town to the bus station. Maria has by now 500 pounds of tiles in her backseat. A nice walk in the night air and a 1½-hour bus ride with Lisa sounded pretty good. And it was good. The bus stopped every kilometer or so to let someone off in the bean field. We got home at 9:20.

Our parting words out in front of Guillén's in Málaga had included an invitation from Francisco that we should drop by their house in Nerja directly upon arriving. I knew what would go on over there, the rehash of what Guillén had to say, how brilliantly quick and lucid he was.

And I also was beginning to figure out that we just might be not too much more than an excuse for Francisco to drink all he wants under the pretense of being a good host, and that it was not easy to get out once you went in. I didn't want to go over; I didn't want to bother telling them because that was the same as going over.

Finally we decided that Lisa would go by to tell them we couldn't come; if they insisted she come in she would and if they insisted she get me she could call me on the phone and I would hear it from my study. I was hoping she wouldn't call. But she did and I complied as I said I would.

When I arrived Maria and the others told how they had assumed we had missed the bus in Málaga and had had to spend the night there; they were feeling awful for us. And now of course we felt awful that we made them feel awful.

Francisco fetches me a whiskey and tells me how Guillén's revelations today of his mild resistance and months in jail really transformed everything he had ever thought about the man. He was a comrade all these years and no one knew it. And now it could do a lot of good, him speaking the truth like this, it could encourage others to do the same. But Francisco was having trouble being coherent tonight. I was noticing more and more how plates in his brain slipped and he could blank out of some subject that greatly interested him a half sentence ago. His attention strayed.

He was asking Lisa over and over if she would please let him fix her another drink. Lisa didn't want another drink. Francisco was acting as though she had rejected him, she had "shut the door on him" as he put it. He was about to convince himself that he was falling for Lisa. He declared that the name Liselotte had been brought by Napoleon to Sweden; we all waited and then he went off on a tangent about his mother Eliza. He kept saying, "Did you say your name is Eliza, do they call you Eliza? My mother's name. . . ." No, we'd say.

Then the evening took a really awful turn. We were all saying how we were tone deaf; none of us could carry a tune. Everyone had their anecdote of how the choirmaster asked him or her to please not sing but mouth the words at an important recital. So I jokingly suggested that we should form an Anti-Singing Club; we would get together and murder songs that we would never be allowed to sing in public. I suggested that right then each of us should take turns singing one song that we knew, and I assumed that most of us wouldn't know more than one anyway.

I started off by torturing "It's a Sin to Tell a Lie," 1953 smash hit for Somethin' Smith and the Red Heads. I thought I gave a proper air of low standards to the fest. Francisco followed next with some moony Spanish ballad. Then Lisa butchered the Santa Lucia song good-naturedly. Maria said she absolutely did not know one song and kept repeating how tough it was for her, imagine, with a husband like Carlos who could and did sing publicly very beautifully. It broke my heart.

Maria Louisa volunteered to give us a little turn-of-the-century kitsch, precious poses with her follies-girl hands, eyes upturned and blank tinkly voice. She gave us one of these songs after another. She thought she was endlessly amusing. She rapidly became an irksome bore. Maria Louisa would not be turned off, twenty songs, then tangos.

Meanwhile Francisco had become utterly obsessed with the challenge to convince Lisa to let him fix her another drink. He is a romantic old slouch, somehow has the image of himself as a woman killer, when in fact he looks like Grandpa on Beverly Hillbillies.

Lisa wants to go, she has had enough. To have been invited over and treated to his imprecations and her tangos. She says good-bye. F. walks her to the door and for 15 minutes pleads with her to allow him as a Spanish gentleman to walk her home. She refuses, it's only a few doors, anything but dangerous, absolutely not necessary. She finally gets away and he returns looking dejected and wounded as a lover. I'm about to shout what the hell is going on here! This whole scene is crazy!

A few minutes later there is a knock at the door and Francisco leaps to his feet, knowing it will be Lisa and perhaps she has had second thoughts about him. I jump to my feet as well, knowing also it will be Lisa, and determined to put a stop to this nonsense right away before I say something terribly unpleasant to the man. Lisa has forgotten her key. Immediately I say well then I think I'll just go along home with you now and hastily made apologies to F. who is muttering vagaries to himself.

FEBRUARY 12

Finally saw Francisco and the rest of that crew tonight after 2 weeks. They were leaving for Madrid the next day and it would have been a shame not to manage a good-bye. Lisa and I went looking for them around 10. They were at Maria Angula's. She had invited them all to dinner and then asked Suzannah if she would cook the dinner at her own home and bring it over; she said her stove there was too hot. Then of course Francisco brought over the liquor. . . . And Maria got a nice homemade dinner delivered to her table cooked and free drinks . . . not a bad deal.

I was glad to see Francisco especially. I was sad that things had turned out the way they had. I knew that he liked both Liselotte and me very much. A warm and sentimental man, weak in some ways perhaps; but real and generous, vulnerable, good.

Laura Lorca was there and we met for the first time. She's a handsomely tailored and coiffed tank of a woman, graceful, gentle. I liked her immediately and was sorry to hear that she was leaving the next day with Feo and M. L. She asked us to visit her in Madrid.

Feo looked wholly changed, rather emasculated by having shaved his beard. It was mainly Laura who had urged him to abandon his shaggy salt-and-pepper six-week beard. Too bad, it was so attractive on him, and went well with his black-and-white poncho. Now I see him for the first time shaven; how sad it is, veritably chinless, or a baby's chin, soft and breakable. It was a dramatic change. The women keep punching him in the jaw, poor soft jaw. Feo is an irresistible child at times. He is not too uncomfortable having these several women telling him what to do.

For some reason we were to move the party across the street to Feo's place, Maria was perhaps afraid we would wear out the tiles on the kitchen floor. Francisco kept insisting that I tell him what happened to our friendship. I very much wanted to tell him the truth. And I did.

After Maria left, Feo told Maria Louisa what I had told him and we all discussed it in a proper tone of remorse. Maria Louisa let it be known that she had had several experiences with Maria that belonged to this description.

Then, for some unknown reason, Francisco leapt and went to his bookcase, came back with a vellum-bound 1842 edition of Byron's 500 page *Don Juan*. Before I could say anything, he had inscribed it to Liselotte and me and handed it to me. Maria Louisa I know was cringing, but it was too late now; inscribed I had to accept it.

A crazy ending; I will miss Francisco; hope we get to Madrid to visit them before we leave Spain.

APRIL 16

Semana Santa always brings in the tourists and all the part-time residents to Nerja. So there were Francisco and Mapissa once again (so soon) with Laura and Isabel Lorca there as well, and Carlos Angula visiting his wife Maria for the first time since New Year's, and Paul and Hannah. And the Texadors still in Nerja. They were all set for two weeks of gossip, food and drink, especially drink.

When I first spotted Francisco on the street again, our greeting, embraces and so forth, felt artificial and full of defeat and dread. Somehow I knew we couldn't attempt to carry on as we had during their last visit. Too many problems. And he seemed more down now, really drained and depressed.

We invited the group to one late-afternoon cocktail gathering on our patio. It went well enough, a bit restrained. Mainly Carlos and Laura Lorca carried the conversation. Mapissa and Francisco were silent; Lisa and I didn't contribute much beyond food, drinks, and service; Isabel and Laura were planning a tour of Russia with Steve and Teresa Gilman. They also wanted to return to Cuba. They both despise communism, are in fact very moderate, perhaps right of center. Laura is built a little like Kate Smith; she is attractive and articulate, well dressed and respectfully old-fashioned, with a lively curiosity. Isabel, once the light of her brother's eye, even more Old World, small and potentially severe; that is, she can and will sting if her code of behavior is broken. Laura is more humane and more diplomatic as well.

As we found out later, the whole group was under a hideous black cloud at that time: Carlos had told Maria that he had been having an affair all year with a 33 year old street poet who is now pregnant with his child, the very thing Maria could never give him, to her great sorrow. He tells her that he wants to leave her and marry this divorcée with a child of her own. Maria's reaction to this blunt, cruel information is to attempt hanging herself in the bathroom of Mapissa's house during dinner, and then again at a restaurant later in Torre del Mar.

Carlos brought additional grief by hitting a boy chasing a ball across the highway. Nothing was broken, but the wreckless violence seemed to follow him on this trip back to Nerja.

Maria babbled hysterically to all her group through the week and everyone was numb. Now she has followed Carlos back to Barcelona and is apparently hiring a detective to follow him.

The affair began, by the way, when this 33 year old street poet approached Carlos in a bar and told him she would write a poem on any subject for him for a fixed price, I forget what, 100 pesetas I think. Carlos requested a pornographic poem and they have been happily collaborating since.

Carlos has decided the only way he can make his weighty decision is to fly (literally) around the world, in two days or something like that; only touching down in airport lobbies; the rest of the time 40,000 feet above the ground, sealed into his capsule, with his thoughts free to consider without harassment of sneaking gumshoes or cackling wife or swaying mistress. . . . Maria is on the end of her tether calling friends daily in Madrid and Nerja.

Fred Chappell

STARTING FROM THE WRONG END

I had imagined that I wanted to write a short story, perhaps a longish one, using the theme of conflict between the individual citizen and the law. I did not imagine characters or situation or story line. Instead, I set down some abstract propositions about the subject matter. Here they are, as inert now as they were on the day they arrived stillborn.

We don't confess to crimes but to having done wrong.

Crime is the first thing sanctioned by law. A body of laws creates criminals, a social class that never existed before the advent of laws.

Only an uncomprehended law compels obedience; to the laws we understand we merely assent.

Upon entering a picturesque and unpeopled wilderness, one feels the presence of laws he is unable to obey.

"The law is no respecter of persons." So that as individuals, we cannot respect the law. The obverse bromide might be: "The law is a respecter of citizens." When we think of ourselves as citizens, we do respect the law.

In public we assent; in private we dissent.

Even the man who most believes in the law protects his privacy from it. At long last he begins to think of privacy as a criminal condition.

A man who trains his private talents—whatever they are—to the highest degree writes his own laws. Later, he writes the public laws.

Where there is individuality there is inequality. Laws written to protect the individual protect inequality.

Laws which protect property protect a philosophy of history in which injustice is recognized as an inescapable human condition.

In the long run, every law a state makes for its own protection subverts its security.

Metaphors and images for law: sun, seasons, natural cycles (Auden); drab uniforms; prisons but also keys; swords but also plowshares;

blindfolds but also eagle eyes; city plazas; fog (Dickens) but also *plein air*; cops *and* robbers. New metaphors: clipboards, file drawers, battered cluttered desks, one-way mirrors, sirens after midnight, printed forms, singles bars, alleyways, microphones, chewing gum.

The Best-Laid Plans...

F. Scott Fitzgerald

From The Crack Up *(New Directions, 1945)*

IDEAS

Play in which revolutionist in big scene—"Kill me," etc.—displays all bourgeois talents hitherto emphasized, paralyzes them with his superiority, and then shoots them.

Lois and the bear hiding in the Yellowstone.

For Play.
Personal charm.
Elsa Maxwell.
Bert.
Hotels.
Pasts—great maturity of characters.
Children—their sex and incomprehension of others.
Serious work and worker involved. No more patience with idlers
    unless *about* them.

Helpmate: Man running for Congress gets hurt in line of other duty and while he's unconscious his wife, on bad advice, plans to run in his stead. She makes a fool of herself. He saves her face.

Family breaks up. It leaves mark on three children, two of whom ruin themselves keeping a family together and a third who doesn't.

A young woman bill collector undertakes to collect a ruined man's debts. They prove to be moral as well as financial.

**** **** running away from it all and finding that new ménage is just the same.

Widely separated family inherit a house and have to live there together.

Fairy who fell for wax dummy.

■

Three people caught in triangle by desperation. Don't resolve it geographically, so it is crystallized and they have to go on indefinitely living that way.

Andrew Fulton, a facile character who can do anything, is married to a girl who can't express herself. She has a growing jealousy of his talents. The night of her musical show for the Junior League comes and is a great failure. He takes hold and saves the piece and can't understand why she hates him for it. She has interested a dealer secretly in her pictures (or designs or sculptures) and plans to make an independent living. But the dealer has only been sold on one specimen. When he sees the rest he shakes his head. Andrew in a few minutes turns out something in putty and the dealer perks up and says, "That's what we want." She is furious.

A Funeral: His own ashes kept blowing in his eyes. Everything was over by six and nothing remained but a small man to mark the spot. There were no flowers requested or proffered. The corpse stirred faintly during the evening but otherwise the scene was one of utter quietude.

Story of a man trying to live down his crazy past and encountering it everywhere.

A tree, finding water, pierces roof and solves a mystery.

Father teaches son to gamble on fixed machine; later the son unconsciously loses his girl on it.

A criminal confesses his crime methods to a reformer, who uses them that same night.

Girl and giraffe.

Marionettes during dinner party meeting and kissing.

Play opens with man run over.

Play about a whole lot of old people—terrible things happen to them and they don't really care.

The man who killed the idea of tanks in England—his afterlife.

Play: The Office—an orgy after hours during the boom.

A bat chase. Some desperate young people apply for jobs at Camp, knowing nothing about wood lore but pretending, each one.

■

The Tyrant Who Had To Let His Family Have Their Way For One Day.

The Dancer Who Found She Could Fly.

There was once a moving-picture magnate who was shipwrecked on a desert island with nothing but two dozen cans of film.

Angered by a hundred rejection slips, he wrote an extraordinarily good story and sold it privately to twenty different magazines. Within a single fortnight it was thrust twenty times upon the public. The headstone was contributed by the Authors' League.

Driving over the rooftops on a bet.

Girl whose ear is so sensitive she can hear radio. Man gets her out of insane asylum to use her.

Boredom is not an end product, is comparatively rather an early stage in life and art. You've got to go by or past or through boredom, as through a filter, before the clear product emerges.

A man hates to be a prince, goes to Hollywood and has to play nothing but princes. Or a general—the same.

Girl marries a dissipated man and keeps him in healthy seclusion. She meanwhile grows restless and raises hell on the side.

Jim Harrison

BIG WOMEN

Not that many years ago, during a difficult time, I was in Rio (Brazil) working on a movie project. The project was about the soul of Carmen Miranda. In that the movie is somewhat unlike the literary business I was living alone in Ipanema in an extravagant apartment with 7 servants. I didn't know how to talk to them. The only book in English I found among a 200 piece Lalique collection was Louisa Alcott's *Little Women*. I read it over a period of a month while watching the cat break a half-dozen of the Laliques. I went to Umbanda rites and changed my life frequently. I had lunch with Sonia

Bragga and almost fell in love. I feared death and mayhem at every moment as Carnival was approaching.

When I returned home I began to brood about *Little Women* and conceived the notion of writing a novella to be called, quite naturally, *Big Women*. I had signed a contract to do a book of short stories and though I had 18 titles I had no contents. *Big Women* was to be the lead item. The story concerned 2 daughters of a Scandinavian missionary to Brazil. The daughters in question were called Emma and Emily. They were both 8′6″ and weighed exactly 500 pounds apiece. One was bad and one was good. The narrator was to interview the bad one, Emma, in an insane asylum in Northern Minnesota where she was being confined because she had killed a half-dozen deer hunters during a sex binge at a remote cabin.

I blame this entire idea on Brazil. It's not my fault. I have abandoned the project for the time being, though if I return to Brazil I might start writing it again.

Elizabeth Spires

I was living in London three years ago [in 1986], working on various poems, when the first section of what I thought would be a sequence "wrote itself," as they say. I wrote the lines in longhand in one sitting, as if by automatic writing. (My normal writing process is to take a poem through dozens of drafts over several weeks.) The voice in the poem was not my own and I had no idea what the rest of the story was. I waited, in vain, for weeks, then months, hoping the voice would dictate other sections or chapters of the story. But alas, it didn't. I am left with the mystery implied by the narrative: an unhappy love affair—possibly a love triangle—and a suicide. Perhaps when I least expect it, a year from now, or ten, that ghostly voice will return to inform me of the poem's outcome.

FROM AN UNTITLED, UNFINISHED SEQUENCE

If it be now, 'tis not to come; if it be not to come, it will be now; if it be not now, yet it will come. . . .

Shakespeare

I

What in this world can ever truly vanish?
The letter you waited for and now are burning
can never be destroyed; watch how it changes
form—bright metamorphosis!—as the fire
licks at the paper with ravening tongues,
until pale sheets collapse and curl inward
like the palsied fingers of an ancient hand
in which your destiny is written. See
how the words change to ash, to smoke rising
in spirals to inform the heavens of your tragedy?
Now pairs of lovers looking at the stars
will read your message in the constellations
and choose, as lovers always do, to ignore it,
falsely believing that they, and they alone,
cannot be touched by misfortune. Except for one,
that is, as solitary as you are, who stands
under the stars and reads their meaning plain,
its bitter application, goes calmly home
and lays the cool barrel of a gun against
a fevered temple. You are, by your impulsive action,
responsible, and soon enough will pay for it.
(only extant section)

Louise Glück

What I don't use is prose, of which I write two kinds. I write funny
short stories of domestic complaint. I also write pithy opening paragraphs for essays on various great themes.

Daniel Stern

*This is an outtake not only from a book but from the body of my work.
That is to say, it is the beginning of a nonfiction book which I never wrote
and never will. I had written and published eight novels and a publisher
friend suggested that the time had come to write a nonfiction book—and she
had the perfect subject for me. It was to be a book about the conflicting
ethos and styles of life characterized by New York and Los Angeles.*

*I had lived a bi-coastal professional life for years, having worked at both
Warner Bros. and CBS. The idea attracted me. I wrote a two-page outline
and received a $25,000 advance. (And this was, mind you, about six years
ago.) But then I had to write the book. And what I found out, definitively,
was what I had always known: that in the deepest part of my self I cared
only about writing fiction. I paid back the advance (not such an easy matter because I had already spent it) and never looked back.*

*Recently, after another first—my first book of short stories, Twice Told
Tales, I came across a beginning I had written for the bi-coastal book. It
dealt with the time when, having been newly hired as head of advertising
for Warner Bros. Motion Pictures, I was first told I might have to leave
New York to live in Los Angeles. Surprisingly, I rather liked what I read. I
offer it as a brief outtake from the life of a fiction writer.*

I KNEW AT THAT MOMENT
THAT NOTHING WOULD BE THE SAME, AGAIN

After the lunch with Ted Ashley and Steve Ross at the Gloucester
House I am shaky. Nothing firm has been stated, but the move has
been mentioned. Over my striped bass and white wine I am discussing
the possibility of moving the entire department to Hollywood.

"It's a matter of dollars," Spencer Harrison says. Spencer is the
executive vice president in charge of money for Warner Bros. "If the
savings can be measured in millions—and they may be—then we'll
do it. Otherwise—"

"Otherwise?" I say hopefully.

"We'll stay put," Spencer says dourly. He is a dour man with one
eye that wanders, making it difficult to argue with him—about money
or anything else. Ted seems matter-of-fact about this as about most
things. Steve smiles and appears to be thinking about more important
matters. Outside, the sun shines; it is May. My wife and I have rented

a little house on a large silvery pond in Water Mill, on Long Island. Los Angeles, the Studio—which I have only seen on the run ... quick flying trips to view prints of films for equally quick marketing decisions ... the guard at the gate waving me through, the famous WB logo contained in a shield, memory of many Bugs Bunny cartoons— all seem distant and unthreatening. But a thrum of menace moves in my blood. All afternoon, in my office, I wonder what to do. Then I ask my secretary to bring in a piece of paper. My contract, I recall, consolingly, specifically states: "Mr. Stern will serve his term of employment in New York City." Who thought to put that life preserver around my neck? Was it my lawyer or me? I seem to recall it was put in, gratuitously, by Spencer Harrison. How strange. I was safe. If they moved the department to the Coast, I could settle my contract, take the money and—.

And, what?

And go back to real life. Advertising agencies, writing books—the way everything had been before I'd succumbed to the excitement of my friend Ed Bleir's eloquence; Ed, who had led this bi-coastal life in its heightened movie-studio form for years.

"It's a very different way of living, Danny?"

"I know."

"No, maybe you don't. It means that you'll be in your office and Ted or Steve or somebody will say, 'We'd better go to the Coast' and that means right then, right there. Not sitting back and planning a trip. It means calling your wife and saying you won't be home and heading downstairs into the limo while somebody calls the airport. You'll keep some clothes at the Beverly Hills Hotel, so you're always prepared. You go from freezing, dark cold to hot smoggy sunshine— just like that ... and back again—just like that."

I put my contract in the Out box on my rosewood desk—inherited from Benny Kalmenson, Jack Warner's right-hand man and president of Warner Bros, the Seneschals of a vanished era I was to inherit. Unless—. The phone rings and I remember Spencer Harrison's "Otherwise—we'll stay put." I breathe easier.

I leave work and walk into a smoky Fifth Avenue twilight. It seems to me, suddenly, that this simple walk, a tired one with attaché case in hand and coat snugly around my throat, through the streets, yellow-stained with lamplight, neon-brushed and chill, is a walk through an enchanted landscape. The sentiment is overwhelming— even though I recognize it as just that. The young, bone-skinny girl playing the violin in front of 666 Fifth, the doorman standing hopeless guard before the apartment building at the corner of Sixth and

Fifty-sixth Street, the bookstore clerks at Doubleday's: all seem like figures out of fairy tales—they are the dramatis personae of my epic of nostalgia which will begin by my saying nothing to my wife, to-night—and end in Los Angeles, in Brentwood Park, in sunlit anomie, barely glimpsed temptation, the temptation to be someone else, al-ways an exciting possibility; in an earthquake and money and separa-tion and panic.

But for the moment, I am a still-young newly baptized movie mogul, tempted away from any thoughts of the serious literary work which has been my constant companion since age sixteen. Here are the noises of the city; car tires and brakes, hissing and squawking, the steady stitch of near and distant voices; I am Baudelaire's *flâneur*: the man of the sidewalks, of the boulevards, living in the reflected glasses of passersby, potential enemies or lovers, sources of income and danger. My heart pounds. I am the animal delicately at home in its jungle—a New Yorker at home in New York.

I decide to say nothing to my wife that night.

FROM THE *DAILY NEWS*' MANHATTAN SECTION

Because Manhattanites "whirl at such a pace," says a fifty-seven-year-old photographer, "it's hard to remember what age you are." (Later I will read, and experience, a similar effect of the West Coast. New York and Los Angeles, two cities where age is willed into irrele-vance.)

"The purpose of Manhattan," says a forty-six-year-old fund-raiser who has just taken a new job in Brooklyn, "is to make money and have a good time on the fast track."

And: ". . . the best talents from all over the country, if not the world, are attracted here, and in fields where talent is the determinant of value, where professional age is no guarantor of respect and talent surfaces so quickly, because the professional striations are not so rigid or hierarchical and it's nobody's company town, you have to keep looking down as well as left and right and that certainly keeps you on your toes."

Thus speaks the popular culture which supports me. Like most popular "truths" it seems to me to contain truth but is not necessarily "true." It does not contain, for example, the truth of the years when, an unemployed musician-turning-writer, I closed the Russian Tea Room, night after night, after long table sessions with friends and drop-ins: Lou Jacobi, a Canadian-born actor, telling jokes, Hershey Kay, tiny, competitive, gifted, telling nasty stories about out-of-town musical openings, Zero Mostel baiting Hershey, Jerry Lurie, the show-business lawyer telling sometimes wonderful, sometimes terrible jokes, Sidney Kaye, the owner of the Russian Tea Room, telling stories about Agnes de Mille never getting the right table, about the Russian émigrés, now long gone from the Restaurant banished by age or death. True, some sort of career ambition rustled beneath the surface of all the talk—but so much was talk for its own sake, that it continued onto the one-A.M. sidewalks, into the Stage Delicatessen or uptown on Fifth, Sixth or Central Park West, depending on who was walking home with whom.

Yet memory also confirms the journalism. Age was irrelevant; we were the children of New York, would-be or accomplished artists, but mostly artists of the quick retort, the literary insult or the borrowed twenty-dollar bill.

Long before it was a question of moving to Los Angeles, while I was young enough for age to be truly irrelevant on either coast, I was almost arrested on the long streets that separate the busy, westward-moving car flow of Santa Monica Boulevard and the more desolate winding ribbon of Sunset Boulevard. I am waiting out the publication of a book so that I can repay my father the $6,000 I owe him and start again, from scratch; the waiting—called *writing*—is being done at an artist's colony: the Huntington Hartford Foundation. Shangri-La behind an electronic gate in the Pacific Palisades.

Gene Kelly's ex-wife, an actress who likes writers named Betsy Blair, has given me refuge. I can't call it anything more than that. I have no money, no status (outside of a few published novels which of course was a kind of status-currency of that subset in Hollywood; those were more innocent days), *and no car*. This last is bad enough; no one would have suspected the worst; that I *have no driver's license*, do not know how to drive a car.

Fortunately, the only people to find me out are the police. In the peculiar, vacant coolness of a Los Angeles summer evening, I am dropped off by the Foundation's station wagon and left to walk what is known in Beverly Hills as "the flats." After a few moments, I notice a police car slowing down behind me. No sirens, no whirling lights, just slowing down. Gradually, intimately, the car eases over next to me and paces me at exactly the same rate at which I am walking. Finally, the cop next to the driver speaks to me.

"You want to come over here, please?" (A very different style than in New York.) I am still walking, they are still in the moving car, but I am being accosted by the police. I walk over to the police car and stop. The car stops.

"Can I see your driver's license?"

"I don't have one, officer." I am ashamed of that "officer" now so many years later, but I was a stranger in a strange land.

"Why not? Where is it?" All questions. Not one declarative statement or command from them, as yet.

"I don't have one. I don't drive."

This ends the overture to the charade. The policeman is out. The car is no longer moving.

"What's in the package?"

It is, in point of fact, an etching given me by an artist to "swap" at a party that night—a cause party, hangover of the early fifties, the Hollywood Ten (one of whom would be at the party) and of Betsy Blair's circle, many of whom were black—listed in the McCarthy chill of the fifties. I decide, wisely, to say nothing to the Beverly Hills policeman pointing his hand at me. Some instinctive Jew/Cossack equation tells me to silently hand the package to him. He unwraps it, stares at it for a moment without reaction, then hands it back.

All around us sprinklers are whispering to lawns; but there are no witnesses. In New York such a scene would draw spectators, commentators, at once. I do not even have the sense that people are peeping at us from behind window shades or curtains. Cars crawl past, incuriously on their way to the Stop sign at the corner.

"Where are you heading?" the policeman asks.

"Six twenty-three Rodeo Drive."

"Whose house is that?"

And like the New York naïf I am, I tell the truth.

"Gene Kelly."

"Okay," the policeman says. "You walk to the house and we'll follow you. Just knock on the door when you get there and go in." He gets back in the car, which seems somehow too small to hold his long legs and arms. Policemen are smaller now than they used to be in New York. In Los Angeles they have stayed the same. (Unless I simply feel smaller in Los Angeles.)

I continue my Rodeo Drive walk, praying that I have not gotten the nights mixed up, that the party actually is tonight. If no one answers the door, I sense it will not be a pleasant night for me. All the remembered jokes about the Beverly Hills Police Department having an unlisted number and toy poodles instead of German shepherds do not ease my pulse.

The bell rings. After an endless instant the door opens. I cannot restrain myself from looking back. The shadowy street murmurous with trees is empty of official cars. As in a dream, I enter a room full of movie stars.

Robert Olen Butler

NOTES ON THE RAMBLER. The Rambler *was begun in late 1979 and got only as far as a great deal of free-floating reverie and these 1,400 words. I stopped work on the book when* The Alleys of Eden, *a novel which I'd finished over a year earlier, finally was accepted for publication. These two works represented vast and separate bodies of material in my artistic unconscious. Alleys comes from my year in Vietnam, a year in which I spoke fluent Vietnamese and fell in unlikely love with a country full of people. Rambler is from my childhood, my blood kin, my hometown. This is the material usually associated with the first novels of serious writers. But Vietnam had intervened in my life and was the more insistent subject. The problem was that in 1979 no one seemed to want to publish more than a few token books on that subject. Alleys was drawing ecstatic rejection letters (twenty-one of them) admitting every virtue in the book except its marketability, a problem which was usually blamed with surprising candor on Vietnam. Consequently, though I had more Vietnam-inspired books that wanted to be written at once, I turned to material that, though not as insistent in 1979, I knew one day would produce good books. When Ben Raeburn of Horizon Press soon thereafter took up* The Alleys of Eden, *I was freed to return to the sequence of books that my unconscious desired.*

With my fifth book, Wabash, *published by Knopf in 1987, I finally went back to my hometown material, though in that novel it is Abraham Cole's son, Jeremy, who is the center of the book and Abraham appears only as a memory, though the memory does include the Indian fires mentioned in this piece. I turned to Abraham in 1979 because he is the closest figure in my imagined world to someone from real life, my great-great-grandfather, William Roland Hall, who did indeed make caskets all winter for his wife to sell during the spring and then packed his carpetbag and rode off into the Ozark Mountains to write a newspaper column under the name of "The Rambler." He also worked as a carpenter in the construction of the Eads Bridge and played violin in the St. Louis Opry House and sold snake oil in the small towns of Missouri. In rediscovering these fourteen hundred words, I hear the old man talking to me again and I expect someday to catch him in the center of a circle of Indian fire and write his book.*

THE RAMBLER

ONE

At a certain time in my life I was a man who loved horses, the smell of them and the feel of them beneath me, the way they nickered when they were feeling gentle and shook the sweat off themselves when they were feeling tired. Horses and printing presses. The sound of the presses' joints and the ripple of the paper taking the words and the smell of the ink. I'd go and get my hands dark with the ink even later on, when I had men working for me to do that. I loved horses and printing presses and the folds of the hills in the Ozark mountains, and when I was ready to go home at the end of each spring and rode out of the mountains to the prairie land near the Kansas border, I loved the turkeyfoot grass with its purple claws clutching as high as a man's head and I loved the haze on the horizon of some fire going some-where. I'd stop and make camp with my own fire at my feet and I'd think of the stories I'd heard from an old muleskinner living up in the mountains who'd been born on the plains. These were the stories of the Indians, before the war, setting their autumn fires. The Indians would torch the prairies in a great ring to drive the buffaloes into a killing ground. The Indians would use fire as a weapon and they could barely control it and sometimes it would turn on them and sweep them away. But when it worked, the world that was ringed in fire just got smaller and clearer and the things the Indians needed to live off of were there in the center waiting for them. And I'd sit by my campfire and I'd concentrate on all that I loved and these things were like a ring of fire inside me and I'd start to get clearer too, like there was some animal in there that I knew I should hunt. Maybe I couldn't see it yet for all the flare and the smoke but I knew if I just let the fire burn long enough, I'd know what it was inside me.

This was at a certain time in my life and at this time I was married to the former Winifred Ruth Gaines who I did not love, and she did not have my son yet who, when he finally came into the world, I loved more than the horses and the printing presses and the tales of the Indians. But when Winifred and I were still barren, I'd leave her every spring. There was nothing else for me to do. It was my calling and maybe I created this feeling about her myself. But her daddy had fixed her good. He'd loved her just a little and then left her young and her momma had loved her not at all and had stuck around and filled her full of a religion that for all its fiery words made it so that Winnie herself could never feel the flames. Not the flames of hell, not the Indian fires, not the flame of the love of anything, nothing at all to throw a circle around what was inside her so she could find it and live.

So what I did was I'd work all the winter long, making caskets in the stable behind our house in St. Louis. My own daddy and momma were long dead. I bear his middle name. He was Joseph Abraham Cole and I am Abraham Jeremiah Cole. He was a trader and he left me some money and this house on the St. Louis riverfront and the other things he left me are part of what I've always had to say. In a way he made me the newspaper man I became. In a way he made me love and made me kill and finally understand what the real difference is between the two. Not that he ever understood any of that himself.

But I'd make caskets all winter and leave them for Winnie to sell in the spring. This was a big time for dying in St. Louis, the winter turning into the spring. And me, I'd pack my carpetbag and my violin and I'd head for the Ozark Mountains. This was the middle seventies, you understand, and feelings ran pretty high the farther south you went. My "carpetbag" was leather and I knew how to keep my mouth shut when I needed to and in the mountains I would write words. At this certain time I loved words. They were horses to ride. I wrote good words in the mountains and I sent them to a newspaper in St. Louis and the newspaper published them and I was called "The Rambler."

Winifred would never read a word of what I wrote. She didn't believe in the newspapers. There was too much of the world in them. She felt if the words weren't written in the Bible, they weren't worth reading. I could never talk to her about this because I knew the Bible as well as she did and there were good words there, too, but some of them didn't fit whatever beasts were roaming inside her. Like when Solomon said, "There be three things which are too wonderful for me, yea, four which I know not: the way of an eagle in the air; the way of a serpent upon a rock; the way of a ship in the midst of the sea; and the way of a man with a maid." Solomon would've loved the turkeyfoot grass too and the Indian fires. They'd've been too wonderful for him. And he had his way with a thousand maids, I think, and not one of them was like Winifred Gaines.

Why did I put my hands to Winnie Gaines and have my son by her? I had taken for myself the freedom of the Ozarks, why not the freedom of some other wife? But all I knew was that Winnie was the woman I'd married, and though I have lived to see an age when marriages could be put aside very casually, this idea never came into my head in 1874. Late one afternoon in early April of that year I passed by a settlement and slept in an abandoned log cabin high on a fire-scarred ridge. The roof was made of oak shakes, but they'd been put down loose and ripped by the wind and the cabin was open to the sky in long thin slips. As I lay there I felt in the bones of my feet that there'd be an April frost in the night. Still, I didn't regret passing the settlement by. I was happy to watch the stars, and because the open spaces were thin, the stars seemed to come and go quickly. I felt

What is the most interesting or amusing idea, line, title, or passage
you have not been able to find a place for in your published work?

I have not yet written the novel
called "Fourth Person Singular"
which is a   phrase in my first
novel "HER". But I am working
on it.

Lawrence Ferlinghetti

AUTHOR'S NAME *Lawrence Ferlinghetti* Oct '87

the sky wheeling over me like it was in a great rush and there were no sounds on the ridge, only a faint hiss, like the stars were shedding just a little of their fire as they moved. Finally I pulled the blanket over my face and went to sleep.

When I woke, though I had not moved in the night and the cover still lay on my face, I could sense that something had changed. I pulled the cover down and lifted my head and my chest seized up because I'd died in the night and they'd buried me and I was peeking up out of my grave. Damn my eyes if that's not what I saw, and it took me a long grapple with my breath to realize that it was snow. A snow had come in the night and had covered the bedstead and the shapeless mound of my body. But I still felt like I was floating there, watching from the afterlife, cut off from the body that lay beneath the snow. I put my head back down and closed my eyes. The cover of snow was warm and it made me want to just let go and return to my sleep and never wake up, and that scared the juice out of me. I could feel the weight of the snow and now I wanted to jump up and stamp around the room, but I couldn't. Instead I waited. And it was then that I knew I must go to Winifred and have a son.

Lawrence Ferlinghetti

I have not yet written the novel called Fourth Person Singular, *which is a phrase in my first novel,* Her. *But I am working on it.*

False
Starts

Mary Elsie Robertson

For me, a novel usually starts with an image, and this is the way my novel What I Have to Tell You *(Doubleday, 1989) began—with the image of a white doorknob shaped like an eyeball, the kind of doorknob sometimes found in old houses. I knew that the doorknob opened the door of a room into the past, into my character's childhood, and I also had the notion that it was through paying a visit to a psychic that the character suddenly remembered that doorknob and saw it clearly. This, then, is the way my novel originally began:*

It was the doorknob she saw first, shaped like an eyeball, white with a shiny film like oil covering it but not purely white either because when she looked closely she could see the pale blue lines—little cracks so fine that not even her fingernail could find them. It was above her head, that knob that would fill her hand if she clasped it, sticking out from the door on a long stem that leaned toward the floor. She knew it would rattle when she touched it as everything else did in that house, all those joints and four-sided nails creaking and groaning. She reached up her hand to the knob, feeling it cool and slick in her palm, and turned it clockwise, slowly, until Sophie loomed up suddenly out of the shadows on the other side of the pie cupboard. "I see what you're doing and if you know what's good for you you'll stop right there in your tracks, missy," she said.

Quickly she pushed on the door, it swung open, and she was back in the room she'd shared with Jordan until they were ten. It was the time they'd had scarlet fever—they were four—and she was in bed beside him, his face inches from hers, his eyes so blue they looked almost purple. She could see her own eyes grown tiny inside his.

"When you scratch it my skin comes off," he whispered. "See?"

"I'm sick too," she told him, outraged. "Just like you. But I'm sicker. I might die."

Under the sheet, Jordan kicked her, hard, and she could feel the heat his skin gave off. "No you won't, either," he said, pounding his legs up and down. "If anybody does, I will. I'm the one."

In the next version of the novel, there is a first-person narrator, the doorknob has taken on less importance, and the scene has grown longer. This time, it's the psychic who sees the doorknob first. And this scene no longer opens the novel; it comes in chapter two.

Settling back in the chair with her hands over her stomach, Phoebe already had her eyes closed and even before she spoke I could feel her sliding off into that state where whatever it was she saw behind her closed eyelids was more vivid to her than anything she might have seen in the here-and-now world.

"A white doorknob," she was saying, and as soon as she spoke, I could feel it cool in my palm, shaped like an egg, my fingers closing over it.

"And a heavy door," Phoebe said in that faraway voice, "swinging high on its hinges, and down at the bottom there's a corner chewed away and some black lines somebody's made with a crayon."

As she spoke, I was suddenly squatting in front of that door with the black crayon still in my fingers and when I pushed, the door swung open, and there was Jordan in the big bed with a ram's head carved into the headboard with his face red and broken out and the smell of fever in the air. I was so intent on looking that I didn't hear Sophie come up the stairs to swoop me up like a hawk on a pullet and lift me squealing into the air.

"I know what you're up to, missy, and don't you think I don't," Sophie said in that hill-country drawl I'd know anywhere.

I kicked and spit all the way down the stairs and when Sophie got me outside the back door she swatted me on my behind before she left me lying in the dust having a screaming fit, drumming my feet.

"You keep that up and I'll come on out there and womp you another one," she said through the screen. "Give you something to carry on about."

After a while I got up out of the dust and ran around the house to the front door where I slipped inside and started making my way up the wide front stairs, being careful to put each foot down right so the boards wouldn't creak. When I got upstairs to the bedroom which was just as much mine as it was Jordan's, I scooted him over in the bed so I could have my side back. His eyes had little lights far down inside them.

"Your face is all red, Jordan," I told him, but I could see he wasn't listening. He was excited about something, his breathing quick and fluttery.

"The spider came out of her hole and saw me," he said, looking at me from his pillow with those little lights in his eyes. "She waved her legs wide"—he circled a hand in the air—"and she said hel-loooooo. Her eyes are red, and listen, JayJay. She's got a whole pile of fly bones in that crack in the ceiling behind her web."

Jordan talked funny the way we both did at Christmas that time when we got into the eggnog.

"I *know* that," I told him. My eyes were so close to his that everything went fuzzy. "She chews up the flies and spits out their bones."

There were lights in Jordan's eyes because there was a fire in his head. I could feel it hot in his cheeks and I wondered if it might burn him up the way the manure piles got so hot deep inside sometimes that little wisps of smoke came out.

I wanted a fire like that in my head too since I always wanted to be the same as Jordan. We were twins and just alike.

The spider lived in the crack in the ceiling above our bed and sometimes we could see one of her long hairy legs awaving slowly in the air below the crack when we went to bed at night. There were words we had to say to keep her from coming down from her crack and taking slow walks across our faces when we were asleep. The ram that was carved into the headboard and who never slept was our guard against her. We ran our fingers over the ram's head every night in the dark after Mama came in to tell us goodnight, reminding him to keep watch. For two nights, since Jordan had the fire in his head, I hadn't gotten to pat the ram. I reached up and ran my fingers over his curly hair.

"Oh, he doesn't like *you* anymore," Jordan said. "Now he just likes me."

"That's a lie!" I told Jordan.

The little points of light deep in his eyes glittered, and I remembered other times he had hurt my feelings. Tears came to my eyes, but I wouldn't let him see.

Instead, I clamped my teeth down hard on his arm, on that hot, cushiony skin I realized was just made for biting. I closed my teeth more deeply on it in a fit of pleasure. Jordan didn't yell, but even so the door suddenly opened and Sophie loomed with the shadows from the linen closet behind her.

"Just can't wait to have your face all broke out like hissen, can you?" she said. "Now you git yourself right out of that bed and on down that stair before I break your tail with a stick."

I was already half out of the bed before she stopped talking, but

I took time to look with satisfaction at the marks—reddish purple—my teeth had left on Jordan's arm.

"I don't want you! I don't want you!" Jordan said to me, kicking his legs. "Go away!"

Yelling, I ran through the door past Sophie, but not fast enough to miss her hard, wiry hand coming down on my backside.

"I wish a hog would eat you up, Sophie," I shouted from the foot of the stairs. "Right down to your ugly old feet."

"Git out of here!" Sophie said. "Git! Git!"

Under the copper beech tree I cried with rage and hurt, with the taste of Jordan's skin still in my mouth. I couldn't stand it when he was mean when all I wanted was to lie with my head on the same pillow as his and be just the same.

Standing on one leg like a heron in the shallows, bringing to mind all the magic words I knew, I shut my eyes and thought about Jordan's face swelling up fuller and fuller like a red balloon until it burst and of Sophie being slowly chewed on by a hog while she cried oh, oh, and tried to crawl away.

In the final version of the novel, the doorknob is mentioned in chapter three, and there are a few sentences about the time when the narrator and her brother had scarlet fever, but this scene has been cut, as well as others I had written about the narrator's childhood. I decided, in the end, that it wasn't necessary to include so many scenes; I could suggest in a few sentences all that was crucial.

Elmore Leonard

Two false starts on Killshot *(Arbor House, 1989)*

ONE

When the Degas brothers were young boys they would come to Walpole Island in the summer to visit their grandmother, an Ojibway medicine woman. At that time her cottage was painted a bright blue. The city boys from Toronto loved it here, an Indian reservation on an island that was all trees and marsh. During the day they'd hunt for muskrats with a single-shot .22. In the evening they'd watch the big ore carriers and ocean freighters go by.

Walpole is on the Canadian side of the shipping channel that cuts through islands at the mouth of the St. Clair River: on the waterway between Lake Erie and Lake Huron, not far from Detroit.

ONE

Victor Degas said that after he finished the job he'd like to stay around there and visit his grandmother. The old man he worked for said, "Sure, of course, long as you want," handing Victor an envelope with $5,000 in it, the down payment.

"She lives on Walpole Island," Victor said. "You know where I mean, the Indian reserve? Close by Detroit but on this side, in Canada. I'm going to drive down there so I'll have a car."

This man Victor Degas worked for in Toronto was Italian, born in Calabria seventy-five years ago. When a commission investigating organized crime asked him what he did for a living, the old man said he was in the pepperoni business, he sold it to places they made pizza. He had heard that Victor was half or part Indian, but always thought of him as one of those French-Canuck tough guys they hired to do the dirty jobs. Victor had that build, that short thick body. Maybe Indians did too. The old man didn't know anything about Indians or care to hear about Victor's grandmother. But Victor was about to do a special job for him, so the old man allowed him to speak.

"My brothers and I would visit her in the summer, when we were boys. We like to watch the big ore boats pass in the channel, so close you could throw rocks at them. Or we go hunting for muskrats, wade in the marsh with a .22 we had, a single-shot. We hardly ever saw any, so on the way home we'd shoot at dogs and cats. Oh, it got people mad, but they never done nothing to us or told the grandmother."

The old man, patient, said, "No? Why not?"

"Our grandmother was a medicine woman of the Ojibway. They were afraid of her," Victor Degas said. "On a day you don't even see the trees moving, she could make a wind come in under the door and stir the fire in the fireplace."

"She could burn a house down," the old man said.

"She could do it easy. You know what else?" Victor Degas said. "If she wants to she can get a bird to shit on your car. If she don't like you. She does it best with seagulls. A seagull flies over, she points to the car. That one."

"I could use a woman like that," the old man said.

Ann Arensberg

From Incubus, *a novel-in-progress: opening paragraph of Chapter One*

On the night of July 21, 1972, the Northern Lights were visible at the forty-fifth parallel. They appeared over Raymond, Maine, as hanging draperies, shining white with a tinge of blue, the color of glaciers. The Manning house, which was screened by tall red spruce trees, had no view of the lights from the upper or lower windows. Inside the house, there was no electric light. The real-estate agents had shut off the power and water. Since the drifter who slept on the porch had broken camp, leaving behind a pile of burnt-out matches, the house was uninhabited by human tenants, although other forms of life had gained entry to the interior. Flies were breeding in the space between the screens and windows; flat brown beetles nested under warped linoleum; silverfish hatched in the blanket chest in the storeroom. Age and decay continued to take their toll, natural processes working on organic matter. Dust gathered; brick crumbled; paint peeled; fabric faded and rotted; woodwork expanded and contracted according to the season. Other processes took place on their own eccentric timetable, irregular incidents defying the laws of nature. A candle in a pewter holder sent up coils of smoke, as if someone had passed through the room and snuffed it out. The wall clock struck the half-hour and the hour, although its pendulum had been removed to a place on the mantel. On the brightest days, shadows collected in the mirrors, darkening the glass and canceling any reflections.

Many experts believe that Spirits resemble ham actors, who pull out the stops when they have a captive audience; yet the candle, the clock, and the mirrors played to empty houses, like a priest who celebrates the office with no congregation. Spirits are also known for missing their entrances, leaving onlookers waiting in vain for a scene to be enacted. The next owners of Manning House might be treated to nightly entertainment, or remain unaware they shared quarters with bodiless thespians.

This was a false start. The tone is too ironical; and the story is not about the haunting of a specific place, but about a freewheeling Entity.

INTRODUCTION TO THE
HERO OF THE STORY, HENRY LIEBER

Lorraine Drago was a practical person. She liked solving problems as much as she disliked uncertainty. When the old privet hedge at the Manning house grew tall and untidy, she hired a landscaping firm to improve its appearance. If the well ran dry, she would make an appointment with a well-driller. If the well-digger failed to find water after several attempts, she would not have had the slightest objection to calling in a dowser. Recurring bloodstains in one of her real-estate listings were a practical problem, more specialized than wells or shrubbery, demanding the services of an expert, a dowser of houses. Mrs. Drago approached Ruth Hiram, a specialist in legends, which were nothing more than gossip of the kind that was besetting the Manning house. "I want someone to get rid of them," she said, "someone with good references," as if these oddities were rodents in the baseboards, whose holes could be baited with poison and plugged with steel wool.

Like most librarians, Ruth Hiram believed that knowledge can be found in books. Her own books, collections of folklore, came from other books. She had never witnessed, firsthand, the bandaged British soldier who limped across the Dartmouth common on winter nights; or the bearded white moose of the Allagash with one spiraled horn; or the lighthouse at Naskeag, abandoned since 1865, which lit a troop ship to safety in 1944. Mrs. Drago's appeal sent her back to the stacks of the library, where she searched through the volumes numbered 133 ("Occult Sciences"). She picked out a book by Henry J. Lieber, PhD, published in the late 1950s by Portland University. The monograph in question bore the title *Number 9, Warren Place: Consensus and Conflict in Reports of a Present-Day Haunting*. Beside it on the shelf was a smaller book protected in clear plastic, the popular edition reissued by a paperback reprinter, which had gained notoriety under the title *The House That Went Crazy*. The paperback cover carried a three-line biography of the author, giving his age (forty-eight), his standing (doctor of psychology), and a reference to fellowships from Stanford and Duke Universities. A much-reduced photograph showed a broad nose, high forehead, square chin, and a smiling expression Mrs. Drago might find reassuring. As it happened, Mrs. Drago never read either version of the book. She studied the picture of Henry J. Lieber's mild face, went directly to the telephone, and fired off a night letter to Portland.

∎

Academics are putty in the hands of commercial publishers. They are accustomed to dealing with university presses, where their manuscripts are edited by scholars like themselves, and where the process of publication is slow and leisurely, lengthier than gestation in an elephant. Financial expectations are modest on either side: a term like "marketing" is rarely, if ever, uttered. When they hold the finished book in their trembling hands, it is jacketed in wrappers that are soberly designed and colored, with the author's name in smaller print than the title, an object which is valued chiefly for its contents. When the people at Viva Books first approached him, Henry Lieber quelled an inkling of suspicion. They were offering him a sum that equaled half his salary for a book which had sold 630 copies. Furthermore, they wanted to publish it "on a crash schedule," and were quite unconcerned about bringing it up to date. "They" were a scrawny young man in his middle twenties, with a receding hairline, pointed ears, and wire-rimmed spectacles, wearing the attire of a serious college student, faded blue jeans, rolled-up shirtsleeves, and a dark-striped necktie. His garb had the effect of earning Henry's confidence, or, more to the point, of lowering Henry's guard. He agreed to the young man's request for "a few minor cuts," and rewrote the Introduction for "a general trade audience." Since he made no demands and asked no bothersome questions, the young man praised him for being an "easy author."

When Henry opened the package containing his ten free copies, he decided that "willing dupe" was the fitting epithet. The book which had established his reputation, the definitive work on interviewing victims of hauntings, was decked out in a four-color print job and Gothic lettering, with a Victorian mansion pictured as a demon's face, two windows on the upper story like bloodshot eyes, the door like an open maw, fangs bared and glistening. It was several minutes before he noticed the title, changed without his knowledge or consent to *The House That Went Crazy*. He called his perfidious editor in Manhattan and showed him what a "difficult" author was made of. Giving vent to his rage was his only satisfaction. The books had been loaded on trucks and shipped to the stores. Henry was slow to act; but he acted decisively. He went to the office of the dean of graduate studies and pledged any forthcoming royalties to a scholarship fund, earmarked for students of promise in his department who exhibited a serious interest in parapsychology.

Judging by his colleagues, the book might not have been published. Whatever their reactions—envy, hilarity, disapproval—they never referred to the subject in Henry's presence. Perhaps they kept silent out of genuine fellow feeling; or perhaps the Dean had told them about the scholarship. They may have been unaware of the book's existence, since they seldom entered the kind of stores that carried it, brightly lit markets with wide aisles and capacious display racks, filled with tempting fresh wares which could be reached without using a stepladder.

Henry's associates might not have frequented these chain stores; but it quickly developed that they were the rarefied exception. Henry heard from his colleagues' wives and their teenaged children; from his students, the secretaries, the Bursar, the chaplain, and the soccer coach; the steward at the faculty club; the staff of the campus cafeteria; his landlady, his barber, a bank clerk, and an usher at the symphony; and every member of the English Department, tenured and untenured. His assistant, Cora Whitman, who was helping him with an experiment, offered her heartfelt condolences and a bottle of champagne. The Director of Admissions asked him who would be starring in the movie; and one excited girl student yelled out, "Hey, Dr. Lieber, I bought it!"

By the end of this chapter I realized that comedy was boxing me in; and that I would have to choose between being humorous and being scary.

Jane Bowles

Editor's Note: The beginning of an unfinished story, found in the author's notebooks

FRIDAY

He sat at a little table in the Green Mountain Luncheonette apathetically studying the menu. Faithful to the established tradition of his rich New England family, he habitually chose the cheapest dish listed on the menu whenever it was not something he definitely abhorred. Today was Friday, and there were two cheap dishes listed, both of which he hated. One was haddock and the other fried New England smelts. The cheaper meat dishes had been omitted. Finally, with compressed lips, he decided on a steak. The waitress was barely able to hear his order.

"Did you say steak?" she asked him.

"Yes. There isn't anything else. Who eats haddock?"

"Nine tenths of the population." She spoke without venom. "Look at Agnes." She pointed to the table next to his.

Andrew looked up. He had noticed the girl before. She had a long freckled face with large, rather roughly sketched features. Her hair, almost the color of her skin, hung down to her shoulders. It was evident that her mustard-colored wool dress was homemade. It was decorated at the throat with a number of dark brown woollen balls. Over the dress she wore a man's lumber jacket. She was a large-boned girl. The lower half of her face was long and solid and insensitive-looking, but her eyes, Andrew noted, were luminous and starry.

Although it was bitterly cold outside, the lunch room was steaming hot and the front window had clouded over.

"Don't you like fish?" the girl said.

He shook his head. Out of the corner of his eye he had noticed that she was not eating her haddock. However, he had quickly looked away, in order not to be drawn into a conversation. The arrival of his steak obliged him to look up, and their eyes met. She was gazing at him with a rapt expression. It made him feel uncomfortable.

"My name is Agnes Leather," she said in a hushed voice, as if she were sharing a delightful secret. "I've seen you eating in here before."

He realized that there was no polite way of remaining silent, and so he said in an expressionless voice, "I ate here yesterday and the day before yesterday."

"That's right." She nodded. "I saw you both times. At noon yesterday, and then the day before a little later than that. At night I don't come here. I have a family. I eat home with them like every-body else in a small town." Her smile was warm and intimate, as if she would like to include him in her good fortune.

He did not know what to say to this, and asked himself idly if she was going to eat her haddock.

"You're wondering why I don't touch my fish?" she said, catching his eye.

"You haven't eaten much of it, have you?" He coughed discreetly and cut into his little steak, hoping that she would soon occupy herself with her meal.

"I almost never feel like eating," she said. "Even though I do live in a small town."

"That's too bad."

"Do you think it's too bad?"

She fixed her luminous eyes upon him intently, as if his face held the true meaning of his words, which might only have seemed banal.

He looked at the long horselike lower half of her face, and decided that she was unsubtle and strong-minded despite her crazy eyes. It occurred to him that women were getting entirely too big and bony. "Do I think what's too bad?" he asked her.

"That I don't care about eating."

"Well, yes," he said with a certain irritation. "It's always better to have an appetite. At least, that's what I thought."

She did not answer this, but looked pensive, as if she were considering seriously whether or not to agree with him. Then she shook her head from side to side, indicating that the problem was insoluble.

"You'd understand if I could give you the whole picture," she said. "This is just a glimpse. But I can't give you the whole picture in a lunchroom. I know it's a good thing to eat. I know." And as if to prove this, she fell upon her haddock and finished it off with three stabs of her fork. It was a very small portion. But the serious look in her eye remained.

"I'm sorry if I startled you," she said gently, wetting her lips. "I try not to do that. You can blame it on my being from a small town if you want, but it has nothing to do with that. It really hasn't. But it's just impossible for me to explain it all to you, so I might as well say I'm from a small town as to say my name is Agnes Leather."

She began an odd nervous motion of pulling at her wrist, and to his surprise shouted for some hotcakes with maple syrup.

At that moment a waitress opened the door leading into the street, and put down a cast-iron cat to hold it back. The wind blew through the restaurant and the diners set up a clamor.

"Orders from the boss!" the waitress screamed. "Just hold your horses. We're clearing the air." This airing occurred every day, and the shrieks of the customers were only in jest. As soon as the clouded glass shone clear, so that the words GREEN MOUNTAIN LUNCHEONETTE in reverse were once again visible, the waitress removed the iron cat and shut the door.

Elizabeth Tallent

A fragment that never quite amounted to a short story

LIKE ICE

The morning they moved was, predictably, chaos. It was winter, and for the last few nights the narrow painted radiators had been silent; the house was alive with a drafty cold. Gus had guessed wrong about having the heat turned off. He'd guessed they'd be out of the house by Wednesday, and had even left the heat on an extra day for good measure, not wanting to seem to be rushing them, but it was Saturday morning and they still were not gone. Lisa woke early enough so that her room, with the U-Haul boxes pyramided in its corners, was still dim, and went into the dark downstairs bathroom. The first thing she touched—a faucet—was like ice. So rare was it for her to be awake before either her husband or her son that her mood immediately, unreasonably lightened. There was nothing about this morning or this day to take pleasure in—it's a despairing day, she warned herself, but the sensation of happiness persisted. It would have to wear itself out against the facts. She saw herself in a nightgown, ISU sweatshirt, and a pair of Gus's old socks dirtied from her wandering through the house last night, worrying over the little that was left to be done, knowing how every unfinished detail weighed on Gus's shoulders. Even now his irritation rankled, not as if it was his mood, ineffectually hidden from her, but as if it were her own, felt sharply and simply as she stood shivering, her arms around herself, her hair messed, sleep in the corners of her eyes so that they felt bracketed by a dry scratchiness. The bathroom was too cold to stay in long, far too cold for a bath, though for the moment she had it to herself; she had the whole quiet downstairs to herself, and herself to herself, as she never did once Wesley was awake. Gus, too, as long as he wanted anything from her, wanted everything, the same degree of attention demanded by their young son. Now she wondered if Gus was even in the house. If Gus stayed the night, that made it one kind of morning. If he didn't, that made it another. Lisa sat, cold porcelain against her heels, her braced feet, even through Gus's thick socks, taking the chill from the floor and translating it upward until all of her felt cold, and she urinated in an urgent grateful rush.

Lisa resented the cold itself less than the way Gus had guessed wrong in turning off the heat. His guessing wrong was a form of wishing this was behind him, or so she understood it, though what he told her was: he would stay as long as it takes.

Hearing him say, "As long as it takes," she'd understood that it would soon be possible to hate him. Once nothing could have seemed more implausible than hating Gus; once she wouldn't have been able to imagine how much she would have to change to be able to hate Gus. Closing her eyes to wash her face, she remembered the way she'd had to wash when they first moved into the house. Because Gus had disconnected the plumbing, they'd run a garden hose in through the bathroom window, and she'd bathed in its needling spray, standing up, the water warm for the first few instants and then, without any lukewarm transition, cold as snowmelt. She understood: a longer length of garden hose was left uncoiled in the sun for a few moments' more warmth. Wesley had loved those baths, though they set him shivering. The day his father finally got the plumbing right and working came as a big disappointment to him, because it meant his funny baths were over, so she'd let him keep the garden hose strung in through the window to wash with—it seemed such a small pleasure, so easily granted. And then one day he'd lost interest, which was just as well. It was fall, and too cold to leave the window open any longer, even a crack.

With the washcloth she did under her arms and between her legs, drying herself with the only towel she'd left unpacked, the towel they will all three have to use if they *are*, all three, in the house. He'd wanted this entire thing to be over fast, faster than she could stom-. ach, faster than it was reasonable to expect, though he'd denied wanting that. It was no help to hear him deny wanting her out of the house. It merely meant he saw the same cruelty she saw, and she'd known that. She'd divided herself into two parts to get through the last few weeks. One part, which showed, which was all she let show, was economical, efficient, familiar, intent on getting things done. The other part panicked. For that, the hidden part, panic was a full-time occupation. Sometimes she heard its voice. Its voice was harsh and frantic, blaming Gus, blaming herself, blaming even—absurdly— Wesley for being a wild four-year-old, for being sometimes pretty hyper. Last night, she knew, he'd kept his father in his room until at least two. Two was when she last climbed the stairs to hear, through the half-open door, Gus's voice, before descending the stairs to her room with the boxes in its corners to sleep. Gus must have fallen asleep on Wesley's bed, because she didn't remember waking during the night, and the way she was lying across their two sleeping bags, he would inevitably have disturbed her, getting into his. When she first saw the way he'd thrown his sleeping bag down, in their room, not only in their room but right beside her sleeping bag, she'd thought he meant it as charity, and she'd resented it enough that asking him to move—to find somewhere, anywhere else in the house to sleep—was on the tip of her tongue, but then, just in time, she'd thought that it was their last night together for him as much as for her and that very likely in the placement of his sleeping bag, which seemed so careless, he'd only meant to acknowledge that fact. To celebrate it, in a sense, in some crazy sense. Then, too, maybe lying in the dark together knowing what they both could not help knowing, that they would never sleep together even in this platonic way again, they would talk. So she'd left his sleeping bag where he'd thrown it down beside hers, and he hadn't slept in it. He might not even be in the house this morning at all. She didn't know what the new rules were and whether it would have caused trouble for him to stay overnight with them. But then, she thought, if he hadn't meant to sleep there, why unroll his sleeping bag in the first place? There had been so many contradictions lately that she shouldn't find herself amazed to come across one last contradiction. What she was doing, now, counted as a form of self-torture, because she didn't know him well enough recently to derive any good from wondering about what he would do or when he would do it or why. It was best when she let her neutral, competent self handle questions about Gus, because that self knows enough not to waste energy wondering about Gus's motives or behavior. If Gus wasn't in Wesley's room, he wasn't in the house. She didn't want to go look into Wesley's room—because, she told herself, in looking into Wesley's room there was a risk of waking Wesley, no matter how you warned yourself to be quiet, and once Wesley was awake she would no longer have this degree of self-possession, which seemed, just now, so important. Wesley had a sort of sixth sense for her presence. This sixth sense seemed to operate even in the deepest kind of sleep, when his expression was one of angelic remoteness.

In the living room she folded an afghan her grandmother had knitted them for a gift, slid it in over some quilts, and masking-taped the box shut, standing to kick it into the corner because she could not lift it. Though she kicked violently, the box moved in shuffling strokes, rasping like sandpaper. Because the house was old and only partially renovated when they bought it, Gus convinced Lisa they could do the last of the work themselves, arguing that it was the one and only way they could afford then, or probably ever, to buy a house. The big rented sander roared down the living room like a siren, but the little sander was a mosquito, a shrill small-scale annoyance. When she had wandered into the room where he was working on his knees, the room was intensely pleasing in that blank-slate way of emptied, unlived-in space, with drifts of apricot-colored sawdust from the ponderosa pine in the corners, faintly sour-smelling. His face was masked in the sawdust that caught in the fine hairs on his cheekbones, the nearly invisible hairs that shaded into the blond of his eyebrows, and the down that grew even on his straight nose. His eyes against the sawdust were very blue, very quick and alive; the flour-fine coating was so thick she once drew her initials on his cheek as she lay beneath him, her head pillowed on his balled-up, sawdust-caked Levis. Once they were done he observed that the plank she was lying on creaked slightly, and he would have to dowel it. Late that spring, she found him kneeling over some last perfectionist detail, the finest possible grade of sandpaper snugged like brass knuckles around his hand, the small sander with its umbilicus of electrical cord wrapped around it lying nearby, and she'd squatted and pulled the tuft of cotton from his ear to tell him that she was pregnant. Four years ago, or—put it the way Wesley likes it put—this is the house they have lived in since before he was born, though "before you were born" means nothing to Wesley, because at four he did not believe in time before he existed. He only pretended to.

Suddenly she couldn't stop herself from running up the stairs to see whether Gus was still there. He was. He lay with a leg across Wesley's body, Wesley turned away from his father, one of Wesley's hands flung out so that his fingers touched the blank wall from which his drawings and paintings have been removed, the other in a fist against his upper lip, his mouth open, his legs scissored. Under Gus's elbow, a Babar book. So he did sleep in the house: Lisa felt strangely reassured, even giddy with this reassurance that he had not yet been able to go. He fell asleep still dressed, an arm crooked in front of his face, a Levi'd leg thrown across his son. They both looked as if they'd fallen from a great height.

Gus was up, and all tension between the two of them mysteriously vanished. Maybe they had lived together too long for this not to seem another ordinary morning. She tucked the filter into the Melitta cone and dashed the fragrant dark French Roast with hot water until it rose, rinsed to a glittering, darker, almost black silt, and fell away, like compacted sand mimicking a vortex, coffee ticking into the pot. Gus tucked his shirt into his Levis, the same Levis he'd slept in; because he'd troubled neither to shave nor to change, he didn't look like anyone's father or husband, but a young lover who got out of bed to run to the corner for the *New York Times*, say, and bagels, and who had going back to bed on his mind. He wouldn't go back to bed, not in this house, but who knew what it was like with his lover? None of them got enough sleep. This made Wesley crazy—there was a reckless high he got the mornings after being up far too late. Gus drank his coffee without looking at her and she drank her coffee without looking at him. Wesley ran naked and barefoot, then T-shirted, then at last sweatshirted, blue-jeaned, and sneakered, through the house. For some reason the fact that it was emptied of all signs of them, of their lives, delighted him. He couldn't get enough of the empty house, and ran from the living room into the bedroom that had been theirs, through the bathroom, down the hallway into the kitchen, past the two of them at unseeing, blissful four-year-old speed. Then from the living room came a sudden sharp thump and the thud of his fall. He must have picked himself up again, because Lisa from the kitchen heard his caught breath, sharply sucked in; he was running and then again came the thump echoed by the fall. Gus said, "What's he—?" but she shook her head. They went to look. He was careening from room to room, throwing himself into walls. For another moment she was tempted to leave him alone: What harm could a child do an empty house? But then without thinking she was on her knees, her arms out, and when he came running he meant to pass her but she swung on her knees and, with her whole body, caught him.

Alix Kates Shulman

Lucky was flipping through the *Malomar Morning News* en route to the funnies and suddenly came upon her own face looking out at her—serious, intense, fanatical. Her lips were closed, almost pursed, in concentration, hiding the gap between her teeth; her unparted hair half covered her cheeks; but there was absolutely no mistaking that face.

Excitement spread over her, tickling her skin like bubble bath. "Look! Look! I got my picture in the paper!" she shouted, racing toward the kitchen to show her mother.

Anna's hands were wet, but she peered down at the open pages Lucky placed on the counter. "Where, dear?" She looked puzzled.

"There!" said Lucky, pointing to a picture at the bottom of the left-hand page. "See? That's me!"

"Why, so it is, Lucky. That most certainly is you. Well!" said Anna, bending down to examine the picture. "See if you can catch your father at the drugstore before he leaves and ask him to bring two more copies. No, better make it six."

The picture showed Merlin the Magician performing what looked like the multicolored scarf trick before a group of schoolchildren at the Malomar Public Library. The photographer had erred, for Merlin in the foreground was slightly out of focus while Lucky in the background was precisely, sharply revealed. There were other children in the picture as well, but somehow each of them was unclear for a different reason, leaving Lucky, by default, the unchallenged star.

When Steven came home all he could say was, "Why so serious, Lucky? Couldn't you have smiled at least?"—after which he went on to criticize Merlin's technique. But it was clear that he too was pleased to see his daughter's picture.

Lucky took the paper to her room that night, frequently glancing at it till lights out, then continuing every few minutes to turn on the light and look at it, for an hour or more. The next day at school several people remarked, with almost as much respect as surprise, that they had seen Lucky's picture in the paper. She gloated before them. All that day (a Friday) she walked more upright than usual, a bit more aware of her expression, her hairpart, her hem, reflecting a shift in self-esteem, though she covered as best she could with appropriate demurrals and false modesty.

By Monday the photo had been pretty much forgotten by everyone else, yet she herself had been subtly altered. Whenever she pictured herself after that, into her mind came a blowup of herself intently watching Merlin perform the scarf trick. She had seen herself framed in newsprint; she couldn't let it go. Her face had been featured as an example of something. It had to happen again, she decided. And the next time the caption must say her name.

May Swenson

From my folder, quite thick, of unfinished prose

MORE AFTER THIS

It was later on that she remembered she had forgotten to look in the mailbox. She had called the taxi too far ahead of time. Without a railway schedule, she did not discover until at the station (where the ticket window was closed) that the 10:30 train had been canceled, so that she would be at least an hour late, no matter how early she managed to leave the house. Locking the front door, she was startled to see the taxi man had already arrived. He kindly took from her left hand, as she opened the little purse in her right hand to drop the house key in, a plastic bag. Opening the cab door, he placed the plastic bag on the backseat. "No, no," she said mock-severely, and laughed. "I don't want to bring the garbage to New York!" He was quite a nice man. He caught on, and twinkled, as she lifted out the plastic bag and transferred it to the garbage can by the gate, seeing to it that the lid went back on tight. Then she climbed into the cab, feeling relieved, almost settled already. But as the cab swirled on up the curve of the hill and she braced herself so as not to be knocked from one side to the other, the feeling returned of having to hurry. Leaning her head on the back of the seat, she became conscious of the seven separately shaped pills swallowed at breakfast, that were just now getting acquainted in her stomach: the little orange bullet, a time-release tranquilizer, the white circle of oyster-shell calcium, the smaller vitamin C, the thin dangerous oval Medrol, the four-sided (but not square) shrimp-pink blood-pressure pill, and the tan migraine fix (really miraculous) with a gray diamond imprinted on its smooth hump. Well, the Lord knew, she might need each of them before the day and night were done.

She was ready with the money as the cab pulled up to the station. A $50 bill. "Nothing smaller?" But he did change it, counting out nine $1 bills, then, thank goodness, a twenty, a ten, a five, but then three more ones. She tipped him $1, rolled up the bills into a tight sausage and crammed it into her change purse. She bore down with all her strength on the door handle until nearly the whole right side of the cab gave way, letting her carefully get out and give the heavy door a slam.

She went into the railway station, which was empty. The hours of peak travel being over, all tickets to be obtained were not at the window but on the train. Which would not be along for fifteen minutes. Outside, beside the tracks, was a lean-to with a scarred bench. She sat down beside an end wall heavily inscribed with ink, pencil, spray paint, knife cuts: "Fucked by the Fickle Finger of Fate"—"*Jesus Shaves* 0 0 0"—"Lil Orphant Annie Got the Cutest Fanny"—"JESUS IS ONLY WAX!!!" The ting-ting-ting of the semaphore bell finally sounded, and she emerged to stand exactly where the first car behind the diesel engine would halt. It rumbled in and she hoisted herself up the four iron steps by grabbing the handrail. If another train should hit from the rear, this car would be safest, or if *this* train hit another in front at least the heavy engine would help sustain the shock. There were only three other passengers, she was in a nonsmoker. At last she felt a sense of accomplishment as she sat back to look out the window, holding her little change purse of black rhino hide, bought in a Tucson thrift shop so many years ago, ready for the conductor when he came along to issue her ticket. She was riding backward, as she preferred to do, in this way getting, she felt, a wider view of the backyards of houses below the tracks. The train passed over wooded gullies, then village cross-streets, rows of shops, then clapboard houses with fenced-in gardens, washing on the lines, alleys with parked cars, schoolhouses, white churches with their peaked steeples, graveyards. More than parks, or golf courses, or playgrounds, even ponds, she enjoyed the white and green of graveyards, the rich shade of their ancient trees, sunlight on the gravel paths, the exclusiveness and privacy, almost never anyone seen walking within the labyrinth of headstones and tombs. A rural graveyard was like a spacious, clean, fresh, beautifully made bed. Its atmosphere untampered with, stayed the same, reliable, restful, whether under winter snow or at the height of summer's ripeness. She drew a deep breath, and smiled.

It was just after entering the long tunnel leading to Penn Station that the train stopped. Which often happened, and did not cause anyone worry until about fifteen minutes had gone by. She would be very late at the dentist's, of course. "Equipment problems," a conductor finally confessed, moving through the cars. There would be a delay, and "if the lights should go out, no cause for panic. They'll shortly come on again, and we'll be under way."

A man wearing a flat, fine-haired black toupee, holding a *Newsday,* made a grouchy face across the aisle. Beyond the grimy windows was blackness, and now the train lights dimmed slowly, then went entirely out.

The effect was unexpected. Not scary or uncomfortable particularly, not producing anxiety so much as a set of new sensations. Total blackness. Not a hint of light within the sweep of her eyes. Were they open or shut? She blinked, or believed she did, but took hold of her eyelashes and pulled the eyelids down. Under closed lids the dark was not so dense. Squeezing her eyes shut engendered wriggling spots of different colors. Opened, her eyes seemed almost to touch a high, thick wall, something like black rubber, that stretched beyond the width of the train out into the tunnel where the distant signals of red or green were also extinguished. She concentrated, hoping to hear sounds, or smell odors, or sense, perhaps by echolocation, while swiveling her neck, any movements, breathings, anything at all being done, or spoken by the other passengers. But silence, a paralytic stillness, was complete inside and outside the train. Deliberately she decided to let go of tension, and relaxed in her seat, after checking that her purse and other things inside her carrying bag were safe, the three zippers closed. Might as well go to sleep. Wished she had her little transistor radio along. In bed at night it habitually helped her to drop off. She'd dial a talk show, the phone calls from all over the country offering personal problems for solution—the word "relationship" invariably figured in these calls—and they were somehow soothing, as long as she alertly excised the aggressive voices, with their accompanying snatches of music, of the advertisers. This was done by clicking off the volume immediately on hearing the words, "More after this. We'll take a break. Stay with us." Hours could pass, on a near-sleepless night, with her mind peacefully afloat among the various voices setting forth their troubles, with the show's host promptly delivering capable suggestions, advice, gentle or crisp reprimands and, finally, sensible remedies summarized at great speed, down to the bottom line: "We'll take a break. More after this." And during one of those clicked-off breaks, she'd fall asleep, innocent of ever finding out the names or messages of any of the sponsors.

The train stopped with a jerk. Not very extreme, but it woke her up. "Pennsylvania Station. Last stop. Please be sure to collect your valuables before you leave the train."

Somewhat bewildered, she found herself on the platform, moving within a jostling crowd toward the escalator. A clock high on a pillar showed 11:15. Her appointment had been for 10:00 A.M.

Dave Smith

Opening paragraph of an untitled essay

My first one was a model-A Ford. Two-door coupe, standard issue black, no frills, scarcely drivable. What did any of that matter—to me this was the world. It appeared in our driveway. It was mine. My father, between his backing-and-filling and his new regulations, said so. I felt as if, in the idiomatic expression, I had died and gone to heaven, so great was my joy. In fact it would not be all that long before I discovered the "gift" of an automobile meant more likely dead than gone to any place remotely like Heaven.

John Hollander

What follows is a rejected first thought from my Rhyme's Reason, *a guide to the structure of verse in English (Yale University Press, 1981, 2nd rev. ed. 1989). I eventually wrote two more complex self-descriptive sonnets, one for the Shakespearean and one for the Italian form, but this one was never used. Like all examples of verse forms and structures in the book, it is about itself.*

WHAT A SONNET IS

A certain kind of short poem's called a sonnet—
Its first two lines will only get to rhyme
With the next two—see, now, you've come upon it,
These four lines hold together every time.
So take another group of four more lines
That end in rhymes like those that went before:
The final words of one of these designs
Sound something like the closing of a door.
We're in the last act of the three-act show
(Sonnets have fourteen lines arranged like this one—
Count down and see there isn't far to go.
This line's the twelfth—it's very hard to miss one.)
Then, at the very end, you'll find out whether
These last two lines can finally get together.

Donald Justice

This started as a verse play back about 1958. I always had a certain af-
fection for this beginning but could not go much further with it.

MONOLOGUE IN AN ATTIC

[*Enter* ARTHUR, *a man of about 30,*
through a trapdoor.]

The sad aroma of mothballs—
What a beautiful smell that is!
But where can the flies have got to
Now, that used to buzz at the pane
All summer, making their music?
I used to sit here admiring
Those ridiculous, long-drawn-out
Wagnerian death agonies
Of theirs for hours; once in a while,
One might stand up and stretch his wings,
Revived like the heldentenor
By demands for an encore.

[*A buzzing of flies is heard.*]

Strange,
How nothing ever seems to change
Up here but the weather. Downstairs,
My mother's radio would be
Tuned to another opera.
Mother had tempests. Still, one could
Always escape to the attic. . . .

Cast-Off Lines and Fragments

Robert Coover

PARTY TALK: UNHEARD CONVERSATION AT *GERALD'S PARTY**

Quotes abstracted from vast quantity of "outtakes" and sorted alphabetically.

"(Like this?)"

". . . And it's a knockout!"

". . . And the lusty impression they have exercised on the popular imagination, but . . ."

". . . And then there's her rather unusual childhood . . ."

". . . At the synapse . . . !"

". . . But of course it was Orpheus who looked back, wasn't it, not . . ."

". . . Frozen into senseless self-contradictory patterns."

". . . It is the effect that seeks always the cause."

". . . Once you—heh heh—get the hang of it . . ."

". . . That got such a rise . . ."

". . . The unbreathable silence . . ."

". . . To shut things down . . ."

". . . Was the hush just before . . ."

"But the way that it whistled when ris!"

"Got our firss piece a tail together!"

" 'Ass my boy!"

" 'Ass our Janny!"

" 'Ass Big Glad's baby brother."

" 'N Hoo-Sin. 'N' so on . . ."

"A bit tight . . ."

"A busman's holiday . . ."

"A little—?"

"A long time ago, long ago . . ."

"A star is born and all that!"

*Simon and Schuster, 1986.

101

"A unique adventure!"

"A what—?"

"Above all else, they should be trained to the point of self-confidence and have a professional pride and interest in work."

"After what he said to me?"

"Ah. Is that so . . . ?"

"Ah! That young man! Well, it wasn't its size, you know . . ."

"Ah! Well! Well!"

"Ah . . ."

"Ah, baysay my feces, Hugly!"

"Ah, the plot grows a complication."

"Ah, when will we ever learn?"

"Ah, you dumb twat! Pick 'em up yourself!"

"Ah, Fats, when you gonna get some learnin'?"

"Alas, a soft file cannot clean off ingrained rust."

"All style and no substance."

"All that running around in the streets—I just couldn't keep up!"

"All I mean to say, is that Ros was about the only person in the world who didn't treat me like a dummy!"

"All I want is for you to find true happiness, with all my heart I do!"

"Always—?"

"An hour! We had to wait longer than that for the goddamn fuzz to show up!"

"An . . . an accident, my mother—she broke her legs, her collarbone, her jaw, front teeth, one wrist . . ."

"And then she'd get confused and say it was for darts and all you had to throw were beanbags!"

"And they're filming it all on some kind of portable TV!"

"And yet . . ."

"And I'm not sure I haven't done it again!"

"Any that shit left?"

"Apparently, while they were going over a bridge at fifty miles an hour, Ros just opened the door and stepped out."

"Are you feeling better, Miss?"

"As I thought, a complete mystery."

"Assume the worst and . . . and . . ."

"At least there's no mystery about that one."

"Aw, hell, Ger, I'm on a, you know, a cunt hunt for some class ass!"

"Bande de cons, quand même! Tout le monde s'en fout . . . !"

"Beautiful from front, worm-eaten behind."

"Besides, who knows, maybe the little tads have all gone back to the promptuary."

"Big brains here prefers to abuse the living."

"Birth and death, the two great ego trips . . ."

"Blah! Somebody's sprayed it with deodorant or something!"

"Bordel de merde . . .!"

"Bullshit! That's not the point!"

"But if everything we call reality is also a kind of mask, then . . . then . . ."

"But maybe not. Maybe they'd simply preferred to keep quiet about it and try to forget."

"But that's what I've been trying to explain."

"But we both grew up in such happy families."

"But we—we can't take this, Mr. Trainer."

"But who's this punctured scumbag you dragged in with you, Beni?"

"But you'll never guess who's Zack's newest discovery!"

"But I got a pump!"

"But I'm not kidding myself. I know how you look at her and how you look at me."

"But, listen, get your tonsils tuned, sweetheart, the kid's writing you some new songs!"

"Button, button, Jacko!"

"By golly, y'know I haven't had guacamole since we were in Mexico, Iris and me."

"By the way, there's this young guy I want Tania to—pop!—meet, one of my clients' sons, a painter, very sweet . . ."

"By the way, who's that heavy lady over there scowling at us?"

"By the way, Ger, you got any more of them party favors?"

"Ça fait mal . . . !"

"C'mere, you kinky fartbrained yodeler—gimme a hug!"

"C'mon, Vadge, cut the goddamn muggin' and give us a hand with Zack."

"Certainly my mother never walked just right afterward, but always had to twist her hip a little as she moved."

"Christ, he even sounds like one!"

"Close your eyes, everybody! I got nothing on but a smile!"

"Cyril said to tell you . . ."

"Cyril?"

"Damn right!"

"Dead body?"

"Defloration's not a light undertaking, I thought you knew that."

"Dickie said that—?"

"Dickie . . . ?!"

"Dickie? He took Naomi up to the bathroom."

"Dickie? Well, he's got a cute ass for one thing, tight and narrow, but not too hard, with soft blond hair all over it."

"Did you see Malcolm's crazy séance?"

"Did I mention his high moral character?"

"Didn't she come with the Scar and Prissy Loo?"

"Didn't you notice how quiet it was back here? He fixed the upstairs toilet, too."

"Didn't you see?"

"Do you chew it or suck it?"

"Do you remember the time Louise jumped all over him in that restaurant for the way he sucked up his spaghetti?"

"Do you think it was really Ros's ghost?"

"Don't ask me. Ask Mee."

"Don't be cruel, Geoffrey."

"Don't do that, Fats!"

"Don't pay him any mind, sir, he's just a bit excitable—it's so difficult, don't you see . . ."

"Don't pretend, Geoffrey! I love you too much for that!"

"Don't try to explain, just do it again . . ."

"Don't what—?!"

"Don't worry about Louise. She means well. But she's not very happy."

"Down to, more like! Ho-boy—hot as a junked-up canary!"

"Everybody lives by one lie or another . . ."

"Except the walls both reflect and let you see through at the same time, don't ask me how."

"Excuse me, but what do you feel about the breakdown of law and order in our society?"

"Feels good."

"Ffooo! To piss 'n' to fart, it's good for the heart—ain't that so, Doc?"

"First one tonight."

"First one?"

"First, she'd complain that you invited her down to play pool, but your cue stick was bent or broken or something . . ."

"For that guy, love's just a passing fanny."

"Form is emptiness and emptiness is form."

"Forwards and backwards!"

"Fred always was one for acting things out."

"Frock? Frock?"

"Fuck that."

"Funny?"

"Ger, are you there?"

"Get down!"

"Ghosts don't salivate."

"Give love a chance!"

"Go up and see for yourself, it don't cost nothing."

"God's had his little joke on us, Gladys, I don't see why we can't have a few on him! I mean, 'ass fair, isn'it?"

"Goodness sake, you bachelors!"

"Grandma used to slip us bits of food, but she was simple and Mother always found out, so that just made it worse."

"Ha ha! Haven't seen one of those things in years!"

"Hair lacquer."

"Half past a . . . pig's ass, friend, and . . . losing ground . . ."

"Hang in there!"

"Hang on to it!"

"Haven't I seen that girl somewhere before . . . ?"

"He and Peg were in the kitchen a while ago."

"He came in the door and fell down the well, that's it, all she wrote."

"He came tearing down through here like a wild bull with a banderillo up its ass."

"He did an imitation of the Captain at our Christmas party that had the whole force busting their britches!"

"He did it, Gerry! It was Dickie!"

"He did. But you can make it well, Gerald."

"He doesn't have enough character to hold his fucking face together."

"He just married the wrong girl . . ."

"He knows something."

"He looks a mite like that feller got caught in the milkin' machine."

"He possesses the dangerous combination of too much physical vigor and too little mental inhibitory power."

"He used to punch tickets all day on the railroad."

"He was so . . . so crazy . . . !"

"He was such a polite, elegant, intelligent man!"

"Hé! Ho! Vous m'écoutez ou quoi, merde!"

"He's got a full set."

"He's got a mean fist."

"He's plowing the deep, got a bone-on like a fencepost, and the most beatific goddamn grin on his map you ever saw!"

"Hey! That clock! It's moving again!"

"Hey—hah!—'dj'ever heara one about the young bride'na baloney skin—?"

"Hey, bring that pearl-diver in here, lady, I got some rotten pipes need reaming out!"

"Hey, heard any good jokes lately?"

"Hey, if it ain't Beni the blimp!"

"Hey, if you're gonna start making fucking rules, I'll get my own."

"Hey, it's okay, Vic, the boat don't sail till midnight!"

"Hey, kid, we got a book yet?"

"Hey, look at these old-fashioned sugar cookies!"

"Hey, look who's here!"

"Hey, wait a sec, Pop! Where you going?"

"Hey, what is this stuff, Una?"

"Hey, Charley, ya like them bazooms?"

"Hey, Doc, I wunner if you could gimme a helpin' gland."

"Hey, I want you two kids t'fine alla happiness inna world, I mean it, juss like me'n whatserface here!"

"Hoary but true!"

"Hold on to it!"

"Honest, I wish I was your heart's desire, Geoffrey. It would make me the happiest girl in the whole world."

"How about the Dropper?"

"How little is actually known of the subtle ways in which one's conduct is determined!"

"How this young fella'n me—this prince 'n me—a long time ago—long ago—"

"Hugues's done his number, Zack."

"Hugues?"

"Hugues's kaput. Fee-nee."

"Hung up?"

"I admit, it has its drawbacks."

"I can't get in it, but I could wear it like a hat!"

"I caught his eye."

"I didn't think of that . . ."

"I don't have a lot of fun at these parties, but I think I have more fun than I'd have in a revolution."

"I don't know what I would have done without him during my last divorce—I was such a wreck!"

"I don't know what Jim has her on, but it sure gives her a hell of an imagination."

"I don't know, it seems to me he's just explained why he can't stop clutching bottoms as though he were trying to milk them!"

"I don't like religious jokes . . ."

"I doubt it. Anyway, I'll—say, where did this bottle of scotch come from?"

"I dunno, but I could eat a whole one right now! Startin' from either end!"

"I dunno, I got a one-track mind—I can't concentrate on two things at once."

"I dunno, I think some old lady made a hole in the fucking bathwater up there or something."

"I forgot to look."

"I hadn't realized your wife had had a cesarean with Mark."

"I haven't seen one of these things in years!"

"I heard him say he was going to do it!"

"I heard though he mighta hung it up."

"I hope I still have some capers."

"I knew they'd get back together . . ."

"I know of course there is a strange contradiction between the discomfort with which such creatures are commonly regarded . . ."

"I know you're the world's most faithful husband, but, hey, if your wife ever gets tired of you, lover . . ."

"I look like Christmas all by myself."

"I loved those kitchen shots, ma'am!"

"I mean, maybe what they were upset about was just the poor treatment or something . . ."

"I once tried to paint that, love's sigh . . ."

"I reckon what always moved me most, eh, since you ask . . ."

"I said, hah!"

"I see. Well, I'm in travel myself."

"I should be grateful, I suppose, that he didn't bray or oink."

"I should be so lucky, Axel!"

"I think he was trying to tear a piece of it off for a souvenir!"

"I think we're almost there . . ."

"I think I just saw that on the screen!"

"I thought he was meant to represent the overturning and misuse of reason . . ."

"I told her I knew where they were, I'd seen them just last week, and she only laughed at me—"

"I want to see the nude man anyway."

"I want to, but I can't!"

"I wasn't talkin' to you."

"I wondered why Talbot kept going back down for a second look!"

"I . . . I was still thinking about Dolph and Louise."

"I—I forget . . ."

"I'll bring you one, Daffie, if you'll promise to stop using your pudendum for an ashtray."

"I'll get it this time, I need one myself."

"I'm going into this with my eye open."

"I'm going to explain it one more time . . ."

"I'm not finished yet!"

"I'm not so dumb I don't see what people think of me, and sometimes it hurts."

"I'm not surprised, that runt was pushing his luck all night."

"I'm ready now."

"I'm sorry about that, Dolph, but if I didn't wear one, I couldn't get into this dress."

"I'm sorry."

"I'm sorry, buddy . . ."

"I'm sufferin' from frontline bottle fatigue! Nothin' works good anymore but my right elbow!"

"I'm truly sorry."

"I'm working on it, Mr. Quagg!"

"I've always loved you, I thought you knew . . ."

"I've never saved anything . . . all my—kaff! foo!—life, I'm not going . . . to start now . . ."

"If he doesn't want to get in it, then stick it at the back there, it'll add to the illusion."

"If you wanta see something funny, you should go check Knud out."

"If I had three wishes—or only one—"

"If Vic's brat's around, tell her 'very funny.' "

"Im—kaff! foo!—possible!"

"In fact there's something almost beautiful about her life. As with many unhappy lives . . ."

"In the front parlor, Beni. It's a fucking tragedy, man!"

"In the old days they forced the priests to do it as a kind of penance, though later, of course, the practice got misunderstood."

"In the sphere of perfect harmony . . ."

"In Venice . . ."

"Intimate as soap, man . . ."

"Is he here?"

"Is it some kind of joke?"

"Is that fair?"

"Is that what you want, a collection of memories like dead butter-flies?"

"Is that where the tall guy drags the dwarf over and swings him between his legs like a croquet mallet?"

"Isn'it?"

"It can't—hack!—be done!"

"It could have been worse."

"It happens to the best of them, you know!"

"It just goes to show . . ."

"It might be catching!"

"It should be easier than this."

"It was strange, but for a moment in there I felt somehow . . . anchored outside time . . ."

"It's a convention. Conventions—whoof!—change."

"It's a strange painting, so beautiful in an unearthly kind of way—yet . . ."

"It's all . . . kaff! . . . happening . . ."

"It's dark and dangerous out there."

"It's hangin' in the balance!"

"It's like hugging a teddy bear, all the girls love it."

"It's like something's . . . taking over inside, some fucking con-spiracy . . ."

"It's not easy for her, I suppose, being married to a theologian . . ."

"It's party time, baby, give us a hug!"

"It's still hanging fire."

"It's the second law of thermodynamics, you can't make heat flow from a cooler body to a warmer one without a fucking pump!"

"It's the worst kind of hangover!"

"It's . . . it's going numb on me, Jim."

"J'ai la patte cassée, bon dieu!"

"Jim—?"

"Jonathan, you old scoundrel! What have you been up to?"

"Just a strange premonition . . ."

"Just don't turn the other cheek, dear, you'll lose it, too!"

"Just garbage, Zack . . ."

"Just like Grammaw used to make! Here, take this one: eat your heart out!"

"Just relax for a moment before you try to get up . . ."

"Keep your eye skinned, Noble."

"Lather, rather."

"Let us see how observant you are . . ."

"Let's get to the bottom of this!"

"Like a hairy Valentine!"

"Like a pucker to a pothole, Gerry!"

"Like smoked oysters?"

"Like something in a supermarket! Unreal!"

"Like the mandala in that icon of the tortured saint in there."

"Like Dolph, I'll stick with the beer."

"Like Howard's finger, Gerry, I guess I was in the wrong place at the wrong time."

"Lissen! The bride's at a—whaddayacallit?—goddamn partya night before, see'n she—"

"Liz's act of course was substantially different . . ."

"Love. Death. Time. Truth and beauty."

"Ma jambe, c'est pas un boulevard, nom de dieu!"

"Mais ils vont m'écraser ces cons-là!"

"Mais qu'est-ce que je suis venu foutre ici, d'abord?"

"Mavis? She's into those wonky tales of hers again."

"Maybe this'll make up for that scarlet flush we hit on the last one."

"Me neither!"

"Memory may be expunged . . ."

"Menopause. Woody still looks so young."

"Merde alors—!"

"Mmm. Right after the teddy bear."

"Moo-ooo!"

"My god, can't she even do that by herself anymore?"

"My mind's a blank."

"My, how observant you are, Gerald!"

"N'whuzza madder w'your shoulder? Somebody take a bite?"

"Naw! Haw!"

"Naw—hee! hoff!—it's funny, lissen—!"

"Neither . . ."

"New one—?"

"Next it was Ping Pong and she tried to claim that there were no balls to play with . . ."

"Next thing to it!"

"Next time he does that to you, Wilma, just pinch his pecker—I read about it somewhere, and it works every time!"

"No kidding! Fat Fred? An actor?"

"No kidding, in their tails or in their heads?"

"No kidding, what does she do for an encore?"

"No matter what happens, it's always easier if you can share it."

"No noose is good noose!"

"No one ever marries the wrong girl."

"No. Pay attention, Gerald."

"No, a knight."

"No, but—"

"No, it's this guy's partner! The stubby one!"

"No, she left!"

"No, Gerald, that's from some other party—I saw Archie in that group . . ."

"No, I hope it didn't."

"No, I said . . ."

"No? What's wrong with it?"

"Noble knows how to turn a blind eye to trouble."

"Noble's got an eye to the main chance."

"Nom de dieu de nom de dieu de bon dieu de merde de pute . . ."

"Not likely—it's pure aged malt. Must have been Cyril and Peg."

"Not now, Charley. Please."

"Not to mention those valuable pearly white gates, if you don't fall right."

"Not to Dickie."

"Not tonight, son. I'm retired, hadn't you heard?"

"Not yet, thanks. Catch me later."

"Nothing is ever wholly concealed."

"Nothing to worry about. We'll work it out later."

"Nothing wrong with your pipes, baby."

"Now you see it, now, you cunt!"

"Now, don't jump around like that, Howard, or I won't be able to tuck it in!"

"Now, if you don't mind, ladies and gentlemen, your watches . . ."

"Now, where's Hugues?"

"Now, who'll play the heavy?"

"Nude?"

"Of course."

"Oh no! Don't tell me! I bet it's her vaginal muscles!"

"Oh putain! Pouvez pas garer vos pieds ailleurs, non?!"

"Oh! Was that Susanna? I thought . . ."

"Oh!"

"Oh . . ."

"Oh, is that what he was supposed to be . . . ?"

"Oh, that one—he didn't try, he succeeded."

"Oh, I know, I am a dummy, she was just flattering me, but I needed her, she helped me through some bad times . . ."

"Oh, I see, they're like different card suits . . ."

"Once she stuck a long rubbery thing down my throat that quivered and made me throw it all up!"

"Only very careful probing uncovers the subtler influences to be found in suggestion, hatreds, fatigues, innuendos . . . !"

"Oops, sorry!"

"Or anyway you couldn't seem to find them, something like that."

"Or maybe I'd read about it happening to someone else and just borrowed the story . . ."

"Or, who knows, an argument with the doctor or the wrong drugs or even just the bill . . ."

"Pardon!"

"Pardon?"

"Patient! What's there for an old scumbag like me to be patient for?"

"People marry the wrong people all the time—I should know, I've made one stupid mistake after another."

"Plastic sandwich bags or something. Her hands and feet and even her head—it's spooky, man!"

"Poor Yvonne."

"Pop? Yeah, last I seen he was in the next room there executin' a slide show."

"Put this between your legs."

"Quagg's goon squad, Mee and Hoo-Sin, Prissy Loo, Regina, and the rest of that freaky lot."

"Quel est le con qui me marche dessus?!"

"Really it's all about Roger the singer, Beni, and that's where you come in."

"Really!"

"Reminds me of that young man from Cadiz!"

"Reminds me of the old barrel-shirt punishment for drunks . . ."

"Right in the chest like that, he said!"

"Right . . ."

"Roger handled everything, he was a real jewel!"

"Saloperie d'escalier! Je me suis cassé le cul . . . !"

"Save your breath!"

"Say, huh! if birds that bring babies're called storks, what're the birds that don't bring 'em?"

"See what, Daddy?"

"She must have a whole jar of hand lotion packed in here, it's thick as transmission grease."

"She must mean that one whose pecker was big in show bizz . . ."

"She only wanted company."

"She powders, and I puff."

"She seemed so lifeless . . ."

"She was badly bruised and hurt inside, too."

"She was in too bad a mood to think straight, I guess."

"She was the model for Susanna—that painting in the next room."

"She'd not seen the script."

"She'll know what I mean."

"She's all right. Even lucky in a way."

"She's been like that all night."

"She's filled out some since then, of course."

"She's upstairs, I think, Vic."

"Shouldn't that be Keith from Cadiz?"

"Sit down! Sit down!"

"Slide it on there for me."

"So delicate is the balance in one's makeup that what seems but a very slight occurrence may determine the event in conduct!"

"So that was what . . ."

"So this—yuff! huff!—young bull's mountin' one a them heifers after another, see . . ."

"So who we headlining now that Vaych is gone?"

"So I tell ya what I want you to do . . ."

"Society's first line of defense is the police."

"Someday! Just you wait and see!"

"Somebody brought it, Fats and Brenda maybe."

"Something that happened. Or maybe didn't happen."

"Sometimes, Gerald, I think beauty is the most frightening thing in the world . . ."

"Sorry if I jumped at you, Vadge, you know how I get when there's a show to put on . . ."

"Sounds more to me like Tight Tillie from Brussels!"

"Speakin' a milkin' machines, Earl—haw!—'dja hear 'bout the farmer witha two ole bulls . . . ?"

"Speaking of the, ah, corpus delicti . . . ?"

"Suchness conceals itself from the peeping intellect."

"Swallow it."

"Ta-DAAA-AA-Aaa-aaa . . . !"

"Tell me, Daffie, what's the secret of his success?"

"Teresa?"

"Thanks for . . . helping out—do I owe you any—?"

"That and money, power, status, connections, big cars, a smashing pad, and access to the best dope in the Western World."

"That clock's been stopped for nearly three weeks now, where have you been?"

"That day, I told Ros she should simply sleep it off, and I sent her home with some theater friends."

"That mutht have been pretty!"

"That poor woman. Her face looks scratched away like that painting on your landing."

"That was when Louise got all red in the face and left, and to tell the truth, I was getting a little tired of it myself."

"That's a cute paint job, funkybuns—but you better watch out someone don't run you up the flagpole!"

"That's because of what Jim did."

"That's better!"

"That's enough now!"

"That's fair, isn't it?"

"That's funny! The clock—!"

"That's me, a very heavy thinker."

"That's no good, Zack."

"That's not a heart, it's a spade."

"That's the kind of story you'd remember. Watch out for the good guys and all that."

"That's true. I think I heard someone else say . . ."

"That's what friends are for, sunshine!"

"The end of patience is the goddamn boneyard, Jim!"

"The essential truth is as untouched by distinctions of the mind, as space is by light and darkness."

"The old Barbarossa syndrome! Aha! The red-folk neurosis!"

"The point of masks is that they are masks."

"The prince of piece."

"The promptuary?"

"The rest is just mechanics, really . . ."

"The what—?!"

"The Doc's tole me to stop all drinks 'nso I haven' let a one get pass me all night!"

"Then something happened in the hosptial afterwards which no one would talk about . . ."

"Then there are the sick ones like flannelmouth here who try to pretend they don't."

"Then, I didn't tell it."

"There was a man with a harelip once who—"

"There's two sides of the Nile, don't you know, and we took in both of 'em, Iris and me, but it was, eh, the west side I most—"

"They try to hide it, but they all got a hump hid away somewhere."

"They used to roll 'em down a hill, y'know, until the staves busted—"

"They're carting her corpse around in there like it was Our Lady of the Bleeding Goddamn Heart."

"They're insured."

"They've turned the interrogation scene into this weird rubber-and-leather number, see . . ."

"This one's about some city all made of ice—like one of those funhouse mirror mazes, you know . . ."

"Those who kill tend to be about three years younger than those who are killed."

"Too bad."

"Tragic?"

"Très, très chic!"

"True love is like a light that can never be hidden!"

"Try it and see!"

"Uncle Charley gave it to me."

"Vair's de boose?"

"Very domestic, if you know what I mean!"

"Wait a minute, sweetie, let me have a suck on that pretty thing before you take it away."

"Wanna hear me really chop out and cut the buck, Zack, or just noodle around, romantic-like? Hey, Zack?"

"Watch out for the fat lady, she'll wreck your marriage if you give her half a chance."

"Watch out, that's probably what he tells all the girls."

"Watches?"

"We gotta get t'gether 'n play some squash, ole Ger."

"We need you for the cracker!"

"We tried to stand on the very spot, but the traffic nearly ran us down."

"We'll use Hugues, give him a new image."

"We're merely the flesh of time, after all, so who knows, cutting through, what we might discover?"

"Well . . ."

"Well, actually, I shouldn't complain, I suppose . . ."

"Well, if it was dead, it ain't no longer! Hot spit!"

"Well, it was the plot of a play . . ."

"Well, it wasn't Tania who—"

"Well, maybe she don't know that."

"Well, what the fuck you lying down here for, man?"

"Well, your balance for starters."

"Well, I—"

"Were you there?"

"Whaddaya talkin' about?"

"What a cute green suit, Patrick! We look like Christmas together!"

"What have I got to lose?"

"What party favors?"

"What time is it, do you know?"

"What you call Dolph's deep-seated anal-lyzing."

"What you need is a good back rub . . ."

"What young man?"

"What I need is a quick kick! And not where I got the last one neither!"

"What . . . time is it?"

"What—?!"

"What—?!"

"What—?!"

"What—?!"

"What? Oh, not with Mark actually—the first one . . ."

"What's ever enough?"

"What's it say? Turn around, lemme see—'Tight Split End'! Ha ha, that's cute!"

"What's that supposed to mean?"

"What's that, Tania, another one of your riddles?"

"What's up with Jim's wife?"

"Whatsat? What's his act? I can do it, gimme a chance!"

"When Hughes ducked, he—ha ha!—ducked his silly French cool all the way down the goddamn stairs!"

"When I heard this one, it was about a young girl named Liz . . ."

"When I leave, I'm always afraid we may never see each other again."

"Where was Fats when Ros's body was found?"

"Which saint is that?"

"Who? Brenda and—?"

"Who's tragic?"

"Who's Noble making eyes at now—or eye, rather?"

"Whoo . . . !"

"Why did you tear up Mark's picture?"

"Why don't you learn the goddamn language, you ass-eared lump of frog shit?"

"Wonderment. At the awesome workings of man's mind, even when perverse and loveless . . ."

"Yeah, and all packaged up."

"Yeah, he's a natural hoofer! Outasight!"

"Yeah, something between a spigot and a gizmo."

"Yeah, sperm—they bear the principle of the soul, some Greek with a beard said so—"

"Yeah, spigoting of the witch, I think that Latin plank-spanker musta forgot me."

"Yeah, that got such a rise . . . !"

"Yeah, that's why modern man is such a fucking disaster—always trying to sublimate!"

"Yeah, there is, they're fulla some asshole's shit."

"Yeah, well, he's had a good run."

"Yeah, well, not my cup of tea, as they say."

"Yes! How did you know? In the Navy—"

"Yes . . ."

"Yes, it's the same with my wife."

"Yes, like a wart, like a fever blister."

"Yes, thank you."

"Yes, that plumber fixed it. The new one."

"Yes, that's so."

"Yes, the famous triple tree of Tyburn—nothing there but a busy intersection now . . ."

"Yes, well, you've probably had too many dry martinis . . ."

"Yes, with my folks . . ."

"Yes, yes, I see . . . and the pose itself . . . ?"

"Yes, I've—heh heh!—had a lot of hang-ups in my day . . ."

"Yet, with that little scratched-out area, an assault on beauty at the same time . . ."

"You almost have to envy her dramatic peaks and troughs—it's as though she has more of a life to live than most of us . . ."

"You already told that one, Charley."

"You asking us or telling us, Soapie?"

"You can always recognize a rationalist. They're all drunks."

"You can have it."

"You don't have to get sarcastic . . ."

"You hangin' out here?"

"You know Hugues?"

"You know, that's funny, I was thinking something like that myself, only about my own childhood."

"You mean, for me? A real part?"

"You mean, like twins and harelips?"

"You mean, something you wished might have happened."

"You remain silent and it speaks, you speak and it is silent . . ."

"You saw that . . ."

"You seen tall, pale, and ruthless lately?"

"You still haven't answered my question, lady. Who or what did that to you?"

"You think that's it . . . ?"

"You, too, Daffie."

"You're a fucking ritualist."

"You're all the same—!"

"You're coming around in your old age."

"You're sure we can't help you wash up a few dishes . . . ?"

"You've a wonderful little woman."

"You've been there?"

"You've worked up a very fancy aesthetic, chum, but it's as primitive as a cannibal's!"

"Your one and only!"

"Yuh huh huh!"

"Yuh—'n' 'ass what I was gonna tell ya . . ."

"Yvonne?"

Nicholson Baker

I used to delete all my typos and failures of phrasing as I went along, but recently, out of an excessively curatorial urge, I have begun pushing the unwanted bits one by one to the bottom of the page with the return key, a few lines ahead of the growth bud of my final intention. A concentrated, enantiomorphic, sludgelike parody of each session's prose-in-progress thus gradually accumulates. Once in a while I analyze these precipitates (outtakes in the most rigorous, qwertyuioptical sense) in search of secret patterns and tendencies, much as I occasionally try to identify the source of a certain tint or texture of lint in the filter basket of a clothes dryer. So far I've

*learned nothing from this research except that I seem to have second
thoughts about the colon a lot. Here, for example, is what collected at the
bottom of the last page of* Room Temperature *(Grove Weidenfeld, 1990)
when I wrote it on Father's Day, 1989:*

three days a week oruhizzing bubbling llbbing   e
to finish the article.
turned above her, ent
Bugdolatry
mere six months oldbshe had fallen aseep sucking from a
l;home
hs etcu the Bug, inconceivably grown, Everything wen
s'
owl and nrtz t, which a plastic bagn
mpinrotn
own mouth: eventually, after ten minutes of
   :
in the grass in
direct sun in a stream
unpleasant tickling of the sharp stream of water against the roof
   of your mouth,   a stream fin
sensation the Bug must have felt as she drew in the warm
milk from her plastic bottlehthour r, against the roof
of your
had it as: the   and saliva combined, a taste similar to et
o prove that   ere
fall overand tacar
]   ,   some change and rubber bands at the bottom; and the very
      eom
hourfr:chewed on for several weeks while writing ;
el s and several ix
hterd
from i   once to
, ginni

But I had the bug!

for larice or sehalf r
k crichad changedexpectedhI
but I had the
Bugtact
my energies, colliding with my uncertainty about mlack of

Charles Simic

Some lines that still interest me:

The Cartesian sewing machine
Quick Eats
The president went riding in a cowboy suit.
Metaphysical plague-carrier
What the generals knitted no one knew.
The rest of us kept watching for the umbrella of the funeral direc-
    tor.
A couple of dumb waiters to serve us
Nature's will did not correspond with young Bishop's wishes.
True angels were using back alleys as privies, as tunnels of love.
Maria Dolores, protect my soul from confusion.
Leaves shuddering at the thought of night coming
Gastronomes of endless disappointments
Mr. Emerson's windmills
Devil's emulators steered by black umbrellas
Assyrian pubic beards
Poor American devils brushing their teeth after every meal
A wedding band with a kazoo
I spend my time going to funerals of lofty ideas.
The brown rats crossed the Volga in 1727.
The necessity of error
Ghost stories written as algebraic equations

O ignorantia, o tristia
You make a city
Of drive-in churches, gas stations,
Peeling billboards. . . .

Theodore Roethke

Editor's note: A collection of lines from the Notebooks of Theodore Roethke *(Doubleday, 1972).*

STRAW FOR THE FIRE
(1953-62)

What dies before me is myself alone:
What lives again? Only a man of straw—
Yet straw can feed a fire to melt down stone.

■

To love objects is to love life.
The pure shaft of a single granary on the prairie,
The small pool of rain in the plank of a railway siding . . .

■

Am I too old to write in paragraphs?

■

I need to become learned in the literature of exasperation.
    In my worst state, once I think of my contemporaries,
    I'm immediately revived.

■

I always wonder, when I'm on the podium, why I am there:
    I really belong in some dingy poolhall under the table.

■

O Mother Mary, and what do I mean,
That poet's fallen into the latrine,—
And no amount of grace or art
Can change what happens after that.

■

And what is to be learned from the defilement of the body?
The devil knows a good deal.
From you, devious darling, one can learn the immense gaiety
    of a seat-warmer.

■

I don't know a thing except what I try to do.

■

My courage kisses the ground.

■

Sure I'm crazy
But it ain't easy.

■

For each act of my life there seems to be a necessary purgatorial
   period: even the simpler things, like going to the store.
   What a bourgeois I am.

■

Who hesitates is Fortune's also-ran.
He never leaves who teeters on the sill.
Once I was one; I can be one no more.

■

I seek first and last, that *essential* vulgarity I once thought
   charming.

■

Feeling's a hard
Thing to do well—
And slightly absurd;
I'd rather smell.

■

Of all pontificators, those who prate of poetry are among
   the most tiresome . . . including those aging Sapphos
   who speak as if they had invented integrity.

■

If you can't think, at least sing.

■

In the very real and final sense, don't *know* anything. That
   is what saves me—from you, dear class, and from
   ultimate madness.
   In every man there is a little woman.
   A teacher needs his students to stay human.
   Suppose you master one cliché—
   You're a step beyond the horse: a horse's A.

■

Anything that's longer than it is wide is a male sexual symbol,
   say the Freudians.

■

O ye apostles of refinement.
   They wander, empty in their skin,
   And see themselves but now & then,
   And cannot tell you why or how
   They got the wrinkles on the brow.

■

I'm so poor I can't subscribe to my own downfall.

■

A breath is but a breath
And the smallest of our ties
With the long eternities,
And some men lie like trees,
The last to go is the bark,
The weathered, the tough outside.

■

I'd like to be sure of something—even if it's just going to sleep.

■

God's the denial of denials,
Meister Eckhart said.
I like to forget denials
In bed.

■

I feel like a pig; but there are worse ways to feel.

■

Who adhere to the central
Can yet be subtle.

■

One the keeper, one the guide,
One that merely stays outside;
One the one that will not stir,
One the expert fathomer,
One the wheel and one the spoke,
One a vaster cosmic joke.

■

For we need more barnyard poets, *echt Dichter* of *Dreck und
   Schmutz*, poets who depart from the patio, the pent-
   house, the palladium.

■

What words have good manners? None.

■

Wake to my praise, you dead!
The old crow wheels and cries;
The cold night purifies
The rich life of the wood . . .

■

Me, I don't want to die: I want to live to a long self-indulgent
    happy productive dumb old age.

■

I sang a most uproarious song,
A tune a dog could understand,
Digging in this prodigious garden
For a long-lost bone . . .

■

I was betrayed by my own hardihood.

■

All bushes can't be bears.

■

A cloud climbs to the moon:
Thought within thought can be
Bleak stone upon bleak stone.

■

My face is running away.

■

By light, light; by love, love; by this, this.

Howard Nemerov

FRAGMENTS

the reason you can't face reality is
it's got you surrounded

a little against
expectation, like seeing the dawn go down

bearing to burying, vulva to the vault
world without end. you get that? without end.

critics who take poor work and make it worse

the university offers a rich menu—you must still choose the meal
and pay for it. I myself, brought up in the elective system,
mistrust the place at which the waiter turns into a dietitian
and requires instead of suggesting.

a circle with a roughly centered dot
is primitive to mind, enough to show
much of what is, along with all that's not.

retributive justice, with the biter bit

the japanese, who can turn a dripping tap
into a work of art. american taps
just drip.

manimals

new model heroes, blown up while they sleep

the homebuilders' apocalypse, the radioactive real estate

soup kitchens, hoovervilles, the bowery
is replicated in every town

the revealed truth of iconography:
sinners are naked, the elite are dressed

it is the still, apparent pool   the still, apparent, and reflective
      pool
powers the waterfall

Ode to Gravity   "no people has ever worshipped a god of
      gravity"—Adam Smith

their sweet disorders, silk or cotton clad,
'scape censure, for their object is their own
in brief possessions not to be possessed

ultraman
the monster, in its muddy tennis shoes

and built up babel of the alphabet
and knocked it down

THE LONG DISSOLVE

  making the movie of paradise lost

the ceaseless sea must be our model here,
banging the rocks and sucking the stones away

we need subliminal imagery in here,
suggestive whisperings too fast for sight or sound
that yet the equal subtlety of the mind
picks up in secret

the flying bodies and the falling bodies
(flying is only a special case of falling
tangential by renewed acceleration;
I think the Red Queen said this better)

how many dead it took
to make homer his poem; how long away
from home he left even Odysseus

having the ego, if nothing else, caressed

he sure did hit the nail right on the point

appearance says, says he,
to his half-brother reality,
"now look, I'm to go first
and show, in elegant verse,
how, bad as things may seem,
they might after all be worse.
and then you follow me
revealing I'm a dream,
and play your single theme:
whatever is, is worst."

the bow of the sun already is less bent
than it was a month ago

the morning paper with its bill of fear

the cumulus across the sky all day
carry themselves carefully, and never spill

it's tantalizing, to see the cumulus
carry themselves from west to east all day
without spilling a drop; no wonder that the field-
folk are the bible-reading ones—imagine
being left alone with nature all the year
and unprotected by a Book.

Anne Waldman

OUTTAKES FROM ''THE MUSE''

She has some cunning as she wishes to meet fame in your words
of her. She is a scant truth, she is a hair's breath away from
it. In the philosopher's scheme she is all you could ask for.
She gives orders
She obeys them
She forgets to acknowledge that that poem in herself has
been forgotten.
No, it is never forgotten!

She lies down with the bear with the buck with the stallion
she will be anything you want her to (not to be held against her)

She is a virgin in her heart

One time when you thought you could get ahead of corporate
time by flying to Tokyo she met you there, bargaining
at the stock exchange. You were traded back.

Your stock went down. She kept upstaging you.

William Stafford

Read my lips, forget my name.

Harold Brodkey

I'm not sure I can feel my estate as anything but fallen, my life as anything but a fall. I live daily as if I were falling in a dream—the astonishment, the doubt, the fear are like that, the disbelief, the question of, Can I undo this, the conviction that I cannot, that it was set long ago, that I could not outwit fate or predestination. The shock and foretaste of death, the sense of animal brotherhood—all of it set in the helplessness of a fall.

But if someone else is falling near me and I am kind to them in some totally unexpected and foolish and even extravagant way, that's not set: so, my will is a rudder, my free will is the posture of my fall.

Jill Eisenstadt

Two fragments

Marge and Jewel sound like two different months but watching them down on all fours doing doggy-style leg lifts can convince you they're the same one. A swollen, humid, thirty-one-dayer without holidays.

It's these big brains. Big brains spend all their time creating complications if not finding them if not avoiding them. And what if there really is reincarnation and he and Fred [twins] are stuck together forevermore—twin sand dollars or eskimo girls or those mutant, Siamese vegetables?

"My head hurts," Oscar says.

"No," Fred corrects him. "My head hurts."

Larry Woiwode

The following is from one of hundreds of pages removed, of my own volition, from Born Brothers *(Farrar, Straus & Giroux, 1988), not necessarily because I didn't care for the content of many of these pages but rather found it necessary to consider my patient reader.*

"An important lesson to learn is your pace," Dad says, "in drama and elsewhere. When we were on the farm, we often hayed or shocked grain for the neighbors, who then would help us. I'd walk out in a field in the morning and hear people say, 'There goes that slow-moving Martin.' But my pace was steady, and faster than it looked if you were trying to keep up. Littler men, like your Grandpa Jones, would be running and dashing at the bundles and tossing them up in shocks, and soon would be pooped, but I'd take the shortest line to each, hooking them by the twines in each hand, and keep up my walk, never slower or faster than at first, and by the end of the day I'd still be going at that pace and have all the field shocked but the last round, while a couple of others would be fighting to finish up a corner of it. If you lie down to take a nap, the earth keeps right on going, and you wake up thousands of miles from where you began."

Kim Wozencraft

It's November again, and November has become a schizophrenic month. The merchants seem to have mixed up Thanksgiving and Christmas. I imagine that some year soon the two holidays will become one, and we will celebrate Thankxmas on some Monday early in December. There will be windows full of red and green turkeys wearing Santa caps and the idea will be to stuff your face and overextend your credit cards all in the space of a single long weekend. Or it will be scheduled for December 7th and we'll be able to get Pearl Harbor Day in there with the rest of it. That seems appropriate somehow; the Holiday Season as Sneak Attack.

Susan Minot

These two pages are an early version of a scene from Monkeys (Dutton, 1986). *What finally made it into print was:*

> Dad sat behind the girls in a rickety chair he'd found on the beach, wearing sneakers and socks. "No balls in the house," he called when Caitlin got beaned by an overthrow.
>
> ("Allowance," p. 53)

"The sand doesn't look real," said Sophie. "Look at it up close."

"Can we go into town later?" said Caitlin. "I want to hit the stores."

Mum had her needlepoint. "Ask your father."

Caitlin lifted herself on one elbow, careful to keep in the sun. "Can we?"

Dad was standing behind them, smoking a cigarette. "Certainly," he said vaguely, glancing out to sea.

"Am I getting red at all?" asked Delilah. "I never get red."

"You're lucky," said her mother, poking a needle. "You just get brown."

"I wouldn't mind getting pink once, just to see what it's like."

"You wouldn't like it," said Sophie. She and Caitlin were both blonde. "But none of us have to worry about it because here comes another cloud."

Mum started humming.

"You're a little off," said Caitlin with her eyes closed.

"What?" said Sophie. " 'Here Comes the Sun'?"

"I can hum whatever I want," her mother said and began to hum louder.

Gus screamed from down near the water. "Hey, Dad! Watch this!" He hurled a tennis ball; it soared high over Sherman's reaching hands, straight for the picnickers, and bopped Caitlin on the head. She swore in a loud whisper and jumped up.

"Now cut that out," said Dad. He had found a rickety ship-wrecked beach chair and was sitting behind his family, reading a book.

Caitlin leapt up and went tearing after Gus to pelt him one, but he scurried off as fast as a sandpiper, grinning. When she finally threw the ball, Gus was far off and she missed by a mile.

"Dad," she whined. She collapsed on her towel. "They always hit me. Every time."

Dad could make out his sons—tiny figures way off down the beach. "All right," he yelled to the ocean which was closer. "No balls in the house." The boys turned around, with startled innocent expressions.

Shelby Hearon

Here are the last two paragraphs of a short story I liked a lot and rewrote a zillion times that never made it into print. Pieces of the early parts of it seeped into a novel, but the end, the point, was left behind. The story was called "Firm Widow."

Margaret went outside. Back on schedule, she dug the caladium and stored them; set out the Chinese blue delphinium in moistened beds; cut back the dahlia. When the breezy December day warmed her back she made the mix of sulphur, copperas, and Epsom Salts which fed the red azaleas.

All morning she worked, in mixed relief and grief that widows, no longer under employ, were not, like a man's clothing and title, passed along.

Hugh Nissenson

Complete draft of an entry from The Tree of Life *(Harper & Row, 1985), a novel in the form of a diary*

8 Oct. 11 P.M. Ten nights ago since I fell unconscious from my stool while writing in this Waste Book. My subsequent resolve—no more booze—holds, spite the necessity of polluting myself abed every night before I can sleep. I get off by imagining that young Delaware squaw who paints her nipples red. She stands facing me at the S. corner of Park Ave. E. & Diamond St. But in a trance: eyes shut, lips slightly

parted, hands at her sides, the palms turned out & fingers spread. Her naked little breasts rise & fall with each deep breath she takes. Her little   A wind from the S.; the fringes of her greasy doeskin skirt flap. Her brass earrings—wire hoops, a ft. long—jangle.

I imagine that young Del. squaw who paints her nipples red. She stands facing me at the S. corner of Park Ave. E. & Diamond St. But in a trance: eyes shut, lips slightly parted, hands at her sides, the palms turned out & fingers spread. Her painted little breasts rise and fall with each deep breath. She twitches her eyelids, trying to open them. Only I can break the spell.

8 Oct. 11 P.M. *Masturbatus sum.* Imagined that young squaw who paints her naked nipples red. She stands in a trance, facing me at the corner of Park Ave. E. & Diamond St. Naked, save for a necklace of polished elk's teeth. Eyes shut, lips parted, hands by her side, & fingers spread. Her painted little breasts rise & fall with each breath. That particularly excites me.

Kenneth Koch

From "On the Edge," On the Edge *(Viking, 1986)*

Crossing the street with you in nineteen-fifty
A word decelerated from a window
Type evaporated
From a newspaper. Daily Cross—done
Nineteen forgotten
Centuries I was not yet
Twenty-five years old
Figures

Sureness made a conflict
Or rather it was the wish for purity that did
I didn't care—know. Red shoes white linen
Sometimes somewhere
Oh I know it's all so vague but its realism
Was your stocking—in the closet
Blond hair—new dials on these things I instruct you
And you me, variously

Oh I can't say "I wish it would go on" or "Had so"
The skirt bobbing the white tassel and the say-so
Sat white hot summer cement—this action—the sidewalk—
Someone comes out—the street—a cry—"Hey, Babe-o!"
Ducks running for governors, strangers
Eating the silence of the palisades. Oh
For another time! is uninteresting hate
Material. Say so! A goat can't worry. Life can't be late
It just arrives when it arrives. And so it goes.
Summer collapsed on summer like a clothespin
Snap on a piece of clothes.
Oh, sure, my hand on your cuff will instruct you
As peapods die into their shells being the same afternoon
We didn't include you, but—now you can come in—
Waking and clearly walking, this in-deep-with-you minute
Collapses. A car is driving around a rose
A very big one, a kind of traffic highway articularity
In rose shape they generally designate this that as clover
Leaf. But the proud Indian stops him
But the sawdust captain scripts him with his eye
Nothing can even be noticed without the people
Whore here and not all the time

Fantomas, even, somewhere around here, is in my book bag
Oh, I'm full of notes
Notes to tell myself something I was going to do

Well, my dog, my dawn, my overcoat of summer
Shoot up your parties or the hosts will rust them
Avid for seeing huh nap in between
Flying to clown around deshabillé

Where is Bud Inwards, who mailed you a card
Saying If Dan isn't here at eight o'clock
I'll phone Marilyn! She roused up from her bed
Has only time to toss a fluffy stuff on
Then out into the floodlight-tinted yard

Kal says to me Ah you professor—one half minute.
Rodrigo says Watch out! The volcano almost hit me.
We talked about him for weeks. The movement hunts me
And excites me and I am gone—sooner, and in
A way much later, than I think (thought). The movies
Are one hour and forty minutes long. Sweet December.
Shane hides behind Kate (four seconds).

I walk into the eatery—for nothing. Pie sold out.

I go into the train station interestingly—for nothing. I just, then,
    come out.

Robert Bly

Five fragments

OPENING THE HOUSE DOOR IN WINTER

A lawn of bluish and blackish snow,
Five below. The snow had slept all night, undisturbed.
I dreamt of black and white skeletons—
People I knew passing in trains, sliding quietly behind a door.

That means we miss so much each time we step outside!

UNTITLED

Let us all refuse to be the white herons of eternity!
We are the survivors
of mutinous sugar,
and the thirsty remnants of fighting bread!

"MY CHILDREN PLAY WITH RATS"

"My children play with rats
as other's children play with dogs."
The long sweeps of wind
after the Boeing . . .
Forgive us all the wind
blowing about airport buildings,
warehouses, where the goods
are being hurried into Asia . . .

THE AZTEC CODEXES

A man with one eye comes in, talks about Aztec codexes.
"Quetzalcoatl is more powerful than Christ on the subtle plane."
He shows Aztec codexes in color:
"This codex ties you in to the catastrophe."
Shining faces forgotten in a corner of the stubble field;
The Sufis with stolen rose stems under their cloaks . . .
"I know she was coming up the hill,
      I could hear spirits passing in the trees.
I got out of my sleeping bag, and went down
      the mountain the other way."
"The invisible spheres are ruled in fright."
The thump of the heart begins.
We are in Egypt with the dreamer about to rule.

THE WAGON TONGUE

The violets wave like flags over the grave of the sainted mole,
whose nonresistance brought the moon to the garden.

Have you thought about the sureness the wagon communicates to
      its own tongue,
and the tongue, a horse on either side, gives to the road?

The mad straightness that some old fathers
passed on to their sons . . . What was that?

Richard Wilbur

*The following fragment was composed as a short second section for the
poem "Castles and Distances," which I included in my second collection,
Ceremony (1950).*

                    Down from the saddle sway
As you come to the woods verge, with a coin in your sword hand
            For Francis standing there, for the marked man
            Who wends an endless sabbath, and whose way
                  Is every way to find his kin
                  In water, air, and land.

Then ride, although it is said
That old judges, often enough, have sighed and confided
That there is no law, and that soldiers, all unsteeled
By a sudden peace, have shared with the beaten their bread,
Camped in the grass of the last field
Of a long war decided.

Missing in Action

(Chapters, Verses, and Scenes)

Oscar Hijuelos

From The Mambo Kings Play Songs of Love *(Farrar, Straus, and Gi-roux, 1989). A prologue of sorts*

First I'm hearing things. On the street uptown, music coming out of the windows. And not just any single kind of music. Out of one window there's congas and horns and a *cencerros*—magic bells—and a trembling piano, then a Pan-like flute; and from another window, Perry Como in the living room singing "Jingle Bells" to Doris Day in another room [and she's] singing, "Ché Sera, Sera"; and from another window a scratchy 1920s recording of the famed tenor Caruso singing the "Vesbe la Juppe" aria from *Pagliacci*; and from another window, flapper music, the Bix Beiderbecke band and the old lady inside, all dressed up in a pearl-beaded *cloche* cap and in a tassel-hemmed skirt, delicate as a Chinese curtain, in white low-heeled shoes dancing the Charleston in front of her mirror and from another window, the 45 RPM recording of the Cadillacs, famed neighborhood R & B group, singing "Need a Woman"; and from another window in the whorehouse building the real Cadillacs—the fresh-and-blood men—rehearsing with the ardor of widowed gospel singers, banging and shaking their tambourines and singing to the glory of Our Lord and not getting rich. Then . . . a jazz violin and from another window, Roy Rogers crooning "Happy Trails to You"; and then from the hallway of that building with the Corinthian pillars and the black-and-white hectagon tile floors where the junkies come and go with their cream sodas and Mallomars and aerosol cans of whipped cream, the dulcet vibraphone of Cal Tjader and his "Afro-Blue"—as if on cue Cal presses the tremolo pedal and the junkies fill up fat with a warm blue smoke that lifts them through the walls and carries them in loops over the rooftops, like pigeons being trained to circle by that little kid with the red flag, and then from a back window on the courtyard James Brown and his Extraordinary Flames and this is followed by Art Blakey and the Jazz Messengers performing "Three Blind Mice."
   Then from the window of the 1940s couple—she in curlers iron-

ing, he in a T-shirt with his racehorse "blue sheets" in hand—the
Tommy Dorsey Orchestra and "Moonlight Sonata"; and from another window two little girls practicing their piano scales,
doremifasolatidotilasofamiredo, a Dominican nun standing behind
her and idly fingering the dicy beads of her black rosary, perhaps
thinking about love; then from next door, the Kingston Trio strumming banjos and guitars, a wholesome college student who'd just
moved in, hammering a nail into the wall; and from another window,
a ghostly rendition of Matos Rodriguez's famed "Cumparsita," the
tango that started it all, the two sisters in that apartment, Cubans,
dancing across the floor much to the amusement of a homosexual son
of one of them; and then from next door the voice of the mellow-
toned crooner, Nelo Sosa and his Havana Orchestra performing a
ballad to the sea—the love-enriching sea—and then on the same
floor, the Thymes' "So in Love" and from the window down below,
the harps and violins and marimbas of a loving song, "Cielito Lindo,"
a hammock rhythmed Mexican lullabye that Mrs. Gonzales plays for
her son, Benny, a thin diabetic whom we'd often tormented for no
reason, tying him up to trees and pouring warm soda over his head,
and from the basement there's the one-eyed plumber Leo, a nice
Sicilian fellow who had once played in the Artie Shaw orchestra
before the Army and Europe and shrapnel in the head at Normandy,
strumming a one-four-five sequence of ninth chords on the guitar.
. . . And speaking of guitarists, there's the fireman up the street
playing "Stardust" on an old jazzmaster, indifferent to his family
watching TV around him and drunk, drunk, drunk like so many of
the fathers in that neighborhood, cats and dogs are running around
in his living room and his pretty wife wants to move back to the quiet
town in Pennsylvania where they first met; and next door a Puerto
Rican rock 'n' roll band, smooth-looking guys with slicked-back hair
and thick sideburns and wraparound shades rehearsing in their living
room for all the kids who are climbing the ledges of the building,
edging close to listen. The group played "La Bamba," "Louie Louie,"
"Twist and Shout," three-chord songs wailed out through a big La-
fayette ball microphone, while up on the street the fellows harmonize
"Ebb Tide" and from upstairs I hear a recording of Xavier Cugat's
orchestra with his vocalist, the great Miguelito Valdez, singing "The
Lady in Red," while three doors away the mournful strains of a violin
followed by a sad voice intoning, "adonai, adonai"—people say the
woman living there is Jewish—while downstairs on the stoop children
mark the walls with swastikas and strange numbers, dates and names:
"June 1944, 122,000 dead, Auschwitz"—swastikas that my uncle,

Cesar Castillo, superintendent and former Mambo King, has to remove with solvent. . . .

And in another apartment, a lady sitting in her darkened living room; she's dressed in white and twirling a Chinese parasol, as she listens to Nelson Eddy sing to Jeanette MacDonald; then the black man with the limp, an elevator operator, plays "Stormy Weather" on his Hohner harmonica and the Right Reverend Jones of the Last Incarnation of Christ's Disciples' Church on an electric organ playing the gospel song, "I am the Light of This World," and then from the Catholic Church with its immense red doors and golden angels, Bach like a sky filled with bells, and then a funeral service, Gregorian chanting, gloomy and comforting; then 11:30 choir practice, shattered at noon by the air-raid sirens. . . . Civil defense signs everywhere saying: "Fallout Shelter." In every basement, right next to the doorway, down the rickety stairway. . . .

Then whistling the beautiful melody of one of his own compositions, my uncle Cesar Castillo, who's hauling heavy incinerator-ash–filled cans out the basement, and up the stairs. Up over the final step to the sidewalk with a hoist that provokes a groan and "phoomph" go the ashes and he's about to turn around to go back down the zigzag hallway past the ticking electric meters when he stops. . . . Somewhere, some buildings away, a young musician is practicing his trumpet. He plays happy-sounding scales that stop my uncle in his tracks, my uncle who once had a grand orchestra, the Mambo Kings, with my father back when. As he listens he begins to figure out the scale and then he begins to imagine that the young man is just like his dead brother, Nestor, my father: sitting framed on a windowsill daydreaming about lost loves and Cuba, so far away, poor Nestor knew how to enjoy nothing, not his home, wife, and children, while my uncle in that epoch was an arrogant, braggardly womanizer who crooned and really knew how to enjoy life, who snapped his fingers and picked up broads at dances and clubs and church socials, now hauling garbage, now drying his sweaty forehead with a handkerchief. . . .

Mona Simpson

An epistolary section and a passage cut from the novel Anywhere but Here (Alfred A. Knopf, 1987)

Dear Ann—

Hope you are well—got a call from Adele yesterday just at noon and she said she was so sick—had the flu. It seems it is just all around. We had it here too—was in bed a few days and didn't eat at all. I believe it was for the best and just drink lots of liquids. She also mentioned that she got the shock of her life the day before. The building in which she lives was sold and her rent will be raised 100 and she just doesn't know what to do. Was thinking of taking someone in with her or moving into a room and junking all her old stuff. I wish she would call in the evening when rates are cheaper. She also mentioned that Erv would see what he could do. Oh Carol was sick longer than I was and just didn't get better. I feel fine now—was to the mailbox yesterday and today.

Oh my back porch was just covered *high* with snow. We had no mail for 3 days but the poor little paper boy got thru. Well Mary-across-the-street got it shoveled Sunday. There was no way in getting out. Suppose you are busy with homework.

Well that's all I know and must get something for dinner—have some left from yesterday but must get it warmed.

Well take care of yourself.

When you were here you wanted to see a snowstorm. Well you should be here today. The snow on the back porch is already as high as the railing by the steps. The winds are at times as high as 30 to 50 miles per hour. All schools, everything is closed. The snow plows in some places have even stopped running. Now they even notified people not to use phones unless emergencies. Now the plows have to have another larger plow ahead. The airports in Milwaukee and Chicago are closed but the one here is still open but no planes coming in. This is really a blizzard—worst I have seen. The storm a bit more south of here is supposed to be worse, visibility down to zero on account of blowing and snow.

Hope your violet is still blossoming. One of mine wasn't for about 3 weeks but some buds are coming again. Oh water them from the bottom about once a week. This is my Saturday morning job. There was a talk on TV one day. Also no direct sunlight. Only in winter sun. Violets bring back memories of our flower picking days together. Now they said they really can't get help for emergencies. Plows not running in Kewaunee or Manitowoc and very few here. West side has been blacked out—a tree fell, broke wires, but they are working on it.

There are some drifts up to 8 feet.

I am still awfully weak and haven't dressed and lay down most of the day. Today is the first day I feel a bit better and washed dishes but am really ready for a nap. Carol brings over some good dinners and lunch. Mrs. Roznowski was just here for a few minutes with the mail. She brings it in every day. Today it was 10 below and there is some snow on the ground. Really haven't any more news and don't feel much like writing. I love you.

Bye now.

Dearest Ann—

Was so nice reading your letter and hope your eye is OK by now. Seems allergies do cause so much trouble in different people. You do read and use your eyes a lot and maybe too much strain. You wrote about your cat watching the birds. Is she tied when you have her by the window? Oh I had Mittens clipped and he is only half as big and doesn't like the snow too much and is out only as long as possibly necessary.

I feel real good and have been driving about two weeks now. I just couldn't wait to get into the car and it works so good. Now I can do my own shopping and errands.

Am so glad to hear your mom is cooled down. She really had me up in a jitter and all rileded up with her calling twice & 3 times a day.

Does your new boyfriend go to school with you. Now your troubles begin. Which one do I really like best. What does Jason have to say about this?

I didn't know that Carol was on a yogurt diet but she is always talking about losing weight but she likes to eat too much. One day she diets and the next day she eats 2 doughnuts with frosting & coffee. Oh talking about dieting—I listened to Phil Donohue on T.V. this morning and he had a dietitian on the program. She eats no meat or sugar. Talked about a dish made with Barley (pearled) and vegetables and water and bake it for an hour at 350.

Well this barley is similar to rice and I had some here from making soup. I put in ½ cup barley 1¾ cups water, salt, and I had only carrots, onion, celery and I have dried parsley and dill here and put this in and it was OK but I wouldn't want it too often. There is this recipe on the box and includes green pepper (didn't have any) and mushrooms. She also added some oil and I put in a little margarine when I ate it. I have also gotten one frozen slab of fish (believe it was cod)—browned about ½ chopped onions—a little Worcester sauce, a little water and the fish, then slow boil until fish & onion is done and it is real good. Don't add salt because sauce is plenty salty. One of those slabs of fish I make 3 meals out of it. I take it in the basement and pry a screw driver into it in 3 places and chop with hammer— otherwise I couldn't cut with knife. If I would make it all at once I have too much left over.

Well Ann sure hope your eye is better. Really don't know any more to write.

Love to you and boyfriend.

Dear Ann—

Well by now you should be well on the way of the routine of home-work and working. We have a beautiful sunny day, a bit chilly in the low 40s but beautiful outdoors. We had frost for two nights so far but Carol's flowers in front are still red and beautiful. Well Carol and Jimmy had an accident Friday evening. They went up to the trailer after work and stopped for something to eat on the way. When they got up there and started carrying something in Jimmy turned on the heat in the trailer. There was a *loud* bang and the whole thing was in flames. The explosion banged out the door and blew it quite some distance away. Well Carol ran up the road and woke some people up there and she was unconscious and taken to the hospital. Also Jimmy. It was some time before the Fire Dept. got there and it is all burned down and she had so many pretty things up there. Carol says she doesn't remember anything only running up the road. Well Carol's hair and entire face and on her ankle got burned. Her eyelashes, eyebrows all burned and entire face is thick and puffed up and practi-cally all her hair is burned. Her hair just feels like straw (whatever is left of it). Her ankle has some big blisters and soreness. Jimmy's hair also got burned but not as bad as hers. They came home Saturday and slept until about 5 o'clock when she told me. Now they had to go to the hospital here today and maybe everyday this week for treatment so no infection sets in.

Here for the good news. Well at Amy's school they had a pitza selling contest. She sold the most (really Hal and Merry) so she won

25 as a prize. I didn't even order any but Hal knew I would take a few so now I have 3 pitzas in the freezer. Carol also took 3. I forgot how many Hal has but he says he will have a pitza party sometime and have his friends over. Suppose I will have Hal and Carol over also for a pitza. Well I feel happy for Amy. I told Hal he definitely must put this in the bank for Amy.

Oh I was talking so about the sunshine and now it is beginning to get cloudy and rain predicted for tomorrow.

That's all for today. Take care of yourself. We all love you.

Dear Ann—
Received your letter this morning and always glad to hear from you. Oh it is a beautiful afternoon but was quite foggy up until noon. Well Carol is getting along real well but she is very upset & crying spells at the least little thing. I imagine she must get over that shock from the fire. Jimmy's hand is still all bandaged and sees the doctor. Well Carol got a wig and at first it was just too much hair but they trimmed it and looks real nice. Her real hair is only about 1 inch long. She was at a birthday lunch with her club girls today. Yesterday she and I had lunch at the Holiday Inn and sure was good. I believe you were along one day at this place. They have a style show every Wednesday and that always adds.

I don't know if I told you that Jimmy won a trip for the two at Las Vegas from those cleaners. They are leaving Sunday and I believe it is a week or 10 days. She is looking for a fall coat & clothes as hers burned. What makes you think that it might not be O.K. if you came Christmas? You know we are all happy to have both of you come. There is plenty room. Sure hope it won't get as cold as last year but that was the coldest we have had since the 1890 I believe—25 to 30 below but we fortunately didn't have too much snow. Sure I would love to meet & see Jason and you.

Those pictures turned out real nice only the picture on the wall is hanging real crooked. Thanks for sending them.

Well that's all I know but will write if something exciting turns up. All my love to both of you.

Gram
Oh your Mom called Carol which was real nice.

You almost made me hungry talking about your peach pie.

Mary Griling cut the grass again and burnt the dry leaves. It looks a little better now.

Was with Gen and her new husband and Flora out to lunch Wed.

and then to see Em Clusman. She was just 90 and is failing very fast poor Em. I always liked her. Rain practically every day this past week. Am so happy we didn't have more rain when you were here, although the day we went to Algoma made up for it. It sure is interesting about the balls of fat on ferns. I bet my big fern is loaded with roots and fat. I never transplanted it and the pot is quite small. The pot must be full of roots and all. I think I will tackle it some day. First I must get a larger pot and good soil and that will be a job because it is so large. Oh I got a sort of grayish tan suit with a rust sort of larger stripe check and a rust T-shirt and it looks real nice. There is a little shop across from the filling station and I found it there. Had it on three times already. Was your kitty happy to see you when you came home? I bet she was. It has been cold and windy and rain all week and Mittens doesn't stay out too long. Will write more when something comes up and thanks again for coming.

Dear Ann—
Suppose you think something seems strange for me having something to write about again. Well there is. Adele called twice the beginning of the week—first time that she had the flu and the second day that she had been raised & 100 on her rent. The place was sold and the new people raised it to $300. Then I said "I suppose you are calling for money" and after talking a little more I hung up. I just was so upset. She is going to cause trouble—I know that. All she ever did was take, take, take and never a give. She also said you were talking about buying a used car for $300 and *"Where does she get this money?"* I also told her I had taxes and insurance to pay now and had nothing to give her now. I have to budget my money so that I have taxes and insurance. All she ever did was spend. She also talked about the two of you are talking about going to Europe and again, "Where does she get that money."

Oh yesterday Carol took me to get my hair fixed, then shopping, then to the clinic to get all the Social Security and doctor bills straightened out, then we took my tax papers and all the dope to the accountant and it was then 10 to 12 o'clock. We had lunch along the way and she takes in all the groceries. Maybe I shouldn't have written all this but that is the only time I ever hear from her. When you were here she called but I really think that was all to put up a good front. Believe she is old enough to take care of herself. I would have been ashamed to ask my mother for help all the time. Well Ann take care of yourself. Hope I didn't get you down too but she is just beyond me. I love you.

Dear Ann—

Just have to write & tell you Carol, Jimmy and I just came back from Malgoma. You know we met and saw every body at Helen's. *Mary*, Billie and Billie Joe. Well today it was for the burial of *Mary* (Billie's *Mary*) and just 52 years. She died just a week after we all saw her. Well Jean and Harold came again from Texas and today we saw Lorraine, her husband and children too. It was a nice funeral and all went to eat at Town & Country and it was real good. Oh it was sleet when we left this morning and snow in spots so we came right home after dinner. Oh uncle Bill sure broke down (much worse than Helen). Bill is 82 and really has been sick for some time. You know I wrote about the flu around in Wisconsin. Well Mary & Billie were both in bed with the flu and sick only 4 days. Billie sure was sad. Mary also was diabetic which I didn't know but Carol said she knew. Oh I am so glad we came right home because it is blowing and snowing.

Really don't know any news, wanted to tell you how quick something happens.

Don't study too hard and take it a bit easy.

Dear Ann—

Well by now you should be past Chicago and on the way. I watched a while for the bus, but it was still too foggy so I went back to bed and woke up at 10:15. The sun was out for a few moments this afternoon but still foggy in a distance. It really seems quite lonesome here. I must get busy and in the swing of doing a bit of work to pass the time this next week. Had the paper to read this afternoon but still am not dressed and in my robe. Seems everyone around here is gone today. The only one happy to see me is Mittens. Time just passed too fast when you were here, especially to see you going with all the luggage. I believe that weighed more than you do. I see Dicky (across the street) must be a bit lonesome too—he is sweeping out all the garages and cleaning up. Suppose you will be loaded with work at school soon, but you do really enjoy it I know. Suppose Jason was happy you were back and missed you—let's hope so as you are a *fine* girl and I enjoyed having you here so much.

That's all I know & will write again. Thanks & so much for coming—we love you.

Oh my violets are all blooming yet—some more flowers than others but all very pretty.

Got the sheets on beds upstairs all washed & folded & waiting for your next visit. Sure was nice.

Dear Ann—

There are so very many getting aid for college and sure hope you get some. Am enclosing this little clipping from paper and hope it applies to you. Ordinarily I don't even pay attention to that but as it applies to you that is different.

Dear Ann—

I think about writing every day but just don't get to it. Playing cards is my weakness. Oh I was just looking at your picture—the one Carol brought along for me. Sometimes I think you still look the same and then again you look different but still a very pretty girl.

Oh how would you like to be here right now? It was 27 below zero for a few nights and predicted again for tonight. Oh Madison had 22 below a few times lately and yesterday it didn't even hit zero for high. This has been going on for Nov., December, and January so far. The coldest on record so far. You just don't see anyone outside. I feel sorry for the little paper boy but he seems dressed good and warm. The wind chill is 37 to 40 below today.

Went to church yesterday with Carol and then had breakfast later at Big Boy. Oh we have about 7 or 8 new little restaurants out this way now. Won't have to be hungry anymore. Most are hamburgers & short orders. There must be money in that or they wouldn't pop up all over and so close and one sees cars at all of them. I always stop at one on Fridays after I have my hair set. The hot coffee & lunch tastes good.

■

I drove then. She asked me to. She held her hand on the other shoulder. "Oooeeeuu," she said, "my arm just hurts. It feels almost like a nerve."

She said she wanted to show me a plot of land she wanted to buy. We were on Ocean Avenue then, in Santa Monica. She directed me, east, up toward the canyons.

"This little Jim that I told you about gardens up there. That's how I even found out about it. It's just a little road off of Sunset."

By the time we came to Sunset, clouds of fog were blowing up around us. It was suppertime, five o'clock, the houses looked pretty, eveningish, as we drove. I knew the curves even before I saw them. One thing every kid who grows up in LA knows is Sunset Boulevard. Even a kid like me who didn't drive. You know it like your own hand.

The banks of the canyon, gray dirt, ragweed, dusty eucalpytus, attenuated with pretty ranch houses, curtains up in the windows, clean driveways, before closed garages.

"I hope I didn't go too far," my mother said. We kept on toward the Palisades, eventually Malibu.

"I did. We've got to turn around. I don't know where it is until we're right there, until we're just near it."

My mother told me the land she wanted was a deep lot, narrow but deep. Apparently, it stood between two mansions, old stone buildings, each with a pool and a tennis court.

"There is a running stream and it's all woods. And along one side is all National Park. So they can never build there. It's just the little road and up above there's a yellow fence and they even ride horses."

It was getting whiter and duller with fog and the dark and we headed back toward town, the other way on Sunset. My mother shoved her sunglasses on and looked close to the windshield.

"It's called Evan's Road," she said.

The houses we were passing had lawns and basketball hoops and yellow lights on behind kitchen curtains. When I was a child here and went home sick from school, there was a cookbook I read. It was old, with a red-and-white gingham cover. We'd taken it from Wisconsin. I read the recipes, but we hardly ever had food in the house. Most of what I read were the hints, the warm paragraphs before the lists of ingredients.

We were driving on the wide avenue, up Sunset. We passed, on one side, two boys playing languid basketball, their shots liquid and slow in the last light, the basket looking low and too easy, as if anyone could top it in, and that seemed right.

A little further up a man and a woman stood a few yards apart on the other side of the road. Between them was a child on a bike, wobbling precarious. He veered and tilted until the woman chased up and held the steering wheel, turned him, set him right in the other direction, toward the man. The child knew how to ride but hadn't yet learned to turn. The man and the woman each stood, then ran to catch him, turning him around and he stayed up aloft, going as long as I could see.

As the small leaves, the ferns by the side of the wide road collected, grayer in dark, we rode back for the third or fourth time. We kept driving the curves, looping, then finally turning the other way. I don't know how many times we've turned around. But my mother keeps looking for Evan's Road, and as we ride the sky is darker, all the cars around us have headlights on now, but I can see it, clearer and clear, the spread of land, once we turn in. It is a canyon with old trees, eucalyptus, willows, cottonwoods, pine. The brook is blue black and cold over sharp rocks. It is all low bush, manzanita, and chaparral, pointy, and on a dirt road just over our left side is a yellow fence and a dusty path. Three horses, brown and strong and dull in the late sun.

Charles Johnson

After digging through an old box of drafts for my second novel, Oxherding Tale *(Indiana University Press, 1982), I came up with a scene I dropped from the end of Chapter 3.*

FROM CHAPTER THREE

And when at last the hour of Flo Hatfield's party came, I descended the uncarpeted stairs slowly, like Daniel tipping into the lion's den, wearing a pair of striped duck pantaloons and a black jacket, stepping into a haze of tobacco patchouli incense and opium so thick I could taste as well as smell these powerful odors as I paused outside the parlor, my knees banging together, carrying the book of philosophy (Aurelius) I'd been reading earlier to steady myself—I was always thinking metaphysically at the moment Reality reared back to swat me into stranger waters. All Flo Hatfield's guests were actors or musicians who brought their instruments, or poets who had to be seen to be believed. One swanlike gentleman, a book reviewer who resembled woodcuts I'd seen of the Devil, with a tightly drawn mouth and conical nose between his spectacles—this dry fellow nodded sideways at one of Flo's still lifes and told his neighbor, "It's beautiful, all that balance and clarity, but it's obviously an illusion, a *lie,* because we find nowhere in Nature anything that unambiguous," then he slipped into schoolroom French, rolling his r s softly, for the benefit of a few brittle scholars. Two playwrights at a tulipwood table drained off Boilermakers in a gin duel. By a window, a group of actresses— they called themselves actresses, at least, and all drank Bloody Marys—were composing verses for a poem, very pornographic, each contributing a line. And Flo?

She entered the room provocatively, sashaying a little, the fingers of her left hand on her hip. Yet what baffled me most that evening were the elegant gentlemen, the powdered women who worshiped beauty and achieved only the grotesque, who were witty because they could not be candid, who in the parlor's glimmering green-gold lamp-lights—in this claustrophobic gourd of old dry smoke—favored me-chanical dolls pieced together from paste and bailing wire, puppets turned loose, as in an E. T. A. Hoffmann tale, where the marionettes murder their creator. *Dead,* Reb's voice whispered through my mem-ory, *All dead, Freshmeat.*

A Pink Lady took two sandwiches from my salver, and said to a Cup of Bitters, "You know, the last time Arthur and I made love, he wouldn't give me back my *clothes,* not a stitch. He made me chase him into town, into a saloon before he gave them back to me," and Cup of Bitters, one hand on her throat, confessed, "Well, Richard, the ass, used to *wear* my underthings. You don't blame me for leaving him, do you?" Sweat began to stream inside my clothes. My throat tight-ened. Flo Hatfield's necklace. Too snug. But I didn't dare remove it, for as my employer she had me by the short hairs. All that evening her eyes ranged over me. She lifted her head and laughed like a young, young girl. I felt a kind of torpor, a languor or marshiness like sleepiness in my limbs; I was aware of her eyes grabbing at me, an object in the midst of other objects, her look a beacon or ray that realized something corrosive in me, as if it was not I who made a meaning for myself—as I swore to do that night in Jonathan's house—but rather the meaning was already there, preceding me, waiting like a murderer at a boardwalk's end. As if, to speak plainly, all my possibilities had shifted to the skin's seen surface. The thick-ness of the world's texture thinned. The room was, in a single stroke, epidermalized. In this state, transfigured, my fingers were so stiff and fumblesome, without feeling, that I spilled my tray on a Tom Collins, who swore like a blacksmith and started to strike me. Apologizing, I began mopping up the mess, and cursed Master Polkinghorne for sending me here.

A few men, wearing the black silk cravats then fashionable (they all spent, I suspected, a small fortune on clothing) argued politics, and with their wives and mistresses, who seemed so comfortable in the World Cave, nibbled at the eggbread and grilled fowl Zilphey brought from the kitchen. "You find," remarked one Lemon Cooler, an art patron in barbaric jewelry, to a very confused Hot Buttered Rum with a lump of food stuck to the seat of his trousers, "so few people who truly know *how* to eat. Most are pigs. They dump anything down their esophagus. Like," she lowered her voice, "this guacamole. Now, in Nice, they prepare food lovingly, as if Christ Himself were coming to dinner." Helplessly, Hot Buttered Rum asked, "Who? The *pigs?*"

Two feet away, Cup of Bitters told Pink Lady, "The *only* punishment equal to the crime of rape is prefrontal lobotomy. I've researched the subject of rape thoroughly. Would you care to hear my conclusions?" Pink Lady said she was dying to hear this but preferred to wait until Cup of Bitters sold it as an exclusive interview to the *Abbeyville Register*. I placed my empty tray on a long table of wine and sweetmeats, gulping for air, my back to Flo Hatfield and a pale, wounded-looking Whiskey Neat—a frail, teacup-passing fellow— whose head was tipped toward Flo as she sat before the fireplace, feeding it letters from her husbands to help it burn. "Boy," he said to me in a voice just short of demand, "please freshen this glass for me." For an instant I was distracted by a Brandy Alexander who told Two Fingers of Rye, "These colored bruise so easily! It so chanced that yesterday a boy asked me if I knew where City Hall was, and—" Whiskey Neat pushed his glass into my hand. "Can you hear?" I did hear him, but could not speak because this little pismire regarded me with such disdain, and because, for all my self-control, my body reacted to this slight. Whiskey Neat waited for me to speak. He waited, in fact, for me to stammer, slur my words, brutalize the language as a signal of my Negroness, a sign that we in our bodies were not the same. My motions seemed to be slowing down. "Can this boy speak?" he asked Flo, and I whispered a *Yes* lost in the blitz of laughter, chatter, and the big, hectoring voice of a Rum Grog whose argument for the necessity of Negro slavery drew from the most recent scientific studies, the Old Testament, from history, and the subordination of one creature by another in the natural world. Beneath his voice, one of the Bloody Marys whined, "Every theater director I've met already knows someone who looks *exactly* like me, it's like *everyone* is so anonymous these days." Dizzily, I made my way toward the door, frowning and fighting to stay polite, over the Boilermakers, both heaped on the floor after consuming forty-eight ounces of straight gin in fifteen minutes. But now I could not perform the simplest act, such as pouring water, without causing catastrophe all around me.

"So," roared Brandy Alexander, "this colored boy looking for City Hall nearly fainted, and I couldn't figure out why. All I said was, 'You're a block past it,' and *he* thought I said, 'You're a black bastid.' Why," he asked me, "are Negroes so sensitive?" I closed my eyes, counting twenty. "To speak frankly, sir, I have no idea. I don't know many of them."

The entrance was blocked by a Rum Grog, a fat man wiping condensation off his glass with his handkerchief, puffing at a

Tequila Sunset. Rags of smoke hung in air hot and rubbery. Wind outside changed pressure inside the room. Suddenly, I could not breathe. Rum Grog would not let me pass. "This country, in my view, runs on economic fact," he was saying, "not goodwill. We brought these people here as one essential ingredient in an agrarian society. Their purpose as a group, and every group has its teleology, or sense, is tied in the Negro's case to a specific form of production. . . ." Rum Grog inflated his lungs. "*If* the Abolitionists have their way, and if the North, then South, move to manufacture and no longer *need* the Negro, what then? Of course, we shall always need him poetically, but they will be, as a people, without a national purpose, if you follow me. It will be centuries before the nation discovers what to *do* with them. Can we ship them all back to Africa, eh? Answer me that. Be careful now." Before his neighbor could answer, he hemmed, "Not on your life. For I put it to you, is it reasonable to suppose that they are any more suited for a life in Africa than they are for full participation in an America that no longer needs slave labor? They are *here*, but not truly here. Do you see the dilemma?" His neighbor did not, so he turned toward me, and asked, "Do *you* see the problem?"

Pulling free, I stumbled, tipping over a table of pastries, then struck out from this morgue, the party roaring on behind me when I came crashing through Zilphey's kitchen, then lumbered, full of rage, my thoughts tangled like twine, onto a back porch that bellied out, low, into the yard. . . .

Gordon Lish

From Extravaganza (G. P. Putnam, 1989)

Smith comes home and Smith goes and finds Mrs. Smith in the kitchen, and Smith sees Mrs. Smith sitting and eating a plate of soup in the kitchen, and Smith says to Mrs. Smith, Smith says, "Listen, I just this instant come in up here from down there in the street where guess who I just this instant finished having myself a conversation with, because the answer is none other than the man of science, the famous physician Dr. Dale."

"Very nice," says Mrs. Smith.

"Sure, sure, very nice," says Smith. "You said it, very nice," says Smith. "But I ask you, is this the whole story," says Smith, "just a conversation? Because I promise you," says Smith, "this conversation which I, Smith, the layman, just had with the famous physician, Dr. Dale, was not, I guarantee you, just a situation where there was a mutual exchanging back and forth of the various different types of unimportant inconsequentia which your common ordinary people exhibit such a habit of constantly talking about when they got nothing more intelligent to discuss on their minds."

"Very nice," says Mrs. Smith.

"You hit the nail right on the head, very nice, very nice," says Smith. "Because, I promise you," says Smith, "this conversation which I was making reference to—namely, the one with the distinguished medical practitioner—just so happened to be, believe me, a terrific personal scientific godsend for you individually as my beloved sweetheart for—who is even counting, am I, Smith, counting?—sixty, sixty-five harmonious years of wonderful wedded bliss."

"Very nice," says Mrs. Smith.

"So far as I am concerned, you couldn't say it enough, very nice, very nice," says Smith, "because if Dr. Dale and me didn't just this instant have such an intelligent scientific conversation, you think that you, Mrs. Smith, would have the benefit of the latest up-to-date information as regards the brand-new disease which they just discovered for the old people?"

Mrs. Smith puts down her spoon and she says, "So which brand-new disease did they just get for the old people?"

Smith says, "Don't kid yourself, you didn't even hear of it yet, this is how totally brand-new it is, this particular disease which they just two seconds ago found out about for the old people—thank God that I as your husband have over the years been doing everything which could conceivably be done to keep up perfectly civil acquaintances with a certain very important private practitioner who lives right here, God love him, right in the neighborhood."

Mrs. Smith says, "So at least tell me, it's got a name, this brand-new disease which the scientific practitioners went out and visualized?"

"Sure, it's got a name," says Smith. "What kind of a disease do you think it would be if it didn't have a name?" says Smith. "I give you my solemn promise," says Smith, "this disease wouldn't have to go ahead and be a disease without a name," says Smith. "Don't worry," says Smith, "they gave it, as a disease, a name," says Smith.

"So do me a favor and tell me the name," says Mrs. Smith.

Smith says, "Listen, the name of this particular disease which Dr. Dale just took the trouble to inform me, Smith, your husband, as to the nature of, is called, for your information, the Elzenheimers."

"The Elzenheimers?" says Mrs. Smith.

"The Elzenheimers!" says Smith.

"So tell me," says Mrs. Smith, "how would a person know if they were sitting there and they suddenly got afflicted with the Elzenheimers?"

Smith says, "In other words, you, as Mrs. Smith, are asking me, Smith, your beloved husband, what, pray tell, would a certain person detect in their mind as the so-called syndrome if a certain person should suddenly all of a sudden be beset by this affliction?"

"This is my question to you as your sweetheart who is sitting here and eating a plate of soup," says Mrs. Smith.

Smith says, "Talking to you as a layman, what's doing with the syndrome of the Elzenheimers is like I, Smith, your adoring husband, sit here and tell you something, whereas two seconds after I tell you, bing bang, you wouldn't have the first idea of what it was I told you, not even if they came and put a gun to your head. So did you hear me describe to you the syndrome of the Elzenheimers, or did you hear me describe to you the syndrome of the Elzenheimers?" says Smith.

"Who couldn't hear you?" says Mrs. Smith.

"Then if you heard me sit here and describe to you the syndrome," says Smith, "I as your husband will take it for granted you are also hearing me when I now say to you will you do me a favor and be a sweetie and go get for me a nice piece of herring when you finish with your plate of soup. So tell me, you could or you couldn't do this for me, your pussycat sweetheart of a husband?" says Smith.

"You want herring, I will get you herring," says Mrs. Smith.

"Make a note," says Smith.

"Make a note?" says Mrs. Smith.

"Sure, make a note," says Smith. "You could be catching the Elzenheimers," says Smith. "You think you couldn't be catching the Elzenheimers?" says Smith.

"I'm not catching it," says Mrs. Smith.

"Sure, you're not catching it," says Smith. "Thank God you're not catching it!" says Smith. "But you think it makes sense to take a chance? Be smart," says Smith, "don't take a chance," says Smith, "it doesn't pay to take a chance," says Smith. "Write it down, what I said, a piece of herring," says Smith.

So Mrs. Smith puts down her spoon and writes it down, a piece of herring.

"And listen," says Smith, "be a darling and when you go get me the herring, slice me a few slices of a nice onion, yes?"

"You want onion, you will get onion," says Mrs. Smith.

"Thank you," says Smith. "And let me tell you something," says Smith. "Maybe I am just your husband, but in my modest opinion as your husband, you are some wonderful person whatever they ever come and try to say to me to the contrary," says Smith. "But listen," says Smith, "I wouldn't, if I were you, even speaking to you in the context that you are such a terrific wife, make the mistake of not writing it down what I just this instant said to you about the onion, because who could tell when you went to get the herring and when you went to get the onion that in the next instant before you got them you wouldn't be a woman who suddenly all of a sudden, lo and behold, got a case of the Elzenheimers? So as your husband, be a sweetheart and stop eating your soup for two seconds and play along with me and just to stand yourself in good stead, please God you will hurry up before it is too late and make a little note, onion."

So Mrs. Smith puts down her spoon and makes a note.

She says, "Did you see? I made the note," she says. "I didn't need to make it," she says. "But you think I wouldn't make it?" she says. "Because," she says, "which wife in her right mind couldn't afford to humor such a lovely matrimonial individual such as yourself?" says Mrs. Smith—whereupon she finishes her soup, puts down her spoon, goes and gets a dish, comes back and says, "Okay, so here's your cigar?"

Smith says, "You, my wife, are standing there and telling me to my face I didn't also say to you to bring a match?"

Madison Smartt Bell

A chapter cut from Soldier's Joy *(Ticknor and Fields, 1989)*

John Thomas McCarthy was dressed as if for the stage in a black satin jumpsuit studded all over with costume jewelry, the pant legs tucked into fire-engine-red boots. He was a heavy-set, compact little man only a little gone to fat. Take the jewelry off that suit and he could have gone in the ring as an All-Star wrestler, one of the smaller ones, at least. He'd had his hair done for the occasion too, or recently, in a big blond bouffant rolling four inches out from the back of his head and then sloping back in two wings to the point of the ducktail. The fake gemstones worked a big treble clef on the breast of the suit and across the shoulder blades they spelled out JOHN THOMAS! There were a couple of stones sprung out of the *T,* but if you overlooked that he was ready for Vegas. Laidlaw wondered who the hell he was trying to impress, since there was nobody there but the sound men and Rollo Fox and a handful of bored studio musicians who'd been rounded up to put a quick fix on the *John Thomas McCarthy Christmas Album.*

The musicians were spread out around the edges of the room, while John Thomas McCarthy rocked from one foot to the other behind a mike stand in the middle. Laidlaw stared out at him across the edge of his music stand. Next to him was Terry Baxter, sitting on a red leatherette stool with a black Les Paul guitar across his knees. Against the right wall was the pedal steel player, William Pike. On the left wall near the door was a pale-faced woman with thick black hair, strapped to a long-necked electric bass with a transparent Lucite body. She only went by the name of Julia, never telling anyone her last name. Even her cards said nothing but "Julia," alongside a few phone numbers where she could be reached.

The red light over the door was on, but they were all waiting for John Thomas's signal. When his left index finger went up, Laidlaw broke into a banjo intro to "Deck the Halls with Boughs of Holly." He had concocted the thing himself and was not proud of it, though it stood to earn him a little extra on the job. Terry Baxter thunked along behind him on the Les Paul. When they came to the end of the fourth bar, Pike and Julia chimed in simultaneously and then John Thomas McCarthy opened his mouth, but all he did was let out a husky cough and then drag his finger across his throat. All around the studio, the musicians stopped, and after a second the red light went off.

"I don't know, Rollo," John Thomas said.

"Now what is it you don't know, John Thomas?" Not much had been spent on the intercom, and it took all the tone from the producer's voice, but Laidlaw could guess he was getting impatient. He glanced up at the big window high in the wall but there was too much glare off the glass for him to really see through it. He sat down on a stool and lowered the banjo drum to the floor between his feet. Terry Baxter, mouth pursed in a silent whistle, swung around on his stool and shot him a wink. John Thomas McCarthy coughed again. His voice was a little throatier than usual today; he'd said he was just getting over a cold.

"I don't know but what we might ought to open that one up with the pedal steel instead," he said.

The intercom hissed, but no words came out.

"Rollo, why don't we talk a minute?"

"Okay." The intercom sighed. "Everybody take five, then."

Julia was the first one out the door, and Laidlaw and Baxter filed after her, William Pike bringing up the rear. The pointy toes of Rollo Fox's boots were coming down the steel stairs from the sound booth. Julia turned into the office and poured herself coffee in a Styrofoam cup. Terry Baxter hung back in the hall.

"Anybody care to step out a minute?" he said.

"Too cold," Pike said, and went by him toward the coffee pot. John Thomas followed him into the office. He leaned across the desk toward a mirror hung on the wall behind it and began to rearrange his hair with both hands. Sighing, Julia leaned back on the wall and struck a match to her cigarette. The coffee machine fizzled out a few drops of hot water. Rollo Fox stuck his thumb in his belt loops to hitch his pants up the lower curve of his belly and turned back in the doorway to face Terry Baxter.

"You hadn't got time to go nowhere," he said. "I said take a five-minute break, is all."

"I'm only going just out to the car and see what I can hear on the radio," Terry Baxter said. "I'll be right out there whenever you call me."

"Just don't get a notion to take any ride," Rollo said, and went past Laidlaw into the office. "All right, John Thomas, what's on your mind?"

"I'll go with you," Laidlaw said to Terry Baxter.

"That's the spirit." They walked out through the front lobby. Violet, the receptionist, sat behind a desk on a raised dais, her head lowered to blow on her nails. Terry Baxter blew her a kiss as they went past, but she didn't look up from her polishing job.

"She don't love me," Terry Baxter said sadly.

"She don't love anybody," Laidlaw said. "I believe she's sharpening her nails to tear human flesh."

Outdoors it was chilly enough to make Laidlaw wish he'd thought to put on his jacket. He trotted quickly after Terry Baxter to the mint-green 240Z, which was parked facing out the drive toward Eighth Avenue South.

"Can you get some heat on in this thing?" Laidlaw said.

"Have to let it warm up a minute," Terry Baxter said, turning the key. The car started with a smooth murmur and he reached for the radio, pushing the button for KDA FM. Laidlaw tucked in his shoulders and rubbed his hands together. Terry Baxter pulled down the sun visor and plucked a thin joint from an elastic band behind it. Fixing it in his mouth, he turned to grin at Laidlaw. He had a reddish beard and freckles and there was a glint in his light green eyes.

"Strike a light to that for me, will you?"

Laidlaw extended a lit match, then pulled it back to his own cigarette. KDA was playing the Beatles. Terry Baxter took a long drag and held it and hung the joint under Laidlaw's nose. Laidlaw shook his head.

"It's good stuff," Terry Baxter said. "Came a long way to find you, or so I'm told."

"I don't doubt you," Laidlaw said. "I just don't use it that much, is all."

"Suit yourself," Terry Baxter said. "What'd you come out in the cold for, then?"

Laidlaw laughed.

"I don't much like to be shut in a small room with Rollo," he said. "Not when he's wearing his after-shave."

"You got a point there," Terry Baxter said with a sigh. "How's Adrienne been getting along, she working?"

"Okay," Laidlaw said. "We're both getting by."

"I sort of looked to see her here today."

"They're planning to dub in a string section on this one, according to what I heard," Laidlaw said. "The rate they're going they'd be better off dubbing everything else in too."

"It is starting to look like a kind of long day," Terry Baxter said. He had a flat Arkansas delta accent, and spoke in a steady near-monotone. Laidlaw reached out to put a fingerprint on the fogging windshield.

"He could just as well lay in the vocals to a rhythm box or something," Laidlaw said. "And not pay all this many people to watch him change his mind."

"Well, that's John Thomas," Terry Baxter said. "He likes to have that more realistic atmosphere."

"Yeah," Laidlaw said. "And he likes to fool around and burn up money."

"You're not paying him, are you?" Terry Baxter said. "He should be paying you if everything's the way it's supposed to be."

"Sure," Laidlaw said. "I just get a little bored with it."

"We just get through this one and that'll be the end of the carols, at least. I expect we'll be into the original material before we go home."

"God help us," Laidlaw said.

"What, you don't like it?" Terry Baxter said. "I'm getting kind of fond of the one where the little girl dies in the snow in the end."

"Brings a big fat old tear to your eye, don't it?" Laidlaw said. "We'll see if it still does the fifteenth time around, though. You know this record is going to be an atrocity, nobody in their right mind ever would buy it. I don't understand how he pays for his studio time, if you want to know the truth."

"It's kind of a mystery." Terry Baxter leaned forward to turn on the heat, then cracked a window to let out some smoke. "I don't worry about it all that much myself, not when I got my car payment to make."

"Just kind of curious," Laidlaw said. Terry Baxter shrugged and dampened a run on the joint with his index finger.

"Pike went out with him on his road trip once," he said. "He told me he's a pretty good draw out there in the West. Maybe that crowd buys his records too. Else he's just living out some kind of long contract."

"I reckon," Laidlaw said. "Wonder what time we'll get done tonight?"

"Do like me if you want to stay happy," Terry Baxter said. "Every time you look at your watch you also figure out your check. Money's as good for this one as anything else."

"I know," Laidlaw said. "Sometimes I just hate to think of putting my name to it, is all."

Terry snorted and sucked on the joint.

"This is John Thomas McCarthy you're working for," he said. "Your name's bound to be in the *small* small print."

"Principle," Laidlaw said.

"I wouldn't get excited about that on this kind of job," Terry Baxter said. "Go on have a toke and try to settle yourself down some. Rollo's the one with his eye on the clock, and I believe he's getting tired of watching that fool blow his cues. A little more like this and he'll be looking for somebody to take it out on. I know you don't want to run up against that."

"I guess you're right," Laidlaw said. "The dope wouldn't settle me much, though, I think I'd just as well let it alone."

"It takes hold of everybody different, I expect," Terry Baxter said.

"Yeah," Laidlaw said. "It mostly just gives me the heebie-jeebies. I'll get drunk when we get done, if I feel in the mood."

"To each his own." Terry Baxter balled up the dead roach, flicked it into his mouth and swallowed.

"Do your damnedest now, John Thomas," he said. "Bore me to death if you can."

A short while passed in silence, except for the radio. Laidlaw rubbed a hole in the fog on his window so he could see out. The studio was a gray brick building with blue trim and mustard-colored lettering that read "MELLOWTONE" over the broad glass doors. Left of the entrance, his truck was parked, and he squinted at it, thinking for a second that a tire had gone flat, but he saw he had only parked on uneven ground.

"Some more fast action in Music City," Terry Baxter said. "We'd had time to go for a hamburger at least."

"John Thomas kind of robs me of my appetite, seems like," Laidlaw said.

"But it's still a living, right?" Terry Baxter said. "You all still playing at the Clawhammer?"

"Not regular," Laidlaw said. "The old band finally came back."

"Too bad."

"For us it is," Laidlaw said. "Not that I'd wish them any harm, they had a bad time themselves, some of them did. We sure could use another steady gig like that, though."

"It's a common condition." Terry Baxter reached to twist the rearview mirror toward him. He prised back his eyelids with thumb and forefinger and dribbled a little Visine in.

"I don't see much use in that," Laidlaw said. "They'll smell it all over both of us anyway, smoking in a closed car."

"I doubt Rollo could smell too much of anything over that jive juice he wears," Terry Baxter said, working on his other eye.

"Maybe not, but what difference does it really make?"

Terry Baxter tossed the Visine up on the dashboard.

"I don't know but I think he's starting to really get touchy," he said. "I just don't want to give him a chance to start in on me, is all."

Laidlaw rubbed away a fresh accretion of mist from the glass and looked out. He could see Julia standing inside the doors, hooking at them with one arm.

"Time to go," he said to Terry. "They're calling us in."

Pike kicked off "Deck the Halls" with the pedal steel and after only one false start John Thomas managed to come in singing in the right place. Laidlaw had to wonder how he managed on the road; studios just made some people nervous, he guessed. The John Thomas voice was a deep hollow bass, more or less in the style of Conway Twitty, though he seemed to have to work hard to sustain it, puffing himself up like a toad before every line. Laidlaw pattern-picked his way through two verses. In the middle of the tune there was a lull in the instrumentation during which John Thomas was intended to deliver a spoken homily of some kind, but after Julia's bass had thudded across two measures all on its own it became apparent he had choked again or dropped the cue. Laidlaw started playing the line he'd written for the intro, just to fill in. The intercom let out a feedback screech, the red light died, and everybody stopped.

"Laidlaw, what in the hell you think you're doing?" Rollo's voice squawked from the box.

"Filling in," Laidlaw said.

"Where you think you're at, a square dance?" the intercom said. The others were leaning back away from their instruments. John Thomas was lipping a bottle of Coke. Laidlaw adjusted a string and said nothing.

"You just play the score like it's wrote, Laidlaw, that's all you need to worry yourself about."

Laidlaw glanced up at the window of the sound booth. He could just barely see Rollo's silhouette.

"You already threw out the score, remember?" he said. "I don't see what you're tearing your hair out for anyhow, the take was already shot before I picked the first lick."

"Was it now?" Rollo's disembodied voice said. "I reckon I'll just be the judge of that. All I need you to do is set there and do your best to keep time."

"Well now," Laidlaw said. "Maybe you ought to hire a clock."

The intercom sputtered.

"That's it," Rollo said. "That does it. You pack up."

Laidlaw stole a glance at Terry Baxter, who closed his eyes and blew an imaginary smoke ring toward the ceiling. On the rear wall behind him, Pike looked just as much like a dead fish as he always did.

"Go on," the intercom shrieked. "You think I'm fooling with you?"

Laidlaw unslung the banjo and lowered it into the case, which he'd left propped open near his feet. He shucked the picks off his fingers and put them in the plush box under the neck, rolled the strap and tucked it in and closed the lid. By the time he got the catches shut his fingers had begun to twitch with anger and he had a little trouble fastening the length of rope that attached the handle to the case. When he had finally got it done he stood up and walked straight to the door. There was no one on his way but Julia, who shrugged at him and looked off at the other wall.

Rollo had come tumbling down the steps and was waiting for him in the hall.

"Now where the hell you think you're going?"

Laidlaw stepped around him, went into the office, picked up his jacket and put it on. Rollo was standing in the doorway, holding the frame on either side.

"You want to just write me my check now?" Laidlaw said. "Or would it be easier on you to mail it?"

"Come on and get back in there," Rollo said. "I'm serious now, this is *studio time.*"

"You're always serious," Laidlaw said. "You're the boss, you hired me, you fired me. Now all I got to do is pack my traps and go home." He lifted the banjo case and went toward the door, but Rollo didn't step aside. Laidlaw hesitated, looking at him for a moment. He was losing hair and what remained of it was carefully arranged in oily mounds around his head. On his cheeks two purplish patches were rising—maybe he was allergic to his after-shave, Laidlaw thought. He wore a red satin shirt with mother-of-pearl snaps and a cowboy yoke touched out in white piping. White jeans came tight over his pear-shaped belly and his boots were a Tony Lama snakeskin special.

"Five hundred bucks for the boots alone," Laidlaw said, and shook his head. "You sure are a beauty, Rollo."

"Cut out your monkeyshines and get back in that studio," Rollo said.

"You best move before I have to move you," Laidlaw said. When he began to walk forward again, Rollo got out of the doorway. Laidlaw went out through the reception area and swung the glass door wide. He could hear Rollo's boot heels clacking after him, but he didn't turn back before he got to the truck.

"Don't be a damn fool, Laidlaw," Rollo said. "You really think I want to replace you this late in the day?"

Laidlaw jerked open the passenger door of the truck and slid the banjo case in on the floor.

"Hell, you don't need me anymore anyway," he said. "You already got tape of anything you'd let me do, just make a loop and dub it in. Besides which, you couldn't save this record now if you had a harp from heaven." He walked around the front of the cab and unlocked the other door.

"Goddamn your eyes, Laidlaw," Rollo said. "You think I can't get along without you, well, you're mighty wrong. You won't work for me again. Time I get through with you, you might not work for anybody."

Laidlaw smiled blandly down on him.

"Don't lose any sleep over that," he said. "One way or another, I'll get by."

"I bet you will." Rollo's face was red all over now, either from anger or the cold. He raised up on his toes and then settled back down some. "You go on back out in the woods and scratch you out a garden. You better learn how to dig roots too, son, because I'll tell you one thing, it's a long way to summer." Rollo spun around on his expensive heels and stalked back toward the studio.

Laidlaw lit himself a cigarette as he climbed into the truck, and sat there a while smoking it before he put the key in the switch. The stone cold of the seat came right through his jeans; the weather was turning fast now, no doubt about it. Through the big show window of Mellowtone Studios, he could see Violet angling her head one way and another as she talked on the phone. His anger had passed and now he just felt chilly and empty, his stomach slightly shrunken and sour since he hadn't really eaten that day. He put out the cigarette and sat a minute longer, watching a stray dog trot across the parking lot. A potato chip bag came blowing over the concrete and the dog looked up at it for a hopeful instant, then dropped its eyes and went grimly on. On the road, the traffic kept crashing by, and the dog made to cross, gave up, and turned the other way. When it had gone around the corner of the building, Laidlaw shivered and turned the key. The truck answered him with a dry grinding noise, and it took him three more tries before the engine would start.

Lee K. Abbott

What follows are two scenes from a story of mine called "We Get Smashed and Our Endings Are Swift," which appeared in the fall 1982 issue of The South Carolina Review. *Curiously, the scenes were written after the story was published, when I was thinking of expanding the story to something like a novella—a thought, and a project, now thoroughly abandoned.*

One night Zion called. I had been dreaming about squalor and came to the phone still dirty from sleep.

"Hey, white boy," he said, through the static, and my heart wobbled up and free.

"Where are you?" I hollered.

"Is it safe?"

I could see Daddy outside. He was stringing barbed wire, and unhappy about it. He'd told me there was a woman on the phone. Or a child with a large vocabulary.

"Let's talk code," I said.

"What do you suggest?"

Food, I told him. Vegetables.

"Commodities," he said. "Pork. Lamb. Cow."

"State capitals."

"Opera."

"Religion," he said. "Worship. Heavenly appeals."

"Z-words," I said, "zinky. Zebu. Zoid."

We settled on women's fashion.

"Valentino culottes," he said. "Ungaro satin."

"Crepe evening dress."

"Sephardic, variations on black and white, quilted, slinky, hopeful."

This last was a complex-compound sentence that brought to mind old times. In the mind's eye, I could see him again—that swift, soaked, limping black man vanishing in a swirl of rain and deeper darkness.

"You're here, aren't you?"

"Maybe," he said, "I'm everywhere. I'm Santa Claus."

Outside my daddy was kicking a fence post and saying naughty things about man.

"Meet me, Zion. We can do it."

"No can do, Herkie. I just got lonely for a while."

I knew the feeling. If it were geography, I told him, it would be here—featureless, full of sky and harsh light, dusty—or it would be the North Pole. Loneliness, I told him, had a texture and a taste and a sound one couldn't ignore.

"You're being poetic," he said. "I like that."

"The Major's teed at you, Zion. He takes it personal."

"I sympathize," he said. "The Major's a troubled man."

"He used the words prejudice and bias. He wants us to drink something and tear you up."

"What do you want, Harold?"

I tried, in my imagination, to hold myself at arm's length. What, indeed, did Herkie Walls want. Money, I thought. Nookie. A ranch-style home as in *Life* magazine. Offspring. Neighbors.

"I don't know," I said. "The Major says I ought to want you."

"The man has a one-track mind. Lift him up, Herkie. Show him the light."

"He says you cost him plenty. He figured it up the other day, made me check the numbers. Three hundred sixty thousand dollars, give or take. He aims to recruit more guys."

"What're they like?" he wondered.

They were all named Buzz, I said. Or Duffy. The other day, I told him, the Major came by with a Cajun named LaTouche. He was sixteen, in love with his sister. He was built like a tree stump, spoke mostly with his hands. We discussed Nate Hawthorne and the pineal gland.

"You were scared."

I was petrified, I said. This was a new generation, only ten years from our own. But like bird and spoor, not related.

"What happened?"

The kid took Norbutal, liked the way it made his face swell up like a pumpkin. He had green teeth and only one ear.

"I got to go, Herkie."

"Wait," I said. I was thinking of him as he was the time we went into a Detroit bar called the Cavern. Proud and grinning, he'd stood on a table, made a speech about Fizzies. It was a metaphor, I knew, about the kind we were. Gamete, zygote, being that grew up to multiply. That's how we started: effervescent and grape-colored.

"Call me again sometime."

"Maybe," he said. "I got sentimental, is all."

"I miss you, Zion."

Outside, Daddy had put all the elements in one hell, humans in another. He was so loud I had to choose which voice to listen to.

"I miss me too, Harold. I really do."

Two nights later, I had dinner with Daddy Ben and Buck. They ate in the TV room, absorbed in broadcast America. For a time we watched electronic beauty reel by—vehicles, conveniences, smells New York likes.

"Eeefff," Buck said when a pretty woman came on. "Eeeefff."

They could take females apart like puzzles. Women were meat, is all. Raw and lovely parts you got at a cafeteria.

"Bosoms," Daddy said.

"Flank," Buck said.

"Lips."

"Mons." Rapt, Buck was eating string beans. "Labia," he said. "Majora."

"Eeefff," Daddy said.

I let another hour go by. I had grown up in this room. On the walls hung things we were once proud of: ribbons from the state fair, my honor rolls from high school, the gray pelt of a coyote Daddy had skinned, a tree I'd made that showed who we grew from. We were from sodbusters mostly. A race of Walls named Cooter and Joe Ben and, way back in sooty England, Ebenezer. We had fought Indians and Spaniards and rainstorms and drought. We looked at life directly and spoke what we knew without shame. "Scum," we said. "No." "Yes." We married women named Rilla and Marva and Faith, and they died early or went on toward death like the men. We lived here, in Texas, in the dry, wind-whipped sections we own, and chased off those from the larger world.

"You're going now, ain't you?" Daddy said at last.

I was.

"Where?" he said.

It was classified, I said. I gave him hints having to do with swamp things and what you find in third worlds.

"Need money?"

I didn't, I said. I had a rich, olive-colored uncle who could meet my needs.

"You're a son-of-bitch now, ain't you?"

We looked at each other, one animal to another. I could see into his brain, which was smooth and glossy as ball bearings.

"I'm a true bastard," I said.

In the front yard we took leave of each other. In one direction lay heaven, in the other the underworld they taught us about in college. Between them were Daddy, Buck, and I, kicking the dust and trying to put our hands away. The night had warmth and odor to it and way off stars were flickering on like Xmas lights.

"You coming back?" Daddy said.

I didn't know.

"Well, bring a present if you do," he said. "I'd prefer something expensive. Gold maybe."

In the pickup, Ben played KMOX and made up the lyrics he forgot. He said, "Hard times," then was quiet. He said, "The Lonely Crowd." He beat his foot on the floor. He said, "Oo-la-la."

Ahead I could see the Greyhound station. I would be in El Paso in seven hours. Two more and I'd be in San Diego. More and in Hawaii. Time after that had no direction or way of being known.

"They want me to play football next year," Buck said. "Cisco Junior College."

"Who's they?"

"Coach," he said. "Name of Oscar Tweego."

I knew the name. Around here he was famous for halftime talks in which he ate live fowl and talked about God. His face brought to mind the words "sulphur" and "pitch."

"What does he want you do?" I asked.

"Violence," Buck said. "I'm to be the one running around bashing heads."

I had a thought, possibly warm and complete. And another.

"I got to take classes though," Buck said. "I've seen the list."

"Hard, huh?"

He pulled into the parking lot, hit the brakes the way he likes.

"Calculus," he said. "European history."

On the radio a group was singing about the soul and the ice it rests on. "You can trust the Communists," they sang. "You can trust the Jews."

"I had a meeting the other day," he said. "They put me up in a Motel 6. Some boosters came over. All dressed in red and black, the colors. They showed me their wallets. Asked me about fortitude. Said what car I'd like."

I'd seen the same thing at TCU: many sportcoats with currency falling out. White shoes. Cocktails from foreign lands. Parties with themes attached.

"I told them I'd need a tutor," Buck was saying. "They showed me pictures. Patti. Darlene. Debbi. Audrey."

My bus was waiting and we headed toward it.

"Pretty, huh?"

He grabbed my hand, shook it like a hammer.

"Eeeeefff," he said. "Aaaaarrrgghh."

Richard Stern

This is an outtake from a novel in progress.

THE BEAUTIFUL WIDOW AND THE BAKERY GIRL

Venice was in a stew, at least the Venice of the rich and pretend-rich who spent hundreds of hours finding out who'd be coming to town, what parties they'd be coming to, getting invited to them. The exciting visitant now was not a head of state—just as well, the summit conference of '78 had been a social disaster—not a great actor or beautiful actress, not a literary, musical, or pictorial genius, but one of the fifteen or twenty super-super celebrities of the world, *La Bella Vedova,* no longer quite so beautiful—indeed, had she ever been?—but still mysteriously recessive, sexually piquant, and high-lit with the beauty derived from the luminaries who'd paid her court when she'd been mistress of the Great American Court.

Betsy, a sucker for the rich and powerful, was enormously excited. The American prince whose violent death had turned the young beauty into the beautiful widow was one of the lights of her pantheon. She'd made a life-size bronze of his head and sent it, unsolicited, to his grieving parents. (It was never acknowledged.) She was in love with the beautiful widow, with the images of her grief and bravery, her artistic consolations, her temporary exile from the country which killed the prince and killed his princely brother and which, she believed, wanted to kill, break, or humiliate their children. In exile she'd become a widow twice more, marrying first an official prince—one of the few who had survived the great wars with part of his family's fortune—and then an industrial prince, a charming international gutter-rat whose unscrupulous persistence led to his becoming one of the richest men in history. The Widow was not rich, in fact, for years had thought of herself as a pauper. Her marriages had risen from and declined upon mountains of legal paper. She said to a friend whose leaky tongue was the source of much of what the world knew about her, "The mountains labored and brought forth church-poor me." What had these husbands, or their families, spotted in her that they had, independently of each other, willed their money out of her hands, leaving her with funds which would barely pay for her clothes and jewels? Poverty—the poverty of insufficiency—was a family curse. Her father had drunk, gambled, and gestured away his small fortune, had died in the Pierre's slummiest room, barely large enough for his three suits and hundred empty bottles.

What the Beautiful Widow had was the radiance of celebrity that had for decades thrilled people as celebrated as she. She was a class of one, and like Wallace Stevens's jar, drew the eyes of everyone in the social landscape as if she were the only significant creation.

Rumors occasionally had it that she was a dear person, an adoring mother, a loyal friend, brave in the face of assaults on her privacy and person. Other rumors had it that she was avaricious to the point of mania. Some claimed she was brilliant, immensely learned, polylingual and soaked in the poetry and culture of a dozen countries. There were counterstories of her naïveté, stupidity, laziness, callous disregard of suffering, inequity, and anything but the happiness of those closest to her. Stories piled around her as they had about the Holy Grail. (She was pursued almost as religiously as that old receptacle of narrative surplus.) Years after the last of her husbands left her, she remained one of the chief icons of Western celebrity.

No wonder Venice couldn't contain its excitement. There were fifty stories about the time of her arrival, where she was staying—the Grand Canal? the Lido? the Torcello? a villa on the Brenta? Surely, she wouldn't stay at the Danieli or the Gritti. Was she coming incognita? Was it possible she was already here? Every well-dressed woman between thirty and sixty was inspected.

"She'll be at the Mulligans' party," Betsy told George.

That afternoon, George had gone with Betsy to a bakery in the Calle degli Fabri. Betsy loved their almond cakes and dark spiral rolls. She also wanted to show George the girl behind the counter, one of those beauties that look as if they've fallen out of a Renaissance canvas into Venetian streets. Behind the counter was—my God, the Beautiful Widow. Or so, for a second, it seemed. No, this girl was more solid, a Vermeer, a Veronese girl, her colors red and gold. The redness had oven heat in it, the gold was pocked with sweat. A working girl with marvelous solid arms and powerful wrists. Her white uniform sported work stains at armpit, breast, and belly, her hands were rough, the fingernails short. Her nose was blunt, the eyes dark with green glints, her complexion extraordinary, something off a mosaic. Dark gold hair looped in chains around her head.

What, she asked, did the *signore* desire? George Share could not speak, could hardly breathe. The bakery, full of hot bread smell, dizzied him. He inhaled as if the warm smell rose from the girl's pudenda. Finally he managed to point to a spiral roll. "*Questo.*"

"*Quanto?*"

He held up both hands.

"*Dieci?*"

He nodded.

"*Cinque mille, trecento-cinquanta.*"

He handed over a five-thousand-lire note.

"*E trecento-cinquanta.*"

He handed over another five-thousand-lire note.

When he took the change from her fingers, their rough touch made his heart skip. She knows, he thought. She's used to what she does to men. "*Grazie, signorina.*"

"*Grazie lei. Buon giorno.*"

"See what I mean," said Betsy.

"Do I." He walked Betsy back to Santa Maria del Giglio, went through Campo San Stefano, crossed the Accademia Bridge, and made his way through winding *calli* to the apartment, his head and body full of the girl. She would be through at three, would walk home, at four she'd be in her bath. Lucky tub. If Fellini had come into the bakery, he would have spotted her power instantly. Who could escape it? There were a thousand beautiful Venetian girls, maybe more, and thousands of visiting beauties. At a table in the artists' café in San Barnaba, he'd seen Del Plunko talking with a black-haired beauty in a red dress. How could that be? Del Plunko had seen and ignored him. As he passed, he heard him say "Montale." Up the *calle* walked a blonde girl in a short blue dress, bare-legged, carrying a plastic sack in each hand. George watched her bare legs as she headed for the bridge. Would he see her again? Would he see the girl in the red dress, the bakery girl?

At Mulligan's party, the bakery girl stood in the center of an adoring crowd. Astonishing. Who'd had the inspiration, the social guts to bring her, this Venetian Liza Doolittle? God bless Venice. God bless the democracy of beauty. In a dress that looked like one of Colonel Qadaffi's gaudier. outfits—a kind of sand-colored tent, with all kinds of sleeves, real and phony, and a long skirt—the girl made theatrical gestures and spoke like a child who'd swallowed a bassoon. What a voice, an innocent, burping buzz, but it was accentless English, for of course it wasn't the bakery girl at all but the Beautiful Widow.

Meg Wolitzer

A section from This Is Your Life *(Crown, 1988) in the father's point of view, that never made it into the novel*

Dottie and Bud: two names that seemed to fit their owners, she so crazed and sprawling, he so tight and closed. He would think about this as he lay in bed at night, smoking before sleep. Actually, he and Dottie had been referred to more often as Jack Sprat and his wife. It was humiliating—not Dottie's weight, really, because there were many times when he simply loved the heft of her, loved the way her body seemed to swing around him like swirls of cloth—but the contrast between the two of them. When they walked into a restaurant together he could feel people look up from their dinners and stare. He liked it when they went to Cookie's Steak Pub, because it was a family restaurant, and everyone was preoccupied with their children. You could settle in at a big varnished table and not feel you had to be presentable. You could reach over and wipe your daughter's face with a napkin. You could say, "Sit still, girls!" and not feel embarrassed.

Parents looked at each other in sympathy at Cookie's. "I know how it is," a woman at the next table said once, when first Erica started crying, then Opal joined in. All parents understood. This big, paneled room with its many mealtime dramas—everyone here understood. You could smell steak cooking, and if you turned around you could see the kitchen, exposed by a picture window, and inside the cooks with their high hats were flipping steaks, the flames climbing dramatically before them. The flames, the heat, the smells: it all made Bud feel agitated and compelled, as though he were a kid at the circus.

Everyone began to crowd around the salad bar, whole families lining up to fork pale lettuce into their black plastic bowls. Bud stood in line with the rest of them, waiting, looking around the dark red room, smelling meat and smoke and something underlying, something sweet and almost alcoholic. There was that woman again, smiling at him from the other side of the salad bar and helping her two sons pump ranch dressing from a huge jug.

"It's hard," the woman said simply.

"Don't I know it. You're telling me," he answered in his best good-natured voice, which he automatically used for talking to women he did not know. They thought him polite, enjoyed the lilt in his speech, his deferential way of addressing them. It was different from the way he spoke to men, the few men he spoke to. When he gave it some extended thought, he realized that he spoke to very few men. The ones at work—did they count? They floated through each other's peripheral vision every day, passed each other in the hallway and groaned about tax season. And then, when it came time to prepare the returns, they shored themselves up for the long haul, making ape-faces of commiseration.

One fellow, Phil Mercer, taped a sign to his door announcing that everyone was welcome to stop by his office for a little "IRS cheer." Bud could hear the sounds of people talking and beer cans pipping open as he went past, but he didn't know if he should go in. He hung outside, doing a tentative little shuffle. Finally Connie, the receptionist, pushed him through the doorway and wrapped his hand around a can of Budweiser.

"A Bud for a Bud," she said, and he was confused, but then understood the joke.

"Yup, Connie, thanks. Yup," he said. The room was filled with all the faces from the office, only now everyone's ties were loosened. Men in groups didn't interest him—not that he was interested in women in groups, either. Once he walked into the house when Dottie had three friends over, three neighborhood girls, and just the sound of their voices, the way they seemed to rise and rise, made him anxious. He closed himself in the bedroom with a double-crostic. It was groups in general that he hated. The men in Phil Mercer's office were all decent people, but they didn't talk about anything except the IRS. He didn't think he could bear another joke whose punch line was, "April fifteenth!" Jokes were saved for Dottie. That was her exclusive territory.

When they first got married, she had showed him her high school yearbook. She was pretty in the photograph: a wide, young face with a dab of dark lipstick, her hair pulled back. Underneath the picture it read: "Dottie Lubin," and then, "Look out, Fanny Brice."

"You should do something with all your jokes," Norma from around the corner told her, and Dottie reported this back to Bud.

"What do you mean, 'do something'?" he asked. "What could you possibly 'do' with jokes? Solve world hunger? End the Vietnam War?"

She was offended. "Well, what are you 'doing' with your skills at accounting?" she asked.

He sprang up in bed. "For one, I'm supporting this family!" he said. "Can you do that with your one-liners?"

They would bicker like this on and on, and then she would turn away and weep, her shoulders moving. He touched her shoulder on the spot where her aqua nightgown strap formed a little bow. A little bow on that wide strip of freckly skin.

"Dot," he would say. "Dot. Come on." And sometimes she would roll back to him, in one swift motion roll right into his arms and press herself against him. Sometimes she almost knocked the wind out of him with the weight of her, the surprise, and he would gasp and feel himself getting excited. This was the danger of sleeping with a woman like a boulder, a boulder on the edge of a cliff.

But other times, he would say her name and she wouldn't even turn around or acknowledge that she had heard him. Her shoulders kept working up and down like a piston, and he said, "Ah, what the fuck, Dot! What the fuck do you want, even?" And then he would jump off the bed and go into the den, where he would smack on the television. If he was lucky, "The Rockford Files" might be on. He loved this show with a furtive, childish appetite. He told no one about this love. Years later, when Dottie was already famous and Bud lived alone, he got himself a VCR, and taped every single episode of the show, kept a complete library for his own personal viewing.

Now, after a fight, Bud arranged himself on the couch, watching television with a real fierceness; he focused on the commercials as well as the shows, and he realized that he knew all the jingles by heart. But late at night, the only time he ever watched, just low-budget commercials were on, the ones from local outlet stores, where they couldn't pay enough money to hire decent singers or dancers. There was one place called the CynDee Shoppe, on Ditmars Boulevard in Brooklyn. The spelling of both "CynDee" and "Shoppe" made him almost cry out in pain. He pictured some corroded storefront, some tiny place with the elevated train thundering by overhead, making all the terrible, frilly dresses tremble on their hangers.

Three girls jumped onto the screen, and began to sing:

"Oh, the Cyndee Shoppe is the place to go, we have great fashions don't you know."

Now one girl had a solo here, and she leapt into the front in her red jumpsuit and sang, "You'll love our styles. . . ."

Second girl: "And you'll browse awhile. . . ."

All three in unison: "And you'll find our prices are oh-so-low!"

Why should these three ridiculous girls make him so sad? Why should their hopeful, smeary faces make him feel desperate about the world? There was no reason, he knew. But now, like a curse, the song was lodged in his head, and he couldn't release it. After the television station had signed off for the night and Bud pulled an afghan over himself on the couch, he kept humming it. This began, for him, what would be a long career of humming. He held onto tunes, whether he liked them or not, and he found them relaxing. He didn't even need lyrics, or a context.

A few days later he was humming as he drove to work—some pleasant, jazzy little tune—and he realized, with horror, that it was unmistakably the song for the CynDee Shoppe, and that it would be with him forever.

Toby Olson

From Dorit in Lesbos (Simon & Shuster, 1990). Jack finds himself a stowaway aboard a yacht heading south from Long Beach toward Panama. He hides in the anchor well, fearing the potential danger from mysterious figures aboard. In cutting these sections I recognized, yet again, that I was carried away with detail, something that happens quite often. But what else is there but detail? I ask myself. Well, there are a few other things, and in this case obsession got the best of me.

There was nothing between me and the man sitting at the desk down and a few yards beyond me, his back to me and his head in the glow cast across the desk surface from another of those gooseneck table lamps. I could tell the room had things in it, file cabinets and bookcases, but my eyes were fixed on the man's back and head, his thin and graying hair, movements in his left elbow as he did things with his hands on the desk surface.

I held my bag and racket tight against my leg and turned my head slightly, glancing away from him then back again quickly, checking the space on either side. On my right there was nothing, only a railing and the room a few feet below it, but on the left the wall extended out to the front edge of the platform. It was a tight space, and the door opened into a slight indentation in that wall, the only way it could be opened completely. There was a hook eye protruding from the forward edge of the door-shaped indentation, and I guessed that there was a hook of some sort close to the door's frame behind me, a way to hold the door fully open, maybe to get air into the place. I looked quickly over the cabin walls and saw that there were no portholes or windows. It was an inner cabin, a space I had a hard time placing within the not-yet-sure picture I had of the yacht's layout.

Then I heard something, and at the same time my stomach turned as the man shifted in his chair, the metal swivel squeaking slightly on its bearings. I felt my racket head come up as I tightened my grip. Then the man sighed, hunched his shoulders down a little, and continued his work. I have to get out of here, I thought. He'll turn soon and see me. I'm too damn close. This is crazy.

I started to turn, to reach back for the handle. Then I heard the sound again, distinctly now, the click of sure steps over the engine drone beyond the door. I stepped quickly to my left, squeezed back into the shallow indentation, my bag and racket pressed in tightly against my leg, and lifted my free palm up and waited. I heard a cough and a quick shuffling of feet and saw the opening door coming toward me. I braced against the indentation and stiffened my arm, watching the door move quickly toward my eyes. It stopped an inch short of my palm. Then it was closing, and for a moment I saw the thick arm and figure of the man on the platform no more than a foot from my body. He looked back as he flicked the door toward the frame, his head turning away from me over his right shoulder, catching the handle as it passed behind him, shutting it. As he came back around, he was descending down the few steps to the cabin floor.

I held the fixed image of his thick forearm, that long snaking tattoo, vines and flowers, that I had seen coming around as he swung the bat at my head so long ago now with Chen and the others outside the trailer. I fought against the significance, watching his broad back, something strangely familiar there as well, as he reached the cabin deck, moved to the seated man, and bent down over the table. I reached out to the door handle and pulled it back toward me, pressing myself into the shallow indentation behind it.

I could see them, hear the man's talking, sound of the other's muffled answers as he kept his head down over the table. I wondered if he could be Janes, but I didn't think so. He seemed younger than that, thicker through the back than he should have been, and taller I thought too. His hair was graying, but it could have been premature. It was someone else, possibly another of the men from the trailer, and these were possibly the same men who had come at me in the ski masks near Congress Park, but I couldn't be sure of that.

Morning came with fog, a heavy line of it obscuring the shoreline completely, and dark and low rain clouds in the sky, moving quickly in the same direction we were heading.

I took an inventory of my bag, setting the food aside, enough for four more days if I was careful, and enough water too if I counted on the juice around vegetables and fruit to supplement it. What I had was the length of nylon rope, the penlight, pencil, and the ten sheets of paper I'd taken from Janes's cabin, eight now that I'd used two of them. I had the Porsche's keys, both bent and ragged from their use as can openers. I could have used the screwdriver or the pliers for that purpose, but in my anxiety and vagueness I'd forgotten them. I had the headband, the key and emblem. And of course I had the racket, a big help so far, and the blanket and Janes's tweed jacket. I had one bent cigarette, a half book of matches, and some loose change that I found along the bag's seams in its bottom. What I didn't have was my wallet, credit cards, substantial money, phone numbers. I'd left all that in the glove compartment of the Porsche, thinking then that it would be good to be anonymous if I was caught, a foolish consideration altogether, I now thought. I had the legal pad, my underpants, my sweat pants and shirt. I had my filthy socks and my tennis shoes, and that was absolutely everything. I put the objects and the food back in the bag, looking at each thing, remembering it as I did so. I only kept the legal pad and pencil out. It had started to rain, but there was no strong breeze. Still the rain drifted into my space at times, mist and a few drops dampening my clothing again, and I squeezed against the metal, getting as far from the grate-covered opening as I could, and began a rendering of the yacht.

I drew two rough outlines, one a side view and one from overhead, thinking back to those two sightings that I remembered, the one brief one I had had from Janes's house and the other from the catwalk before I'd sneaked aboard. I guessed the paper's lines to be between a quarter- and a half-inch apart, probably two-fifths or so, and figured the scale roughly against a hundred and sixty feet, what I guessed was the length of the craft.

I figured at its widest amidships it must be thirty-five, though that seemed off, too broad, the scale wrong. And yet when I remembered the cabins, the passageway, the engine room, it seemed even broader than that. And of course it seemed deeper than it should have been as well. I tried counting the ladder steps as I remembered them, the space between different levels. I couldn't remember much from my brief look at the superstructure, but I remembered some of it and filled in what I thought would be there.

I scratched out, erased, and began again. Then I stopped censoring myself and went ahead with it, bringing each space and passage up from memory, translating it to scale and getting it down. The rendering, when it was finished, looked monstrous, but once I'd drawn a wavy line to represent the sea along its length, I saw that most of the monstrosity was below the waterline, and that the rest could be taken as conventional miscalculation.

From above, the broadness of the craft seemed only slightly exaggerated, and the squares that represented the cabins and spaces of superstructure seemed right enough. But looking at the side view, everything began to slide into disorientation. The first thing that I noticed was that I should be a good thirty feet below the yacht's deck and that that should put my space a good twenty or so feet under the water. And yet I was at least ten feet above the sea. I looked out and confirmed it.

And the rest was faulty too. Those cabins across the passage from the one I'd hid in, how could they be at a lower level from the others? And what about the two descending stairways, the fact that the cabin where I'd seen the two men, Janes's study or whatever it was, was lower down than the other cabins on the same side? The bottom of the boat, following my scale, had materialized as a series of blocky hernias, the rear of the ship extending down into the ocean a good distance farther than the portion from amidships to the bow, and when I extended a smooth line down deeper than the herniated one I had gotten from my scale and brought it forward to contain every-thing in a conventional-shaped hull, the craft was rendered as extend-ing down a good fifty feet into the sea, a clear impossibility.

I tore the sheet away and began another one, decided to accept the weird structure, and penciled in the places I had been in and on, then drew in the unknown areas, the ones I thought I'd better find out about.

I'd been in what I thought were Janes's two private cabins and had been in the cabin of someone else, maybe the man who had come so close to me in the doorway. Though I couldn't be sure, I figured there was at least one more person aboard. Surely someone had been on deck when the man had been in my sight in the cabin. He hadn't hurried when he was there. He'd been quick and intent with his information, but he had not been rushing to get back above to the helm of an unmanned ship. So, at least one other, and there was no reason to doubt that he would have a cabin in the same bank of cabins, unless there was another passage like the one I'd tentatively penciled in, directly above the one I'd come down into. There'd be a galley below decks, more storage spaces, maybe a lounge of some sort or a living room. I'd seen enough of what should be the bed-rooms. Above the deck would be at least a wheelhouse, someplace for electronic gear, maybe a bar and another lounge of some kind. I remembered that there had been a row of windows in a bulkhead above deck level, with curtains drawn over them.

After I had studied the renderings for a while and made a tenta-tive plan for exploration, one that would take me first to Janes's study, then above decks if I could manage it, I began to think of what I might do if I was able to get to shore. The thought embarrassed me, imagin-ing myself in the state I was in, going somewhere, searching for help of some kind, carrying my bag and racket, smelly in some foreign country.

Nobody knew where I was, but they were counting on me. Chen especially. I must be a few days late at least for our appointment. Donny was to take me to the airport, and I hadn't shown up for that, either. And then there was Waverly. She might have called. Or Chen might have called her, wondering about me, thinking I must have gone back to Congress Park on some emergency. It wouldn't be like him to call. It was not his way to intrude into family matters that way. But I had let him in on some of the difficulties I was facing back there, and I could tell that he took them seriously. And if he did call, that would be a concern for Aunt Waverly.

I thought if I got ashore I could call her, then realized I didn't know her number. I had very little Spanish and was heading down to countries where they spoke that, and I wasn't sure I could manage information. It would have to be Chen then. If I could reach him.

It was in the early evening of that day that the yacht bent in a little and headed gradually toward shore. The sky had cleared, and I could see the full moon again, faintly in the dusky sky, high up through the grate. I began to gather my belongings, but even before I had them ready, I felt the engines cut back, the craft begin to settle, and then heard another droning from somewhere ahead of us.

I pressed against the grate and looked out, craning to see along the boat's side ahead. I heard voices in the distance above me, far up, and picked out three of them. They were yelling over the sound of the sea, calling out what I thought might be directions. Then I saw something massive coming at me and lurched back from the grate. It came slowly, really, but my angle was such that it was across from my grate before I could judge or measure it. The hull of another boat, I realized, and when I edged back to the grate and got my head down and looked up the hull, I could see the edge of a railing, feet and legs moving. A rope flew across, and there was more calling out. Then I smelled the fuel.

We stayed beside the other craft for a good half hour, and I thought I could feel my space lowering gradually as the fuel was pumped into our tanks. The hull of the other craft was rising up at the same time, and in a while I saw the letters painted low on the hull come up enough so that I could read them. There was a word I couldn't read, then a symbol of some sort, then *Puerto Escondido*. I knew the name. There was an Escondido near San Diego, and I remembered this as a sister city. It was near the bottom of Mexico. Next stop Guatemala. I'd heard three voices in English, three distinctly. At least that many aboard then.

It was that night, in what I judged as best I could were the early morning hours, that I went out again and made my way to Janes's study.

Ishmael Reed

From Kaifuku *(Reclamation), a novel*

CHAPTER 1

Haven't seen my chin in ten years. Look at that hair. Got to clean it up; I guess loneliness can get to you. What did Otis Redding say. Ms. Loneliness won't leave me alone. Won't even get into that part. Let's see. Onions. French fries, just about done. Food is no problem. Enough in the supply house to last another ten years. Got liquor and books. But I don't have nobody to talk to. Can't spend the rest of my life looking up at the stars, walking up and down artificial streets and artificial gardens, in some massive bubble revolving around the Earth. Watching the same old cassettes and reruns. Been up here so long that I've watched the planet change from a white and blue to a mud brown. Watching meteorites whiz by. That's why we all came up to this damned station in the first place. Try to find out if those guys in geophysics were right about this asteroid that's supposed to collide with earth in 2020.

Ten years from now. Last time it hit, it wiped out the dinosaurs. Said they could tell by some iridium they found at the bottom of one of the oceans. The space boys felt that they could send up some of those Star Wars gadgets and blow it up before it reached earth, send it spinning off course, and keep it from destroying all life, and turning earth into a barren planet. I won't be around to see it.

Us and the Ruskies were sent up here to examine the thing, and were supposed to benefit all of mankind. Wasn't up here for four months before the arguments broke out. Those two American women didn't even reach the station. We had to push their bodies off into space about two weeks after blast-off. One of them went into depression because we didn't have any shrimp salad on the menu. The other one discovered that she'd left her eye makeup kit at home. Then all of the fellows were left with this Russian astronaut. Helga. Used to be a farm girl before she got a science scholarship at the U of Moscow. Huge tits and thighs like those on half the monuments in Paris. Thought we'd get lost in those tits. She had a cleavage like a valley nestled between the Alps. Then the guys got into fights over who was going to bang her. She was multiorgasmic so she was ready all the time. Then that night we were all drunk. And horny.

Poor Helga. Next thing you know, we and the Russians were at each other with these Rambo semiautomatics. Had to bury her, too. There was a lot of disagreements. Fights. Clash of tastes. They liked chess, we played checkers, we wanted to watch baseball, they wanted to watch the soccer games, we drank beer, they drank vodka. Then we lost contact with Earth and things really freaked out. Now I'm the only one left. My last meal. Hamburger with everything on it, Pepsi, and a pumpkin pie. And then I'll swallow the cyanide pills. I can't take another twenty years of this. What. What the fuck is that? A ship. A big ship. Coming this way.

CHAPTER 1, SECTION 2

It's been up there for twenty hours. I been screaming my head off and waving flags and I get no reply. What? An exploratory vehicle leaving the ship and heading this way. Hey, over here. Here I am over here. Look. They're docking. Two of them entering the station. Who could it . . . God, all out of breath. Running down the steps. They're coming down the street toward my compartment. Little guys. What are they doing all that bowing for. God am I glad to see you fellas. They're taking their helmets off. What the fuck. Japs. Japs in space ships? Japs got their own space ships. They're bowing. I guess they're friendly. Probably can't speak English. You take me to Earth? More bowing. They're saying yes. I'm going to go home. No. Look. Me want to go home. Me lost.

"Yes, Captain Yardley Globe. We know all about your space experiment. Though it's primitive by our standards."

Son of a bitch making fun of American ingenuity, but I ain't saying nothing. Want them to take me back home.

"Yeah, well, it was a start. Nice ship you got there. Who made it for you, the Russians?"

"This ship was made in Japan, Mr. Globe. We have the biggest space fleet in the world now, the most superior army and navy with, because of our alliance with the Chinese, the largest army."

"The what? You mean the Japs—I mean the Japanese and the Chinese have gotten their heads together? Well, I'll be." The two men turn to each other and smiled.

Boy, what liars. Don't want to offend them, though. First thing I'm going to do when I get home is take a shower. Next thing. Read all of the newspapers.

CHAPTER II

It took us three weeks to return. Boy, was I disappointed. Expected to see a big turnout of the press, and my folks and thousands of flag-waving Americans. A brass band and maybe the President. After all it was twenty years. No, the Japs blindfolded me and gave me some kind of pill. When I woke up I was in this apartment. They're feeding me alright, and bringing me books and magazines, but they're all about Japan. When are they going to let me see my people? They keep telling me that they just want to keep me a few more days to ask me some more questions and then I can go home, but that was four weeks ago. We must be in Japan. Maybe they'll take me to the embassy and they'll arrange for me to get home. Been holed up in this apartment for eight weeks now. They keep asking me a whole bunch of questions. Said they'd turn me over to the Americans after they finished. Won't let me make phone calls or nothing. No television. This debriefing is taking a long time.

Paul West

Three sections cut from Lord Byron's Doctor *(Doubleday, 1989)*

There followed a coach-borne dream of a humming and glowing English fireside, beside which I was asleep with a naked houri crouched doglike beside me, inhaling the aroma of my calves, but the dream died as someone said, "They have lost their way," meaning the coachmen. Out I leapt, ever willing, to ask at the big house only steps away. No one answered. I smelled something afoot, amiss, and so went back to the coach for a pistol, then again hammered at the door, to no avail. The postilion and I approached another house, this one lit up, but he then slunk away. I knocked. No one to answer. Now we distributed sabres to the servants and went on with our knocking chore until, at last, someone came and answered us, gave us the way to Gand.

Eerie as this circumstance was, as if some plague had descended overnight, it was hardly the fearsome event our postilion thought. He ran and hid. He knocked and hid again. Then he ran again and waited. Next he ignored the instructions given us, to go right forward the way we had been going, and reversed course for Bruges, back across the bridge we had already traversed several times in looking for advice. Our servant stopped him. On to Ghent, the postilion still inexplicably frightened. The gates were closed, but a few francs took us in, our passports unneeded. Hotel des Pays Bas. Rooms august. Butter, cheese, Rhenish. All but Milord slept, who went prowling the corridors for venereal game, a partridge or a dove. All the knocking had stirred him up, he said.

Gand Cathedral was lavish, and I was determined to do it justice in my diary, observing that it was here that Charles the First of Spain had come to quaff his last draught of worldly joy. Streets *not so unpleasantly regular as London.* And the interior of the cathedral neither Catholic *tinselly* nor Scottish plain. Statues not contemptible. Beneath this cathedral lay the first Belgian church built in the reign of Charlemagne, some eight hundred years after Christ. The one sat under the other, somewhat like Polidori under Lord Byron. I took notes while he spoke forth at large, lauding colors mixed with white of egg, extolling the fine detailed work on a certain tomb which had a carved bishop thereon and every thread of the vest cut separately. Up 450 steps we toiled, Milord puffing from those extra stones of his, but even the exertion failed to silence him until at last we stood atop a map of Gand, with Bruges on the horizon like a child's toy. I made a small bet with myself that he would say the word "Olympian" within the next twenty breaths, but stertorousness got the better of him. Down we came, almost toppling, it was so easy. We took a fiacre and aimed for the Ecole de Dessin, where two students, quite oblivious of the crowd milling about them, went on with their work, neither of them offering to move his machine, one of which covered Rubens's *St. Roch Amongst the Sick of the Plague.* "In faith," said Milord, "the tail hides the dog in this place." No entreaty in no language could budge them or bring them to their senses, or evoke in them the least sense of public considerateness. On they copied, and Milord made so bold as to pass his flattened hand before their eyes, several times, to no effect. "Ha," he cried in the hearing of these dolts, "The Flemish invented painting with oil. These two paint in arrogance." They had no idea who he was. Told, they showed no sign of knowing the name. Milord was as little discriminated there as his Polly, for all the fame of his reputation. I had noticed how certain sorts of persons became well known for being known. There was no more to it than that; all it took was a title, a bearing, some wealth. And scandal, of course, which presumably might be bought by the bucketful once you had established which sins you wanted bruited abroad.

On we went, touring, from a depiction of Charles V with Dame Africa to a Vandyck depicting the effect of Christ's last sigh: an interesting enough idea perhaps applicable to other sighs, to screams and protracted sayings of such syllables as "No" and "Ah" and "Yea." What were we doing, I wondered. Chatting the while, but hardly conversing, and I thought how *touring* had become an excuse for not talking. I no sooner got him started on the theme of the local people, who showed us the way and then swept off their hats as if we had done them some enormous kindness, and the way in which civility fosters itself in this or that population, than one of the wheels refused to move. Much hammering followed, ample cause of yet another headache, with which I had to ride in a *calèche* to Ghent and bring back help. I came back on horseback while the *maréchal* took a *voiture*.

■

The return through Soignies forest was an end to the world. Pitch black amidst the silken play of twilight. Our local coach was jogged, so we gave it over to this same Gordon, but the coachmaker tried to make Lord B. pay in full, which Milord deigned not to do, upon which the coachmaker got himself a warrant officer to seize another vehicle belonging to us. We left a trail of broken conveyances behind us, putting me in mind of an old thought of mine: we are better at killing than at mending. During his musing, his apparent sulks and huffs, Milord had been composing in his head, and then these lines, perhaps some twenty-six stanzas, did not abandon him (like the ten napoleons I myself thought to have lost), but surfaced on his paper like well-fed dogs. And so we lived through Waterloo, as unscathed as the colonel who, asked by Lord W. if he would fly from or to the battle, boldly faced about and trotted off to Brussels, once furnished his by-your-leave. We soon went off to dine with the Gordons, L. B. taking only an ice, returning with Mrs. Gordon's little scrapbook in which he had promised to "insert a verse" before he slept. After all, only a few months before, Sir Walter Scott had done the like, of whom, Milord told me, he had said, with telling authority, I thought: "Scott is a fine poet and a most amiable man. We are great friends. As a prose writer, he has no rival; and has not been approached, since Cervantes, in depicting manners." How tenderly Scots stuck together, marooned from the rest of the world in a pigment or raiment of porridge. Post-journal, I installed in my mind, for *me*, some saliences adjudged worth lingering over, like Napoleon, during a single glass of wine:

1. Pryse Gordon nicer than I thought (I was feeling poorly, too early risen from fatigue): he introduced me to his son by blowing a trumpet.
2. Wellington: too much the soldier when he should have been the general, and too much the light-limbed dancer when he should have been the soldier.
3. Three French riding together were all struck in the jaw, the same place, all dead of it.
4. Post-battle: Where, someone asked, was Napoleon? "There," said a sergeant, indicating his feet. True.

On these Milord eventually opined as follows:

1. "A deuced busily sociable fellow; I had asked him that there be no party, but behold, when we arrived, there glowed a brace of accomplished, talkative gentlemen, one my meat and the other my pudding. By previous arrangement."
2. "Had I had such an opportunity, I would not have danced or map-theorized."
3. "Thus the Scottish idea of economy."
4. "But his soul, where was that? Above? Or elongated across the empyrean like some guidon? I wonder."

"What," I asked him, "did you think of the bed in which Josephine, Marie Louise, and the queen of Holland had fast succeeded one another?" Snorting, he answered "I had as soon have all three with me on the same occasion. A man cannot develop sexual style until he has an excess of orifices to disport him in." We had bowed before the eagles left behind on the chairs of empire. In my journal I wrote, *I sat down on two chairs on which had sat he who ruled the world at one time.* The servant raised both eyebrows at this, but not at

What I had got:

The novels of Abate Casti, a gift from Mr. Gordon.

The memory of a Rembrandt painting (of his wife or mother) owned by the Gordons, full of zest.

The works of Casti were lubricious; what was he telling me? What did he think he had discerned? A need for fantastic excitation?

Lord B. gave the Gordons' son a doll, and Walter Scott, who had written in Mrs. Gordon's book "For one brief hour of deathless fame," a poke in the eye, reading: "Oh, Walter Scott, for shame, for shame." Oh to be gone, to be in yet another breaking-down carriage. Oh for Italy, I whined.

■

Under the red canopy of a jubilee in Tirlemont, itself under a dirty
Indian-ink sky, we saw sinners and saints: God's full motley on the
move, and in every street there were fir branches sixteen or seventeen
feet tall, every five or six feet. A sylvan arcade, to be sure. In Trond,
or rather St. Trond, the avenues had a more majestic look because
of the long swells of ground and the straight roads; but such misery
we saw there, in the mud-houses. To enter, you must tread on a
dunghill, there not to remind but to keep the house from filling up.
We ate there, our breath held, and perhaps we slept the same way.
What a comedown after Waterloo. You said Tron, to make it shorter,
thus exposing the inside of your mouth to the stench for a smaller
period, but it were better to say *Trn* or nothing at all, or to honk with
nose closed.

As my journal advanced, I found myself keeping a ghost journal
alongside it, full of things having nothing to do with Milord, and
wondering if I would ever have a chance to write this second one,
amend the other. Was L. B. keeping one of his own? Not that I could
see; it was part of his lordly stance that others should collect the
crumbs of his table talk, the choice morsels shifted to the brink of
his plate, the little brilliants of his spittle as he made some point too
vehemently. This, I instructed myself, was just what a doctor had been
schooled to do; it was another way of cleansing Milord's liver, purging
his eyes of ambergris, and I yearned to be better at this impromptu
amanuensis kind of thing; I would have been better at taking tiny
samples of his bodily fluids or flakes of skin, wax from his ears,
bunions from his feet.

■

No, the true baths (as I was meaning to say) were hot sulphuretted-
hydrogen-impregnated, which gave them an aroma of the baby cot.
If you wanted to see the sulphur beds themselves, you had to be a king
or a duke. So much for rank. Milord would have qualified, but off we
chased to St. Juliers (May 8), where they wrote down our names as
we entered and departed. There were lovelies here, with dark eyes,
darker hair, who left it to the men to curl hair and sport earrings (an
old custom reported in Tacitus). The women took their hair straight
back and crown a square of linen, a decisive-looking style whose touch
of austerity got me thinking the men a peck effete.

As we entered Prussia (no line to cross, no sign), people began
to look cleaner. They let the filth pile up on their possessions and
dwellings whereas the Belgians let themselves sink into the superven-
ing filth. I had never, I told Milord, seen a more manured-looking race

than the Belgians, to which he quipped, "How dreadfully soon one becomes inured to the manured." I did not think it was a hint of any sort. After another bad road, both sandy and sludgy, we landed in Cologne, whose towers and battlements sprang out at us like a long-delayed dream. Its inns were full, but we at last laid our bodies down in the Hôtel de Prague, breakfasting almost no later than dropping off. Writing in my journal, I said *Just done, we heard some singing. Enquiry told us, buyable. Got them up.* (I showed Milord this entry, asking if he did not think its concision admirable, something along his own lines, at which he brayed, saying, "Well, damnit, where *are* they? Where are the musicians?") They came, a harp played by a pretty dark-haired German (these the best of their breed) and two fiddlers. We heard *The Troubadour,* making the Scotch part of us homesick, and then a German thing, which fast restored us to the delights of homelessness. They followed with a march, in which the music died, then poured forth again. They ended with a waltz, far superior to the stained glass that followed as, once again, we did our duty, eyeing the piles. Oh, the stained glass was fine, of course. Polly just felt out of sorts: *unconfided-in* by Milord, and then tripped on the steps, smashing a glass for which I made them take three francs. "Our Pol is dizzy again," Milord said without caring much. *Kept countenance amazingly well,* I pounded into my journal. Was the whole tour going to be thus?

In St. Ursula's Church they showed us a mass of some 11,000 virgins' bones all jumbled up, male with female, some in gilt, some adorning silver-faced busts, some set out in little velvet-lined cavities. Some had names. All names had skulls. We asked for a sample, a souvenir, but a finger pointed out an admonition in Latin, which neither of us could be bothered to read. It was astounding to be alive in the presence of so many relics, much more so there than at Waterloo, where all the detritus of battle had been gobbled up. Poussins, Claude Lorraines, a Tintoretto. All kinds of masterworks. *Cologne,* I wrote, *has stamped more coins than some empires, and has coined twenty-six kinds of gold.* The art was serious, from Titian's four designs for the Polenham Caesars to Dürer's sketch of Christ's head. They told us they had lost many missals to revolutionary Gauls, and asked for any copy of Caxton's printing, after hearing which it was only just to go and buy books, from a Miss Helmhoft, who declaimed much German poetry I did not understand. I laughed at her gestures during declamation, and she thought the poem had amused me—something to do with a shirtless poet. Hardly Lord B.

I began to feel I was improving at the journal business: pithier, brighter, more Byronic. Perhaps not sprightly enough, not often enough witty, but at least as inviting as a German poem about a shirt. Perhaps it was predictable, in an area where the French had knocked about as many ruins as Cromwell himself, converting whole convents into places for promenade, that the locals could not tell us for what we were: not English gentlemen at all, but servants or merchants, even Frenchmen. Were we too mild? How uplifting it must be, I thought, to be notorious, like Lord B., to have done all manner of abominable things and yet to be able to go forth unknown, unrecognized, undenounced, as if one were not a monster after all. Yet, within the lamb's clothing, the wolf had that delicious sense of knowing who he was, and what, unpursued by police or wife. Oh to have no rivals in ignominy, to be casting about for the next unmentionable thing to do, all while preserving the quiet, schooled mien of the Cambridge man, the lord, the connoisseur of Albanian customs, the well-read man about town. Had milord been a doctor, what dreadful things he might have done, and not got away with; the pageant of the bleeding heart would have had a different meaning as, with scalpel in hand, he haunted the stairs of the nursing homes and hospitals, yearning to reshape the human race.

"Behold: the Rhine," he said, "at last."

"As wide," I responded, "as the Thames some way below Blackwall, if I am not mistaken. As fine a mass of wetness as we will see this voyage."

He laughed abstractedly, saying the river here was deeper than any English poet.

"Saving one," I said, but he cared not about that and said, again, "*any* English poet. Or Scotch too. We fumble for the riverbed, but end up making castles on the sand."

"I had been wondering, my lord," I began, "if your traveling companion and physician might be of even further use to you."

"Nay, Polly," said he, "what with carriages breaking down and the almost total lack of decent roads, I fear you are exercised enough. Pray rest, and drink in the Rhine."

"In quite another matter, my lord, than those at present besetting us, but nonetheless of great moment."

"*Childe Harold*? No, you cannot mean that."

He peered at me, waiting, willing.

"In the matter of Lady Byron, sire."

"In the matter of Lady Byron? *You*, Polly?"

"In the matter of the thing unmentionable—"

"Polidori, I know you jest. Kindly desist, I am not in the mood. There has been too much pain."

"I was wondering if I might help in the matter of ascribing a name to the dread offense."

"Oh," he said. "And your natural tact, having quite expired, you choose to bring up that. You do not choose or try to interfere with something private; you choose something that has no bearing on the heart of anyone who matters—really, this is too much." His voice was ice and broken glass. "If Polidori wants a ball shot through his skull, let him talk on. Let him meddle even further. I command you, doctor, cease."

His choler shocked me. After all, were we not drinking friends? Fellow swyvers? I had put the matter politely enough, every bit as politely as your Hobhouse and Company, so what was the rub? I was a mere slip of a lad, twenty only, yet nonetheless a *doctor*. Surely the greenness of the one mellowed the impersonal sagacity of the other. Lord B. was in no mood to listen, but perhaps he had all the same divined a shred of my good intent, as when I offered to lend him Casti's salty novelle (which he poo-hooed). I would have to come back to the matter on another occasion, possibly with medical text in hand: an Anatomy, to substantiate my serious aspiration. Where the lawyers had failed, Physick might prevail, though I dared not tell him this, he who glowered now at the Rhine as if it had all issued in a torrent from his nether body. Perhaps all Milord had done was bellow at her, only *threatening* half a dozen of his pet abominations, and she had quailed at this assault from the coarse and bumbling world of men, where a penny upright was all that mattered, to be rubbed into submission by a drab in a lane. At that instant I longed for London, for the cries of its violet- and lavender-sellers, for the sound of hooves on cropped turf in some park or other. The farther into foreign parts we went, the more foreign to himself Milord became. I let him be. We saw our first vines. The Rhine was a valley of sweet waters.

We had never seen so many crucifixes, of stone or wood, as if the whole world—Cologne as far as Bonn—were being crucified bit by bit. An innkeeper made us fill in his book each night with name, profession, and age, as if through some devilish alchemy all three had changed in a few hours. I could tell that Milord, vexed by this, had some kind of retaliation in mind, but in the end he did nothing after some mighty brooding. All this put us in the mood for ruined Drachenfels, once a storied castle, close to which was a monument commemorating the place where one noble brother had slaughtered another. Gradually the landscape was becoming softer, more southern, thank goodness. It pleased me to think that Lord B. had paid much the same sum for his thundering, lumbering, fake Napoleonic

coach, green of darkest oak leaves, as Murray had offered me to keep
my journal. Where were his wild Albanian songs now? He was sulking
on the verge of paradise (surely not at my civil offer of intimate help).
All about us spread the geometry of cultivation: hedgeless beds rather
than fields; women at work therein; oxen and horses ploughing; the
peasants jolly-faced and working with a will on the swollen river's
flank. Aurelius, Theodoric, Napoleon came this way. In particular,
the last of these was everywhere; they had not forgotten him. At the
tomb of Hoche we read "The army of the Sambre and the Moselle
to its general-in-chief Hoche." *There* was a dry inscription for you,
among the broken marble slabs and the scars where the reliefs were
torn away. What I wrote next seemed to me exact and quotable,
although I dared not show it to Milord:

> After Andernach the Rhine loses much. The valley is wider, and the
> beautiful, after the almost sublime, palls, and man is fastidious.

Perhaps the commas were too close together towards the end, but this
was a Physician writing, not one of your whoremastering married
poets. Lord B. kept looking behind as if expecting something to gain
on us, perhaps brewing some lines that began "The castled crag of
Drachenfels / Frowns o'er the wide and winding Rhine," which was
an obvious-enough beginning. At the Trois Suisses inn, we mused on
how many cannonballs had passed through it when Marceau stayed
there (his tomb a mile from Coblentz). It was here that the Cossacks
crossed by boat, making their horses swim across. (Marceau dead in
1796 at twenty-seven, and Hoche, whose monument we saw, rots *in
the same tomb,* as I briefly exemplify the massive present tense of
Outre-Tombe, which we occasionally allow ourselves. Hoche only
twenty-nine.)

No sooner up than looking at the view, we went off to the bath, at
a maltster's, costing us thirty sous. Then into a Catholic church
where children were singing to an organ. The effect was that of an
awning of sound. One copy of a Rubens. After breakfast, to Marceau's monument by calèche, thence to the Chartreuse: *deserted,
ruined, windowless, roofless, and tenantless.* Lord B. would have said
"Polly is piling up the epithets again." The best part was the flying
bridge done with moored boats on a rope and deft rudder. All those
peasants, in head-dresses of crimson and gold, or green with steel pin,
carried crosses and kept bowing to roadside Calvaries. At Ehrenbreit-
stein everything had been sundered by gunpowder; immense lumps

of stone and mortar hurled fifty yards. The whole place was in ruins and it was hard to miss the grandeur, now silent, but it set me wondering about the sheer waste of war that would devastate even such things as the canoes, almost Otaheitan, in which we passed the Rhine. In the carriage again I wrote three "splendid"s on approaching St. Goar—cocked hats and big buckles. Vines for all to harvest. One column revealed Napoleon's name erased. Mayence was lovely, with a red sandstone cathedral; garrison of Hessians, Austrians, and Prussians; our best view since Ghent. Was it only yesterday that, as one of our postilions blew a horn, twin rainbows appeared, as if summoned up by sorcerer's apprentice, one of them up close atop the trees and shot through with greens from the leaves. It was as if we had lumbered over into paradise. Lord B. wrote to his sister about this or something else. Family secrets. *Half-*secrets, anyway. I drew a squiggly map of our journey, I having some skill with a pencil, but the coach's motion jumbled it, so I tossed it out into the breeze, knowing it would soon help some traveler to get from Aix to Ghent. We saw the house where printing was supposedly invented, but the French, who had much to answer for, had pulled it down; then the cathedral, roof pierced by bombs during the last siege of Mayence. We beheld beheaded reliefs and one German marshal gravely jutting his head forth from beneath his tombstone: "I am here," he said, and we wondered if he wanted to be hauled out entire or pushed back into fame and peace. It was here that things began to go truly wrong, in all ways. Mayence to Mannheim, for all its loveliness, jarred my serenity, and his. We crossed the river on a bridge of boats, and then a fever struck, rendering me unable to write, unable to observe, unable to make sense of anything, as if a sulphurous, acid, narcotic damp had eaten into my brain, and I saw bridges where there were none, and Lord B. where only a fly buzzed.

Only a little recovered, I set off (May 15), among ample alleys of Lombardy poplars and horse chestnuts, with crisp, rather Scotch villages. To Karlsruhe I clattered through a grove of Scotch firs, only to enter the (non-Scotch) inn reeling and perspiring, jelly in the knees, and needles in the eyes. Heal thyself, I said aloud in bed, and dosed myself with ipecac, *Cephaelis ipecacuanha,* with fifteen grains of opium. There followed vertigo, headache, and a tendency to syncope, none of these helped by magnesia and lemon acid. I cheered but felt worse, in some phase of my dementia imagining I saw a long shelf with my life's works (books) all arranged with titles in alphabetical order, but I could see only the first letters of these titles. Someone had dusted the gilt tops of the pages. The books looked as if they had never been opened. The shelf was a shrine. Only peasants would bow at it.

So why then did I force myself to go out touring with Lord B.? In and about the town, the glare of all the white stucco made my eyes burn and the headache worse. I took some stewed apples (local delicacy approaching fetish) with more magnesia and lemon acid, to no effect. I lay down without sleeping, then got up after two hours of it. I was on the point of going out again, to escape somehow from myself, when Lord B., observing that I had in hand a plated candlestick, took it from me and gave me a brass one instead. After a few steps more, I fainted, crashed to the stone, which noise brought the servants to me in a hurry. Now I took four pills and witnessed Lord B. once again exchanging candlesticks, this time making the servant take brass for plate. Again I went to bed, trying to persuade myself that Lord B. had wanted me, on each occasion, to have the candlestick with the longer candle in it. Surely he had no intention of insulting me. What he had in mind was an invalid's needing a candle that would burn night-long. And light him into the next world if need be.

More medicine gave me slicing pains in the abdomen. I vomited. Then I slept, waking weak. When at length I made to leave my chamber, there at the door stood Sir C. Hunter, full of my almost dying. I invited him in without more ado, apologizing for the fug of a sickroom and assuring him that the windows had been open an hour. He was a bosom friend of the Grand Duke. Lord B. entered, and they carried on a conversation for which I had not the strength, the upshot of which was that Sir C. sent us a few hours later the *Guide du Voyageur en les pays de l'Europe,* begging in return some of Milord's poems. I went out again and stared at gilt-thick columns, Corinthian and regular as fir trees.

On the eighteenth, feeling much better, I was able to enjoy the journey from Karlsruhe to Offenberg, although I did sleep through half of it and kept the blinds down for the rest, which, in effect, is to say I took no notice at all of our surroundings. It was indeed a very blindfolded excursion behind yellow-coated postilions. After Offenberg, however, I watched again, urged in this by Lord B., and I made myself note things in my journal, such as Freiburg steeple, *pervious* to the top with trelliswork showing the light. Our postilions, like all German ones, talked to their horses, which, Lord B. said, made far better conversation than was to be had back in London. He may have been right, my own best part of attention having gone to women in short wide red petticoats and hats of straw wide as wheels. They looked like tops waiting to be made to spin. All of a sudden we had a view of the Alps, the Rhine, the Jura mountains, all in one; we crossed the river and lo, we were in Switzerland, just like shifting from metaphysics to physics. "Must we?" said Lord B. We went anyway to view a panorama of Thun, a Raphael, a Rembrandt, and much more, at a *marchand d'estampes* finding *Nelson's Death*, Chatham's same, and other vignettes of England. Milord looked to be seething, although he said nothing, except to commission a *voiturier* to take our carriages off to Geneva in five days. He wanted badly to be away, aimed at some new way of living; he the wanderer with the brand of Cain wanted to settle in some idyllic town where Cains were welcome, which could only come about, I mused, if our Cain were to slaughter nearly everybody else.

Asking in French for milk of a goatherd, we found we were not understood until we guaranteed to pay for it, and then our French became effective. High up, between bald mountains and those fringed with trees, we did some giggling and much hoping, then descended to find servants playing bowls where we took dinner. I read the *Arabian Nights* to get me in the mood for delectable visions, whether of houris or not. I felt much better from the air high up and slept as well as if I had been heaving on the carriage from behind.

Feeling even better on the 22nd, I was soon making notes on the Jura mountains and, more interesting, the short petticoats (again) and the black crape rays the women affix about their heads, giving them a certain spidery aspect. How far the roofs extended at the slant, offering all passersby shade and, I dared say, a certain sense of safety, even of invitation. How slowly we went, mostly from the *voituriers'* having eight francs of drink money each day, almost six times the amount specified in the *Guide*.

Xam Cartier

This excerpt is from what would have been a sequential chapter to the end of my first novel, Be-Bop, Re-Bop *(Available Press/Ballantine, 1988).*

. . . In the way that it looks, this particular lounge of today bears a dingy resemblance to those neighborhood nightclubs of yore, with yellow hanging overhead lights which pride themselves on durable

dimness cast on determined drinkers scattered below. Back behind
the bar there's a stock stocky barman with taciturn face so recognizable in expression that instantly I know that somewhere in the gloom
up ahead a weary waitress scuttles between territorial tables, her
diocese, where she's merciless missionary to thirsting lone strangers.

What's the Hawk think of this dungeon as site for our talk of
marital truce or divorce? "Does this place seem OK?" I say to the
Hawk.

"It'll do," says the Hawk. "A bar is a bar." This last he says with
head turned to the side as he walks toward a table in shadows beyond,
till he's caught up short by circumstance; he steps into something
sticky underfoot and stops to dig it with accusing concentration in
the way that all humans do when we trip, we're forced to hide our
chagrin and seek understanding from fellow stumblers around us—
*It's not me see, it's this unforeseen thing in my way here; it tripped me
up*—till knowing approval returns to absolve us: *That's OK, we can
dig it; we too have bumbled into unforeseen stumps.* . . .

"One thing I want you to know is, it's not personal," the Hawk
says to me when we've reached seats in outback of the bar. We're
sitting thigh to thigh on the same side of the table at my suggestion—
Well, what of it? I hedge to myself; it means nothing, just shows reflex
need for access to his body when he's around. But wait, the Hawk's
talking, he has Something to Say. . . .

"I've got to be head of my household, that's all," the Hawk's
saying. "I've got to be the one to call the shots. That's how I *am*."

What can I say? Where to begin? We could storm and stalemate
from now till next doomsday, unless I say . . .

*Now wait just a god-docile minute! You know good and goddamn well
I come from a long line of spirited women . . . and spirited men, truth be
told—spirited men who wanted a spirited woman, not behind 'em or beneath 'em, say beside 'em, so they could be twice as tough and ready
theirownselves, could double the pleasure and double the fun! I mean to say,
hey. Is you hip? Can you dig?*

But naw, don't say that or anything of the like at this truce talk
where the object is peace or said possibility. My object's to see if truce
can be had, just show me or tell me, I'll take my cue, though I've
missed a few; yeah, yeah, don't I know it— After two months of split,
just show me the following: In the wake of raw wounds of the past,
Can This Marriage Be Saved?

(Well now, just what the F do you think?)

Aw now wait, don't be dismal. Stay tuned to the Hawk. See? He's
talking again.

"... is all I'm saying," the Hawk rambles on. "What I mean when I say I'm gonna do what I have to do, with you or without you," (this was a sore point starting to scab) "—all I mean is that I'm going to do *this*" (meaning scale through medskool), and *no* one can stand in my way, not just *you*."

Satisfied now, the Hawk looks away and I see at this juncture how our roles have blurred within their barbwire borders so that here I am now not as loud-shouting talker but as listener-digester while the Hawk spouts shredded dictates to me, though it's easy to see he expects no intestinal changes in our onwarring maneuvers, just retreat to original trenches with a new containment treaty.

What this was, what this is, is a boundary dispute where the Hawk's on guard against subversion which he expects from me; it could undermine his forward advance toward a stronghold in the future which he has to claim, it's the core of his campaign. Our way is cold and clear, it's so objective it makes me want to scream, not for the hell of it but because shouting still needs to be done, it's way overdue in our discourse. What this scene needs is high-pitched shrieks of gripe from me, and the Hawk stalwarting like "Shhh— Don't air our dirty linen in public" so I can yell, "Yeah, it's linen time! Here, catch your *draws!*" I'll proceed to wail out my woe without cover-up, right out loud in public as I know now the Hawk would hate; my shows of emotion have always enraged him, he'd be speechless with spite while I on my part, I'd be sick of his silence and grounded practicality; he's caused me to damp down my dreams!

Joyce Carol Oates

The following poem was originally published without the first stanza, in The Yale Review, *and is included in Ms. Oates's poetry collection* The Time Traveller *(Dutton, 1989).*

EDWARD HOPPER, *NIGHTHAWKS*, 1942

They are sitting at the luncheonette counter,
a man in a gray fedora hat, a red-haired woman
in a summer dress, coffee cups before them.
There is one other customer, a solitary man,

seated several stools away, his back to us,
and there is the counterman, blond, stooping,
in his white uniform and hat, looking
toward the woman who has never once looked
at him. It is that time of night
when everything is still. No traffic.
No voices. The street is empty as if swept
clean, the sidewalk too is clean, a dreamy stasis
to the red brick façade of a facing building
and to the wide oval of the luncheonette counter
where each tidy object—salt and pepper shakers,
napkin holder, sugar bowl—exists in perfect
proportion to the others.

The three men are fully clothed, long sleeves,
even hats, though it's indoors, and brightly lit,
and there's a woman. The woman is wearing
a short-sleeved red dress cut to expose her arms,
a curve of her creamy chest, she's contemplating
a cigarette in her right hand thinking that
her companion has finally left his wife but
can she trust him? Her heavy-lidded eyes,
pouty lipsticked mouth, she has the redhead's
true pallor like skim milk, damned good-looking
and she guesses she knows it but what exactly
has it gotten her so far, and where?—he'll start
to feel guilty in a few days, she knows
the signs, an actual smell, sweaty, rancid, like
dirty socks, he'll slip away to make telephone calls
and she swears she isn't going to go through that
again, isn't going to break down crying or begging
nor is she going to scream at him, she's finished
with all that and he's silent beside her
not the kind to talk much but he's thinking
thank God he made the right move at last
he's a little dazed like a man in a dream—
is this a dream?—so much that's wide, still,
mute, horizontal—and the counterman in white
stooped as he is, and unmoving, and the man
on the other stool unmoving except to sip
his coffee but he's feeling pretty good,
it's primarily relief, this time he's sure

as hell going to make it work he owes it to her
and to himself Christ's sake and she's thinking
the light in this place is too bright, probably
not very flattering, she hates it when her lipstick
wears off and her makeup gets caked, she'd like
to use a ladies' room but there isn't one here
and Jesus how long before a gas station opens?—
it's the middle of the night and she has a feeling
time is never going to budge. This time
though she isn't going to demean herself—
he starts in about his wife, his kids, how
he let them down, they trusted him and he let
them down, she'll slam out of the God-damned room
and if he calls her SUGAR or BABY in that voice
running his hands over her like he has the right
she'll slap his face hard YOU KNOW I HATE THAT: STOP.
And he'll stop. He'd better. The angrier
she gets, the stiller she is, hasn't said a word
for the past ten minutes, not a strand
of her hair stirs, and it smells a little like ashes
or like the henna she uses to brighten it but
the smell is faint or anyway, crazy for her
like he is he doesn't notice, or mind—
burying his hot face in her neck, between her cool
breasts, or her legs—wherever she'll have him,
and whenever. She's still contemplating
the cigarette burning in her hand, and
the counterman is still stooped gaping
at her and he doesn't mind that, why not,
as long as she doesn't look back in fact
he's thinking he's the luckiest man in the world
so why isn't he happier?

Philip Levine

"The Receiver" was written in the summer of 1963. For reasons I can no longer recall, instead of publishing the three sections in the next book I published, Not This Pig (Wesleyan University Press, 1968), I chose to use only the first section and within a few years forgot there were other sections. In 1976 an old friend of mine, Henri Coulette, who had helped me with the first version, asked me why I'd never published the entire poem: by this time I couldn't even locate the entire poem, but fortunately Henri had kept a copy of the final draft. I would like to publish the entire poem, which I have never read in public before and is known by almost no one.

THE RECEIVER

I

I waken with the television on
And no one here. It's Sunday afternoon,
The phone was ringing but it's silent now;
Only the television and the sun,

Which burns along my arm, have been awake.
This is impossible. There is no phone,
Only a play receiver in my hand,
An unconnected one, efficient, black,

That always gets its man. I dial you
And listen to the customary rings,
And then more rings and more until I know
That everything suspected must be true.

I hang up and unscrew the listening piece.
What would you have me find so close to home?
A Chinese message? or a little man?
Or a small mirror that refused my face?

The surprise was that there was nothing there,
Nothing at all, nothing, not even ought,
And thus it was that in my 35th year
I learned that by these words I hid my thought.

II

A time came when I couldn't sleep or think,
Thus I have been reading Benedetto Croce
Alone at night by a small boudoir lamp,
Reading and soaking my hemorrhoids in the sink

Until the water cooled and the house creaked
And my mind seemed like something else again,
Something useful that might entertain a friend
If there were friends, or ease the enduring pain,

Or simply name the pain and make it known,
Familiar, hateful, like a relative.
Pain is my daughter Rachael, I could say,
And I'm her father, Edgar Allan Poe.

The mind is useful, and that's how I use it.
Right now, wrapped in a towel, barefoot, I stroll
In my small garden under the fixed stars
Tasting my luscious taste before I lose it.

Croce is with me in the cheap edition,
Under my arm, drawing the richest heat
Through the warped binding and the mildewed pages.
Old college hero, imperial aesthete,

How will you make it in America
Here in the armpit of the bourgeoisie?
His answer is the answer of the stars,
The long dead stars that know their destiny.

III

A woman's voice says, Hello, is this you?
I answer, Yes, it's me, who wants to know?
She asks me if I feel like talking now,
She knows it's late, she knows that the great slow

Unwinding of the stars has preference now.
Who wants to talk to me? I ask again.
It's Leo Tolstoi calling from Berlin.
Well, put him on, don't keep him waiting, ma'am.

Speaking, she whispers. I say nothing back.
She's in a phone booth near the central gate,
She heard me breathing, heard me toss all night,
Get up and read a book I couldn't bear,

Walk in the garden thinking that the stars
Might speak to me or that a bird's low call
Could tell me something that she couldn't tell.
Edgar, she says, I speak as man to man

Across the acreage of my suffering,
Life is not a novel, life is not
The great upheavals that I said it was;
I put it somewhere in a little thing,

A private memo or a shopping list.
Put what? I ask. Misplaced, she says, somewhere.
What was it you lost? But now I hear
Her breathing mounting on the other end,

Gasping and catching like a summer storm,
And then the voice, but different now, now deep
And without gender, without words or limit
Wailing in my dark house, "Oh, go to sleep."

Phillip Lopate

Three episodes from the original manuscript of Being with Children.
(Poseidon Press, 1975)

1. TADPOLES

I was getting the guided tour. The principal, Mr. Jimenez, took me
into room after room, showing off his school, but I had the feeling
his mind was elsewhere.

Mr. Jimenez wore a pink shirt and a flowered tie, which suggested
possible friendliness to audacity and originality. On the other hand,
it might not mean anything. He was one of the new breed of principals who had been swept in by the New York City decentralization
ruling in the late 1960s, which gave communities a stronger say in the
appointment of school officials. Puerto Rican, tall, still in his thirties,

he carried himself with the proud, self-conscious, uneasy air of a renegade not yet used to being the authority figure, like a member of the Opposition party who is suddenly taken into the cabinet.

I would have sympathized with him at the time had I not felt so watchful and on trial myself.

He spoke all the time. The information he was giving me was extremely detailed—too detailed for my needs, in fact, as if he were practicing a speech he intended to give later on. His conversation was filled with frank remarks about the problems he was having.

In each classroom he scrupulously introduced me to the teacher. "This is Phil Lopate from Teachers & Writers Collaborative. He'll be directing a program of several writers coming to our school to work in the classrooms, and if you're interested in having a writer you should talk to him." The teachers mostly nodded in a martyred way. Their routine was being interrupted again for God knows what reason. I could have been an astronaut who'd dropped from the skies. I tried to use every opportunity to make knowledgeable, "telling" comments. After all, how were they to be convinced that I was who I said I was?

I thought I looked young to be a program director. I was twenty-seven.

"This is a fourth-grade classroom," the principal said, pausing outside the door. "The teacher is George Sanchez, he's in his first year. He's coming along well, but he still has problems with control. Some of the bigger kids have been taking advantage. I had Hector Rivera down in my office last week. . . ."

I had the feeling the principal would have continued his analysis of the freshman teacher's problems inside the classroom, but we were stopped by a strange arrangement.

Near the front of the class, all the tables were pushed against the windows. The children were hunched underneath the tables or seated on top of them. They stopped giggling when Mr. Jimenez walked in. The center of the room had flooded. All the school desks were pushed to the underneath side the windows. A young sad-eyed teacher was mopping up the water.

He glanced up and saw the principal. Then he returned to the flood, not saying a word, as if he were thinking that of course the boss would walk in on the day he had a catastrophe.

Mr. Jimenez started to walk over to him, then looked at the puddle he would have to cross, changed his mind, and turned to the children.

"What happened here?" he began in a surprisingly gentle, pleasant tone.

The children looked at each other, to see who would answer.

"The goldfish bowl fell!"

"The goldfish bowl fell," repeated Mr. Jimenez. "How did that happen?"

The children were so small and wet, squeezed together under the desks, they looked to me like tadpoles.

"Juan did it!" a boy yelled out. Everyone agreed it was Juan.

"No—no—I don't want you to tell me who did it," Mr. Jimenez waved his hands; "I don't want you to tattle on each other. The important thing is not who did it but how it happened. And whether you can figure out how to prevent it from happening again. You see,"—he turned to me—"I'm saying, we can turn this into a learning situation."

As far as I could see it was a mess. An irretrievable, inconsolable mess. But I had to admire him for giving it the educational try.

"Now can anyone think of a way that we might stop this from happening again?"

"You could make Juan never go near the goldfish," one boy said brightly.

"Yes, that's a possibility. Anything else?"

"You could lock certain people out in the hall during recess. Like Juan," said a cute, curly little girl. A Spanish boy in back of her dug her with his fist when no one was looking. Juan? I wondered, or a loyal friend?

"Punishing is one way," nodded the principal. "That seems to be what most of you are saying. But can anyone think of a way which is not punishment that will stop it from happening again?"

Silence.

Even the teacher stopped mopping to listen.

"You could," one cooperative boy said, "you could, uh . . . you could make a bigger table with a fence around it so that it wouldn't fall off."

"There's a very good suggestion. A bigger table. That's useful. Any others? Well, I think you should give this serious thought. Maybe write a list of ideas for how to keep the goldfish bowl from breaking. You could even make it a homework assignment," he said, turning to Sanchez. They spoke a few sober words in Spanish which I didn't understand, and Mr. Jimenez left with me.

In the principal's office, we said nothing about the incident. Jimenez told me that if I had any difficulty I was to come to him, and if I wanted anything or had any insights to share I was also to come to him.

Since I had met the two assistant principals on our tour I wondered aloud if I shouldn't bother them instead, as he was so busy.

He thought for a moment. "No, I want you to come straight to me. This is a program I'm very interested in."

I sensed he did not have complete confidence in his assistant principals. He had a mistrustful air that isolated him—a bit like Ivan the Terrible in the Eisenstein film.

2. THE LOST STORY

There were three boys who always ran up to me whenever I came into the schoolyard. They hopped around me like monkeys and pulled on my arms, although when it came to talking they were shy and never had anything to say to me. It was a curious kind of romance: they seemed as much involved in competing among one another for who could wiggle closest to me, as in actually communicating with me. I noticed that they were often excluded from the punchball game because they were frailer and less coordinated than the other boys. They carried themselves in a painfully cautious manner, as if worried that their bones might break.

I have no doubt that they would have been less eager to see me had they been chosen for the punchball game, instead of just standing around, knocking each other with their bookbags. The game they passed the time with was for one to poke the other and irritate him into chasing him around the yard. My heart went out to these boys: Jamie, Gregory, David. One of them, Gregory, was a mild, good-looking black kid who came to school every day dressed like a miniature CPA, in sweater and tie.

He had invented a superhero named Sir Lancelot Dubernickle, and he wrote a story for me about Sir Lancelot's adventures and noble deeds. The story was quite good. I had compiled a scrapbook of stories from Miss Phifer's class which I left in the classroom for the children to read, and I pasted Gregory's into it. The next week it was gone. Gregory wanted to know where it was. Someone had stolen it out of the book. I suspected who the thief might be (a boy who didn't like Gregory), but I didn't have the heart to conduct a witchhunt, and so I did probably a stupid thing, I stalled Gregory by telling him I thought I had left the story in my house. Meanwhile I tried to retrieve it by questioning several kids. This was done to spare Gregory the knowledge that someone disliked him enough to rip out his story, but also to spare the guilty party. I have a horror of those mass school investigations which make a public example of one-child thief for the good of all.

I was unable to retrieve the story. At a loss for what to do, I made a search of my house, though I knew quite well that I had pasted the story in the book. I began in a strange unconscious way to believe my lie, and to feel guilty for having "lost" Gregory's story. I had never lost a child's written work before, and I was proud of that; but I always had a nervous feeling in the pit of my stomach when I thought of it ever happening.

In any case, I told Gregory finally that I couldn't find it and he seemed to accept the loss. But I felt I had to make it up to him somehow. That same day, I had to go and pick up a big chair which had been donated by a parent to the Writing Room, and I asked him to come along and help me move it. The chair was at the parent's apartment, two blocks away from the school. This may not seem like much of a favor, but he was pleased to do it. It gave us a chance to be together. It also showed I thought him strong or "man enough" to help me move something.

It was twenty degrees outside. Gregory explained to his friend Andre that he was going to help me.

"What are you going with *him* for?" Andre said. "Don't go with him."

Gregory gave him a peeved look. Andre, whose face was covered by a woolen ski mask to protect him from the elements, tried throwing his pudgy body onto Gregory to slow him down.

"Quit it," Gregory said with some embarrassment, pushing Andre gently but solidly away. Andre grabbed his arms from behind. "Don't go with him," he said to Gregory. "It's too cold."

"Quit it. I have to help him move something," Gregory answered.

Andre, whom I had never met before this time, made no attempt to hide his hatred of me. I had the feeling that I was watching in embryonic form a lovers' jealous quarrel.

"Why don't you come along?" I said to Andre.

"Why should I?" he said sullenly.

"All right then, leave us alone."

He followed a dozen paces behind us. Then he did the same thing, catching up and flinging himself on Gregory's back. "Stop that!" said Gregory, with more vehemence than I had ever seen him show.

Andre fell back; but then a few steps further he was alongside us again. "How much longer do we have to go?" he demanded.

I laughed at the tacit, belligerent way he had acknowledged my offer to join us. "It's just a block away."

"It's too cold to walk!" he whimpered.

"Isn't that ski mask warming you?" I asked him. Andre ignored me; he went back to pretending I wasn't there. Meanwhile, Gregory was looking up at me with bashful pride, as if to let me know that he wasn't complaining.

We went into a building with a large lobby and the doorman stopped us at the intercom; then we went up in the elevator to Mrs. Masters's apartment. Mrs. Masters welcomed us into her house, which went on and on for several rooms: one of those high-ceilinged, twilight West End Avenue flats that have the closed air of a doctor's office. Mrs. Masters told us laughingly that her mother-in-law had given her the chair ten years ago when she was first married and she had always wanted to get rid of it. Now that she was divorced she could. She showed us into the den. A delicate girl with golden ringlets, about nine, curled up into the chair as if to demonstrate the way to use it.

"Nancy, please go into the other room." Nancy wouldn't. I thought this was odd. Why was she sitting on the chair like a sofa advertisement? Her mother repeated the order more forcefully and this time she ran out of the room in her bare feet.

As we started to lift up the chair, Gregory at one end, I at another, and Andre holding the chair cushion, we heard the little girl weeping through the walls.

I started to set the chair down.

"Isn't that strange," said Mrs. Masters with her finger on her lips. "She's crying because the chair is being taken away."

"We can leave it," I said. "Really, we don't need it that much."

"Certainly not," said Mrs. Masters.

"She's crying about a piece of *furniture?*" Andre asked scornfully. I gestured him to be quiet. But he had to say it again—suddenly he had become the exponent of toughness. "How could anybody cry over *a piece of furniture?*"

"Shut up, Andre. —Really, if you'd like we can leave it."

"No, don't be silly. This is just something . . . momentary. It will pass in a few minutes." She opened the glass-paneled doors to the foyer so that we could back the chair through. She was a well-groomed woman in her middle thirties, and she stood watching us with a meditative, apologetic look, as if she owed us an explanation for her daughter's tears. "I wonder why that is," she said finally. "I guess she's sad because a piece of her home will be taken away."

Then we backed the chair into the service elevator and, thanking her a million times, said good-bye.

■

In the street it was bitter cold, and Andre kept whining about the weather and refused to give us any help. Gregory was panting and sweating but made no complaints. I couldn't help thinking how many of Lois's more robust boys, like Roberto or Sammy, would have zipped through an expedition like this. For Gregory it was an ordeal, another one of those largely senseless tests of manhood that had seemed so brutal to me when I was growing up. But he put up with it, he was genuinely brave, and I admired him for it as I would not have admired someone to whom physical tasks came easily.

A few days later he gave me this, his own account of the incident (taking the trouble to fictionalize names and locations first):

THE LOST STORY

Once there was a boy named John. He goes to P.S. 157 every day. There is a writer who comes to his class, 5-607 every Wednesday. One day the writer said "Why don't we make a class newspaper." So John went home and wrote a story for him to print. The next day the writer brought a typewriter to class but John did not get a chance to type his story. When he came to school his story was not there. When the writer came he told John his story was not in the box. The writer said "he thinks he had taken it to his house." When it was time to go home the writer asked John if he could help him bring a chair to the school. The next day the writer said he could not find the story. So John went home and wrote another story.

By Gregory

3. A VISITOR

Last week I was in the auditorium rehearsing *West Side Story* with the kids when a bearded stranger came and sat down in the first row, looking patiently toward me. He had a crumpled *Post* under his arm and the rumpled look of someone waiting out a week of jury duty. When I had a minute to spare I asked him if he had come to see me.

"You're Phillip Lopate, right?" he said. "My name is Marmot" (not his real name). "I know Such-and-such and So-and-so" (naming two distant acquaintances of mine). "I'm working for ——— [a mammoth publishing company], as a free-lancer. . . ."

I could barely hear what he was saying because he mumbled so much and his eyes kept roving away. I thought he might be on junk, which worried me because of the kids. His striped white shirt was incredibly wrinkled like a derelict's. But he kept his rap going and I realized he was who he said he was.

"What do you want exactly?" I interrupted.

"I want to see all the children's compositions."

"Can you wait forty minutes?"

"No, I have to be going. . . ."

"Meet me here tomorrow at twelve-thirty. Upstairs, room three twenty-four."

Somehow the phrase "all the children's compositions" wouldn't leave me. I called Karen Hubert, my colleague, and told her a man would be coming to our room tomorrow—a leech—and if I was late a few minutes, to tell him to wait.

"What does he want?" asked Karen.

"He wants to see all the children's compositions."

"*All?*"

"Most likely he is a police spy."

"What book have you been reading now?" Karen said astutely.

"*Hope Against Hope,* by Nadezhda Mandelstam," I answered, "the widow of the great Russian poet Mandelstam who was hounded to his death by the Soviets. In those days if a man came to you with an obsequious or fawning manner, saying he would love to see your latest works, Nadezhda knew he was a police spy."

The next day I came to my classroom and saw Marmot sitting on top of a desk. He was again extraordinarily passive in his body posture. I had seen visitors to the school sink into this dazed lethargy before, becoming suddenly very childish. Maybe it was the high degree of energy and noise that frightened them. He looked out the window, toward the West Side Highway, and then he saw me.

Just then the room emptied for lunch. We were alone which gave him if not me a sense of relief.

"I brought you these three magazines of children's writing. This should give you what you need."

"Can I keep them?" he said.

"Of course. That's why I'm giving them to you."

"Let me explain a little about the project I'm doing," he said expansively, looking me in the eyes, although the main business had already been transacted. "I'm writing a new creative writing curriculum and it's in the form of a story. . . . See, this kid is wandering around after school and he runs into a friend. Then there's the usual junk. You know, 'You look kinda down.' 'Well, my teacher wants me to write a composition about my neighborhood and it's such a boring neighborhood, I don't know what to do, you know, this neighbor-

hood is blah . . . nuthin's ever happening, I hate this neighborhood.'
So his friend says—the usual crap, like—'Well, that's because you
don't know how to use your eyes, you don't know how to focus in
on detail. . . .' We do a lot of sensory opening, awareness. This
package is divided into three parts: the first is Detail, then comes
Imagination, then Feelings."

All this while Marmot was backing into me and lurching away;
or maybe I was imagining that part; but he certainly had more energy
than I gave him credit for, a kind of malevolent insistence underneath
the apologias. I knew I was in for at least twenty minutes more of this.
Then I saw a simple way out.

"This project is ridiculous. I'm a writer and I don't understand
what any of these categories mean, Imagination, Detail. That's not
the way writing works. Imagination springs out of detail which springs
out of feeling, they're all entwined. Why are you trying to sell them
in separate packages?"

"I'm a writer too. I agree with you," he said amiably.

"And another thing. I'm tired of having people come around here
and rip off the kids' stuff and never get back to us."

"Oh no, no . . . ," he shook his head. "———— takes care of that.
The Permissions Department."

"Even so! I don't want to help ————, I don't want to help
Macmillan or Random House or McGraw-Hill or Doubleday or any
of those educational conglomerates get rich. Don't you see that when
the big corporations make a curriculum of "Feelings," it's practically
all over? These kits are baloney! They're dead cards, they don't respond to what's going on in the classroom or at that minute in the
kids' lives. Let's say two kids had a fight, or it's a pretty day, or
something is weighing on your mind—how does the card know that?
The only way to teach writing is to teach the flow."

"I agree with everything you're saying. I wouldn't be doing this
if I weren't getting fat off of it."

I looked at him. He had lovely blue eyes, really gentle, and that
brown shaggy beard. Why was I so irritated with him? And that same
yesterday's wrinkled, wrinkled shirt. There was only one way a shirt
could get so wrinkled. You would have to take a wash-and-wear and
bunch it together while it was still wet, and even that wouldn't go far
enough, you'd have to leave it in a waffle iron.

Which was precisely why I was irritated at him. He had no self-
love. He didn't take care of himself.

I was all set to accept him on grounds that, given our comparable
educations, I could easily be in his shoes, when he added defensively:

"The fact is that we're trying to put some nourishment into the baloney."

"Oh no! Not that one! Go talk to ———— at Random House, he said the same thing. In fact he looks like you, those same kindly eyes, that mumbly voice . . . and he's got all the children's writing you need."

"I can't go to my competitor," he groaned.

"*Your* competitor?" I started gathering my papers to leave the room; perhaps we would continue this over lunch. "The point is, this kit is not the way to get people in touch with their selves. A person has to teach out of his individual obsessions and the daily concerns of the kids." I don't know what I said; the adrenaline was talking in me, I couldn't shut up.

"But if you depend on individual obsessions," he objected, "the lady in the Midwest will be teaching patriotism and menopause."

"Better patriotism than canned pap! At least it's authentic."

"You see, the way I look at it, at least this package will give some kid fifteen minutes to get away from his teacher."

"But they're used as punishment. 'Johnny, stop talking, take out an SRA card in the corner.'"

"At least they're getting away from their teacher," he persisted. "The difference between you and me is that you seem to have more faith in teachers than I do."

"That's appropriate!" I laughed. "You work for a publishing company, I work in a school, it's to each of our advantages to think the way we do. Come on, I have to turn out the lights."

I locked the door behind me. Wondering, do I want to have lunch with this guy? It would only soften my outrage. I didn't really want to know that Marmot was human, that he had a family to support or wrote short stories on the side. Let me keep my fresh impression of repelling the Devil. The Lying Joe came to Ivan Karamazov in the clothes of a shabby relative. Mine visits me in a disheveled wash-and-wear shirt.

"Well, I wish you good luck in any case," I said, and patted him familiarly on the shoulder.

"Thanks. Really, it doesn't matter to me. I'm just getting fat off of it." He patted his shrunken stomach. Even that was a lie.

May Sarton

Material left out of The House by the Sea *(Norton, 1977)*

MAY 4, 1973, WILD KNOLL

I have slipped into these wide spaces, this atmosphere of salt and amplitude, this amazing piece of natural heaven and haven like a ship slipping into her berth. Every single thing looks marvelous in this house . . . and there is, here too (as in Nelson) the delight of *looking through* from one room to another . . . looking through from the smoky-gray paneled walls of the porch to the mustard yellow of the kitchen . . . and through the cozy room to the solid chestnut shine of the *bahut* in the library. The library is simply glorious . . . the shaggy yellow rug a triumph, with all the blue and white objects around.

The animals are perfectly happy . . . no risk of being run over. We all sleep together: Tamas, Bramble, and I in my big bed and wake to the light and a wonderful silence. Lately Nelson had become less silent as big trucks use the road now . . . here there is only a distant ocean murmur and many many songs of birds when I wake at five. The birds are one of the biggest thrills. I have seen a scarlet tanager, an oriole, flocks of gold and purple finches at the feeders. Song sparrows, swallows. . . .

And of course it is *the* moment of transparency when the leaves are not yet out . . . the field garlanded with daffodils as it sweeps down to the sea. There must be twenty or more kinds of narcissi and daffodils here!

Yesterday was my birthday and I was so touched that Raymond, the gardener, brought a tiny bunch of wood anemones the night before (he didn't know it was my birthday but it was really the dearest present of all). Late that evening four huge boxes of flowers arrived . . . such an excitement in the lonely dusk. I must say I am pleased when the dusk comes and the workmen building Mary Leigh's house leave for the day. Then I am filled with secret joys. Mary Leigh and Bev brought a great dinner of lobster, and a supreme Italian *dolce* dessert, and we had a glass of champagne in the library first. I could hardly wait for their reactions to what I have done here but I am thankful that both seemed truly pleased by all the long-dreamed "effects," such as the large planter in one long bay window. Anne Woodson brought a hanging fuchsia and it looks splendid hanging there.

It has been rainy or foggy most of these first days (I moved in in a wild drowning Northeaster!) but I love the soft grays and greens . . . and then sometimes the sea is shot over with silver as light breaks through a cloud. There have been two or three glimpses of real *blue* sea—ah!

I am still not settled into my study as Malcolm, the carpenter, only left two days ago . . . so it is hard to write and I long to unpack once and for all.

[a preface written for The House By the Sea *but a different one was used.]*

MAY 10, 1973

There have been three wild Northeasters since I arrived here, the first the very day the movers arrived! But I love all the weathers . . . the marvelous changes of light every day and every hour. Today after the storm, I see distant white surf from up here. The sea has a broad band of dark gray at the horizon and then pales out as it nears shore . . . a curious light that brings out the bright green of the pasture. The hosts of daffodil and narcissus that garland the field are terribly beaten down, poor things.

The house is very livable though huge, my only problem planning always to take something with me when I go up or down from my study here on the third floor—and often I forget. But now I have a phone up here at least I don't risk my neck stumbling down to answer, and I have three calendars marked with appointments, one on each floor.

Yesterday in the downpour I had a truly quiet day here alone, without workman or guest (Beverly Chamberlain was my first overnight guest and did a terrific job helping me set up all the records. It would have taken me hours alone). After I had written a lot of letters, I got at making a bulletin board with photographs of Nelson: the house, winter and summer, and my dear friends there. It's lovely to know that Mildred Quigley, Tami, and Randi (her daughter and granddaughter) are coming this Sunday to bless this house. Yet it is strange that I have not had *one* moment of nostalgia for Nelson since I left. It makes me think of something Marynia Farnham said, "We don't lose what we have wholly experienced." I have Nelson in the marrow of my bones and always shall have it.

Good moments lately: hanging the photographs of my mother and father in my dressing room. That act seemed to set a seal on my having really arrived here. Going out in the wet grass to pick daffodils and white and blue violets (a tiny exquisite bunch; getting my hands in the earth for the first time day before yesterday when I planted two bleeding heart, some English daisies and forget-me-nots, the latter I trust will spread as they did at Nelson and make blue carpets in every flower border in spring; my daily walk down the field to the sea with Tamas after lunch, or sometimes we make a tour of woodsy roads. The great charm of the place is that it combines so many natural worlds . . . has that open spacious feeling of the ocean view, but also the sheltering woods at the back. Great moment when I put on the first record and there was music here at last. It was a Brahms sonata to celebrate his one hundred fortieth anniversary, but somehow it didn't work. A Boccherini violin concerto just melts me this morning.

I am so physically tired that one of the very good moments these days is getting into bed, Bramble purring and Tamas curled up against my back. They are having a glorious time.

Against all these joys is the perpetual ache about Judy's having to stay permanently in a nursing home. But I shall soon be able to have her here with dear old Scrabble, our fifteen-year-old pussy, for two weeks.

[Unpublished entry]

MAY 12, 1973

Every morning I wake up happy . . . amazing! It has been years since I woke with this sense of anticipation, a whole rich day being born. And this is true despite almost constant bad weather and yesterday again heavy rain and wind . . . the poor daffodils! As soon as the sun comes out I go out and lift their heads, hundreds of them beaten down in sad bundles. But they revive. This morning I woke at six to brilliant sunlight, got up and spent a good half-hour just watching and listening to birds. I have counted twenty-one kinds since my arrival two weeks ago. This morning I saw the catbird and that explains the mysterious varied songs I have been hearing these past days! A pair of cardinals came to the feeder, quite glorious among the many goldfinches and purple finches that zigzag in and out of the crab apple all day.

Yesterday I roughed out the piece on "Flower Watching"* for Leo Lerman and I have been pondering the good talk with Eric Swenson who came overnight on the tenth. By great good fortune he arrived, for once, to a blue sea and clear skies so we had a little walk down to the rocky point and then on woodsy roads making a circle behind the house. The novel** has been turned down by *Readers' Digest.* . . . I had hoped! They said it was a very moving book, but too grim . . . and that is the view also of the magazines, I guess.

Anyway I feel sure now that I can do good work here. That is the word from the fates and furies at present.

Amy Clampitt

The Drawing Room at Rydal Mount, a scene from a play

The drawing room at Rydal Mount. Midafternoon in late summer. Mary Wordsworth, in a black dress and cap, sits at a table under the window overlooking Rydal Water. With her is Isabella Fenwick. Well dressed and tactfully self-contained, Miss Fenwick is a woman of that sterling mold whose devotion is unerringly drawn by the likes of William Wordsworth. Each of the women holds a page of manuscript.

IF   [*reading*]   . . . Or saw like other men with bodily eyes
                        Before them in some desolated place
                        The consummation of the wrath of Heaven;
                        So did some portion of that spirit fall
                        On me, to uphold me through those evil times,
                        And in their rage and dog-day heat I found
                        Something to glory in . . .

MW   I had thought he meant to alter a line here. But it appears not.
       [*reading*]   And in their rage and dog-day heat I find
                        Something to glory in . . .
       Dog-day heat is certainly what we have been having lately.
       And still such *troops* of visitors go on arriving.

*Vogue, August 1973

**As We Are Now (Norton, 1973)

IF   Extraordinary.

MW   At this time of year, they are nearly all from New York. That entire city seems to have broken loose and come here somehow. It is years since I remember quite so many tourists.

IF   Extraordinary.

MW   Of course, it's the railway. Since that came through, everything is changed. A *hotel* on Lake Windermere—imagine! Omnibuses and carriages running from there to Grasmere. You know my husband's feelings on *that* subject.

IF   My dear, given his feelings, and given that the household is in mourning, ought not someone simply to be posted at the gate to turn them away?

MW   Oh, no. He complains, but he wouldn't hear of that. They never stay long, otherwise he would be quite worn out. He takes it all good-naturedly—and to be quite truthful, it is a relief to me that he has something to distract him from so much grieving.

IF   After such a blow—

MW   Yes, for him it has been the heaviest of all. I do not believe, Miss Fenwick—[*A pause. IF lays her hand over MW's*]—that he will ever be himself again, quite. For me, it was not the same. I saw it finally as a blessing. But he could not. He simply could not. You know—I am not sure whether I told you this, but—[*She breaks off*]. I did tell you, of course, about his being presented to the Queen, after he succeeded Mr. Southey as Poet Laureate. And found her charming. A charming little person.

IF   I remember.

MW   Of course, he accepted on the understanding that the appointment was entirely honorary. And then at the time of the royal marriage, it appeared that some kind of observance in honor of Prince Albert was called for. And he simply could not get on with it. In the end it was Edward, Mr. Quillinan—I tell you this in confidence, of course—

IF   Of course.

MW   It was Mr. Quillinan who wrote it for him. Yes, with Dora so very ill—he knew by then that she could not recover—it was Mr. Quillinan, and not my husband, who wrote the ode in honor of the Prince Consort.

IF   I believe that is the saddest thing I ever heard.

MW   He had reconciled himself to it finally—Mr. Quillinan, I

mean. My husband never did. We all had our delusions, of
course.

IF   I still reproach myself sometimes—

MW   For the part you had in their marrying? Oh, my dear, you
must not reproach yourself.

IF   When I heard that he was not at the church to give her
away—

MW   No, no, it was not that he *refused* to go, that he opposed it
any longer—he saw that you were quite right, that for the
sake of Dora's happiness he could not oppose it. It was
simply his nerves—those Wordsworth nerves. You know, his
sister was not at *our* wedding, simply because it was too
much for her nerves. It was a matter of her, of his, being so
greatly *moved*. And Dora understood. No, no, I think she
might have broken down herself if he *had* been there.

IF   For a while, she seemed truly to bloom.

MW   As recently as last September—I can hardly believe it, that it
was just last September that she walked home at midnight
from a ball at Mr. Carr's, across the way. With no ill effects
at all. It was while we were at Carlisle for the winter holiday
that she took cold, and then there was that cough she
couldn't rid herself of. I suppose we ought to have known;
but we all clung to the notion that somehow or other . . .
They tried everything. There was that new remedy that came
very highly recommended—cod's liver oil, doesn't it sound
revolting?—and for a while we thought it might be helping.
But in the end . . . I found it possible to be tranquil, and
finally to see the end as a blessing, she suffered so—and
spoke so cheerfully of getting well, it broke my heart. . . .
My husband, though, could not speak of any but the most
indifferent subject without weeping.

IF   He had you to lean on, and he leaned.

MW   We both of us leaned on *you*. It is the greatest comfort to us
both, to have you here. And for what you have done as a
scribe, an amanuensis—well, we simply cannot, either of us,
begin to thank you.

IF   The corrections he has made on the self-biography, what he
refers to as the poem to Coleridge, are now our main
concern. Has he settled on a title, do you know?

MW   Not finally. I thought it might be called simply *The Prelude.*

IF   There was another passage, near the end. Yes, here it is. If
you will match your copy with this one.
[*reading*]   Child of my Parents! Sister of my Soul!

> Elsewhere have strains of gratitude been
>   breathed
> To thee for all the early tenderness
> Which I from thee imbibed. And true it is
> That later seasons owed to thee no less;
> For, spite of thy sweet influence and the touch
> Of other kindred hands that opened out
> The springs of tender thought in infancy,
> And spite of all which singly I had watched
> Of elegance, and each minuter charm
> In Nature and in life, still to the last,
> Even to the very going out of youth
> The period which our Story now hath reached,
> I too exclusively esteemed that love,
> And sought that beauty, which, as Milton
>   sings,
> Hath terror in it.

All that is apparently to stand. But a little further along, there were some lines that seemed not quite clear. Yes, here it is.

[reading]   With such a theme,
> Coleridge! With this my argument, of thee
> Shall I be silent?

MW   With such a theme,
> Coleridge! With this my argument, of thee
> Shall I be silent? . . .
> I agree: the construction is a bit hard to follow.

[reading]   With such a theme . . .
> [Wordsworth enters. He is noticeably grayer and
> more stooped than in the previous act. He is also
> more elegantly dressed. He wipes his forehead with a
> pocket handkerchief.]

MW More Americans, dear?

WW From New York. Perfectly docile. They merely wanted a look. In such oppressive weather, I wonder at their coming at all.

> [A sigh in the trees outside; faint rumblings in the
> distance.]

MW It will be cooler soon. There is a storm coming.

WW If you will excuse me, I will go up and see to my sister.

MW Be prepared for a storm here too. [to IF] Do you know, she asked for a fire this morning?

IF   And got it?

WW Only a little one.

MW This weather makes her fretful.

WW If you will excuse me. [*Exit.*]

MW He is the prisoner of his sister's every whim. The willing
prisoner. Let me see, where were we?

> [*reading*]   With such a theme,
> Coleridge! with this my argument, of thee
> Shall I be silent?

IF   He is saying, in his way, that having spoken of his sister's
influence, he cannot but go on to speak of his debt to
Coleridge.

MW You might discreetly ask him whether—

IF   It might be clarified a bit? Yes. I will make a note. And here.
Further down the page.

> [*reading*]   And now, O Friend! this History is brought
> To its appointed close: the discipline
> And consummation of the Poet's mind,
> In everything that stood most prominent,
> Have faithfully been pictured; we have reached
> The time (which was our object from the first)
> When we may, not presumptuously, I hope,
> Suppose my powers so far confirmed, and such
> My knowledge, as to make me capable
> Of building up a work that should endure.

MW The text I have reads the same, with only a little mark
beside it. But to draw that particular passage to his attention
again . . .

IF   . . . Would be a matter neither you nor I . . . Of course.

MW How many times Dora or I—or his sister, in those days
when she was still herself—urged him to take up that great
unfinished work! But I suppose it is twenty years since he
even looked at it. And now, of course . . . [*A silence. WW
reenters*]

WW She is coming down. For once, the room is too hot even for
her. Dolly is getting her into fresh linens.

IF   Poor dear.

MW We were working on the fair copy of the poem to Coleridge.

WW I was just turning over in my mind a passage in the twelfth
book, that may need attention. [*He takes up the pages from
MW, and slowly examines them. Sound of the wind in the trees
outside.*] Yes. Here it is.

> Oh! mystery of Man, from what a depth
> Proceed thy Honours! I am lost, but see
> In simple childhood something of the base
> On which my greatness stands; but this I feel,
> That from thyself it is that thou must give
> Else never can receive . . .

[*musing*]   That from thyself it is that thou must give,
> Else never can receive . . .

That was a borrowing, a direct borrowing, from Coleridge himself. It was a sentiment he expressed, rather desperately, in the latter days of our daily association. [*Pause*] Now, that *I am lost.* I am not quite sure what I meant by that. Can't think what I can have meant. Do you think it should stand? [*The two women look at him attentively.*] Should it stand?

MW It seems . . .

IF   [*similarly temporizing*] It seems . . . Would you read a bit further?

WW [*continuing*]   The days gone by
> Come back upon me from the dawn almost
> Of life: the hiding-places of my power
> Seem open; I approach, and then they close;
> I see by glimpses now; when age comes on,
> May scarcely see at all . . .

[*Another silence. Dorothy appears on the stairway. She wears fresh clothes but appears agitated.*]

IF   Good afternoon, Miss Wordsworth.

DW [*ignoring her*] Dearest Dorothy made such a frightful mess. In her clothes. Dolly and Agnes had to change her. Dearest Dorothy has trouble with her bowels. She has offensive habits. She uses wicked, revolting language. Sometimes while there are visitors, she does it.

MW You see, Aunty, what Miss Fenwick and I have been doing. We are making a fair copy of the poem to Coleridge.

DW The trouble always seemed to settle in the bowels. Coleridge had those troubles. And Dora. Dora died.
[*WW turns away. He is crying.*]

MW I hadn't been sure she even knew.

DW They said it was a consumption. It was in her bowels. A diarrhea. And the sores!—the bedsores, horrid bleeding ones. They had to keep changing her.

WW Must our guest be subjected . . .

MW Dolly! Agnes!

[*A maid appears in the doorway at stage right.*]

MAID Mr. Quillinan is here.

MW Show him in, and ask Dolly to please come and take Miss
Wordsworth . . .

DW No! No! I won't go up! [*runs to WW, crying*] My *brother*
needs me, don't you see? [*She throws herself against him and
clings. They are both crying.*]
[*Edward Quillinan enters.*]

MW Another scene of domestic tranquillity, I fear.

Q [*to IF*] I am one of the family.

IF We were just looking at a passage from the self-biography,
the poem to Coleridge. The Poet wondered whether it
should be altered. Perhaps you could offer an opinion.

WW I should be grateful.

DW No, no! [*Thunder, crashing, drowns her voice.*]

WW Is it not ironic, Quillinan? I am Poet Laureate of England. I
stood in the presence of the Queen, of Queen Victoria
herself. But here I am my sister's slave and prisoner.

DW Shall I say a poem for you, Peter Quince? I will say my
prison poem.

> A prisoner on my pillowed couch
> Five years in feebleness I've lain . . .

I must alter that, as soon as I can remember just how *many*.

> Five years *and more* in feebleness I've lain.
> Ah! shall I e'er with vigorous step
> Travel the hills again?

[*She goes to the window. There is a sound of wind rising. It begins
to rain.*]
The hills! Helm Crag, with the moon above it, the crescent
moon. The Rock of Names. On Dunmail Raise, the way
poor Coleridge always took
from Keswick . . .

[*Silence, while the rain comes down.*]
But *now* let me say a cheerful one.

> *No* prisoner in this lonely room,
> I *saw* the green Banks of the Wye
> Recalling thy prophetic words,
> Bard, Brother, friend from Infancy.

Q [*gallant*] Now those are lines worthy of the sister of a poet
laureate. [*to WW*] I should be honored to look at the
passage from the poem to Coleridge.

DW Bard, brother, friend from Infancy. The Rock of Names.
    Poor Coleridge. Helm Crag, with the moon above it, so thin
    and narrow, like an old, old wedding ring.
    [*Thunder echoing among the hills as the curtain falls.*]

Odd Men Out

(Uncollected Pieces)

Annie Dillard

FRONTIER CITY

In the second half of the eighteenth century, Pittsburgh was the last place, the end of the road, the outpost where both Indian fighters and Indian traders loaded up for forays into the west. By 1770 there were twenty houses in town, all made of logs, and there were farms tucked into the hills and valleys all around. Almost fifty thousand people lived in southwest Pennsylvania. During the Revolutionary War, Pittsburgh supplied meat, kegs, boats, and grain to American troops on the Great Lakes and westward. The town was then a weird scatterment of brick redoubts, log cabins, slaughterhouses, a few fine houses, boatyards, and apple trees. Doctors and lawyers were already practicing in town. It was still a small frontier village, but it was a market center, and the gateway to the west.

Those were the days of the flatboats and keelboats. They flourished for forty glorious years, from the Revolutionary War which brought the immigrants, to 1816 when steamboats carried them away.

The immigrants used to drive their wagons clear from the coast into Pittsburgh during the winter, when the mud had frozen hard on the mountain tracks. They bought flatboats there—for a dollar a foot—and waited encamped in the snow on their boats, or in wagons or tents, until the river ice broke up in the spring. They all camped together, by the Monongahela, Scotch-Irish and English and German, French Huguenot, and the so-called "Finns"—any Scandanavians. Some built brick fireplaces right on their boats. They tethered horses and cows about their campsites. From local merchants they bought not only the boats, but also fodder, groceries, dubious charts of the Ohio River, farm implements and woven linen, and sometimes extra corn and pork to trade downstream. Because these men, women, and children were strangers then, stranded, ignorant of the country ahead, sometimes not speaking English, and in possession of their life savings which were to see them through the coming years, the local merchants charged them double prices for everything, and talked them into buying things they would not need.

When the ice broke up, the immigrants broke camp. They loaded furniture, fodder, family, hens, horses and cows onto the clumsy flatboat decks. To the flatboat roofs they lashed the wagons they had traveled in overland from their unthinkably long-ago Atlantic ports. When they got where they were going, they sold the boats for lumber, because flatboats were a downstream craft only. And milled lumber was valuable everywhere, even in the thick of the woods—for wasn't the new world everywhere building?

Upstream traffic required not the flatboat but the keelboat, a shallow-drafted double-ended craft poled by professionals. Upstream from Louisville or New Orleans the keelboats hauled sugar from the West Indies, hemp, tobacco, Mexican copper, Missouri lead, and Spanish wool. Downstream to the Ohio River towns, to Wheeling, Cincinnati, Louisville, Cairo, and on to the Mississippi and New Orleans, the keelboats carried frontier cargo: noggins of butter, corn whiskey, homespun linen, flour, and pork. Pretty soon from Pittsburgh they carried blown glass, too, and bar-iron.

Some keelboats flew a calico flag; they were floating general stores that called on small settlements. The keelboatmen tied up at the little landings on the river and blew a tin horn. The settlers came running toward the calico flag, to barter and hear the news.

There were giants in the earth in those days. They were the keelboatmen. One was Cherry Tree Joe McCreery. If this Pittsburgh giant of a keelboatman took a notion to chase skirts in New Orleans, he just lashed a log raft to each foot and strode off down the Ohio River skating. He kept a panther at home for his kittycat; his wife cooked for him in a frying pan so big it took a side of bacon to grease it. (I learned most of this from writer Lee Gutkind.)

The keelboatmen were braggarts and battlers, and Mike Fink was the loudest and brawlingest of them all. A ring-tailed screamer, as he put it, a rip-tail roarer. Because of Mike Fink and friends, Pittsburghers put on the books an unenforceable law against galloping a horse through town while firing a gun into the air. Mike Fink manhandled people in bars all up and down the western waters, and took pride in gouging out their eyeballs with his thumbs. (Your thumbs get pretty strong when you pole an eighty-foot boat against a river current every day for four months twice a year when the ice is out.) If he couldn't get at their eyeballs, he bit off their lips.

Cherry Tree Joe, Mike Fink, and their keelboat buddies had a touching ceremony by which they pledged friendship. (When Abraham Lincoln was president, thirty years later, he heard about Mike

Fink and the keelboatmen's pledge and professed admiration for it.)
They caroused all night in a bar until, along about dawn, it struck one
of them that this other fellow here was an unsurpassed companion,
to whom he should plight his troth. So by agreement the two rolled
out onto the street, squared off at seventy yards, loaded rifles, and
shot tin cups of whisky off each other's heads.

Pittsburghers launched their first steamboat in 1811, on a fall
Sunday: a side-wheeler, the *New Orleans*. People who were there said
the red-shirted keelboatmen dropped their poles when she smoked by
at eight miles an hour. In a noisy twinkling, the steamer wore around
the big bend of the Ohio and vanished from sight. But the keelboatmen knew—knew with their broad backs and sinewy arms—that the
rivers ran low much of the year. Low-slung cattle could ford the
Monongahela at Pittsburgh's point. The keelboats drew only three
feet. Even on the Ohio, there wasn't always enough river to float a
steamboat.

The keelboatmen were right. They did a mighty business out of
the port of Pittsburgh in the years after the steamboat launching. For
the War of 1812 played into their hands.

The War of 1812, like all subsequent wars to date, meant a boom for
Pittsburgh. The war closed sea routes and wagon routes; all north-
south trade ran the rivers. And the United States, and especially
Pittsburgh, began to manufacture all those goods it had imported
from Europe: things made of brass, tin, iron, lead, and glass, and
steam engines, liquor, woven textiles, hats, and boots. Keelboats
glided up to the factories by the river banks, loaded on these bright
new things, and poled them all away.

Downstream, the going was easy. A fiddler used to sit on the
cargo-hold roof and entertain the crew of twelve. The two rivers that
made the Ohio were of differing colors, green and white; the two
rivers ran side-by-side and unblended for a long way down the Ohio.
The keelboatmen amused themselves by steering gently down the
seam. In spring floods, all the rivers ran muddy, and the reckless
keelboats fairly flew; they covered the Ohio in fifteen days, or half the
usual time.

In 1816, after the war, marine architects designed a steamboat to
carry her big boilers up on deck. Now steamboats could travel in
shallow water; the keelboats' days were over. Some of the keelboatmen found work on the steamboats, or in the boatyards that made
them. Mike Fink, on his part, stalked out to the Rocky Mountains,
where he died of rage.

■

By then, Pittsburgh presented a fair prospect from afar only. Visitors seemed actually to compete in their expressions of horror at the scene downtown. It was almost as bad as Birmingham, England. Black smoke and soot lay over everything, including the residents; coal dust thickened the air. Open sewers ran through town. When dogs died in the street, there was no one to move their carcasses. Workers and their families sickened from typhoid—a disease of filth—and died. The Scotch-Irish leaders of the town fought off all efforts to keep the streets and drinking water clean, lest tax rates rise and the principle of independence suffer.

Even the pigs, people said, deplored the muddy streets. When in the course of their wallowings downtown they got stuck in the mud, they were heard to squeal, just like everyone else in town, "Where's the street commissioner?"

T. Coraghessan Boyle

"The Arctic Explorer," originally published in Fiction International in 1976, was left out of Descent of Man (1979) because it seemed too similar thematically to another story included in the collection.

THE ARCTIC EXPLORER

I. DAY

DEPARTURE

Posing in full dress uniform at the bow of the little brig Endeavor, rigid as the mast looming behind him, he raises a stiff arm in acknowledgment of the small send-off parties spotting the Kings' shore of the Narrows. With his perfect posture, immaculate uniform and manicured mustache, he looks very much the Hero, a reincarnated admixture of Henry Hudson, John Paul Jones, and El Cid.

His solemn eyes scan the bandless, bannerless shore. A paltry crowd, he reflects, for an occasion so momentous. After all, he is sailing cheekily off into the frigid unknown, beyond the reaches of men's maps, to probe regions whose very existence is but rumor. Yet such, he supposes, is the lot of Heroes: all but ignored by the self-satisfied Present, revered by Posterity. Glebe cows. If it were up to them Kentucky would be a wilderness still.

Beyond the Narrows, the open Atlantic, rolling pleasantly underfoot to a gentle June breeze. Captain John Pennington Frank (MD, USN) breathes deeply, closes his eyes, and removes his cap to let the sea breeze tickle through his hair. As he does so, the last spangles of confetti are sucked up in the wind and shot away to starboard (this the confetti that his mother and two unmarried sisters had solemnly flung at him just half an hour earlier when the brig had been launched at the Brooklyn Naval Yard). Like Ishmael too long aland, he feels the salt breeze raking up all the old sailor's pluck: Ah! The Open Sea! Adventure! Man against the Elements! It is then that the brig pitches forward and an icy slap intrudes itself upon the Captain's meditations. His eyelids snap-to like the surprise of a stroke and he lurches forward against the rail: the cap sails out from his hand in a graceful arc, to be sucked down by the frothing waves below. When he recovers himself he glances furtively about before digging out the handkerchief, thankful that none of the crew had been watching. The ceremonies over, and the voyage begun, the Captain retires to his cabin, where the crisp and neatly lined pages of the logbook await him.

Of course he knows nothing as yet of the Arctic Night.

CAPTAIN'S LOG, JUNE 2

Set sail from NY Harbor at 1100 hours Eastern Time. Momma, Evangeline and Euphonia saw us off with a not inconsiderable crowd. As we passed the Narrows, quite ten thousand I should think turned out to cheer us. It was heartening thus to witness the deep reverence and goodwill the people of this great nation show for our venture.

My party consists of fifteen: eight officers (myself included); five crewmen; Phillip Blackwark, cook; and Harlan Hawkins, cabin boy. Our stores include a large supply of navy ration salt beef and pork, hard biscuit, flour, some barrels of an exsiccated potato, two thousand pounds of pemmican, a quantity of dried fruits, and twelve barrels of pickled cabbage. (Surreptitiously, I laid in a supply of party hats and whistles, to cheer the men during our winter confinement.) It is my expectation to reach the northern coast of Newfoundland by the twentieth. There we will supplement our stores with a few sides of fresh beef, God and Governor Pickpie willing.

GLUT AT ANOATUK

Kresuk's bare chest is bespattered with blood, his face a smear, the oily black hair at his cheeks congealed with blood and bird fat. His incisors dig at the purple vein along the breastbone, his lips suck at the tatters of pink flesh still clinging to the pink ribs. As he gnaws, the denuded breast and its few dangling particles flaps flat against his greasy knuckles. The remains of nine eider ducks lie beside his bare thigh, a wet neck and ribcage beneath it. His right nostril is crammed white with fat and bits of raw meat.

Ooniak, his woman, patiently cracks auk eggs and drains the contents into the yawning maw of Sip-su, their defective son. Mouth agape, head thrown back, Sip-su is a birdling in the nest, begging the sky for food. Five winters, thinks Kresuk, looking hard at his son. I give him one more. Then he lies back with a sigh, his head buried in a heap of bloodied feathers. He breaks wind. He picks his teeth. And thinks of walrus, bearded seal, narwhal. He does not suspect the existence of New York Harbor 2,800 miles to the south, nor does he suspect the existence of the brig *Endeavor*, already making its way north to ripple the placid waters of his life. There are legends telling of tribes of gaunt, pale men, but Kresuk has no time for legends—the Night, the season of frozen ice, of terror and of want, is over, and the birds have returned to Anoatuk.

DINING AT ST. JOHN'S, NEWFOUNDLAND

(A dainty tinkle of silverware, china, and crystal accompanies the dialogue.)

Oh, excellent. You know I haven't titillated my palate with such northern delicacies as these since—oh, forty-seven I guess it was, up in Finland.

It's only on special occasions that I can get them myself, you know, Captain. I don't expect you picture me glutting on poached wapiti tongue all the time—

No, no, no. And I'm deeply flattered that you consider our visit one of those special occasions, Governor Pickpie . . . these smell ducky—what are they?

We call them St. John's marbles. The genitalia of the male musk-ox, braised in port. Care for some more wine?

Oh yes, thank you. . . . Quite tasty, these marbles. Ho. Ho-ho.

Have you tried the smoked salmon in soured cream? Cochlearia salad?

Um yes. Superb. You know, Governor Pickpie, I think the memory of this feast alone will sustain us through the long winter to come.

You're very kind, sir. At any rate, I wish you greater success than the last party that came through—Sir Regis Norton's expedition.

Oh?

Yes. Their ship was found by a Swedish fellmonger no more than a month ago, frozen solid as a rock into the ice sheet—all hands dead from frost. Preserved like pickles.

DOWN

Kresuk smiles to himself in the loud sun, mirror-whiteness, bird squabble. He stoops to collect eiderdown from around the eider nests, occasionally pausing to poke a hole in an egg and suck its contents. Ooniak squats on a lichen-crowned rock, stuffing a new walrus sleeping bag with eiderdown and the ass feathers of the arctic tern. Nearby Sip-su sits: circular, drooling, eyes focused on nothing. Work a son should be doing, thinks Kresuk. The seal are back. I should hunt. I give him one winter more.

CAPTAIN'S LOG, JUNE 28

Entered Baffin's Bay, bearing to northwest by north, looking for open water. Great bergs like floating mountains hem us in. We keep in sight of the dramatic coastline, navigating from headland to headland—it takes us steadily westward, and always to the north.

The sixty-two Esquimaux dogs we purchased at Fiskarnaes are perhaps not even half a step removed from their lupine ancestors. One is afraid to go on deck anymore—they surge about one in a snarling pack, nosing about for food, snapping and tearing at each other. Yesterday they pulled down two sides of beef from the rigging, and before Mr. Mallaby could get through the seething pack, they had reduced the rock-hard frozen meat to bare bone, like a swarm of those carnivorous Amazonian fishes. The men complain bitterly of these ravening wolves infesting our decks, and I explain that we shall need them to pull our sledges during the fall and spring explorations. Still the men grumble. Perhaps I shall break out the party hats this evening to brighten their spirits.

UFO

Metek is agitated. He can barely contain himself. Nervously he cuts strip after strip from the walrus carcass and nervously he wedges them in his mouth. Across from him squat Kresuk and Ooniak, their faces slimed with the buttery wet liver that had served as an hors d'oeuvre—they too are now cutting strips of walrus-beef and feeding them into their mouths. Sip-su sits on, an autistic little Buddha. It was big as the floating ice, Metek says finally. No one looks up. The assiduous gorging continues, to the accompaniment of lip-smacks, grunts, booming eructations. It had great white wings, and it flew atop the water like a flock of eider coming in to feed. I saw it from Pekiutlik Lookout where I am hunting. A great creature, of color like the summer fox, and wings that hum like the auk.

Kresuk, without breaking the studied hand-to-mouth rhythm he has established, looks up and utters a single word: sealshit.

BERG-BELEAGUERED

Like a foundling among wolves, a shot glass of Wild Turkey among winos, a bridge over the River Kwai, the *Endeavor* drifts among ice peaks that rear malevolently a hundred feet above the water. The bergs are drifting too: battering together like gargantuan rams, shattering the arctic stillness with explosions as the ship-sized blocks thunder down. The brig rocks dizzily in the concussive waves; the men are panic-struck; the sixty-two dogs beshit the decks in fright. But the Captain seems unmoved, absorbed as he is in thinking up names for salient coastal features. Aunt, Aunt, Aunt? he thinks aloud.

Soon the black channel before them vanishes—two titanic bergs roll gently together and lock with a kiss: the open passage has become a cul-de-sac. Accordingly, first officer Mallaby orders the brig turned 180 degrees. But wait! Even the channel they've just passed through is stoppered tight as a nun's orifices—the brig's wake trails off into the gullets of two implacable bergs, tall and white as the chalk cliffs at Dover. The open sea becomes a lake—no, a pond—inexorably the ring of ice closes in, like a mountain range seen creeping in time-stop photography through ten million years. Captain Frank! shouts Mallaby. Captain Frank! The Captain looks up, and for the first time assesses the situation. How embarrassing, he mutters, and returns to his notebook, annoyed with the interruption—he'd almost had it, the name he'd been searching for—his great-aunt on his mother's side.

Two hours later the *Endeavor* bobs in a puddle, surrounded by the sheer ice faces, kicked about now and again by their feet—the feet which even now, deep in the black and secretive depths, are welding themselves together, freezing across in a grim sort of net.

Five hundred yards distant, from their vantage point in Pekiutlik Lookout, two figures, swathed in the hair of beasts, are watching. One grunts: Hmph. What'd I tell you. The other, incredulous, mouths his reply: Mother of Walrus!

CAPTAIN'S LOG, JULY 17

It is with great sorrow that I must report the loss of our ship. In searching for a northwest passage we entered a blind bay, became beleaguered by ice, and were finally crushed by the shifting floes. All hands escaped without incident, and due to my own foresight, much of our stores were saved, including a great quantity of wood from the crushed hull. She was a stout little brig, and we all hated to see her go—especially as it means making the 800-mile journey to Fiskarnaes, on the South Greenland coast, by foot. I have given orders to establish a winter camp here, as the season is so far progressed as to render any attempt at escape impracticable. About five hundred yards from the scene of the *Endeavor*'s demise is an outcropping of greenstone. I have named it Pauce Point, in honor of my great aunt, Rudimenta Pauce. It is in the lee of this cliff that we shall make our winter quarters with the heavy timber salvaged from the brig, insulating the walls and ceilings with packed ice, Esquimaux-fashion. God willing, we shall live to see the spring, and other eyes will come to peruse what I have written here—the record of our tribulations.

THE GLARE

Out on the floes Kresuk is bent over a tiny hole, no more than two inches in diameter. His ear is to the ice, his fist curled round the harpoon. The seal responsible for this hole is at that very moment gamboling about the ice-blue depths, gobbling fish, undulating sealishly through the water, out of breath now, darting back to the airhole for a heaving gasp of oxygen. It will be his last gasp, smiles Kresuk.

Some distance off, the man with rifle and notebook is busy naming headlands, cliffs, and glaciers after himself and members of his family. The jagged pencil line of the coast grows northward on the paper as each day he hikes farther, ostensibly in search of game. Soon, he thinks, he will have a team of dogs trained and will be able to cover twice the distance in a sledge—but for now he must walk, and haul back meat for the crew and ravenous dog pack. Up ahead he catches sight of a movement out on the ice—he strains his eyes, but with the glare, and his sun-blindness, the object drifts and melds with the red and blue spots before his eyes. But isn't it a bear? A fat bear, rich with meat and suet, bent now over a hole in the ice? The man folds the notebook into his parka and begins his stalk. When he gets within two hundred feet he lies flat, braces the rifle on an ice pedestal, takes careful aim, and fires.

CAPTAIN'S LOG, AUGUST 15

Have made contact with the Esquimaux. I found one of these savages unconscious on the ice, suffering apparently from shock as a result of a recent flesh wound in the gluteus maximus. With the aid of a sledge drawn by six of the crew (we've not yet been able to train the dogs), I brought the poor fellow back to camp, where I was able to perform a crude operation, dressing his wound and treating the shock with a dose of morphine. He lies asleep now in the main cabin the fellows have constructed from the remains of the *Endeavor.* In appearance, he is very much like his Christianized counterparts to the south, but in size he greatly surpasses them, measuring six feet from toe to crown, and weighing nearly one-hundred-ninety pounds. He is dressed in rude garments fashioned from the pelts of his prey—he wears a sort of breeches fabricated from the hind quarters of the polar bear, the claws still attached and trailing upon the ground as he stands. His boots are of sealskin and his parka of arctic fox. He exudes a strong odor of urine.

I am quite anxious to speak with our primitive guest (hopefully through the office of my interpreter, second officer Moorhead Bone), as information regarding the indigenous Esquimaux tribes and their seasonal wanderings should prove invaluable to us in effecting our spring escape.

GAUNT AND PALE

Kresuk awakes groggy, and with a distant ache in his anak, from a dream in which he had harpooned Osoetuk, the great narwhal, God of the Seas, and been dragged through the ice, down to Osoetuk's lair in the icy depths. There Osoetuk had given him a wonderful elixir, the spirit of fishes and heart of walrus, and it had made him warm beneath the ice and the dark waters—warm, and drowsy.

Now he lies still, eyes closed, listening to the beat and wash of a strange tongue, remembering the flank attack and the lost seal. He struggles to open his eyes but the elixir prevents him. It takes all his concentration to crack the heavy lids just enough to catch a glimpse of the ceiling, its wooden beams. Wood! The last thing he'd expect to see at Pekiutlik. Hard and carvable, just the ticket for tools and totems—but up here the best he'd ever done was a forked branch washed up from the south. His conclusion is inevitable: I am dead, he thinks, and lifted into another world. The voices drone. His eyes open, close. He looks again: wood all around him, so precious, so rare, a forest above his heavy lids—the lids which now close as if weighted, while the dream seeps back into his consciousness. When again they open he twists his head in the direction of the voices, strains to see, focuses finally . . . on legends! Men with hair on their faces, gaunt and pale as winter, legends incarnate.

II. NIGHT

CAPTAIN'S LOG, NOVEMBER 7
So cold your axillary hair shatters like glass, and the spittle freezes in your throat.

CAPTAIN'S LOG, NOVEMBER 8
We have just enough light at noon to read the thermometer without aid of a lantern. Temperature at noon today was $-38°$ F., with a stiff breeze kicking up. Mr. Mallaby is lost somewhere out on the floes. At ten this morning he went out to feed the dogs and has not been seen since. I have sent out a search party.

The supply of fresh meat I commissioned from Kresuk in early September is nearly gone. It was well worth the price (some 300 pounds of walrus and bear in exchange for a string of glass beads and six red wooden buttons). Judging from his look of idiot delight as I dangled the beads before his nose, I think I could have got another 600 pounds of meat in the bargain. My only complaint is that the savage has not returned since, and we are in dire need of further barter. I presume he is wintering at Etah, the Esquimaux village sixty miles south of us.

CAPTAIN'S LOG, NOVEMBER 12
The search party has not returned; no trace either of Mr. Mallaby. I regret to report that of the men remaining (five went out on the search) only four are well enough to be up and about. Frostbite has been our biggest enemy, with scurvy running a close second. All the men suffer from the latter, and to complicate matters, our meager supply of dried fruits has been already exhausted. Even the pickled cabbage is beginning to go quickly—yet all of us show signs of scorbutic weariness and bleeding at the gums.

The incessant hacking and wheezing, and the groaning of the amputees, is trying on my nerves. Besides which I am bored witless— nothing to do but tend the sick and wait for the sun—nearly 140 days distant. Nursing is not exactly my idea of an heroic occupation—I long for the more active fight.

CAPTAIN'S LOG, NOVEMBER 15

The remains of Mr. Mallaby's fur suit have been found by Mr. Bone among the dogs: I can only conjecture his fate. The dog pack, incidentally, is now down to twenty-seven survivors—it appears they have been eating one another, as we have been unable to provide them with fresh meat, and the pemmican (unpalatable though it is), we must conserve for our own use. Yet Mr. Bone reminds me that without dogs we should be hard pressed in making our spring trek to civilization. Something must be done.

The search party has not yet returned. I have dispatched a second search party, composed of our three ablest men (Tiggis, Tuggle, and Mr. Wright), to search for the missing search party.

BARTER

Kresuk returns. His round cheeks, white furs, slit eyes. His shaggy frame in the doorway. The stiff seal flipper clutched in his mittens.

The Captain beckons him in, slamming the door against the wind. A dying wood-fire glows in the corner, shadows mount the walls. The men snuff and wheeze. The Captain nods at Kresuk, smiling. Kresuk nods back, smiling. "Bone!" shouts the Captain. "Bone!"

Mr. Bone lifts himself from his pallet, breath steaming around his head like a pot of coffee, and hobbles out to join his superior. "Mr. Bone, speak with this fellow. I feel certain that he's come to exchange meat for beads, and I don't think I need emphasize how sorely necessitous we are at this juncture." Bone coughs, relieves himself of a wad of sputum. "Wuk noah tuk-ha," he says. Kresuk stares past him for a moment, then turns to sift through the murky low room. He pokes into each cabinet, each bed, beneath each man's pillow. "What's he about, Bone?" demands the Captain. "Here now!"

Kresuk is collecting things: fine glittering knives, pewter mugs, pocket watches, axes. A sack of red wooden buttons. He clatters them down in the center of the room, holds out the seal flipper to Mr. Bone.

CAPTAIN'S LOG, NOVEMBER 21

Kresuk has been back. We exchanged a few of our things for a new, if small, supply of fresh meat. The savage drives a hard bargain. He has us, as they say, over a barrel.

Mr. Bone's great toe has suppurated to such a degree that I fear gangrenous infection if it is not removed. Once again, I think, as the surgical blade splashes through to negotiate the bone in a quick down-and-across stroke, the damnable frost has cost us another part of our bodies. We'll all of us be amputees by the time the sun returns to us—a pack of sniveling, scurvied cripples.

No word from either search party. I would organize a third search party to search for the two missing search parties, but there are just five of us here, and I am the only one with two serviceable legs and feet, arms and hands. Really, I feel like chief attendant at a leper colony.

CAPTAIN'S LOG, NOVEMBER 22

Funeral obsequies for Mr. Mallaby today. My bedridden mates hobbled outside where we gathered round a memorial plaque and sang hymns. What with the coughing and slobbering of the men, and the groans of the wind, it was difficult, but we did manage a fairly respectable job of "Art thou weary, art thou languid?"—one of my personal favorites. Young Harlan Hawkins wept as I read "ashes to ashes, dust to dust, ice to ice" (I thought the insertion quite apposite), and scattered the remaining strands of Mr. Mallaby's furs to the wind. It was a pitiable sight indeed—the poor boy swabbing at the frozen tears with his right stump as the soul of his valiant shipmate was set free to be gathered to the bosom of his Maker. The boy's own soul, I'm afraid, will not be long with us either.

LOST ON THE FLOES

The wind howls a gale, the cold shatters steel, splinters wood, transubstantiates flesh to ice. Misshapen ice-hummocks rear up like bad dreams, gray and ghostly in the perennial dark. All living things perish here: only the ice belt lives on—thrives—in the searing winds and falling temperatures.

The search parties, having found one another, are faced with a secondary problem: finding their way back. Their progress for the past six hours has been geometrical—on feet long dead, they have plodded out the shaky hypotenuses of a dozen right triangles, one atop the other. They are drunk with the cold, enraptured with it; cold no longer, they lie down to rest. Pekiutlik Lookout (known variously as Pauce Point) lies but half a mile south of them. Half a mile through the black moonscape of the Arctic Night.

NATURAL SELECTION

In his igloo at the Etah settlement Kresuk and his neighbors are lounging about naked, skin on fur, sunning in the prodigious heat put out by their seal-blubber lamps. At this particular moment Kresuk is bending over to display the tiny circular scar on his anak, the badge of his first encounter with the gaunt men. The badge of his later encounters with the gaunt men dangles beneath his chin: a necklace of red wooden buttons, glass beads and gold pocket watches. His neighbors are threading similar necklaces, chipping away at the icy floor with their steel knives, trying their teeth against the smoky pewter mugs. They look up as Kresuk begins retelling the story of the wound, a story they've heard as many as ninety-seven times. They are fascinated nonetheless. Beads, knives, and mugs drop, mouths hang open. And pairs of quick black eyes follow the necklace twisting and slapping against Kresuk's breastbone as he pantomimes the action of his sealhunt. When he speaks, the gibbous cheeks part to reveal his smile, and his eyes flash like headlights beneath the fleshy lids.

When the tale is finished and Metek sits up to tell his story of the great winged whale that brought the gaunt men, the others turn back to their beads, knives, mugs. Kresuk stretches out and begins picking at his sealhaunch. He chews thoughtfully, only half-attending his friend's narrative, his mind on the glory he's won, glory that will pass down through generations. He sees himself a king, his sons princes. It is then that Sip-su raises himself and waddles over to his father, where he squats to deposit a turd, wet and shapeless, on Kresuk's foot. The friends laugh. Ooniak stares down at her toe. And Kresuk explodes, slaps the fat-headed child across the igloo—Sip-su totters, spins off the kotluk, scalds himself, wails. The neighbors look down at their beads and laps, faces elongate, and fight to suppress chuffles and snorts while Kresuk pulls on his furs, orders Ooniak to dress the child. Wordless, he snatches up the screeching Sip-su and crawls out the door. The old men nod.

Outside, in the wind so sharp it takes away the child's squalling breath, Kresuk harnesses the dogs, straps the child to his back, and starts off toward Pekiutlik Lookout, tomb of his ancestors.

PLAINT

Driven by the insufferable stench of the accumulated slops, he determines to make a slop-emptying expedition. Doggedly he hefts the slop bucket and doggedly he steps out into the glacial dark: the hairs in his nostrils fuse with his first steaming breath. When he exhales he can hear the vapor crystallize, whisper to the ground in tiny pellets. Already the reeking paste has become a bucket-shaped block, no more offensive than an ice cube. He stops, whale-oil lantern in hand, intent on checking the thermometer for his meteorological records.

As he stoops to clear the glass an exceptionally virulent gust extinguishes his light, and brings to his ears the unmistakable plaint, weak and attentuated, of a child in distress.

He drops the bucket, holds his breath, uncovers his ears (the lobes freeze through instantaneously). Yes, there it is again—borne down on the wind from above, up on Pauce Point!

CAPTAIN'S LOG, JANUARY 5

The Esquimaux child is doing well, fully recovered from the effects of his exposure. I only wish I could say as much for the men. Blackwarp and Hoofer are alternately comatose and delirious; young Harlan Hawkins has contracted erysipelas in his left stump; Bone, who could hardly walk in any case, is suffering from a new attack of frostbite. Yesterday he reeled out to chop wood from our scrap heap to keep the fire going. After half an hour I began to wonder what had become of him, and went out searching. I found him asleep in the snow, his cheek frozen fast to the beam he'd been chopping—it was necessary to hack half his beard away in order to extricate the poor fellow. On one of my downward strokes I inadvertently swiped off his left ear. Little matter: I hardly expect the poor beggar to make it through the night.

The child, though about five or six years of age, appears to be defective mentally, from all indications suffering from mongoloidism. He must be hand-fed, and insists on fouling himself. I can only pity the savage heart that left him to the cold.

CAPTAIN'S LOG, JANUARY 10

Disaster. The dogs have broken loose and got at our cache of pemmican—practically all we had left, better than two hundred pounds, is gone. I've managed to round up five of them, bloated as they are. Four will pull my sledge (or be whipped raw) and the fifth will grace our table. I can't see how we'll survive—we've almost no provisions left, and the night has barely begun.

CAPTAIN'S LOG, JANUARY 11

Bone and Hoofer dead, Blackwarp on the brink. I must leave them in their bunks, as I've barely the strength to drag them outside, and I must conserve my resources for the days ahead. With an interior temperature of $+35°$ F., I do not expect an overly rapid decomposition. Temperature outside at noon today was $-54°$ F.

CAPTAIN'S LOG, JANUARY 21

Mad with hunger. The last two days we've had nothing to eat but a broth made from bits of wood and the more tender portions of Mr. Bone's boots. Blackwarp expired early this morning—there were no hymns, as Harlan Hawkins is in a coma, and the Esquimaux child, my only other companion, can do nothing but wail for food and defecate. Clearly, without edibles, there is no hope for us here. As a result, I've come to a decision—I've determined to strap Hawkins and the child to a sledge drawn by the four curs I've spared (what a temptation it's been to roast them!) and make for the Esquimaux settlement at Etah. When they see the condition we're in, and when they see the child—one of their own—I trust they'll help us.

HEGIRA

A Hero indeed! he triumphantly thinks as he brings the lash down across the muzzles of the four dogs. If only Momma and the girls could see me now! But it is dark as Styx-mist and cold as Proserpine's breath—so cold the thoughts begin to freeze in his head. Beneath his feet the ice is a jagged saw's edge, cutting into each agonizing step, overturning the sledge, abrading the hard pads of the dog's paws as if they were wax. Sip-su and the comatose Hawkins are lashed to the sledge, greatly impeding its progress, and from time to time the dogs stop and begin devouring one another and it is all he can do to whip them back to order. But indomitable, he presses on, a navy fight tune frozen in his cerebrum. Ard! he bellows (he had meant to yell "On you Bastards!" but the wind had driven the words back at him, right down his throat and into his shocked lungs). Soon his fingers will become brittle, and the fluid in his eyes will turn to slush.

AT ETAH

Outside the wind tells of a gale as it sweeps smooth over the glassy surface of the igloo. Inside it is sweating hot, and the three seal-blubber lamps, burning simultaneously, circulate a thick greasy smoke which stings the eyes. In the center of the domed ceiling a black helix winds and dances as it is sucked up through the chimney-piece and out, to rush before the deadly gusts.

Kresuk is sitting on the floor, dressed in furs, breathing heavily. His eyebrows white with frost. The carcass of a big bearded seal is wedged in the narrow entrance passage, its head and whiskers and cold dead eyes at Kresuk's feet. The seal's tail is outside, in the wind and dark, the bloated belly jammed like a cork in the neck of the entranceway. Kresuk turns, tugs at the animal's head. He smiles. He'd been improvident in his early dealings with the gaunt men, trading away half his winter cache of meat for a few buttons and beads. And so he'd been forced out on the dark floes, hungry, hunting. There was no choice about it: Ooniak grumbling, the dogs howling, Metek muttering every time Kresuk stepped next door for dinner. But now he looks down at the seal. And thinks feast.

Then the voices outside: Ooniak, Metek, Metek's woman. Kresuk rises to his knees, works a hand under each flipper and leans back. He can feel the others pushing at the seal's fat flank. There is a moment of inertia, effort in suspension, and then a lewd wet sucking release and Kresuk is on his anak, the seal in his lap, Ooniak and his friends scrambling in: laughing.

Later, his belly full, Kresuk crawls over to Ooniak and lies beside her, the string of beads and watches clacking as he throws himself down. She is rounder than normal. He puts his ear to her stomach, and then barks out a laugh: something is moving, just beneath the skin. He sits up, grinning. Metek says something about sons sturdy as bears. The wind howls. And Kresuk looks down, suddenly startled. Beneath the smooth crystal, inching like an insect, the second hand has begun to trace its way around a watch face, and the watch has begun to tick.

A SOPORIFIC

A soporific, it lulls, soothes, spreads its uterine warmth—and you want to lie down on the floes, tired, ineffably tired, impervious now to the sting of it—bed down right there, on the floes. The child and Hawkins are still lashed down, but stiff as flagpoles: a patina of frost glosses their lips. The dogs have given up, iceblood crusting between their toes: they lie doubled, nose to tail, whimpering, and still in their traces. Have you the strength to crack the whip? Hardly. It's all you can do to grip the sledgehandles, woozy and reeling as you are. But warm, strangely warm, and tired. This is no gale, but gentle windsong, a lullaby in your tired ears. If only to lie down . . . for just a moment.

Daniel Halpern

A PERSONAL INTRODUCTION TO BIRDING:
MISCELLANEOUS NOTES

> For all his purple, the purple bird must have
> Notes for his comfort that he may repeat
> Through the gross tedium of being rare.
>
> —WALLACE STEVENS

1.

There are some who own birds and prepare cages in an elaborate way, and soon the birds feel relaxed and trusting and will sing short passages, or talk, or spread their wings to display their colors, if they are colorful birds, and bright.

2.

You might not think of keeping a bird unless you live alone and spend a great deal of time at home. Learning to feed birds is not difficult and cleaning up after them becomes habit after a few months. As their constant chatter, at times shrill, depending on the species, can be trying, it is imperative that you require a presence stranger than that of a dog's or cat's (fish are merely self-contained electrical units). Most of us have been trained to keep the practical in mind, thus making the unpredictable (and uncontrollable) noise of birds unacceptable, as well as their general upkeep.

3.

Of course, birds can be allowed to fly around the house, and there are those who like something erratic in the air, who have allowed their compulsions to ignore the untimely bodily functions that occur so randomly.

4.

Out in nature most of the birds you find are earth-colored and unremarkable. It often happens when you are driving that suddenly, out the side window, you see a flash of some primary color, a splash of real color, but when you look a bird is flying at an angle that prevents any further display of color.

5.

On one of those long-deserved weekends away from the city, you regain consciousness two hours later than my normal hour of reckoning. The smell of coffee arrives, along with onions softening in butter and Canadian bacon. But as you lie there in the cool, slightly damp sheets, it is the sound of birds that tells you you're in the country. This is because birds are involved in what you know.

6.

But can they sleep with you?

7.

It is possible that birds can become affectionate after spending time with you, especially if you've had them from the egg. They tend to become "one-man" pets, snapping at casual outsiders and those uninvolved in the rites of feeding, which is something you'll want to keep in mind if there are children to consider. This is what cages are for, although most birds will understand they have been placed behind bars for unsympathetic reasons, and will adopt the symptoms of depression except during parties—although they will again become morose immediately after the last guest has finally gone—even if one of the guests does not leave.

8.

African grays are the smartest of the talking birds. They possess gray plumage, a white chest, and a tail that is of the brightest vermilion. Green parrots are sweeter as a general rule, less temperamental, but are also more common and so less of an oddity in the home of those whose purpose in owning a bird is primarily entertainment.

9.

Have you ever listened carefully to what people say to talking birds when they think they are alone?

10.

I once knew a parrot who repeated everything he heard during the day after the lights went out for the night: the maid talking on the phone, the service men, the doorbell ringing, the faucets going on and off, the cabinets slamming shut, the old pet cat, and most importantly, the instructions for his own feeding.

11.

Bird guides are often where potential bird lovers begin the romance that surfaces only years later—the pictures, the Latin names, the exact descriptions, the absolute knowledge in those guides whose names themselves are part of the experience:

Looking up: The Bird Watching Handbook
A Watcher's Guide to the Finest Song Birds
Know the Birds on Your Land
What's Up in the Trees

And the information, if at times lacking in the concrete, is always engaging:

BLACK-CAPPED CHICKADEE This plump chickadee needs no introduction. Its call is its name. He is a constant visitor to feeding stations, and will often feed upside down.

BROWN-HEADED COWBIRD A bird with the unusual habit of laying one or more eggs in the nest of other birds. The eggs hatch in a quick ten days—sooner than those of the nest owners. With this head start, the fast-growing cowbird soon monopolizes the nest.

SCARLET TANAGER Identification of this unmistakable bird is obvious.

BROWN TOWHEE This western towhee is as plain brown a bird as any.

And then there are the descriptions of their songs: *chewink*, which identifies the Rufous-Sided Towhee. The short nasal *car-car* of the Coastal Fish Crow. The low-pitched, hoarse *quock* of the Black-Crowned Night Heron. A quickly achieved *pill-will-willet* of the ordinary pasture bird, and so on.

12.

The first bird I heard talk was a myna named Señor Excellent at the Farmer's Market on Fairfax Avenue in Los Angeles. I remember being taken there as a child, and although I was certainly interested in watching candy being made, the elaborate fruit displays, as well as eating a little of this and that, it was our stop in front of Señor Excellent that was the important event of the visit. His vocabulary was limited to a shrill catcall, a few opening bars of a song, and a number of *hellos,* varying in intensity and pitch. What I remember best is not what he said, but the wisdom and irony in the eyes of that myna bird. We would all stand around whistling and clicking, and inevitably one of us would eventually send out a few words of endearment. Señor Excellent would just look at us all, his expression one of agony and disgust, his a life of witnessing the utterances of the human race.

Frank Gannon

MY LOVE STORY

What can you say about a girl in a commercial that's not on anymore?

I remember all the little things about her. How her plastic wrap had a mind of its own. We would sit together and laugh over that, and she would tease me because my plastic wrap never showed any intelligence at all.

I thought that our times together were times when everything was absolutely right. No matter how long I live, I don't think I'll ever feel that way again.

I remember the first time we met. It was a Tuesday night. I had just played softball. We had lost, and I was still in my uniform. I got a beer and turned on the TV. Then I saw her. She turned around, looked right at me, and said, "Hey, I think we're going to make a pretty good team."

I didn't see her for a week. I thought that there was going to be nothing between us, ships passing in the night, and all that. Then I sat down on a Thursday night and turned on the TV. There she was. She was born to rock and that's just what she was doing. She was on the street. She was on the ceiling. She was rocking. Then some jerk drove by and splashed her with water.

It made me so mad, but she calmed me down.

When I think of her sometimes, all I can see is this series of photographs and some vapid music. Every time I look at another photograph, besides the vapid music, there's this sound like a 35mm camera advancing, and then another photograph of her. My love is a baby.

My love is sitting in the mud at the seashore. My love is graduating from someplace.

She's eating all the ice cream while I'm out and then, when I get back, telling me that, if she had it to do all over again, she would.

And then smiling.

I remember her hitting a terrible shot at tennis and then telling me that she can't play well because she's bothered by hemorrhoids. But then she goes back to the clubhouse with a friend of hers and, when she comes back, she's hitting winners with just a tremendous amount of backspin. Then she looks right at me and smiles.

My love. Built to last because she was put together right the first time.

Running down this enormous spiral staircase in slow motion, her hair was so beautiful it always looked like she had just stepped out of a salon, which was, of course, impossible. You could say that nothing was in her class, at least not in her price range.

She knew how good life could be. She knew how to celebrate the moments of her life with some coffee. She did so much so well. She was so versatile that she looked good, no matter where I took her. All this, and she had more than enough power for almost anything you might be confronted with.

She had more than just a beautiful look, she had a beautiful feeling. I could never tell with her. Which of her fingernails were still wet? They all looked shiny to me.

She was that kind of person: extraordinary.

She was trouble-free and perfectly stunning. Everywhere she went, her form followed function. Everywhere she went she turned heads because she was so sleek and everybody could tell that.

She knew how to turn exercise into fun. She knew how to turn cleaning the toilet into hilarity. She knew how to turn cat food into a feast. She knew how to turn a visit to the dentist into a big opportunity to let the world know that love lasts forever.

She knew everything. She was good at the extras because she was so good at the essentials.

Then came . . . well, the rest.

I remember that day when I asked her why she was calling Gilbert and Gottleib, and I remember her telling me that she thought that she deserved *something* for all the pain, heartache, and suffering that I had caused her. And also quite a bit for the internal injuries. And also, what about the loss of all the time that she had spent with me?

But what hurt most was she didn't even have the nerve to tell me herself. No, she hired John Madden to do it.

Preserve your memories, they're all that's left you. Because this is as real as it gets.

Veronica Geng

At the time (spring 1988, I think), this seemed like a much-needed attack on the slave economy and on cultural nostalgia's suppression of history, plus a couple of Bette Davis jokes. My goal was to write something that would actually be embarrassing to read: possibly that's why no one would publish it.

DIXIE'S

> Appetite-whetting, competent, delicious recipes that have made Southern cooking famous the world over.
> —*Southern Cook Book*

Southern cooking is perhaps preeminent among the regional American cuisines that have lately captured the imaginations of top restaurateurs and demanding diners. And at Dixie's Home Away from Home, we offer those classic dishes right here in the heart of New York City, prepared and served by professionals in an atmosphere with all the honeyed charm and hospitality of home, evoking the Old South in all its legendary magnolia-scented competence.

First and foremost, when we publish our address in the phone book or a restaurant guide, you can rest assured that our location is exactly where we claim it is. Because if there's one tradition honored above all in the historic Southland's code of courtesy, it's that well-bred ladies and gentlemen don't say a place is at one address when it's really somewhere else altogether. So no hitch of that sort will prevent your evening from getting off to a gracious start. Just as with your own home, when you step out of your taxi or limousine—lo and behold, we're just where you thought. The number painted on the white pillar of our ante-bellum-style portico is, in fact, none other than the one we said it would be. Some incorrect number has not been put on there by a carpetbagging sign-painter unfamiliar with the area, nor is our publicity handled by an unreliable debutante with a whirl of other numbers going around in her head. Everything having to do with Dixie's is done by our family of employees, whose training hearkens back to the no-nonsense efficiency of the great plantation system of yore.

And once inside Dixie's, you'll find we're not about to renege on the impression we gave you when you made your reservation—that we are open for business, sure 'nuff. There is no chance that the chef abruptly took the night off to defend his sister-in-law's honor in a pistol duel with one of the bucks from the Julep Club who had the unconscionable audacity to use her name in public. All that is simply a myth. Chef Tarleton's sister-in-law retains a lawyer who is perfectly capable of handling the routine paperwork involved in filing suit for defamation of character, leaving the chef free to show up for work every night at the appointed time. And whatever personal problems Chef Tarleton may have, there is no question that once he sets foot in our adequately equipped kitchen, he becomes an effective function-ary who handles the basic tools of his trade with as much adeptness as can humanly be expected from a man of his bulk.

"Dixie" (not a real person) is a name we firmly believe is viable for its purpose—to conjure the picturesque sun-drenched common sense of the Old Confederacy's economic structure. Our hostess is named Virginia, and she'll guide you to your wisteria-twined table. No awkward surprises where she's concerned! You're advised well in advance that her museum-quality reproduction of a Richmond ma-tron's satin ball gown circa 1850 has been arranged for under the auspices of a certified accountant, who will amortize your share of the cost against your annual bar tabs. And Virginia herself will be in-stantly familiar to you as the type of aristocratic belle whose manner and physiognomy trace their lineage all the way back to lemon-sucking fanatic General Stonewall Jackson bearing up as well as he could under stress fatigue near Mechanicsville. She can be polite, and is financially insecure enough so she isn't going to suddenly leave you stranded, searching for your table, while she dashes away to eat barbecue with a bunch of handsome, high-spirited beaus.

And talking of barbecue—is there any better reason to come to Dixie's Home Away from Home than to eat? All our specialties are considered valid examples of regional ingredients and preparation from the Maryland Tidewater to the Louisiana Bayou, and their names are arrayed for your consideration on our menu as legibly as printing know-how permits. Place your order with one of our clean servants. (On special nights, Virginia then reappears to taunt you by saying there isn't any of anything you want—and what could be more comforting than the predictability of her behavior, stemming as it does from early experiences with her father? Just relax and enjoy this home-style mind game, played as ably as our house pianist picks out Stephen Foster songs on the recently tuned upright.)

Surely the primal fear of every gourmet is that there will be some clumsy mixup in the kitchen, rendering the food troublesome or dangerous. At Dixie's, you don't have to worry. No shiftless *sous-chef* is going to bump a pot with his elbow and send the Hopping John plummeting into the sweet-potato pie. All our kitchen help have been examined by a physician to ascertain that they have normal control over their muscular reflexes. What's more, every condiment is properly labeled in easy-to-read letters of the standard alphabet, so there's only the remotest possibility (statistically meaningless) that a secretive, no-'count apprentice harboring a grudge against folks who eat out could slip the pastry-chef a bottle of hot sauce zesty enough to blow your head off when you dive into the Lady Baltimore cake.

"Sakes alive!" (as qualified researchers tell us was once common parlance on the verandahs under moss-draped oaks pruned with the proficiency of those bygone days when all the world knew "King Cotton" as a synonym for sound management)—the entire staff of Dixie's is equal to just about *any* occasion you could dream up. Suppose you're sitting there, you and your sophisticated Yankee fiancée, basking in the afterglow of a meal, sipping a liqueur of plausible pedigree, when all at once a woman from a neighboring table comes over and sinks to the floor at your feet with an ardor potently redolent of inconvenience, her white organza dress and petticoats floating and frothing around her like a sea of beaten egg-whites, her sweet young face flushed and shining up at you with sheer adoration as she says, "I can't believe it's you here. I dreamed about it so long—a lifetime. No, longer than that. It must be an eternity since that first night you kissed me, in the vestibule after we had dinner at that Italian place. I'd loved you for so long—I know now I always loved you. And when you put your arm around me, and then with your other arm you turned me toward you so I was right up against you, and held me close, and kissed me on the lips—you were so brave and strong, and the whole world fell away from under our feet and there was nothin' but us, way out in a great big pure and silent space. The most sublime kiss of my life. The most sacred. That's the truth. And that's why I said that silly thing about my hatpin and ran away. Because I was lackin' in courage. I thought it might all be an illusion. But *that* was the illusion. I know in my heart you felt the same way. You always did and always will. You love me. You know you love me. Don't be afraid. I'm not—not anymore. I learned my lesson, all these months when life was supposed to go on as usual and all I knew was knowin' I'd find you again. I'm wearin' this dress for you. I wear it every night, prayin' I'll run into you and you'll say I look nice. I knew it would happen sooner or later. And now I'm on my knees to you, so you'll know how humbly, how completely I'm offerin' myself to you. Nobody can ever see into my soul the way you do—I see that now. I've always seen it, but I was too proud to tell you. Proud and ignorant and afraid. And spiteful and mean. But now I've come to my senses, and I'm pleadin' with you from the bottom of my heart—tell me you know you love me, just as I'm tellin' you right out where everybody can see and hear, includin' your little nose-in-the-air Yankee. Tell her you know me inside out and love me more than you've ever loved any woman who ever walked the earth. And then take me in your arms again, say you knew all along it was goin' to turn out right, let me soothe away your troubles and make love to you and look after you the way only I know how. All of you—your sweet body, your fine clear mind, your true and noble spirit. Oh, I know you're not perfect. Though you sure know how to pour on the charm when you're so inclined. You know I don't care what way you are. Just so I can see you there. You inspire me and give me courage to face the truth. You make me see how I can be all grown up and still as trustin' as a child. You know we can't turn back now. This is serious. I'm beggin' you—don't say it was nothin'. It will never, ever be nothin'. And that's why I know it's right to give my love to you now, tonight, with all the tenderness and abandon and loyalty you know you see here in my eyes. Cat got your tongue?"

Were this to occur at Lutèce—the heave-ho! But at Dixie's, among the legacies we still cherish from the Old South is the obligation to let everyone choose his own destiny, with all the free will that practicality allows. Our capable bouncers will await your say-so.

Roy Blount, Jr.

WHERE'S THE BEEF?

Some observers feel that this expression's extraordinary vogue during the Reagan administration reflects a repressed mass suspicion that everything solid melts into air nowadays.

I believe the truth to be somewhat different. I believe "Where's the beef?" to be a contraction of "Where's the bee feces?"

Let me explain.

Months before the hamburger people began using "Where's the beef?" in their ads, the sanguine new concept of bee feces settled into the American consciousness, whether we quite realized it or not.

On May 31, 1983, Dr. Matthew S. Meselson of Harvard, one of the nation's leading experts on chemical and biological warfare, announced that "yellow rain," which the United States government persists in seeing as a toxic substance sprayed by Communist planes in Southeast Asia, was quite possibly just bee feces. Toxic—but *innocent*—bee feces.

Or bee excrement, bee waste, bee droppings. All those terms were used in press accounts. But "bee feces" was the most euphonious. Dangerous toxins would indeed appear to have grown on the substance found in Southeast Asian trees, but if that substance was what this expert thought it was, it was dropped by bees, not Bolsheviks.

This hypothesis may not have been comforting to the United States government or to anyone living near large concentrations of bees, but it was comforting to everyone else. Maybe other dread things were actually bee feces. Warheads, for instance. The deficit. The thoughts of Louis Farrakhan. Bee feces might account for a great deal. *"Cherchez la merde des abeilles"* is how they would put it in France.

You can't say "Where's the bee feces?" on television. Nor can you sell products with it. It was shortened, and co-opted, to fit into a hamburger campaign.

There is one more twist to the story, however. The United States Government may be experimenting with bees for military purposes.

Not professedly, to be sure. The colony of 3,300 bees that was sent up above the earth's atmosphere aboard the space shuttle *Challenger* were supposedly there to determine whether honeybees could function in weightlessness.

They could. Except for one thing. In the box where they were kept throughout the week-long voyage, they built a nice hive. Their queen laid eggs. But when the bee box was opened after its return to earth, the bees abruptly sped away. Minutes later, they returned.

It seems that bees can relieve themselves only on the wing, outside the hive. In their box, the space bees' keeper told reporters, "there was not a speck of excrement. They just held it for seven days."

I am afraid that the United States Government, as part of the projected new "Star Wars" defense system, is planning to stockpile constipated bees.

Nancy Willard

This poem was omitted from William Blake's Inn, *a book of poems for children (Harcourt Brace Jovanovich, 1981) because I felt the river rabbit's daughter was too close to the porters in "A Rabbit Reveals My Room." Also, the tone seemed different from the other poems in a way I couldn't put my finger on.*

THE RABBIT'S DAUGHTER
DESIRES SILVER PAWS

"I've heard it said, when travelers meet,
that good luck lives in rabbit's feet,"
the river rabbit told his daughter
skimming sunbeams off the water.
Watching water, she was struck
by the fickleness of luck.
"Just suppose my feet wear thin.
Where is my good fortune then?
Time will take both fur and feather.
Silver paws will last forever.
To William Blake I'll take my best
linen cloak and woolen vest,
my bamboo cage, my two jackdaws
in fair exchange for silver paws."

Blake was eating black-eyed peas
when something small embraced his knees.

"Welcome bird, and welcome beast!
Share my fire and join my feast!"
When she told him her desire
Blake looked grave and poked the fire.

"When good friends meet face to face
silver gives a cold embrace.
I've heard it said that children weep
if rocked by silver paws to sleep.
Silver well becomes a king
but fur is soft and comforting.
But by my bowl of beaten gold
and by my supper growing cold
and by magic's secret laws,
you shall have your silver paws.
Take your presents back again.
Paws of silver on a chain
shall be yours for luck, that you
may use your paws and keep them too."

Leonard Michaels

THE SCANDAL OF HAMLET

So many spend their lives talking about books
That it seems a desirable thing; easier than digging
A ditch or doing work you have to get right, like that of
Accountants and cooks. But why, in all this verbal stewing,
Has nobody said exactly what, in Act V, Hamlet is doing?
It's been over three centuries since he appeared,
For no apparent reason, in the graveyard with Horatio.
No; not for Ophelia's burial—he hasn't heard she's dead.
Isn't it possible, being in the graveyard, he himself is dead?
Ophelia's hothead brother, Laertes, leaps into her grave
As if he had the right. Hamlet, horrified, wants naturally
To fight. He leaps into it, too, and they begin to rave
About who more deeply loves this ground. Hamlet hates
The "bravery" of Laertes' grief, but not a word he says
Is on the money. Only moments earlier he'd asked the funny
Gravedigger how long he'd been at his work, fooling around.

Since "the very day that young Hamlet was born," he says.
That clown, he be digging you grave, Hamlet, since the
Day you born. Is there proof Shakespeare means this
Earthen roof for Hamlet? A clue appears in Act II.
"Will you walk out o' the air, my lord?" asks Polonius.
Hamlet says, "Into my grave?" Act V begins with Hamlet walking
    out
Of the air into his grave. It is plainly what he's doing.
He no longer even sounds the same, referring to himself
As Hamlet. Just the name, the name, not the living son
But the ghost of the hideous ghost who stalked Act I.
Too much woe, too much memento mori.
Demonic Osric, the apposite fop, invites him then
To the duel against Laertes' poisoned tool.
Poor sweet prince, "fat and scant of breath"
—in fact quite dead—must go.
But we persist, like garrulous clients
To their analysts, In talking so.

Jonathan Baumbach

AN INTEREST IN SENTENCES

They had met apparently on the Russian steppes or perhaps on the sliding sands of the Sahara, one traveling by camel, the other, if our reports are accurate, by Fiat. They were both at work on generously commissioned travel books, their approaches as one might determine by their modes of travel, philosophically disparate. After they had embraced in the European manner, Barash mentioned that he had dipped into Anthelm's last novel which had been sent to him as a gift. "And?" said A with the pained casualness he struck up when mention of his novel was in the air. "I liked what I read of it," said B, his unenthusiasm showing despite exaggerated attempts to disguise it, "but it disturbs me that you seem to have lost your interest in the sentence. I'm talking about the sentence as sentence."

    "I think," said A, feeling some defense necessary, "that I am still interested in the sentence as sentence. Maybe you didn't get far enough into the book. I've refined my language, distilled the sentence until its economy is as close to absolute as I can make it."

B's benign smile beamed brighter as if embarrassed for his fellow traveler. "What I mean is, you have sentences in your book about the weather."

"The weather?" A couldn't remember any descriptions of weather in his novel, but he supposed there must have been one or two. "When you write a novel, you plan, I suppose, never to mention the weather."

B shrugged good-naturedly, whistled idly as Lawrence of Arabia might have done (in his day) when confronted on his own sliding sands with unredeemable muddle. "If I wrote a sentence about the weather," he said, "it wouldn't be about the weather." He gestured the uncompromising nature of his unwritten sentence. "I hope you don't think I'm trying to put you down. The issue is philosophical not personal."

A, though he no longer loved the book under question—his deepest affections had transferred to his current project—felt protective of its reputation. If they were anywhere else but the Sahara (or the Russian steppes), he would have walked away in symbolic protest. Instead, he said, "Sometimes, and I wouldn't presume to include you in this generalization, we project our own deficiencies as readers onto the text in hand, which may explain your unacceptable remark on my novel's treatment of weather, which in its own way is like perceiving baby swans out of context as ugly ducklings, a classic though nevertheless embarrassing misperception, for which . . ."

B, who was not all the time, not exclusively, insensitive to the frailer feelings of others, let the subject, which was the heart of his pleasure, slip away.

The two men, conscious of their own spoken music, exchanged paragraphs in the desert until other urgencies intervened. At which time they said good-bye, embraced again, and went off into the greater world to tell their stories, each writing down at first opportunity (with an interest in sentences) his own very different version of their encounter.

William Matthews

RAIN

It wasn't one of those tropical storms that comes at four in the afternoon and routes everyone from pool to bar, but whose last damp stains have evaporated from the poolside and walkways by six. It was a daylong rain robbing from the tourists one day of winter vacation. It was gray and steady and a staunch enemy of cheer. It was like a long harangue, one man in the bar thought; and another thought for over an hour, dreamily and sullenly, about the years in his youth when no man with a good job or who wanted to look as if he held a good job would go downtown, in any season or weather, without wearing a hat.

The rain came down at a constant tilt and one of the men in the bar asked the waiter his name.

"Armando."

"Well, Armando, what happens around here on Christmas Eve, anyhow?"

"We have already hang the lights from the street poles, and we have a small parade, and then we are at home with families."

This news led his listeners straight to silence.

"If you like," Armando began, and he looked embarrassed and full of resolve, both. "If you like," he began again, "you can come to my family and house the day before Christmas."

The idea of a harangue had appealed to Frank, because it led him to think of those long Fidel Castro speeches we liked to deride, we Americans. We'd heard how they lagged on—soldiers in dress uniform at parade attention, one crumpling now and then onto the tarmac in the blistering heat while the bearded one droned on like a long flight. . . .

"Armando, are you sure?"

"I would be honored," Armando said, and stood a little straighter.

Pastries, thought Frank, there'd be lots of pastries. "Perhaps we could each bring a bottle of wine." Gene looked at him slantwise.

"I have a bottle of wine," said Armando, and then he was called to another table.

Frank and Gene barely knew one another. They'd just been nursing ("How are we doing?") a few beers one sodden afternoon, and next thing they knew they were in it together. Then Armando was back, and this time he looked at Gene. "You can come to my house at eleven o'clock with a taxi."

"Eleven in the morning?" Gene blurted.

Armando giggled. "No, hell no, eleven at night."

"Well," said Frank, "we'd have to ask our wives."

"My wife will be honored to have you to our family and house." And then he was gone to another table.

"Here's how you tell the taxi." Armando was back. "Go on Avenue Benito Juarez until Pemex, you know Pemex? Go left, go a mile, and I will meet you there and tell the taxi the rest."

"At eleven?" Gene asked. Frank could barely hear him.

"When you like."

The wind yawed a few degrees and the noise of the rain rose a little in pitch and then slurred back down a little in pitch. It felt like it had been raining all day, all week, raining inside the plane on the long ride south, raining back when men wore hats to work or to look for work, hopeful and smoldering.

Armando wore a thin rind of sweat above his upper lip and waited for an answer. Frank's wife was reading and Gene's wife was reading. Rain pocked the pool and streaked the palm fronds.

Armando was called to another table.

"It can't rain forever," Frank said to Gene, and he was right.

James Kaplan

AVALON

Four forty-five. Harry Minsky, the oldest member of Wonderland Indoor Tennis, in Bonnie Brae, New Jersey, is holding a fanned-out deck of cards before a bored audience of two. Harry—tiny, slender, mustached, dapper—is a gentleman, a remnant of another era. He brims with songs, vaudeville turns, and that bygone quantity, pep. He wears an extravagant rug, like the pelt of some white animal: on him, somehow, it looks good.

"Nothing up my sleeve," Harry is saying, although he's wearing a tennis shirt. His audience consists primarily of two younger men, Dick Schwartz and Jerry Nussbaum. In the corner, Larry Blatt, smoking a cigarette and watching a cooking show, gives some side-of-the-eye attention. Dick, rubicund and bilious, smiles indulgently at Harry. Dick is putting off going home. His wife Sue is off at another one of her organizations, and has left Dick's dinner in a covered dish in the refrigerator, with microwave instructions taped to the lid. Jerry Nussbaum, on the other hand, has never been one to go through the motions. The olive-skinned, piercing-eyed cardiologist is only watching Harry because he has nothing else to do. Jerry's in his own version of limbo—waiting for a court. He keeps glancing anxiously through the picture window to see when something will open up.

"And now, with the magic words—" Harry passes a hand, its fingers disproportionately long and slender, over the cards—"*ekha dekha befayge gomekha.*" He plucks out a card with his first two fingers and a flick of the wrist.

"The three of clubs," Harry says, lightly rolling the *r.*

Dick's forced smile suddenly goes slack. "Hey," he says. "How the hell'd you do that, Harry?" Jerry, one eye on the courts, is clapping—slowly, sarcastically.

"Sorry," Harry says. "I never reveal my secrets."

Mort Handelman has just come through the door from the courts. "Hey Harry," he calls. "Now fix my serve."

"I only perform tricks—not miracles."

"You're off?" Jerry asks Mort. Dick and Harry look at each other: this is Jerry's stock line. Club joke: one of the older members drops dead (God forbid) of a heart attack while hitting a serve; Jerry—a cardiologist, remember—runs over, stands over the body, and yells, "You're off?"

Mort nods. "I'm off, Jerry." Jerry quickly gathers his things and gets up.

"Hey, where's Morris, Harry?" Dick asks.

Harry looks at his watch, concerned. "I don't know," he says. "He should've been here at four."

"Did you call?"

"The phone's out of order. For a change."

"Maybe he's on the way."

Harry shakes his head. "This isn't like Morris," he says.

Dick smiles mischievously. "Maybe he's getting laid, Harry."

Harry exhales through his nose. "Morris?" he says. He reaches up and—discreetly—adjusts his rug.

In the corner, Larry Blatt is watching a commercial as if his life depended on it.

In this, the last week of the winter season, Wonderland has been less and less crowded. It's April; soon people will be playing outdoors.

Now in the late afternoons it's light outside, and the extra brightness, as the planet once more tilts toward the sun, filters in through the translucent roof panels and lends the four tennis courts a strange, dull interior glow—a little bit, it occurs to Harry, who's staring through the picture window at the courts, like the light inside monkey and lion houses at the zoo. He laughs to himself. The comparison is not inapt. Here there is much of the same behavior—the pacing, the shouting, the displaying. Even the smells! While not precisely zoo-like, they are potent, subtly disturbing. The unaccustomed late-afternoon light warms the corrugated roof, and the huge, hangar-ish space underneath heats up so that even with the two emergency exit doors propped open (and the startling, weedy, pebbly, harshly daylit real world revealed to the members—next door, at the factory, workers at their lathes are clearly visible at the windows), and the two ventilator fans going full blast, the air on the courts is dense, tropical. The few players who still show up these last afternoons quickly get drenched with sweat; they complain. They're good complainers, Harry reflects; complainers for the sport of it, but this complaining is a reflex, a vestige. Few of the men seem to remember midwinter, when, with the doors firmly closed, the fans off, and black outside the translucent ceiling panels, the temperature on the courts often hovered around forty-five. The big heater would cut on, it seemed, about once an hour. Sometimes you could actually see your breath. Indoors! *Then,* Harry thinks, there was something to complain about.

Sometimes, last winter, there wasn't even enough hot water in the showers. All right, the club was a bargain. Four courts, a locker room and showers; a Mr. Coffee and a water cooler and someone's old black-and-white TV in the lounge. Period. *Haimish.* But no one expected chintz. The towels, over the winter, grew fewer and fewer; the ones remaining look rattier and rattier. Harry wonders: Is the place up for sale?

These late afternoons, the light lengthens eerily. The members, freshly showered, walk out the door not into freezing darkness, but a strange new world of soft wind, secondary colors, bewitching odors. Almost mockingly, the clump of sticks in the patch of earth by the door has turned into an odd, brightly colored bush, exuding a haunting fragrance that none of these men (and their experience with gardens, or at least gardeners, is considerable) seems ever to have smelled before. It is almost, almost, as if something new, something unspeakable, were about to happen. But in the parking lot, by way of contradiction, sit the powerful cars, angle-parked, their monogrammed license plates like heraldic shields.

Today is the last day. Wednesday—doctors' day. On a midwinter

Wednesday, Harry remembers, you couldn't get into the lounge with a crowbar, so thick were the anesthesiologists, cardiologists, periodontists, gynecologists, internists, psychiatrists, radiologists—there is even one chiropractor in the club, Stanley Stern, held in curiously high esteem by his usually suspicious colleagues, many of whom have gone to him on the sly and had tennis ailments cleared up "like magic." Just last Wednesday, Harry recalls, it was sunny and warm, and attendance was pitifully sparse. Today, though, on the final day of the club's existence, it's been cold and raining—pouring—all day, and the place was mobbed again, for one last time. "You're here? You're here?" they kept saying to each other, and then, "Everybody's here!" The waiting list for courts, on the chalkboard, was immense. Every new arrival, as he walked through the door and looked automatically at the board, slapped his forehead and said—good-naturedly—"Oy!"

These doctors, Harry thinks, are admirable men! All day they've swaggered into the lounge, beaming with goodwill, tennis bags in hand. There is nothing for the self-esteem, apparently, like being a specialist. They wear suits, but with neckties loosened. Many of them have beepers on their hips, slung like holsters. What could be more serious, more solemn? *If you call, I will come.* But today solemnity of a different sort is in order: tennis is to be played. Today is reunion and farewell. Well, not exactly farewell, since a great many of the men belong to the same outdoor clubs, and will certainly meet again in that next world, the sweet afterlife of summer and clay. The real truth of the matter, Harry realizes, is that nobody will much miss anybody else. This is a competitive lot. But isn't a farewell of another order, a less acknowledged one, going on here? For didn't many a doctor and businessman, walking with wet hair out into the freezing dark of three months ago, breathe a small, contented sigh? Isn't what we desire most deeply—what we expect—continuance? Well, any one of them might have said, but isn't it continuing? Tennis, that is. You don't mourn a building. These are sentimental men, but only to a point. Look, they would say, at the old guys—the Harrys, the Morrises, the Irvings. Still playing! At sixty-five, seventy, even eighty! Game as hell and nobody's patsies, they move around the courts like cagy old cats, blocking back even the hardest slams with their oversized rackets, holding their own against anybody in doubles. Has any one of them ever keeled over? Do we keep oxygen at the club? The answer is an emphatic no. See? they would say, these men of the second generation, the Jerrys, the Larrys, the Steves—it goes on. Nothing is ending.

But it ends, even as they stand in the agora of the lounge, in tennis whites instead of chlamyses, discussing the events of the day (all the while keeping a close watch, out of the corners of their eyes, on the availability of courts). Harry Minsky has watched them all afternoon. The first of their number to go went silently. Back in his three-piece suit, hair glistening, he simply threw his towel in the pail and walked out the door. Without saying good-bye. And no one said good-bye to him. The same as every other day, only today there'd be no tomorrow. Was this superstition? Or merely distraction?

Five-fifty. "What'd you do with your silver, hold on?" Arnie Glickman, in the roofing business, is asking Sam Wachtel, an ortho-dontist. Sam nods, ruefully. Monty West, the brain man, recently divorced, is showing all comers a portfolio of his color photographs, enlarged to giant size and mounted on cardboard. The pictures are of gaudy Western sunsets, intricate mesas, autumn leaves, reflecting lakes. Monty's face is hopeful and boyish as he displays his work. "Gorgeous, gorgeous," the men mumble, reverently. "Not a nude in the bunch," grumbles the irritable Jack Pearl, slouched on the sofa, having just been bumped from his court at 5–3, his favor. "I stopped looking at trees when I was twelve." Ed Watts, the psychiatrist, one of the two black members, is throwing his towel into the pail. Ed is wearing a magnificent gray suit. "Ed's dressed for one of his hundred-and-thirty-an-hour patients," someone says brightly, an affirmative-action needler, and Ed smiles—but with a certain ambivalence. The note is flat. He hurries out, past the emptied candy machine, past the disconnected pay phone, without looking back.

And Morris is still nowhere in sight.

Harry presses his nose against the picture window. On court two, Al Levine is starting again. Al is playing Fred Rosen, the contractor. This is a match! Fred is built like one of his trucks, all chest and arms and shoulders and head, no hips. He chews gum while he plays. He hits like a boxer, jumps toward the net, his black nostrils flaring, sweat pouring off his nose, the gold *chai* around his neck dancing. There is no chink in Fred's game; playing him is like being attacked by a brick wall. Al, on the other side, looks like a gladiator with battle nerves. There is a strained intrepidness in his eyes. His hair is crew-cut, the skull underneath narrow and mesomorphic. His nose is long and bellicose. He hits every shot with every bit of his strength, which is considerable, but the ones that Fred doesn't put away are sailing over the baseline. Al has just double-faulted, and now he stands panting, glaring to his left, at court four, where, in the midst of a spirited but inept doubles match, Howie Greenberg, a genial blabbermouth, has dropped his racket. By some freak of physics—could it be anything else?—the racket has landed on its side and balanced there. "Oh my God!" Howie crows, with delight. "Do you see that? Can you believe it?"

"Shut up!" Al thunders, two courts away. Al's voice is bass, and in the cavernous enclosure, it reverberates like the roar of a lion in pain or in heat. "Oh my God," someone mutters. "There he goes."

"Shut up!" Al roars, his hands on his hips. "Everybody! Shut up!"

Harry Minsky watches, through the glass. Suddenly he hears a noise, turns and looks at the front door. Nothing. The wind. The door shudders slightly on its frame, then falls closed. Harry presses his lips together, and drops his racket in his bag.

In the locker room, red bodies are emerging from showers, some with towels held modestly before, some not, catkins and bachelor's-buttons. It could almost be a classical mural, a scene from Herculaneum; except that Steve Frishner, combing strands of hair across his bald spot, is holding forth on General Motors. "Are you saying to buy now, Steve?" asks Larry Blatt. Steve holds up a hand. "All I'm saying," he says, "is that it's very low." Larry, still in his tennis clothes, sits in a Naugahyde chair, a hand on his chin, a forced smile wrinkling his cheeks and eyes. The matter, to him, can be nothing but academic. No one knows exactly what he does for a living, if anything, but he drives a beat-up old Volkswagen, an eyesore in the parking lot. Where will he go now in the afternoons?

"I can't believe this," says Phil Weissberg, the neurosurgeon. "Has anybody seen a pair of shoes? Who would take shoes?" He's standing in his shirt, tie, and pants, his feet bare.

Outside the high locker-room windows, the rain has stopped, and new leaves, the color of fresh chlorophyll, tinted orange by the declining sun, brush the glass.

Harry Minsky stands in front of his locker, humming to himself. Maybe Morris forgot. On the court and off, Harry is a model of equanimity. He has seen the Al Levines come and go; he has seen places like this come and go; he has seen too many things come and go. Long, long ago, before he was born, perhaps, Harry learned a secret, one that has enabled him to live to an unheard-of age, to be sublimely happy. But it's a secret, and he hasn't told anyone, not any of his five wives, all of them gone now, or his nineteen children, most of them gone now, too. Harry is a hundred and thirty-four years old. He hardly believes it himself. He tells people he's seventy-eight.

"Hey Harry," Phil Weissberg says. "What the hell song is that?"

"That I'm humming?" Harry says. "It's an old one; I doubt you've heard of it. Let me see if I can think of the words. 'Da da da da . . .' He shakes his head. "Trying too hard," he says. "Anyway— before your time."

"Jesus, where do you come up with them?"

Harry smiles, with one side of his mouth, and pulls up the knot of his tie.

The courts are dark; the picture window in the lounge reflects the lounge back. Larry Blatt sits, still in his whites, smoking a cigarette and watching cartoons. Out in the parking lot, the last Cadillacs and Mercedeses boom to life. Fred Rosen, prognathous, rosy-cheeked with victory, guns the engine of his silver Eldorado, then shoots out the driveway with a screech of brand-new radials. Home! Harry emerges from the locker room, fragrant and perfect.

"Good night, Harry," Larry Blatt says, from his dark corner.

"Good night, Larry."

"That was an interesting-looking card trick you were doing before."

"Just part of the repertoire."

"Would you mind showing it to me again?"

Harry shoots his cuffs.

"And now, with the magic words—" Harry passes a hand over the cards. *"Ekha dekha befayge gomekha."* He plucks out a card with his first two fingers and a flick of the wrist.

"The three of clubs," Harry announces.

"But Harry," Larry Blatt says. "That's the queen of spades."

The wind rattles the door quite violently, and there's a click and a jingle from the pay phone—exactly as though a quarter had some- how fallen into the coin return.

Harry looks at the card. "I'll be damned," he says.

"Maybe the humidity in the locker room—" Larry says.

"This has never happened before."

"Probably just a mistake."

"Here's the three," Harry says, pulling out the card, frowning. "Another part of the deck entirely."

"Don't worry about it, Harry. By me you're the best."

Harry emerges from the building, sniffs the wet air, regards the orange light, the thick, dripping leaves, the purple shadows, the drooping catkins. He sighs. *Again,* he thinks, as he walks toward his car, a large, late-model, sensibly priced machine. Maybe Morris forgot. Keys in hand, Harry pauses, sniffs the air once more, quizzically. Maybe not. What if this spring were the last? He smiles at the idea.

Things end, he thinks.

Everything but me.

How much would he mind?

He shakes his head and opens the car door. All at once, for no reason, he starts to whistle, the tune he was humming in the locker room. Now he remembers. The song is "Avalon."

Anne Sexton

The following story is collected in a posthumous volume, Words for Dr. Y: Uncollected Poems with Three Stories, *edited by Linda Gray Sexton and published in 1978 by Houghton Mifflin.*

VAMPIRE

I was a perfectly normal man. As a matter of fact a successful insurance agent. I could sell death to anyone. I could sell old age—and its annuities—because my clients felt themselves stiffen (though they were only twenty-nine or so). I could see them make up a movie in their head of the "other"—the other, the aged self—warty, fingers no better than crowbars. I somehow *put* them there (just for a second) so they would buy, buy, buy.

Still, two nights ago just off Route 9 on the Jamaica Way, I struck out. A Doctor, into research, who was just enough of an ass to think he could cure anything or would invent it at any moment. No sale. The shit! Oh, well, I thought, you win some and you lose some, as I scraped off my frozen windshield. Backing out of his unplowed drive, dammit if I didn't back right over his dog. Unlucky dog—a poodle perhaps, I thought as I peeked through the glassy windshield, a flattened poodle lying in the snow like a movie star in too much ketchup. Didn't stop—serves that Mr. Doctor right, he of the cure and the research. Right there in his drive I left *my* answer and drove off thinking, "Not my fault—the dog was in the way and you, Mr. Doctor, when you are going to be in someone's way? What cure? What inventions?"

■

Next day, a new day, a new dollar and the client was a hot one and thus the buy, buy, buy. He had what it takes—the terror of no job. For the terror of no job but the body going on and on, I have the cure—an annuity. For the terror of the body flicking out at any moment, slapped out of you at any age, slapped out like a mosquito, I had the cure—a life insurance policy. Of course I did not insure the life itself, but insured the sudden drop of it and its ability to bring home the bread. I felt like a priest of sorts, insuring them against the luck of it all.

The following day walking down Beacon Street toward the capitol, the sweet gold-domed capitol of Boston, two men (or was it men? I knew right off they were hospital attendants—the white coats to the knee—interns perhaps, or nurses) quickly grabbed me and held both arms to my back in an armlock and shot me with a needle straight through the camel's-hair Filene's Basement overcoat, Brooks Brothers jacket, Brooks Brothers shirt, deep into the skin, through the skin of both forearms (oh the skin!) a needle containing a drug—or a potion?

Now let me assure you I was perfectly normal except for a slight fear of escalators swallowing me up—I was normal and brave enough to defy the escalators, therefore better than normal, having overcome the smallest of neuroses. A normal, normal man selling his goods, bringing home the dough for the seven-room house, the wife, the three kids, and I didn't even dream, even there in the queen-size bed. My wife was a wonderful hostess. My children grew step after step from birth to eight and ten. Nothing unexpected. A registered Republican, a Rotary member, a guy among guys who was making it.

That's all I can remember of the old me except for a flowered sugar bowl on the kitchen table that was my grandmother's. A résumé of sorts and a sugar bowl.

Now I am kept in some sort of darkened room. Or perhaps my eyes are glued shut by my keepers, my daytime keepers. I do not see them come or go. I only know that I am unconscious all day—if there still is a day with a sun in it or a blue sky and all that from my other life. At any rate, what I call "day" is my time of sleep, a drugged sleep but one cannot be sure of such things. I can only note that I do not dream here either.

When I wake twelve bells ring, and I find with my blind fingers a costume folded at the end of my bed—it is a rubber skin diver's suit and fits me exactly. On top of it is an address book. I did not at first know what kind of book but saw in the streetlights when I went forth. There is also a rather surprising loaf of French bread, and I realize that I must put on the rubber suit, the sneakers. And the bread—it is surely the most surprising of all, for the aroma floats upward, freshly baked, still warm to the touch. I am hungry, terribly hungry and yet I realize it is to go with the meal that I must seek. An invisible order that seems to have been written out in my head, and so on with the suit, sneakers, carrying in my left hand the address book and under my right arm the bread I walk forth onto the streets of Boston.

Under a streetlight I inspected for the first time the book, the address book which was entitled *Girls* and there were separate sections, headings such as "Playboy Club" or "Topless Dancers," etc. No names were included but addresses, apartment numbers, directions, and all that was necessary for the job.

Out into the night I went and have done so compulsively from then on, up and down Beacon Hill or Back Bay or even into the suburbs (if I have a feel for it) to find the half-open ground floor window waiting and softly raise it and enter. I have but one purpose.

Zip off the covers—ah, there she is, *this one,* lovely and waiting. Oh the sirloin steak of her! The juice waiting inside the dull-pink flesh (each one, night by night, year by year, I call "this one!").

And as is my custom (I try not to call it a compulsion because I think it would unnerve me in my mission—it is best not to give names to too many things or to dig into the mystery and its rituals) I put my mouth to her belly button—that which held her to her mother to her mother to her mother—back into the eternal . . . I dig my teeth in that belly until I can suck, suck out the red juice. The blood, the darling of her blood, filling my mouth, oh the filling of my mouth—hold it there! Hold it inside the mouth for a minute or two, rinsing it back and forth between my teeth, letting my tongue swim in it like a fish and letting all the taste enter the senses, like tasting the ocean, salty, salty, causing the addiction, falling in love with the addiction and then swallowing. To feed! To feed! There is such love in it—a transfusion body to body. This is repeated three magical times and then a short break for the bread—somewhat like her tummy—also the tough crust that is like the knot of her belly button.

And what of her? Do I only dream that she cries out in joy? There is a cry, but it might be silent, just a gape of the mouth, with a ghost floating out. Have I hurt you? I ask, each time that I rest to munch the bread, but I never get an answer. She is very still, but that is proper. Are you okay? I asked the first time, and when that first one only opened her mouth and no sound issued toward me, my own voice spoke up in my head. Food! Food! It is perfectly proper and absolutely necessary to have food. Think of the starving Armenians, said the grandmothers of yesteryear. I starve. I eat. Plain common sense. Blood and bread, blood and bread, but human blood only, woman blood only. It must be thus. It was ordained.

At first I rationalized, thinking of transplants, and IVs and plasma and the transfusions that save the helpless. I have become a one-man hospital, I am helpless to stop this, this saving my life, myself and with no Blue Cross, no taking up a hospital bed and bothering nurses. Just this little crawl into a girl's room, to borrow, to suck, until I am full for a night. One does what one must and although it's an unusual encounter—navel and mouth—the blood filling me in an hour or two, as my heart does well, pumping it toward toes, fingers, brain, and all necessary parts. I do not know if I use up all her blood—perhaps it is so—but I prefer not to dwell on the results of that. I prefer to think of her blood as a gift, a miraculous gift. When it is over, I tuck her in snugly, smoothing the covers, and as I go out the window, I shut it tightly but softly, lest she feel a bit of a chill.

Hayden Carruth

ASTROFEMINISM

I met her on the beach at Redondo, summer of
  1966. She was blonde, about twenty-two in age,
weighed 118, 5'8", a goddamn near perfect
  replica of the age's lust, who rejoiced in the
name of Marilyn Monroe. She was the "secretary"
  of a young fortyish physicist at the nearby
center for far space probes, where they were
  working on a capsule to send to Venus; my friend
Andy was one of the crew. Earlier that day
  I'd seen them testing a new vehicle in the com-
pression machine; it had leaked once, but now
  they couldn't make it leak again, couldn't
find where the leak might be. "Maybe ain't no
  leak," one guy said. "Shit. You can bet that
fucker goes up she leaks," his pal said. "Yeah,"

and they all sighed. They gave up, took off the rest
of the day on the beach. And the first guy, name
    of Brown, has this secretary, as I said, this yearling
doe nevertheless reeking of oestrus like a four-
    hundredweight sow in a five-foot sty. Yellow
hair, and the hairs on her belly spun from gold,
    and a chin-dimple, high cheekbones, legs for climbing
balconies, no horsing around, she was the genuine
    little all-American fucker in one of the first bikinis
ever seen, even on the west coast. My heart was goddamn
    pounding, the whole beach falling apart, couldn't
find anyplace to put my eyes. But the girl
    wasn't dumb, she knew what she was ambitious for.
(Not many starlets in a far-space probe, baby.)
    Blue? Christ, the sky was empyrean and the sea
as sapphiric as Prakti's navel stone, purling in
    on the golden sand with love-sweats as if the
great mother, Ceres herself, were drenching us all
    in cunt juice. But the lady knew her place. She
stood on one foot and let her belly slack, all those
    golden belly hairs tickling my fingers that were
ten feet away. And she flounced and said, "Shit, man,
    it's all a game, we astrophysicists and gal fridays,
we got to have something going to keep up the flow
    of senaptive juices," and she slouched her
brand-new, scarcely-used, right-off-the-great-
    assemblyline lust forward another walloping notch
in that belly of hers. And the surf pounded in, thrusting
    like a rank of rank bulls with seaweed decorating
their majestic horns. Horny? I doubt I could've
    stifled the family jewels, their inflamed rubicundity,
in a lead container for transshipment of nuclear
    waste. Yet that's what it was, all waste. When my semen
exploded it drenched Redondo Beach and a good two
    acres of Palos Verdes and for two days the stink
pervaded Southern California like a prophecy.
    Never saw the woman again. To be kept and have fun,
is that the evil? To be used for money, good spendable
    funds, is that evil? At my Christly age now, I say
let the pussycats catch a mouse if they can, play
    with him, work him up, then eat off his head,
and leave the tail for evidence on the redwood deck.

Autoclasticism is the way of life in America,
and in Arnhem Land as well. So buy the lady
    another stick of gum. When they launch the probe
to Jupiter, let her fuck herself all the way
    to cosmic epiphany in the roaring gases and roiling
magnetic ion-storms, the nothing girl whose death
    will be somewhat more beautiful and trenchant
than ours, Agnes, though we have transcended greater
    suffering without even rising on our tiptoes.
The white snow does not drift against this window
    like the blue sea at Redondo on the golden beach.

Alfred Corn

THE BLUE RIDER

I climbed up the scale through several states,
Discovery, invention, wrong by right:
When any cadence was sustained, it ended.

Surreason of the ballfield: he takes a stance
On his mound, at the center of a diamond,
Every tier hoping for the perfect pitch.

Serene in our afternoon a blue rider
Arcs through the air, an avatar of speed.
When any cadence was sustained, it ended.

Fear intensifies whenever events
Happen in jags (electroshock, nausea).
I climbed up the scale through several states,

Reaching a twilight of train whistles, showers,
Blue-foiled streets screened through a black umbrella.
When any cadence was sustained, it ended.

Unfamiliar facts may still come true.
By apostrophes, stutters, and gestures
I climbed up the scale through several states:
When any cadence was sustained, it ended.

Marilyn Hacker

Two uncollected poems

APRIL INTERVAL IV

First published in Poetry

There was no spring in Saratoga Springs.
I've spent a month under relentless rain,
uncomforted as I have ever been,
though not in jail, love, anguish, debt, or pain.
No deft phrases or well-proportioned lines
relieve the repetitions of routine.
Sodden, the leaflings spoil. Only the pines
are green. My solace has been buying things:
a white duck jacket, insulated boots,
three patchwork quilts dead countrywomen pieced.
It snowed last week, then thawed. A few released
yellow and purple crocuses uplifted
between shade trees on lawns. The wet wind shifted
and rain battered them back against the roots.

PASTICHE POST-PASTA

First published in Shenandoah

A woman is entitled to a meal
—some more roast lamb?—some more stewed aubergines?
The weight remains, the weight remains and swells.

When she has made a cream sauce for the veal
chops, sautéed dill and garlic with green beans,
a woman is entitled to a meal.

Fraises and *crème fraîche* lose all their sex appeal
the morning she cannot zip up her jeans.
The weight remains, the weight remains and swells.

Elastic shorts and tent-shaped shifts conceal
one-hundred-and-no-longer-in-the-teens.
A woman is entitled to a meal.

"Fast for a week," she thinks, and then she smells
the exhaust of Empire Szechuan Cuisine:
the weight remains, the weight remains and swells.

Perhaps the Fuller Figure Corner sells
trousers that slip up hips sized plus-fourteen.
A woman is entitled to a meal.

Like the two repetons of villanelles
squeezed to suggest whatever they can mean,
the weight remains, the weight remains and swells.

The ninety-three-pound ballerina peels
her apple supper, nibbles two saltines.
"A woman is entitled to a meal;

Art modifies what appetite compels,"
she muses, famished. On the wall, she leans
what weight remains, to wait, remaindered. "Swell!
A woman is entitled to a meal . . ."

Stanley Plumly

Three uncollected poems

A SUNSET, WITH A VIEW OF NINE ELMS

Unpublished, left out of Boy on the Step *(Ecco, 1989)*

At this distance, from the other shore,
looking across the river north and east,
you just can't tell what kind of trees they are,
feathered in those ideal humid greens
in a sort of flow toward the horizon,
and the ocean. In perspective they diminish
to depletion, into the sunset's haw
and haze, as if the water had drained
out of them into water, though closer
to the viewer they tower like a cloud.
This may or may not be Cuckold's Point and

pier—the painter's put in buildings and boats
for reference and to tie the trees to work.
Hence the two men in the boat still drifting out
are fishermen, or no one, one of whom
is standing looking into the water,
while above his head, where the sweete Thames
turns away, is St. Mary's Battersea.
(*after Samuel Scott*)

CLAUSTROPHOBIA

What the eye makes up in the shut dark,
the window icing over over the street,
then ice in the mirror, snow and ice—
waking that way, in a blur, out of a dream,
the wind outside in the iron branching
bringing the night sky in . . . Those long, long
weeks I worked the halls in the mines
I thought I would never sleep again,
would wake up with a diamond in my head
or the arrow shot blind, delicate as ash.
Now the cold air in a train of cold, cold
cupped in my hands; now dust, the taste of dust,
filling the air inside the tunnels, dust
like snow black in the wheels of the coal-cars.

SCHOOLING

I never knew the answer. I'd stand with the chalk
tight in my hands and my eyes closed, the blackboard filled
with the famous impossible names, birth and death
dates, lines across and down, and by the blackboard,
maps and constellation charts. And she'd be talking,
as through a door, to me, to the class, to anyone.
She wanted the word for a flower shaped like a star,
she wanted the color, head-size, height, when and where
it grew, whether the petals fell away or spread . . .
If she knew I didn't know she didn't say, only
her odd voice lifting into the floral octaves.
So that when I opened my eyes she seemed neither
pleased nor angry, just alone, the daylight failing
around her and the small animal objects on her desk.

E. E. Cummings

The following poem was found on E. E. Cummings's desk the day he died, in 1962. It is collected in Etcetera: The Unpublished Poems of E. E. Cummings, *edited by George James Firmage and Richard S. Kennedy and published by Liveright, 1983.*

5.

come from his gal's
alf whistle song
meet frankiegang
"join us or else"
"what for i should"
alf drop like dead

gang grow&grow
grab all the dough
everyone give
who want to live
we small it strong
it right we wrong

so goodbye alf
you just a bum
go fug yoseself
because freedumb
means no one can
dare to be man

Editors Will Be Editors

Sharon Sheehe Stark

I am a pathological reviser. Nothing leaves this house except after endless rounds of fusspot fixing. I revise with abandon, with the joy of having chosen an art that lets me err in secret, rectify at leisure. I revise, with sneaky pencil insertions, the published work. But this is the story of how, once upon a time, I managed to revise myself *out* of publication.

Early on in my career, when every acceptance was an event, I had a story taken by a literary mag operating out of a houseboat off the Florida Keys. The following summer the editor and I happened to be at the Breadloaf Writers' Conference at the same time. In the staff lounge, during the kickoff cocktail party, he handed me what I assumed were the galleys for his forthcoming issue. The story on top was mine. It was called "Seconds," I remember.

Dutifully, I quit the party and went to my room and proceeded to do what I do best. With my irrepressible Bic I made earnest, circuitous arrows from every good word to the better one I'd installed in the margins. Lovingly, I inked out entire paragraphs. It was a heady, satisfying exercise, all the more so for the aesthetic, sensuous pleasure of the "galleys" themselves. I'd never seen such attractive ones. Instead of the usual rambunctious scrolls, these were sturdy things, like oak tag, conveniently page-sized and dapper white. Even more impressive were the tidy, meticulously aligned Band-Aid–like strips already down, pasted over, I figured, printer's mistakes. I tinkered well into the night, and the next morning, bleary-eyed but damn proud of myself, I handed the galleys back at the breakfast table.

To my horror the man threw up his hands. He gave me a sound and very public dressing down. Then, with deadly calm, he went on to explain, as if to a submoron that what I'd done was scribble up something called "camera-ready page proofs."

I could have died. Thank God I had my defenders. A crusty female book editor grumpily observed, "Only a nut would give a writer something he didn't want written on." Another tablemate told the houseboat editor he was being needlessly pissy, that, indeed, he should consider himself lucky I didn't revise the entire issue.

The man was very cold to me after that and, as it turned out, quite unforgiving. Despite my offer to cover the cost of resetting, when the issue came out some months later (a dandy double issue) "Seconds" was nowhere evident.

Time passed. I got busy with new fiction and, to my eternal detriment, busy with business. I learned more than a writer should know about how words go to market. One day it hit me that six years had elapsed since the day "Seconds" was taken. I decided to make polite inquiry as to when the harry it might be coming out. I sent notes and more notes. Nothing. Eventually a writer friend said she'd heard the houseboat had sunk in a storm. There's no end to revision. Now cuttlefish cut and Gulf shrimp refine.

Let them.

Thomas Wolfe

POCKET NOTEBOOK 1, SEPTEMBER 1926 TO OCTOBER 1926

The following two unpublished passages are taken from the Look Homeward, Angel *manuscript in order to illustrate what parts of Eugene's childhood Wolfe was working on in early October.*

He saw that almost everything depended on communication, that communication was founded primarily in speech. But, even so, granted that children were thus imprisoned before they could talk, why had none of them described the horror, the futility, the revolting waste of the whole process, as soon as he had become articulate? The explanation came with electric horror. Eugene found that thought which was not built upon the sensuous images of speech was a house built on sand; he found, for example, on waking from a sound sleep, that what had been clear and sharp in his brain before he slept was now blurred, confused, inchoate, mixed with other thought and other time. For, without language, he saw that even the sense of time became confused.

Thus he was faced with the terror of watching the erasure, day by day, of all his mind had patiently and speechlessly elaborated. The stabbing truth came to him then at once that when his mind had learned to construct itself in speech images, it would be almost impossible to reconstruct its activity during the period when it had no speech.

All the feelers, the tender opening buds of taste and odor, were opening up in him, the cellular kernels of his powerful sensory organization, destined later to become almost incomparably hearty and exquisite, were expanding. He had the rare gift of enjoying the excellence of the common thing—of tasting to its final goodness the quality of a liberal slice of savory roast beef with creamed potatoes. He scented his food like an animal before tasting it: peaches and cream he gloated over sensually. He ate, when he could, on a bare table in the pantry: it was filled with musty spicy odors—the ghost of cinnamon, clove, new bread, vanilla flavoring. There one day, he met first the delights of toasted corn flakes. They came in a huge carton labeled *Force*; there was a picture of a comical, merry old man on the cover—as he remembered, an old man, with a hooked nose and chin, a Punchian and appetite-giving old man. For weeks he lived in hungry anticipation of toasted corn flakes, rich cream and sugar: the savory glutinous compound was the highest pleasure he had tasted.

William T. Vollmann

FROM *YOU BRIGHT AND RISEN ANGELS*

The following passage was deleted from my first novel, You Bright and Risen Angels (Deutsch-Atheneum, 1987; Penguin-Pan/Picador, 1988). My editor, Robert Harbison, and I cut a number of things from the manuscript, particularly from the last quarter or so, where the book suffered from being too "garrulous," as Bob rightly said. Most of our cuts still seem to me to be improvements. However, I do miss some of the material, in much the same way that a sugar addict can be sorry at not being able to eat all the cookies.

This passage was excised from a section entitled "Parker in Love" (ms. page 486, book page 542). Most of the major characters appear in it. Parker Fellows is a plant-like, snakey young man with supernatural dark-

room powers. He and his assistant Wayne are on the side of the "reaction-
aries" in the war which my book describes, and are therefore dupes for the
forces of electricity. Bug Nightcrawler and Milly are "revolutionaries"—in
other words, shock troops for the insect kingdom. Susan is originally a reac-
tionary because she loves Wayne, but becomes a revolutionary later. In this
section Wayne is remembering everyone's childhood. When he used to visit
Parker, he would see angels dancing around on the ceiling like bugs. He
wonders if the angels are fighting over Parker.

But that was none of his business. It was clear to him, however, that
Parker did not pray with his parents, "If I should die before I wake,
I pray my soul the Lord to take," hallelujah, just as I, the author, pray
every hour, waiting in the big blue glow of the screen for the CPU
to judge what I have done in my interactive command procedure. If
it fails, that will be on account of bugs. How strange a transformation
that the bugs had become the saviors of the world! But Bug and Milly
knew that that was true. Susan knew it, too, but she did not like to
think about the bugs too much because bugs scared her. Once when
she was very young she screamed when a cricket jumped on her bed,
just as she had screamed at her slumber party when wicked Milly
jumped on the bed to scare her; when Milly was a little girl she did
many bad things, as will be told in the subsequent volume.—The
other kids, then, hid under Parker's bed. Milly hid, too; she was one
of them. Wayne had told them that Parker's parents would not pray
with him. They had talked it over in Sunday school and decided to
help Parker pray. So they went down to Omarville that night, sneaking along the back roads (they had told their parents that they had
a youth group meeting because their parents would have forbidden
them to go, for fear of spore contamination) and cowered every time
a big tall thin milkweed plant loomed out at them in the moonlight;
but they got to Swamp Street in Omarville quite safely, following the
Boy Scout measures of vigilance recommended by Wayne, namely
staying together and singing "Onward, Christian Soldiers," and they
went to Parker's house and hid under the bed. When Parker came
in to go to bed they all yelled, "You pray with us, Parker; we've come
to help you so you pray with us or else the Devil will get you!"—
Parker convulsed and jerked in astonishment. He got down on his
belly and slithered round and round the bed, peering warily into the
darkness under it, and put his ear to the closet door while he was at
it to make sure that there were no surprises in there as well to trick
him. Then Wayne and the other kids came out from under the bed
and prayed with Parker. Parker put his hands together and wriggled

his lips along with the others and bowed his head and pretended to close his eyes like they did but he was really peeking to make sure that they were out to do him no harm; if they had tried to do him any harm he would have lunged at them. But Parker really did want to be loved. At the same time he was not about to stick his rubbery neck out; so because he seemed to be so viciously suspicious the Cooverville kids had been defensive at first and stayed under the bed and sang (the weaker ones rationalizing that actually they had not come to pray with Parker or anything like that because they mainly wanted to help Parker in the *abstract* or *spiritual* sense; i.e.; to pray *for* Parker safely under Parker's bed) since their parents were always telling them to be decent to the boys from Omarville because coming from Omarville they had no homes as we interpret the concept, poor little terrors (and there had once been talk of establishing a Boys' Home just for them but it never came to anything because they would have had to put special potting soil in the boys' rooms and that would not have met the sanitary codes); but at the same time, the kids from Cooverville had absorbed subcutaneously, as it were, the message that you might help the boys from Omarville but you should never *never* get too close to them*, so while the kids sang under the bed they were trembling and Parker opened his jaws wide and grinned cynically when he heard the wobble in their voices; and Milly was convinced that she would go to Heaven for being out here and risking her life for the sake of Parker; she did not become an atheist until she was twelve and rejected Kant; at the moment she was a pious freckled being who believed, as I said, that she deserved to be elevated for her service to Parker; she was already a vanguardist; and she clasped her white hands tighter at the thought of elevation and uplifted her white face like a wolf howling at the moon and stared up through Parker's mysterious bedsprings overhead and saw glowing bug-cocoons all stuck to the dark coils (not that the bugs had anything against Parker; it just seemed like a good site to settle into a chrysalis or two); while Parker skittered round and round the bed snapping his jaws as if he thought that the intruders might be mice. Finally Wayne came out from under the bed and grinned, a little worried that Parker might be mad at him for presuming too far and exceeding orders and stuff; so Wayne looked tough and yelled, "*Surprise!*" so then Parker knew

---

*"It is the low cultural level of a number of our organizations . . . particularly in the border regions (no offence to them meant) which hampers our Party organisations in fully implementing inter-Party democracy," explained Stalin in his "Report on Immediate Tasks in Party Affairs" (17 January 1924).

that no one was trying to hurt him; and all the other kids wormed their way out from under the bed and prayed with Parker, as told.

This tidbit may also be of interest. When Penguin did the paperback of Angels, *they sent me the standard author questionnaire. Among my responses was the following blurb, which Penguin chose not to use. But I like it, so here it is:*

The world of *You Bright and Risen Angels* is a world of poisonously erotic Caterpillar Hearts, a world whose hero, Bug Nightcrawler, becomes a revolutionary when one of his bunkmates at summer camp is executed for being a beetle. It is also a world of electricity, which is conscious, and controls humanity from every telephone and light bulb and power outlet. In this book we possess the sole authentic history of Bug's revolution in all its stages, from the snowball campaign to the crushing defeat of Operation Hammer Blow, from the battle in the depths of a bottomless swimming pool to the miracle of Electric Emily and the villainies in the Caves of Ice. But Vollmann, who has also interviewed the surviving reactionaries, is no biased Menshevik, for he gives equal time to Bug's archenemies: Mr. White, Dr. Dodger, Wayne with his invincible swizzle stick, and the silently supernatural Parker Fellows. The *New Statesman* (London) calls this book "a fantasia on the emotional mutilations of childhood, on greed and ghosts, all plugged in and powered up and inflated into the monstrous epic simile that is America. Bug is the hero of the revolution, and he is no longer human." Says *USA Today:* "This bold and abrasive act of imagination . . . appears to be an allegory of the struggle between disadvantaged populations and their would-be oppressors." But Bug himself, when asked by a schoolteacher what it is all about, replies, "I suppose we're doing this for the trees."

Frederick Busch

The following passage was edited out of my novel Harry and Catherine *(Alfred A. Knopf, 1990).*

   After almost fifteen years, Harry seeks out Catherine, whom he has maybe never stopped loving during their long separations. Over this period, they have twice nearly decided to stay together, and twice they've run from

*the permanence. This novel is about Harry's trip to upstate New York to
see, once and for all, if they can make their love work long-term. There's a
lot of sexiness between them. This scene occurs in Catherine's kitchen, after
Harry has once more confessed his need for her, and his fear that need,
love, lust will simply not be enough to keep them together. I forced them to
make love here because I was frightened that they would have to part. It
was at first Harry who dragged Catherine outside and all but raped her. I
didn't like the violence—more puling need to seize than to give much—and
so I changed it so that it was Catherine who yanked his shirtfront and
much of the initiative. Still, the scene didn't work. That was when I suspected that their lust was really mine, and that neither their hearts nor bodies were in it—see how promptly the lovemaking declines into the writer's
metaphors about language: it was literary lust. More to the point, my wife,
Judy, said that the scene felt far from essential—overdone, and just one
more damned whine from Harry about his needs. My editor at Knopf,
Harry Ford, reported total agreement with Judy, and so the moment left the
novel and ends up—sad and panting, a kind of embarrassment—here.*

"I'm sorry," he said.

"What the hell."

He wondered how to request that she keep on feeling guilty
because he needed the help. But she was so miserable, her head was
drooping in spite of the anger in her voice, just then, and if you were
going to drop out of the air, unable any longer to lie down upon it
and be received, and fly, then you might as well crash in some kind
of style. So he turned her—rotated her by the waist and shoulder
while stepping back from her, as if he were a fighter she had cornered
on the ropes—and then he stepped into her, as if inside a crisp body
hook, and he managed to get his arms around her hard. He pulled
her in, he pressed his face into the moist hot skin of her neck. He
kept on tightening his hold. For he was desperate, he was beyond the
rationale he no longer could remember, though he'd thought it only
seconds ago. He let her loose, and she, as if fighting in turn on the
ropes, put her hand in to take a bunch of his shirtfront, and she
pulled. He let his arms hang loose at his sides, and he went where she
tugged.

They were at the back door, and then out it, in the darkness and
the cold. He thought he saw stars, and he knew that meant clarity of
skies, and therefore no cloud cover, deeper cold. Let it snow for a
week, he thought. She pulled and he went with her. They stumbled
up the rise behind the house, and toward the several stunted apple
trees that remained of a very old orchard, she'd said. He didn't care.
She clearly wanted distance from the house, and they achieved it. She

walked fast, and she in only socks didn't trip, and then she slammed him, as if he were light, toward the nearest tree. She pulled, then, to catch him, and they swung to it together, not hitting hard. He reached for her belt. He felt her fingers. She was leaning back at the tree, she was unbuckling his pants, which were only partway down, as were hers, and their underpants, when her arms went around his ribs and then his buttocks and she pulled him in. She hissed, and they held an instant, poised. Too confused by what they'd said, by what he'd thought, stunned by his need to say, Harry drew himself back, his knees bent, his body driving forward while it still held away, and labored, under what was left of an orchard, to speak whatever language he had not debased.

Then it was cold night, bright outside with stars, foggy in the kitchen with the spice and steam of the long-simmered sauce. Bob was given a soda with dinner. "Randy has sixteen a day. He told me, on the phone."

"He hasn't talked to you on the phone," Catherine said. "Isn't that what you told me?" There was a large bruise on her forearm from when she had flailed behind her, seeking leverage, a way to push back—to fight back, Harry thought. She looked at the bruise and at Harry watching her, and said, "I wonder where that came from?"

Molly Peacock

To acquire the habit of reading is to construct for yourself a refuge from almost all the miseries of life.

—W. Somerset Maugham

Believing that writers owe a debt to those unable to read, I wrote "Your Happiness" to submit to an anthology of poems and stories designed for teaching adult beginning readers. I still believe that we owe the debt, even though I was unable to pay my share. Learning how to master a task as an adult that the rest of the world seemingly has learned in childhood is painful—and intriguing for what the process reveals to us. I wondered if I could write about such an experience in my own life, one that would connect both to the self-consciousness and to the exhilaration of learning to read. The analogous experience I thought I could share was learning how to feel after I had fought against it so long. Just as in learning to read, I had to acquire a whole new vocabulary for emotions.

Because I myself teach reading to children and teenagers, I thought I knew the vocabulary level and syntax difficulty that would be appropriate for a newly literate adult—and I did, though there was something else that I ignored. The editors of the anthology (teachers themselves) tried "Your Happiness" with several classes of adult new readers, and the students could indeed decode my story word for word—but they couldn't understand it. The psychological twists and turns, the details that the narrator notices, the fact that the narrator sees a therapist and describes the dynamics of the therapeutic interaction were all elements of the reading process that I wrongly assumed the new readers would "get."

I was disheartened because I loved the story, which is to some degree a memoir. In feeling it is purely autobiographical, though in detail it is not. I never in my life have been able to write to the order of an "assignment," and this wasn't any different. I denuded events in order to provide greater accessibility, yet accessibility was just what the editor said the story lacked. The piece was rejected, but the anomaly remained: a complex idea simply said. I saw why the anthology couldn't use what I'd done and also saw that revising it into a more fully developed story wasn't possible, for the piece was what it was: a tender idea, misguidedly expressed, but, to me, somehow persuasive after all. I felt that it would find its audience, if there were an audience for a horse of a different color: so here is a reading primer for those who already know how.

YOUR HAPPINESS

I met Katie because I was desperate and because, as usual, I didn't have any money. I gave money to my drunken father, and I gave money to my babyish, ill, demanding boyfriend, and I gave money to my dope-smoking sister. Of course, I didn't make much money to begin with. I felt I was supposed to take care of everyone, but all I wanted in the world was to be left alone.

I often stared at Katie's shoes as I talked and cried in her dingy office. She wore brown, square-toed shoes that looked Italian, but probably had "Made in Brazil" stamped on the soles. She didn't have much money either, working in the St. Paul's Agency for Mental Health. Together we climbed three flights of dusty, puke-colored stairs to one of several little rooms. They were all painted brown.

I always stared at her shoes, because she always wore the same ones. It felt warm and safe to look at those shoes because everything in my world changed all the time. Drunk people change all the time, and so do sick people, and so, of course, do people who take drugs. And Katie herself changed from week to week. She was pregnant.

All I felt came so alive when I told it to her, because she would name it back to me. "Your grief," she would say, or "your sadness," or "your fear." This was my alphabet of emotions. She was teaching me to read myself. Some people don't think that mental problems are a matter of education, but mine were. I had to learn the names of my feelings.

Some of us have to learn how to feel even though we were born with all our feelings. I was born healthy as an ox, but had to use all my energy to keep myself strong. I worked so hard at keeping strong that I forgot my other feelings. I wasn't going to be like my father or my sister. My problem was that I wasn't sure what *I* was, except, of course, the person they could say had stopped them from having fun. The most alcohol I would drink at a time was a single glass of wine. I passed every joint that was handed to me on to the next person.

What I often felt was confusion, but I wasn't certain of this until Katie said, peering over her large checkered belly, "Your confusion." Trying to pick out feelings was like trying to spell something with the wet, pasty letters of alphabet soup. I could almost form something, but then I couldn't. Katie would have to say, "Your confusion," "your shame," "your wish."

One day she said, "Your happiness." She said it when I told her I just wanted to be left alone. I was suspicious when she said "happiness," just as when she said "love." All I wanted to do was be alone and think. I didn't want to be happy and I didn't want to be loved. I just wanted a rest from driving my boyfriend to his appointments and answering my father's phone calls in the middle of the night, and from writing out checks for them and my sister. When were they going to leave me alone?

I was so big and strong. I was like a picture of an ox. How terrible it was for me to whisper to her shoes, "I'm afraid." I felt sick and weak and ready to puke whenever I said, "I need . . ." Everyone else needed me. Wouldn't the world explode if I needed too? Yet the world came alive when I could feel the pulse of my self inside me. Suddenly I felt buglike and needy and small. Where was I, the ox? But I had been like a *picture* of an ox, a burdened cardboard beast.

I was only a young woman burdened by her own feelings in a brown room up three flights of brown stairs, staring at the brown shoes of a pregnant woman. The window shade crookedly cut off a view of the brown city beyond. Beyond the buildings were the curiously alive, yet completely dead-looking branches of early spring. In spring the brown woods redden and branches take on a violet or pinkish tinge. The buds of leaves are like red puckered baby mouths about to squall.

Spring is a violent season, and there were many violent changes in my life. My boyfriend was very strong when he wasn't sick. After we had a fistfight, I changed the locks on the doors. When he came around again, I crouched in the hallway and shook, waiting for him to get tired of pounding the door and the front window and the mailbox. When he finally left, I thought I had gone crazy. Two days later I threw a drink in my sister's face and left her with the bar bill. I knew I was crazy.

Then Katie had her baby. I talked to her only on the phone. I was alone, but not the way I yearned to be. I was angry and frightened. She said, "Sometimes crazy people make you do crazy things." When she said "crazy people," I felt she didn't mean me.

I bought an answering machine to make sure I received Katie's messages. It dawned on me that it would listen to my father's crying in the middle of the night. After I told my sister to pay her own bills, she stopped speaking to me. My father seemed to vanish because he wouldn't leave a message on the machine. My family shunned me, the cardboard ox, but my boyfriend called and called. I couldn't help myself from picking up the phone when I heard his voice on the machine because I couldn't stop hoping he'd become the person I wanted him to be, though he stopped calling when he met another woman with a car.

Loneliness and fear swept through me like terrible spring storms. I was cold all the time. The weather turned frigid again after the daffodils came out, but I couldn't stand to wear my winter clothes again, so I went around in spring clothes and froze. I was not happy. I was not in love. I was frightened, angry, and stricken into action. I opened a savings account. I was cold and alone and wanted to see Katie's face, the face that I seldom looked at when I had the chance. The phone calls, where I could hear her husband and her baby behind her, felt empty and shattered like a landscape full of rubbish after a storm.

"You made your bed, now lie in it," I told myself, all alone. I was balancing my checkbook. I had added wrong in my own favor! I felt so safe just to add up the columns and have the sums come out nearly right. After I found the fifty dollars I didn't know I had, I drove to a department store and bought new sheets, a corny print of boxes with flowers inside.

Learning how to feel, like learning anything hard, makes you ache with an unused stiffness. I was thirty-one years old on a Saturday morning with an empty day ahead of me. The curtains billowed out from the windows against my legs as I walked from side to side around the bedroom making the bed with my new sheets. It was early May.

"Well, what do we feel like today?" Like a nurse, I asked myself that every morning. Because I was always practicing how to feel, I was surprised when I couldn't say how I felt. I wasn't numb. I just wasn't anything in particular. The May wind played around the room, the bed lay patiently made. Not sad, not sick, not disappointed, not afraid.

Empty of those things, I felt a kind of contentment rise in me, though I didn't recognize its calmness. I thought I might *be* empty. I was like a rusted old metal toy. Could I move again? Oh yes, I found I could move slowly inside this feeling, though I could not name it. On the phone Katie called it, "your happiness."

Rachel Hadas

What follows are never-published parts—each eleven lines long—of a poetic sequence entitled "Generations," which was written in 1985. In 1986, ten of the poem's eighteen sections were published in a London-based new magazine entitled Margin, *edited by the American poet Robin Magowan. I think Robin did a good job of picking and choosing, but I retain a residual fondness for the sections he chose to exclude.*

I

To breathe, read, eat's nostalgia,
habit, fresh beginning,
life-sustaining chore,
refrain, and variation.
The mouse tripes on the floor,
the glow of yellow lilies
against a grey June sky,
the smell of burning wood
and fire's quiet roar,
the cosiness of cold
keeping us in to read.

II

Lift the cat off the clean sheet of paper
and brush her dusty prints off and consider

while automatically jotting down the date
today my father would be eighty-five
or is it *would have been* or even *is?*
Ten years ago today I felt him near me
(long dead already) on a sunny hill
where I was picking strawberries in windy
silence: a closely hovering love,
wordless admonitions, nothing more.
These days I am him more and sense him less.

IV

My needs, my needs! whined the way Mime sings—
phrase whose precise provenance I forget,
but every day its simple truth is plainer.
Needs, needs! Food sleep sex
work anger exercise solitude meditation
mothering (two needs here rubbing noses)—
the need to be told stories and to sing
the baby back to sleep . . .
Look at the sky. See how the devil's paintbrush
has suddenly shot up through sunless days.
Need for the rainbow leapfrog over dailiness.

VIII

We're told that individual death, though everything,
is really nothing, is inevitable, planted
and growing in us. It's the end of all
life, and forever, that the mind's eye won't
encompass. As the train
slides from the dark near Journal Square
and pallor floods the windows, pupils narrow
involuntarily, let in more sky,
more light: a widening that we assent to
under the dome of any world I can imagine.

XIII

Padding by, years pad us with benign
indifference to aging. Otherwise,
a thousand lyrics shout, we couldn't bear it.
Perhaps can't anyway. My mother, falling

asleep each summer sooner after supper,
welcomes that comfort as the cats lie pat,
warm on her belly, her book skids and crashes
and is retrieved . . . the quiet sound of breathing . . .
I don't believe it. I know nothing of
her ever earlier solitary wakings,
seventy years at three, at four, at five.

XVI

At the end of a tunnel I heard you: Mama, Mama!
sound soft a long time, not at all insistent,
and mixed with the sheet's somehow having slipped,
stuff at a yard sale shrouded against rain,
and first light. Mama. And it's morning. Mama.
My child, I didn't answer. This is the word
I may have been waiting for all my life.
I wonder now; but then I covered my head
in the grey dawn, insisting on what sliver
of life left over I could call my own
or only sleep? Your life too had its claim.

XVII

Your father ambles out to check the weather
over and over. Your grandmother
stands stock still at half a dozen stations
of daily meditation, yard and garden,
gazing fiercely at whatever grows.
Ah, the thermometer, the slugs, the baby
swallows on the wire, eft, frog, snail,
butterflies tarnished on the window sill:
to all of these we pay a more or less
worshipful tithe of attention
but only turn idolaters for you.

XVIII

Boiling fruit for jam at the end of *Anna Karenina*—
jostle of recipes, wooden rooms crammed
with in-laws; epilogue of *War and Peace*;
or Mrs. Wilcox wandering across the lawn,

wisps of hay dangling from her vague hands,
while all the others sneeze their way through summer.
Yes. Lines of tension and attachment stretch
their fragile tendrils out, so many spiderwebs
jeweled with dew. Touch one:
each little compartment trembles.

Thank you. The baby's grown into the suit you gave him.

Linda Pastan

*I suppose that most of what I write turns out to be what you call "literary
outtakes." Much of revision for me is paring down, paring down, and three-
quarters of my writing is revision. Here is a clear-cut example.*

*"Trajectory" began for me with the publication of my seventh book,
which coincided with my fifty-sixth birthday. It occurred to me then that I
didn't have time left in my life for many more books. Yet the entire last
stanza of this poem, which deals with just that issue, had to be cut out. A
kindly editor, in rejecting it as it was, said he was sure it was not time to
talk yet of my next-to-last book, and I realized how self-indulgent that
stanza sounded and indeed was.*

*Often a poem swerves from its original direction, and I find it best to
follow where it leads. In this case "Trajectory" is most itself without the
third stanza.*

TRAJECTORY

*In the trajectory
whose arc describes my life
I sense almost precisely
where I am. I see
the patchworked years
spread far below
as if this were an ordinary flight
over farms and fields
unfolding into dusk.*

*And it is ordinary,
ending as it must*

in a single measure of earth
as other flights end,
even those of the bird
with an Indian name
whose landings are marked
by a feather pointing
towards the dark.

[removed third stanza]

"This will be
my next to last book,"
I hear myself say, the wind
of those words
rushing by my ears
as the ground looms up,
and I spread my arms
as far as I can
to keep myself aloft.

Edward Field

In publishing my New and Selected Poems (Sheep Meadow Press, 1987), my editor used only the first section of the following poem, "Take It or Leave It," and the complete poem has never been published.

TAKE IT OR LEAVE IT

While we were dancing, master,
I felt your desire unmistakably hard against me.
You weren't in the least shy about it
and reached for my prick,
but I shrank away.

Then, as if to say So okay, not that, then what?
you lay back, ready for anything,
your pale thin prick waving shamelessly in the air.

I went down on it for a moment
but your young disciples were around,
though not paying any attention—
it was an ordinary thing to them,
their master working with a pupil.

I knew nothing sexual was the least repugnant to you,
you were willing to get on with it any way I wanted,
had guessed what I liked, and offered it.

But I was too ashamed in front of the others,
though my shame came from another time,
a different world that exists for me
more than anything in the present,
more even than you.

So I was the one who broke off,
and lost contact.

■

You were against my poetry,
and I admitted it would never be perfect—
no matter how often I rewrote
there'd always be mistakes.
How could it be sacred, you said, if it wasn't perfect?
But it is, even if in its failure bittersweet.
It was clear we were never going to agree on poetry.

Then came the sex episode, as another possibility.
If I had given in, as totally as in a wet dream,
what possible loss to go to sleep for a moment
and receive a gift
that leaves one startlingly refreshed?

■

The sex part was nothing to you,
but what can you do for one
for whom it's not uncomplicated,
who shrinks away?

His shame is what life taught him,
a refuge against humiliation.
Recognition of that, surely, takes primacy
to being free of it.

But you are reductionist as well as ruthless.
You only say, Get it on.

Then care enough
to make me,
force me even, even if
I keep saying No
like a foolish virgin in the dream.
Free me from whatever
made me what I am,
force me to feel,
free me from shame.

Perhaps, though, it's not enough
to love God.
He's got to love you too,
and just as hard.

∎

Swooning away into total sexual bliss,
it came to an end for me years ago,
and if it ends, I think it ends forever.

So love may not again be perfect
and I'll be wary even in my dreams.
But life, unbearable as it sometimes seems,
is really no harder than I can stand,
and not to swoon away, but wake up,
(or anyway, be more awake),
is still the greater task at hand.

Debbie Cymbalista

Searching for "outtakes" has proven to be unexpectedly difficult. Of course, searching for anything through the cramped disorder of my New York one-bedroom is a trying task; and the word processor's systematic rewrite of history did not help either. But, fundamentally, I was confronted with a real scarcity of valuable outtakes—a limitation intrinsic to short-story collections.

This is because, in most cases, a published short story doesn't differ much from the writer's original version. Editors, as a rule, are reluctant to spend too much time "cleaning up" any one story (though they might not object to sitting through a dozen rewrites of a novel). Theirs isn't an alto-gether unreasonable attitude: a short story's length and its set structure make major editing very difficult. And, since the success of a collection is almost never "made" or "broken" by one single story, the prevailing standard seems to be: "If the story works, fine; if it doesn't, let's just drop it."

Additionally, outtakes from short stories are often nothing more than undigested fiber, an assemblage of unrelated sentences and half-paragraphs. They are simply "there," ideas in a vacuum, words lacking a context to give them meaning and relevance. A few times, while reading my old outtakes, I was moved by the sound of a sentence or by the sincerity of an idea which I had written but had already forgotten (and it was a slightly unsettling process, that of creatively and intellectually repossessing what I had . once consciously created). But even in these instances there was just too little to relate the published story to its orphaned outtake—and the latter did not offer any new connective insights about my own writing or about the story itself.

And finally, regardless of the length of the story, outtakes are annihilated by the word processor which erases possibilities, the "was" and the "might have been," to leave only the "now"—which offers perfection and cleanliness at a price: trading the record of our own writing processes for the sake of the computer's own word "processing." My computer determines the irreversibility of changes; I can't zigzag through the history of my choices or select an alternative from past debris. I am denied (or, better, I deny myself) a memory of the many halting, wavering moments in my writing.

Despite these "obstacles" I did manage to select an outtake. It is the middle story in a trilogy portraying the development of a young girl's sexual awareness. The stories follow her from the ages of twelve to sixteen—from her sudden realization of being more than just a child, to the concretization of her new sexual identity and of the love and the violence she can evoke. Yet only the first and the third stories were published in Danger. "From a Distance" was left out when my editor decided to limit the number of stories about young girls . . . and though I accepted her judgment I still believe that something that belonged in my book is missing from it. So, here is—like all outtakes detached, and very much alone—the "unborn" middle child, now transformed into an only one.

FROM A DISTANCE

This is what to do when they strike you. You stand still. You don't move. You maybe move your face but just a tiny bit and follow the motion of the blow: left-right, left-right. And at every strike there is something less that is left of you. You try not to cry until it's over.

■

I turn left at Piccadilly Circus and enter Soho. "You'll recognize the door," he tells me, "there's plenty of pictures of juicy kittens like you on it."

"How will they know that they should open it?" I ask and I look up at his face and down at his fingers. They're yellow-pink, fat and dimply, still smeared red with the grease of ketchup and chips. I look at his fingers and today the hollow of hunger jumps into my body one more time. Today and yesterday and the day before. I think of Heinz Vegetarian Beans, tins of macaroni and cheese, hot chips with ketchup, doughnuts crusted with sugar. I think please I will do anything, almost anything, to fill my body. I think of my stomach and then I think of my vagina. Fill one up with a cock and then fill the other up with food, these are the rules of the game. "Tell them I sent you," he says.

"And what's your name?"

"None of yer business what my name is, now is it? Pretty cheeky of you, eh?" He pinches my right cheek between his thumb and index. Hard. The pain flies, travels instantly from the cheek to the brain and I shut my eyes to keep from responding. I don't flinch and after a moment I see that he has let go of my face, that he is not squeezing anymore. I feel the hot branding of his fingers, so vivid that I cannot tell what is happening to my body by touch alone.

I whisper, "So. What do I say?" and he spells it out for me. "You just say that you're here to get a job, and you've been sent by me. Now, that's all you have to say and tell, you hear me?" I nod.

He says, "Scat!" and hits my head with the palm of his hand. I run away, deeper into Soho.

It smells of chop suey here, of rice porridge and incense. Of cheap perfume and sandalwood talcum powder. Tangerine body oil, they told me, that's what's hot in Soho now. That and patchouli and sandalwood, of course. If it's a massage parlor I'll stay, if I have to fuck I won't. At least, so I think.

The door looks the way I was told it would. Red with a black frame, covered with pictures of lanky girls in black leather nervously placing riding crops across their breasts or sliding them between their legs, of full-breasted girls in neon-glow bikinis with the tips cut off to reveal the nipples and slits in the bottom to hint at the absence of pubic hair, of childlike girls with white cheeks pouting or opening their mouths just enough to suggest that they could open them even more. . . .

If they want me to be one of them I will be the latter. The matron opens the door and looks me over, judges with her large eyes buried under pockets of fat.

"Yes?" she asks and I say, "I was told me there might be a job here." I don't ask, I state.

She squares me up and then shakes her head, "Sorry, luv. No chest," and closes the door. I bang on it again and again and say "Please! C'mon, lemme in! I'll show ya!" It's not ridiculous, it's very very real and hunger hurts. "I've got it, I've got 'em! Lemme show you!" I yell. She opens the door once again to tell me, "Fuckin' stop being a bloody pest, now will ya?" and slams the door in my face. A man walks out of the door, smiling. The air behind him smells softly of tangerine.

At home I stand still, see hands flying around my face, feel them fall on it. I hear him saying that I am a slut and that he'll get it out of me one way or another. He is right and does not even know it. I wait till it's over and then walk to the refrigerator. I eat so much cottage cheese that I throw it all up, kneeling in front of the toilet, white curd filling blue Kleenexes in my room, rancid yellow globs falling on my blanket later in the night. When everybody is asleep I sit under the desk in my room and eat bananas.

"Dall," he calls me. It's "dall" for "doll" but he's seen too many American movies and now he sounds funny. Camden Town, Northern London. He tells me, "Dall, I've seen *plenty* of punks and *plenty* of little mods 'n' sods and *plenty* of real scum but I ain't seen nothing as cute as you yet." I want to tell him, "Cut the crap and give me a job," but of course I can't do that. He might ask how old I am.

"So, how old are you, hon?" he asks and I barely have the time to lie, "Eighteen," before he tells me, "Don't fuck around with me," so I lie again and say, "Sixteen."

"Sixteen is young but fine," he announces. He presses his lips against mine, his teeth grinding against my teeth, his fingertips searching for my nipples, squeezing and twisting them, his body leaning and pushing against my body. My back is plastered to the wall and I am filled with a horror I never knew could be contained in me. His smells enter into me through my clothes and through my mouth, and I squirm and try to twist away from him. Trapped between his weight and the black wall I have to choose and choose not to escape. His cock is larger, more painful than I expected; it fills my vagina and my whole torso with a thumping, dull, unavoidable suddenness. His mouth is still glued to mine and I cannot make a sound.

"So. Do you want a job?" he asks me. I wipe my face on the sleeve of my purple cardigan. Thin shiny lines of snot glisten near the border of the cuff. "Yes," I tell him. He laughs and walks away. There is a river behind me. They say that more bodies are found floating near the banks of Camden Town than in any other place in London.

An old woman in tatters asks me, "Luv, what's the matter? You look sick. . . ." I do not answer. Behind the markets in Camden Town, behind the leather shops and the tourist barges I sit and lick my fingers, bite the top of my hand, and dream of food, of blue Kleenexes and wool blankets. I pick strands of purple cashmere from my cardigan and chew them thoroughly. I cup my hand under my jeans and let it rest there, pressing lightly to heal the tearing and the numbness. I rock myself back and forth and hypnotize myself into believing that everything is okay.

The water in the night ripples even though there's no wind. The light reflected over the river blinks and shimmers but never rests. I want to stand up but somehow I can't, my legs won't carry me. My head screams at my body to get moving, my knees jerk and order my feet to start walking, my vagina fills my ears with a wailing sound, my brain shouts at her to shut up, my arms help my body steady itself against the wall. Three and four and five pieces of me move through the night of Camden Town. I sit in a coffee shop and wait for them to call the police when I tell them that I have no money to pay for my cup of tea.

"Should have known t'was coming," the fat man with the gray apron tells me. He pushes me out of the coffee shop holding me by my shoulders and says, "J'st gait out of here and don't dare coming back, y'hear?" He spits after me when I am in the street but his mucus does not reach me and I am warm now.

This is what I do when they tell me that I always was and I still am a mistake. I say "It isn't true! You're lying! You love me but you won't say it!" This is what I do when he rises from the living room couch and grabs my shoulders and shakes me and tells me I am not fit to live with them, promises to send me away, to check me into a borstal. I say, "No, please, don't . . ." I ask, "Why, why?" but I should know better than to ask why. I tell them, "It might even be better than here." I run out of the room and from behind the door I listen to them argue about what to do with me, about him being too harsh and her too lenient. I think of myself as the little tin soldier; I don't speak, I don't break, and I fall only when they strike me down too much. I wonder if tonight they will reason or they will strike.

The subway tracks at New Cross Gate cross the railroad line. In the dark you can walk along iron rails and never really know what you are walking on. You must never get caught crossing the rail path or sliding under the station fence, of course. They have wild mutt dogs in the station, trained to keep intruders away. But because the dogs barked too much at the Rastafarian children of Southern London, the animals are now chained in the doghouse behind the station. I slide under the metal fence and hear them growl, useless against my freedom.

First I hear the subway—or is it the train?—coming, then I can see little red and yellow lights growing in the black dark distance and finally I get to see all of its mass and its shape and its power eager to suck me, pulling me under in a rush of wind and traction of emptiness just a second before I jump on the side of the tracks and win again.

From the other side of the fence he yells at me, "Hey, man! You crazy or sometin' . . ." and shakes his head, dreadlocks spinning under orange lights.

"No, man," I say, "I'm no crazy." I say "man" the way he says it, the way a Jamaican pronounces it: with an Italian *a.*

"Come here," he tells me and the *o* when he says "come" is round and full. "I am fine here," I tell him.

"You'll be dead there," he argues.

"I'll be dead everywhere," I explain. I hear the buzz of another train arriving in the distance and brace myself for the jump. I see the lights and I see the shape and I hear the loud piercing sound of the siren and I jump off the tracks just in time, fight the murderous suck of the air. When I look around I see that the Rastafarian isn't there anymore, and I can tell that even he knew I was right.

Kate Braverman

There were thirteen stories in my collection, Squandering the Blue *(Ballantine, 1990), so my editor and I decided to drop this one.*

NOSTALGIA FOR THE EMPIRE

Diana Barrington is thinking about death when Carlotta McKay, her best friend and blood sister, telephones. It is semidark, the sort of incomplete, tainted night that falls across one-bedroom stucco apartments where single mothers live with their dependents, vulnerable and unprotected, on streets punctuated by lawns overgrown with waist-high, unidentifiable vegetation that might have once been sunflowers or corn before generations of contamination. It is the sort of darkness pitted by the erratic sounds of transience, of lovers fighting and slamming suitcases and doors, of cars screeching to violent berths at curbs and ill-defined footsteps on flights of shared stairs. This night is littered with the implications of heartbreak, savagery, and the preliminaries preceding actual betrayal, divorce, and abandonment. There is the not quite tangible sound of drugs exchanging hands.

Diana glances at the clock. It is 9:30. Her six-year-old daughter, Annabell, is sleeping in the bedroom. Diana sleeps in the living room, on a sofa bed. She has been lying on the unopened sofa for days, watching TV without her contact lenses and considering the permutations of death by a terminal form of cancer that often first attacks the brain. A disease of unparalleled virulence transmitted by the act of love.

"It's Carlotta," her best friend says, unnecessarily.

"Carlotta. I know it's you. I would recognize your voice in any guise in this life and possibly in others." Diana lights a cigarette. "And you're the only person who still telephones."

"You're inaccessible," Carlotta points out. "You keep changing your number."

"I can't get out of bed." Diana begins, and abandons the attempt. She remembers that she no longer has a bed.

"You think exclusively about topics that render you paralyzed with terror." Carlotta sounds reasonable, perhaps even reassuring. "Remember when you discovered nuclear war? Recombinant DNA? Now AIDS."

"Don't ever say that word to me," Diana Barrington cautions. Her fist is clenched.

"You should get out of that apartment. American Ballet is coming to town." Carlotta pauses, presumably to allow that information to filter into tattered consciousness, her vast interior region that feels like a kind of ozone layer, pitted and torn, the climate becoming increasingly less stable, edging into the lethal. Perhaps she has had her own greenhouse effect, a certain unpredictable heat, a toxic delirium. "We should take Annabell to a matinee of *Sleeping Beauty*," Carlotta is saying. "We must expose her, inculcate the traditions, and nurture the premises of Western civilization."

Diana finds herself staring at the awkward old-fashioned black telephone receiver that she is somehow holding. "You must be due for a cancer checkup," Diana says.

Silence. "How did you know?" Carlotta's voice is tremulous.

"Whenever you wax poetic about my daughter, it is only the threat of impending malignancy that compels you. The rest of the time, you ignore her," Diana answers.

Diana is without interest in the ballet. What she really wants, she realizes, suddenly and with irrefutable clarity, is a sleek and graceful push-button phone in cream or perhaps pink. It occurs to her that she has spent her entire life longing for what was once called a princess phone. She recognizes that the issue of the princess phone is symbolic, an example of the relentless deprivation that comprises her life as an artist. It is a simple and inexpensive object that she, a poet, has never managed to afford. The injustice of this overwhelms her.

"I have a problem with people who weigh less than I do," Carlotta is admitting. "You buy the tickets."

"They took your Masterscharge?" Diana asks. "Again?"

Silence. "How did you know?" Carlotta asks, finally. There is a wide-open quality of surprise in her voice, as if she had been startled from a dream. Or perhaps, with her awful New Age propensities, Carlotta now suspected clairvoyance.

"I could see it coming," Diana tells her. "Stevie Wonder could see it coming."

Later, Diana orders the tickets by telephone, by her ancient and awkward black dial phone. She immediately regrets it. The contrived cultural excursions Carlotta devices for Annabell are extravagant and counterproductive.

Six months before, on the eve of Carlotta's last cancer checkup, they had taken Annabell to the Cirque du Soleil. Annabell had not been enchanted. She resisted the sophisticated medieval implications and kept asking, increasingly annoyed and confused, where the elephants were. When Diana chanced to glance at her daughter, Annabell was playing with her popcorn wrapper. She seemed mesmerized by the red-and-white-striped cardboard container.

"You keep anthropomorphizing her," Diana accused. She was talking about Annabell and Carlotta's exaggerated sense of what appropriate five-year-old entertainments were.

They were walking from the circus tent. The evening had been an elegance of eroticism, subtle and coherent. Annabell had not noticed this. All at once and concurrently, Diana felt bitter and hopeless. She had purchased the tickets on her overextended Master-charge and Carlotta was increasingly slow on the draw. Carlotta would claim to have no money. Carlotta would remind her that the

IRS was still garnishing her earnings and leaving her sixty dollars a week for after-rent survival. Time would pass, supplying brilliant fresh debris, unforeseen events of such sweep and brutality that the debt Carlotta had incurred would be perceived as insignificant. Carlotta would manage to forget about it and any attempt to remind her would appear tawdry.

"Is it over?" Annabell asked again. Her daughter had been asking this precise question approximately every eight minutes since the performance began. They were walking across a parking lot. This time, Annabell's voice was hopeful.

"Yes," Diana almost shouted.

"Thank God," Annabell sighed with relief.

Diana is lying on the unopened sofa in the room which serves, by economic necessity, as her bedroom, studio, storeroom, and family room. She is aware of a profound sense of despair that feels incalculable in dimension. It has something to do with the absence of aesthetics that informs her life. She studies her room with disgust. The galleys of her new novel, to be published by a feminist press in Oregon at an unspecified future date, are stacked on the floor beside dictionaries, magazines, newspapers, books, and pizza delivery boxes. Annabell's crayons are strewn as if deliberately, almost mathematically, one per square inch of floor. Discarded Barbie doll outfits form odd, nestlike mounds near the coffee mugs and red pencils on the wood surface that serves as her combination desk and family-room coffee table. Her shades are drawn. People pass on the sidewalk three feet from her face, speaking in languages she does not know. Perhaps they are plotting crimes in Spanish and Korean. Somewhere near, teenagers in gangs are spray-painting graffiti across the derelict sides of carports. There is a sense of wind rustling indifferent trees and banks of random, pathetic orange geraniums. Diana lies awake into the night, thinking the same thought, over and over like a tortured mantra or syllables designed to induce madness. She is thinking, I can't go on with this, I can't go on with this.

Carlotta telephones in the afternoon. Diana is not thinking about death. Inexplicably, her obsession with the plague is not the center of her existence at this particular moment. Instead, she is thinking about the course proposal she has just written for the Feminist Center of Los Angeles. She has titled her proposed class "Speaking the Unspeakable." Her focus will be the development of unconventional and forbidden subject matter.

"Until women can murder as well as create, until they demand the same latitudes as their male counterparts, until they give death as well as birth, we will not have a complete vocabulary," Diana tells her.

"I like it," Carlotta says. She sounds like a movie producer.

"I will never be condemned to the hell of writing pretty little nurturing things. I will never be forced to accept resolution when chaos is an option." Diana reads from her notes.

"You can substantiate that with the death goddesses, particularly Kali," Carlotta offers.

Diana Barrington is not interested in Kali. Certainly Carlotta knows her feelings in this matter. The entire goddess concept was a male perversion. It kept women occupied with illusionary tasks like sifting old myths and watching their meter. It was considerably less revolutionary than sewing. Of course, men wanted from their female writers what they wanted from their wives, aesthetically pleasing miniature repetitions, predictable and unthreatening.

Slowly, Diana becomes aware of the silence between them. It was the sort of unnatural quiet that often precedes bad news. There was an emotional climate to this density of silence, something that felt blue, like contaminated rain, perhaps, or her image of nuclear winter.

"It's about Saturday," Carlotta begins, enunciating each syllable clearly and firmly. "I can't pick you up."

"You mean you won't," Diana screams.

Carlotta does not reply. Lately, Carlotta has begun to refuse to visit her apartment. Carlotta prefers to meet somewhere. She intimates that her black Jaguar is unsafe in the fringe area Diana and her daughter inhabit, on a street of two-story stucco apartments adorned with low, crippled trees that pollution has somehow rendered inordinately small and curved. The vegetation looks as if it had turned curiously and deliberately bonsai. Even the obligatory palms seem deformed.

Diana Barrington lives in a ground-floor apartment. The windows are encased in wrought iron. A similar grate is strung across the trash-filled hollow that might once have been a lobby. The small black terraces face a narrow alley crowded with children's bicycles and bedsprings. Yellow-and-red banners announcing NOW RENTING are draped across the sides of the buildings.

Diana stares at the black telephone receiver. Carlotta, of all people, should appreciate the brutal parameters of her literal existence. They had taken feminist studies together at Berkeley.

"They ripped off my antenna last time," Carlotta asserts. "And that street just bums me out."

"How do you think I feel? Living here?" Diana begins to cry. She feels that she is symbolic of the legion of abandoned women with children left in dilapidated border areas, in furnished rooms and trailer parks, in interchangeable urban infestations where the sun glares. In this moment of infinite loss, the clouds seem irrelevant, squalid. The thin blue sky is a brutal mockery. And from the window, across the roofs of identical tenements, she can see women hanging laundry in a slow stalled sea breeze the color of corruption.

"Pull yourself together," Carlotta demands in the tone she used to employ when Diana was having a bad acid trip.

Diana Barrington experiences a sudden intense sensation that is simultaneously homicidal rage and a profound sadness; she feels as if the individual molecules that comprise her are each somehow weeping. The concurrent conflicting emotions: rage and contempt, self-pity and despair, fear and a sense of stain, of something incalculable and utterly tarnished, and an aching, a longing for something like solace or grace or absolution, all of this leaves her breathless and exhausted. And Diana goes back to her bed, which isn't a bed, which is a sofa in a living room in a substandard apartment in a neighborhood too tainted to even visit.

Her mood slowly improves. By Saturday morning, Diana begins to think that survival is an outside possibility. She moves through her miniature combination living room, bedroom, storeroom, dining room, and study with a sense of purpose. She decides that they will both wear similar black velvet dresses with white lace collars. It occurs to her that Annabell needs a white satin bow in her long black hair.

"I don't want a bow," Annabell informs her.

"This is obligatory. You must have a bow for the ballet. They won't let you in without it." Diana stands her ground.

"Oh, I'm really sure." Annabell sneers, one hand on her hip.

Diana begins to comb her daughter's hair. Annabell glares at her. When Diana brushes a tangle near her ear, her daughter screams.

Yes, there are the forms one could still practice, Diana thinks, brushing the black tangles while Annabell screams. Perhaps these pathetic conventionalities are not listless repetitions of a hollow and gutted hypocrisy. Perhaps these small and inadequate acts are, in fact, all there is.

Carlotta agrees to pick them up at a well-patrolled intersection of two garish boulevards several blocks from the dangerous apartment where she lives, in a kind of internal exile. Diana and Annabell hold hands as they walk. White ribbons in a daughter's hair, Diana thinks. Compromise with a best friend. The tangible manifestations of integrity everywhere apparent. Yes, the forms of civilization are miniature illuminations in the emotional barbarism of her life, but a sense of light nonetheless.

It is a surprisingly warm morning. Diana inspects the street as they walk, as if she has never quite seen it before. Diana often pretends she is an anthropologist gathering ethnographic data. She doesn't really inhabit this geography. She is just passing through. After six months of this agony, she will return to Boston or London, an apartment she calls a flat, with a view of stone buildings and substantial deciduous trees, maples and cedars and lindens and oak. Yes, trees you could make into furniture or burn. In the anthropologist fantasy, there are fireplaces and autumn and never a single palm.

Diana glances at the apartments as she walks. They are of a uniformly nondescript architecture, perhaps described as post-World War II indifference and greed. The buildings might once have been a soft beige. They are now the color of haze, smog, and divorce. Beside iron-grated lobbies, apartments wear indecipherable remnants of ornamentation, triangular motifs and circular designs that might once have been sundials or clocks. Perhaps this culture had once conceived of time.

Diana is drawn to a configuration of indeterminate meaning. It is some sort of collective celebration of rubble. The retrograde survivors of the disaster which has eradicated this society are doing something with rags. It is a garage sale in a vacant lot of still yellow grass. Piles of shabby clothing rise beside weeds. Windbreakers on hangers protrude from a bush. There are blond and red wigs on the top of poles like the heads on stakes in Conrad. Of course, any city street is a journey into the heart of darkness, Diana thinks.

"Don't touch that," Diana yells.

Annabell stares at her. Her daughter is standing on the edge of the vacant lot, her hand poised above a mound of seemingly random objects. Diana identifies cookie jars in the shape of bunnies and dogs.

"Don't ever touch anything at a garage sale," Diana cautions her daughter. They are walking again. "Those things have germs."

Diana is thinking that Annabell should immediately wash her hands when Carlotta appears. Diana stares at the black Jaguar, watching it swoop out from the traffic, enormous and assured. It is a dark predator and the waters part around it. Then she is opening the doors and pressing her back against the red leather seat. Her mood is definitely improving. Carlotta shoves a Joe Cocker tape into the tape deck. The tape deck works. "Unchain my heart," Cocker begins, his voice a synthesis of a certain quintessential agony. "Baby set me free."

The Jaguar moves south down Broadway. The air-conditioner works. They are cool and powerful. The doors are locked. The stereo speakers reproduce Cocker's anguished almost posthumous voice without distortion or static. It occurs to Diana Barrington that such speakers cost a fortune. She experiences a flare of rage.

Diana focuses out the window. Beyond their protected environment, the streets are crowded with minority shoppers, men in white T-shirts, women in bright cheap cotton, and ludicrously overdressed little girls in imitation layered chiffon dresses. The Latins carry bags of grocery items and boxes which presumably contain more stiff multilayered pink and yellow and red children's dresses. The blacks carry bizarrely large radios. The people seem simultaneously agitated and disoriented. They walk with fierce determination, as if battling an invisible wind, here where even the elements turn treacherous and betray. Joe Cocker sings, "Unchain my heart, baby set me free."

Diana recognizes that this moment is archetypal. The black Jaguar is equivalent to a litter of jade inlaid with human bone carried by slaves through dangerous streets of lepers and a malnourished underclass. Of course there has always been a caste system. There have always been intoxicants for the poor. They have always had their diseases.

"Look at all the wedding stores," Annabell, who has never been downtown before, notes.

"It's a world where everyone is constantly marrying," Diana says. "It's a manifestation of the cycle of pathetic inadequate seduction and garish abandonment."

"Those dresses are beautiful," Annabell insists.

"They are cheap and flashy. I send you to private school so you can learn that. There is no education anymore, not at any price, but there is still a recognition of class. At least you can have that," Diana says.

"Do you hear yourself?" Carlotta demands, annoyed.

"Annabell has a scholarship," Diana reminds her. "I'm not paying for it. Obviously."

"I'm not talking about that," Carlotta says.

Diana glares at her. They had marched together in the SDS, chanting, "Ho, Ho, Ho Chi Minh, Ho Chi Minh is gonna win," with half a million other pot smokers. Now Carlotta objected to her politics. Carlotta got to wear eight-hundred-dollar suits and go to court where she was addressed by her last name. She had a recognizable career category and all it implied, including regular threats from the IRS. Diana decides to ignore her.

"Look at all the children," Annabell says from the backseat, excited.

It is a Saturday in March and suddenly hot as August. On the street, men and women pass, carrying packages and pulling over-dressed children along by their arms. These people have come from the south, from El Salvador and Guatemala. They have left their families and crossed dangerous borders. They have stopped in Los Angeles and bred. Resignation has replaced a tangible destination.

It is at this moment, precisely, that Diana Barrington thinks of the plague. It is here, on the humid sidewalks they were coolly passing. This is where the virus incubates. It is on such Saturdays in such cities that it spreads. Outside the furnished rooms and stucco apartments embossed with webs of graffiti, outside the trailer parks and brick tenements, the virus. It is at such moments that Diana can perceive it. When all communication seems improbable and the mouth is useless, the lips induce a lurid erasure and hands are a mime of empty gestures.

She closes her eyes. In between, there is the plague, the debasement of history, and in the sky, toxins and planes.

"I can't breathe," Diana says.

Out beyond her window, her locked door, in the heat that is somehow artificial and cruel, she can sense it spreading. It is in the shared syringes. It is in the animal sex between strangers, the terrible flawed attempts to find intensity within the monotony, to be inside and entered, or simply to please. And the lovers and cousins and husbands that keep returning from prison. A legion of junkies and women lying facedown on their bellies, being mated like dogs.

"I can see it incubating," Diana says. Her face feels soft and blurred and distant, as if it were coming from behind a cold screen.

"Careful," Carlotta cautions, her voice suddenly aggressive. "Your phobias are showing."

Like dogs, we are like dogs, all of us, Diana thinks. We are predators of the rubble, in our malevolent clutter, where only our debris is potent, radioactive, with a half-life larger than empires or grace or emptiness itself. The virus of our mutant greed and selfishness. This is what Diana Barrington is thinking, precisely, as they walk into the Shrine Auditorium through a swarm of little girls with white bows in their hair holding hands with their mothers. They are the not-yet-infected. They have to be protected. This is what Diana Barrington is thinking as she sits down and the houselights dim.

Diana is dazzled by the ballet. She is momentarily surprised by her reaction. On the periphery, far away, she notices that Annabell seems tired and withdrawn. Periodically, Carlotta whispers criticisms. Carlotta terms the dancing unexciting, even lackluster.

"You were rapt," Carlotta accuses. They are walking to the parking lot. Carlotta's voice contains contempt.

"I was adding up the cost of the costumes. I was keeping a running tab," Diana tries.

"You were drinking a Tab?" Annabell is suddenly alert and hopeful.

"I'm having a vision," Diana announces as they drive on a shabby street bordering USC, passing frame houses torn by the elements, time, and personal catastrophes. They pass tall thin boys with radios by their heads like oblong appendages. And black women who look like they practice voodoo on a daily basis. The gods are not dead, Diana thinks. They are disguised, are the color of concrete, of vacant lots and parched grass.

Carlotta stops at a red light and stares at her. Yes, Carlotta is staring at her with wide eyes that seem to hold no judgment at all. And isn't it incredible that these tons of steel actually come to a stop when one wills it, one presses a pedal with a leather-sandaled foot and the beast is obedient, docile, mute? Or that the sun rises each day at exactly the moment it was predicted? And it isn't a matter of technology or condos or the poisoned landscape or butchered sky. It is rather that we pretend a sophistication, as if it were possible to inhabit a region where the antiquities had been banished. Isn't the sensibility fundamentally Stone Age, Diana thinks, primal and uncorrupted?

"I believe in sorcery and spells, absolute evil, and the temptations of the soul," Diana hears herself saying. "I believe in prophecy, grace, and hell."

The car isn't moving. Carlotta is still staring at her. "You've got to stop this," Carlotta says. Her voice is soft.

"My vision," Diana remembers. "Yes. I see a resurgence in the classical forms."

"Not based on that performance," Carlotta points out.

"It has nothing to do with quality. It's sociological. As the plague spreads, class distinctions will be synonymous with survival. Ballet. Opera. It won't be enough to drive—"

"A Jaguar," Carlotta supplies.

"A BMW. Class will become caste, as it always has. There will be no social mobility. And, of course, there will be nostalgia for the empire."

"The empire?" Carlotta glances at her.

"The American Empire," Diana says. "We were too young to

appreciate it. Then there was Berkeley. Now, I'm afraid, it's gone."

"America is gone?" Annabell asks. She looks out the car window. "Where did it go?"

On a lawn in front of a two-story wood-frame house, an urban shack, another garage sale is in progress: it is a city of constant garage sales, as if people are relentlessly ripping off their neighbors and selling off the residue, the things even they do not want. The stacks of red-and-black unattractive pants, the lampshades with dents and stains, the aluminum kitchen utensils, the worn stuffed animals baking under the fierce sun, where did it come from and why was it there? The black wrought-iron pedestals that might have once been plant stands, the pieces of vacuum cleaners and stereo speakers, the rolls of chicken wire and fabric and rusted metal racks for records? The virus is there, of course, on the thinning torn lawn and in the residue. Somewhere near, money is changing hands for packages of white-and-brown powder. Somewhere, a syringe is being passed around a room.

"I see patrolled streets," Diana Barrington hears herself saying. "The infected classes wear armbands. The ghettos are enclosed."

"Storm troopers protect the Music Center," Carlotta offers.

"Criminal penalities for fraternization. Compulsory monthly blood tests. Concentration camps for the positives." Diana is trembling. "Bodies burning in the central plazas. In the air, a dirty human smoke."

Carlotta drives, contriving not to look at her. Night is falling on the doomed city in its usual array of postapocalyptic maroons and magentas. The air is metallic.

"I'm finally through with ballet," Carlotta says after a while.

Diana stares at her. "You can afford to be," she says. Diana is aware of the tension between them. In the unnatural silence, she senses a kind of toxic charge.

It is dark now. Soon Carlotta will drop them off at the outskirts of the neighborhood. It is Saturday night. In the city, women are everywhere pulling red dancing dresses over their bodies. Men from prison will mount them from behind. On street corners, in parking lots, and on the edges of lawns overgrown by urban foliage without distinct category, the profits from burglaries, muggings, armed robberies, prostitution, and garage sales are being exchanged for plastic packets. It is here, in the wood-frame cottages and stucco bungalows, along the curbs and by the trash cans, in the blood of sex acts, in the needles, in the rooms and bars and discos. Diana Barrington leans back into the red leather seat and watches the plague spread.

Double Takes

(Alternate Versions,
Titles, and Endings)

hysterical

I saw the best minds of my generation
            generation destroyed by madness
            dragging starving, mystical, naked,
who dragged themselves thru the angry streets at
            dawn looking for a negro fix
who poverty and tatters and fantastic minds
            sat up all night in lofts
                        contemplating jazz,
who bared their brains to heaven under the El
            and saw Mohammedan angels staggering
                        on tenement roofs illuminated,
who sat in rooms naked and unshaven
            listening to the Terror through the wall,
who burned their money in wastebaskets
            amid the rubbish of unread Bronx manifestos,
who got busted in their beards returning
            through the border with a belt
                        of marihuana for New York,
who loned it through the streets of Idaho
            seeking visionary indian angels
                        who were visionary indian angels,
who passed through universities
            with radiant cool eyes hallucinating
            Arkansas anarchy & Blake-light tragedy
                        among the post-war cynical scholars,
who burned in the hells of poetry turpentine + paint
            whose apartments flared up in the joyous fires
                        of their heavenly brains,
who purgatoried their bodies night after night
            with dreams, with drugs, with waking nightmeares,
                        alchohol and cock and endless balls,
Peyotl solidities of the halls, backyard cemetary mornings,
            wine drunkeness over the rooftops, teahed red light
                        distriots, sun and moon and tree vibrations
                        in the roaring dusks of winter
                                    winter dusks of Brooklyn,
who chained themselves to subways for an endless ride
            from from Battery to holy Bronx until the noise
                        of wheels and children brought them down
                        trembling wide eyed on Benzadrine shuddering
                        mouth-racked and brilliant brained
                                    in the drear light of Zoo,
who mopped all night in desolate Bickfords
            listening to the crack of doom
                        on the hydrogen jukebox,
who talked continuously seventy hours from park
            to pad to bar to Bellevue to museum
                        to Long Island to
the Brooklyn Bridge, a lost batallion of platonic
            conversationalists jumping down the stoops
            vomiting out their facts and anecdotes
            ——memories and eyeball kicks and shocks
                        of hospitals and jails and wars,
who vanished into the New Jersies of amnesia
            posting cryptic picture postcards
                        of Belmar City Hall and last years sharks,
who suffered sweats and bone grindings and migraines
            of junk-witdrawel in Newark's bleak frnisjed room,

+ later—
and black of brained
all
brained
of brilliante

Allen Ginsberg

PAGE ONE OF THE
ORIGINAL FIRST DRAFT OF *HOWL*, PART I

        I saw the best minds of my generation
           generation destroyed by madness
               starving, ~~mysticall~~, naked,   hysterical

dragging —————— ~~who dragged~~ themselves thru the angry streets at
           dawn looking for a negro fix
       who poverty and tatters and fantastic minds
           sat up all night in lofts
               contemplating jazz,
       who bared their brains to heaven under the El
         · and saw Mohammedan angels staggering
                  on tenement roofs illuminated,
       who sat in rooms naked and unshaven
           listening to the Terror through the wall,
     · who burned their money in wastebaskets
           amid the rubbish of unread Bronx manifestos,
       who got busted in their beards returning
           through the border with a belt
              of marihuana for New York,
       who loned it through the streets of Idaho
           seeking visionary indian angels
               who were visionary indian angels,
       who passed through universities
           with radiant cool eyes hallucinating

Arkansaw ————————— ~~anarchy~~ & Blake-light tragedy
              among the post-war ~~cynical~~ scholars,

0   s   who burned in the helll of ~~poetry & paint~~ ————— turpentine & paint
           whose apartments flared up in the joyous fires
              of their heavenly brains,
       who purgatoried their bodies night after night
           with dreams, with drugs, with waking nightmeares,
              alchohol and cock and endless balls,
    Peyotl solidities of the halls, backyard cemetary mornings,

                         wine drunkeness over the rooftops, teahed red light
     flying| districts|, sun and moon and tree vibrations
                         in the roaring ~~dusks of winter~~
                                    winter dusks of Brooklyn,
                    who chained themselves to subways for an endless ride
     & batter -   ~~thru~~ from Battery to holy Bronx until the noise
and bleak ~~of~~ brained   of wheels and children brought them down
         all   ~~trembling~~ wide eyed on Benzadrine shuddering
drained of brilliance————— mouth-racked and brilliant brained
                                 in the drear light of Zoo,
                    who mopped all night in desolate Bickfords
     or   ed   listen~~ing~~ to the crack of doom
15   on the hydrogen jukebox,———in the stale beer bar
                    who talked continuously seventy hours from park   of third avenue
                       to pad to bar to Bellevue to museum
                                 to Long Island to
                    the Brooklyn Bridge, a lost barallion of platonic
                       conversationalists jumping down the stoops————— off fire escap
Screaming &—————————— vomiting ~~out~~ their facts and anecdotes   off Empire ~~State bldg~~
                    —memories and eyeball kicks and shocks   ~~& off the Empire State—~~
                       of hospitals and jails and wars,   & off the moor
                    who vanished into ~~the Jersies of~~ the New Jersies of amnesia
                       posting cryptic picture postcards
                                 of Belmar City Hall and last years sharks
ing   ~~who~~ suffered sweats and bone grindings and migraines————— of Tangie
in——————————— ~~of~~ junk-withdrawel ~~in~~ Newarks's bleak frnisjed room,   unde

Delmore Schwartz

These entries were made on November 11 and 12, 1954, and are reprinted from Portrait of Delmore: Journals and Notes of Delmore Schwartz, *edited by Elizabeth Pollet (Farrar, Straus and Giroux, 1986). The note at the beginning is by Ms. Pollet.*

NOVEMBER 11

[The following poems contain some of the same or variant lines finally used in "The Kingdom of Poetry," in Selected Poems.*]*

     Poetry is certainly
More interesting, more valuable
   And certainly more charming
Than everything contained in the zoos, parks, or poppy
                 palaces in Hollywood
It is far more interesting as it is far more
           Coherent & organized
Than the Atlantic Ocean, Niagara Falls,
And other overwhelming phenomena.
It is as useful as light & as beautiful
It discovers and renews the original freshness of reality
Again and again and forever, like the sun and the morning
It is necessary, it is preposterous, it is unpredictable
Precisely, for it is as implausible and true
         As the kangaroo.
It naturally imitates, illuminates, celebrates, and improves
     Upon the raw glory
Of reality's festival & circus.
For as it [is] fecund & beautiful, it is very powerful
For only the faithful, straining
To be adequate to the edge and extreme of dream
      Can lift, carry, or move mountains
Succeeding only as wrestlers, in an overwhelming labor
         Triumphant but exhausted.
It is true that poetry begins in the chaos of pandemonium
[. . .]
Since poetry like nature succeeds through profusion
[: . .]

[. . .] and poetry must be ubiquitous
If it is to be gay, exact, and serious
As it is when it says: a sunset resembles a bull fight,
        The dew upon the grass resembles cuff links,
These are acts of invention & love,
            Uniting experience & heightening consciousness.
Hence poetry makes the past rise from the
        Sepulcher, like Lazarus
It makes a lion into a sphinx and a girl,
As it gives to a girl the splendor of Latin
For poetry invented the unicorn, the centaur, the
        Phoenix, the sonnet, and the limerick
As the sonnet augmented the nature of praise
So the limerick discovered new structures &
                Somersaults of laughter.

Hence it is true that poetry is an
            Everlasting ark
An omnibus of all the mind's animals.
It is the supreme sunlight of consciousness
Making love eloquent, giving tongue to forgiveness.
Hence a short [history] of poetry would be a
            Short history of love
(It would also be a text, a testament, and an epitome of joy)
For love requires the diminutives & the pet names
Which only poetry provides with fullness, with richness
        Spontaneous & original
            Adequate to the advent
                Of the event of uniqueness
And joy requires the soaring choirs of poetry
            Rising as the flames of
                The bonfires of jubilee & hallelujah!
For poetry is like light, and it is light
It shines over all like the blue sky, with the
            Same blue justice.
Since it is the sunlight of consciousness
It is also the soil of the fruits of knowledge
                In the orchards of being.
It is also the fire which burns the black coals
            Of desire
Poetry is quick as tigers, clever as cats, vivid as oranges
Nevertheless it is deathless: after the Pharaohs & Caesars
            Have fallen

It shines and endures more than diamonds
The praise of poetry is like the
                    Clarity of mountains
The heights of poetry are like the
                    Exaltation of mountains
It is the consummation of the stars
                    Of consciousness in the
                    Country of the morning

NOVEMBER 12

This is the time to praise poetry clearly
                              and loudly
For now poets are regarded as having
                         the limited significance
Of flagpole sitters, deep-sea divers, or marathon
                              dancers
They receive the same care as xylophones &
                         equestrian statues
& now they are honored and ignored like
                    famous dead Presidents
Supported like holidays & given less attention
Than a circus, a musical comedy, or a catastrophe.
Hence it is proper to declare the power & the
                    glory of poetry
        It shows us the pleasures of the city
        It lights the structures of reality
        It is a cause of knowledge & laughter
        It sharpens the whistles of the witty
        It is like morning (the flutes of morning)
            It is the first morning forever
This truth must be proved anew unendingly
                    like the truth of love
I will write a poem about the kings of emotion
    The monarchs of the heart & of English
The lords of the joy after the suffering
                    without hope
The children of the new birth after the
                    death of the heart
The type of Orpheus & Lazarus, and of Jacob victorious,
                and Joseph triumphant.
Hence it will be a joyous, jubilant, mercurial poem
It will be full of triumphant repetition

It will be full of stories of light and
                    international romances
[. . .]
It will assert that America is the
                    new world & new Eden
The promise of the freedom to begin again
                    forever at the frontier of hope
It will seek the festival of exaltation
          After the tree of the knowledge
                    of good & evil
Has been struck by the ego's lightning
It will declare that that tree grows
          And is green again in the May of
                    forgiveness & hope
Because America is adventure, as it was
                    in the beginning
Because freedom is existence & persists only
                    as the freedom of hope
& of beginning again after the blessing of forgiveness

W. D. Snodgrass

The poem "Mr. Evil Disguises Himself as Herself with Murder in Her Heart for W. D." appeared in a recent issue of Salmagundi. Since then, however, I've decided to make it part of a Dance Suite I've been working on with the painter DeLoss McGraw. In this cycle of poems and paintings, Mr. Evil (who's been part of several other cycles) decides to go in drag as Miss Treavle and to seduce the hero, who has the unlikely name of "W. D." So, if this was to be part of the suite, it had to go to the music of some well-known dance—there's already a waltz, a tango, a tap dance, a masquerada, a fox trot, etc. I decided a striptease would be the best for this, since Mr. Evil, even in putting on such a disguise, is really stripping himself down to his true nature—so I set this to the tune of "The Stripper"—this involved, chiefly, rearranging the couplets into stanzas, but it also became longer in the process.

MR. EVIL DISGUISES HIMSELF AS HERSELF— WITH MURDER IN HER HEART FOR W. D.
—After the Painting by DeLoss McGraw

Note, please, the elegance of line,
The delicate gestures and the fine
Seductive bias of the torso
Slim as a palmtree. Even more so,
Check out the precious, heart-shaped bib
Accenting the breast cage and rib
With hints of some great passion; watch
These arrows pointing to the crotch.
It's time to welcome our Miss Treavle,
Shaped with all a daughter of Eve'll
Offer a man, then when she's had 'im
Let him be driven out like Adam
Forth from the flaming gates of Eden.
What need for me to visit Sweden?
Right here, I rise up from the norm
Accoutered in my own trans-form,
Designer flanks and slate-gray denims
Sleek as a cobra steeped in venoms,
Slink up the particolored ladder
To his roost, swaying like an adder,
While small black thoughts circle my head
Like gnats crooning, "I'll knock him dead!"

DANCE SUITE:
MR. EVIL DISGUISES HIMSELF AS HERSELF— WITH MURDER IN HER HEART FOR W. D.
Melody: "The Stripper"

Note the elegance of line,
The grass skirt gestures and the fine
      seduc-
      tive bi-
      as of
      the torso,
Slim as a palm tree;
      even more so,

Check this precious, heart-shaped bib
At the breast cage and the rib

suggest-
　ing heart-
　felt pas-
　sion; watch
These arrows pointing
　　to the crotch.

Time to welcome our Miss Treavle,
Shaped with all some daughter of Eve'll
　　give
　　a man,
　　then when
　　she's had 'im,
Drive him forth, stripped
　　stark as Adam

Through the flaming gates of Eden.
What need I repair to Sweden?
　　I'll drag
　　up my
　　new clothes
　　exchange
Into something rare and sex-strange.

Here, I rise up from the norm
Decked out in my own trans-form—
　　design-
　　er flanks
　　in slate-
　　gray denims,
Sleek as a cobra
　　steeped in venoms,

Then slink up the swaying ladder
To his roost, lithe as an adder,
　　while black
　　thoughts swarm
　　around
　　my head,
Crooning like gnats, "I'll
　　knock him dead!"

Amy Tan

I have few extant "literary outtakes" related to writing my first book, *The Joy Luck Club* (G. P. Putnam's, 1989). I went through more than seven thousand manuscript pages, and only 350 managed to escape my garbage can. Aside from those seven thousand pages, there are also many more that saw life only on my computer screen—and only long enough for me to cringe, then mercifully send into oblivion the fancy phrases, false starts, and writerly clichés.

Looking back, I do have to admit that the most significant outtake was one I did not think of on my own. It occurred in 1987, before I even started to write the rest of the book. And it consisted of removing three words and replacing them with four.

I had just signed on with my literary agent, Sandra Dijkstra, with only three short stories in my file. She suggested I draft a proposal: what a whole book might look like consisting of more stories like the first three I had shown her. She thought there was a chance of selling the book before it was even written. I thought she was an optimist in the extreme; pragmatist that I am, I refused to delude myself with wild fantasies of being published so soon. But I also felt the proposal would keep me focused on my fiction writing. In ten years' time, who knows what could happen?

So I quickly wrote a proposal, briefly describing sixteen stories for what was then to be a first collection. I had in mind a set of stories, divided into five sections, each related to one of the Chinese elements that make up one's nature and fate: wood, earth, fire, water, and metal. In it would be separate vignettes told by women, young and old, who lacked one element, had too much of another. I titled my book-to-be-written, "Wind and Water," after the Chinese belief in *feng shui,* the balance of elements which governs one's harmony with nature during life and after death. I also thought it sounded very literary.

My agent called and said she liked the proposal very much. But after a few minutes' discussion, she said, "I don't know, that title seems a little obscure, maybe too prosaic. But in the first story, you talk about the Joy Luck Club—what an unusual and wonderful title that would be."

The words, "The Joy Luck Club," had never struck me as unusual or remotely literary. It was a social club my father had named and to which my parents and their friends had belonged for as long as I could remember. After years of hearing about it, the name had come to sound quite ordinary to me. But after my agent suggested the title change, I could see the stories revolving around a community of women who were more intimately related to one another than what I had originally proposed to write. I changed the title, figuring if it didn't sound right by the time I finished writing the book—which, by my estimate, would be years later—I could change it then. Plenty of time to reconsider.

Within a couple of months, my agent went to New York and sold the book—with that title. I pulled out the proposal and began to write the rest of the book, starting with the first story, "The Joy Luck Club." And when I could see the club and its members in my mind, the characters took over the storytelling—and I mean this in a literary, not mystical, sense. That is, the characters determined the stories to be told, not the proposal. And those stories became increasingly interwoven, past layered upon present, present intersecting with past.

Those characters were also the ones who told me that a word, spoken aloud, is magic itself, a wish that can be fulfilled. And I did feel those words, "joy" and "luck," brought me exactly those elements as I was writing.

Of course, I sometimes wonder what would have happened if I had not changed the title. Because now I realize that a title is not simply an ornament that graces a book jacket. For me, the title gave shape to the stories, provided the necessary force to pull the whole book through from beginning to end.

Peter Benchley

Dear Mr. Dark:
I'm afraid I don't have any outtakes to send you. In an effort to keep from drowning in a sea of paper, I throw away whatever I don't use. And nowadays, of course, in the age of the computer/word processor, the unusable is simply erased.

About the only thing I can think of that might be remotely useful to you is a sampling of the 100+ titles that were rejected before—*faute de mieux*—I settled on *Jaws* . . . twenty minutes before the book had to go to press.

I had toyed with a lot of Françoise Sagan–like stuff, such as *A*

Stillness in the Water. My father goaded me onward with splendid suggestions like *What Dat Noshin' on My Laig?* Then there were *The Jaws of Death* and *Leviathan Rising* and *White Death* and *The Jaws of Leviathan* and *Death in the Water* and *Shark!* and (the French used this one for their version) *The Teeth of the Sea* and *Summer of the Shark* and on and on and on. . . .

Finally, I said to my editor, Tom Congdon, that since we couldn't agree on any title we should concentrate on a single word we liked, and the only word we thought was kind of good was *Jaws.* So screw it, said I, we'll call it *Jaws.*

I ran the title by my family and my agent. Everybody hated it. I didn't think much of it, either. But what the hell . . . nobody buys first novels anyway.

Sorry I can't give you anything better.

yrs,
Peter Benchley

Gilbert Sorrentino

LOST SONGS

"Clime Hot, Four Beers!"
"Blue Ruin to Go"
"That Bold Stealing"
"There We'll Severally a Brother Screw"
"Lou Calls It Badness, Yet Sy Balls a Dove"
"Nuts Hot for Thee"
"Prancing With Leers at Thy Fly"
"Hard Aches"
"Busts Won Romance"
"Pillow Deep for *Whee!*"
"The Poule Regards Her Crooked Seams"
"Go Kiss the Sated Lady"
"Sigh, Cold Dame"
"My Pants Are Parted"
"Dikes *Can* Cream, Rant I"
"Suspenders in the Lane"

"I'll Enter Vile, at Ten"
"Gall and Nothing *but* Gall"
"Tools Gushin' "
"Clues in Her Tights"
"Vi Got Her Lad and Kat Ain't Good"
"Hy Don't Want to Fuck Without Sue"
"Wild December's April"
"Few'll Ever Blow"
"My Shawl and Gloves Glow Crazily"
"I Stood Bare"
"So What's a Sin to Me?"
"These Ghoulish Flings"
"Annie Mercery's Faults"
"Sin, Love, and Pain"

Michael Drinkard

GREEN BANANAS* MISCELLANY

Never-used title for *Green Bananas: Earthlings.*

Never-used epigraphs for *Green Bananas:*

> On any night you can hear evolution happening.
> —Biology: An Introductory Text

> This is the sound of hundreds of thousands of tiny sperm.
> —Channel 13 PBS TV

Never-used book jacket for *Green Bananas:*

> A leading toy company denied permission to use its well-known dolls (standing on a patch of microscopically photographed sperm cells) for the book jacket art.

---

*Alfred A. Knopf, 1989

Sharon Olds

MY ~~DOG~~ ~~MY~~ ~~SUMMER~~ MY OUTTAKES

LENINGRAD CEMETERY, WINTER OF 1941

That winter, the dead could not be buried.
The ground was frozen, the gravediggers weak from hunger,
the coffin wood used for fuel. So they were covered with
     something
and taken on a child's sled to the cemetery
in the sub-zero air. They lay on the soil,
some of them wrapped in dark cloth
bound with rope like the tree's ball of roots
when it waits to be planted; others wound in sheets,
their pale, gauze, tapered shapes
stiff as cocoons that will split down the center
when the new life inside is prepared;
but most lay like corpses, their coverings
coming undone, naked calves
hard as corded wood spilling
from under a cloak, a hand reaching out
with no sign of peace, wanting to come back
even to the bread made of glue and sawdust,
even to the icy winter, and the siege.

"Leningrad Cemetery, Winter of 1941" used to have a nineteenth
line. Its present last line was its next-to-last. It ended like this:

with no sign of peace, wanting to come back
even to the bread made of glue and sawdust,
even to the icy winter, and the siege,
wanting to come back.

When Howard Moss wrote to me to accept the poem for *The New
Yorker* (Dec. 31, 1979), the first one he'd taken out of the many I'd
"offered" over the years (Muriel Rukeyser used to say she preferred
offering to *submitting*), he said he thought I didn't need the last line.
I could end with *siege*. Immediately I saw that it was a "better"
ending—subtler, smarter, less hopeful. It didn't really sound like me,

but it was better. Hmm . . . I had long had a fear of my own imitativeness. I felt it behooved me, especially as a woman, to sound like myself, for better or for worse. But I knew I repeated things too much, partly out of a lack of faith that a reader would get it. I was assuming a reader like myself—patient, emotional, a bit thick, and a salvation addict, wanting to end on *come back,* not on *siege.* But my reader was smart, subtle—was Howard Moss! I would read his note, over and over. Would he still take the poem, even if I didn't change it? I'd hold the little page of stationery up to the light bulb—any secret writing in lemon juice to guide me? And Lord Byron, or Amy Lowell, or whoever that immaculate diffident "New Yorker" on the letterhead was, so little like any New Yorker on West Ninety-seventh Street, would look down his/her long nose. . . .

Finally I decided that it was a stronger poem "his" way, that most readers did not need to be hit over the head with the meaning. And the lesson stayed with me. Since then, many of my poems have been born with a tail that subsequently—like the sperm's when it enters the egg—has fallen off gently on its own.

So as I struggled with "Making Love" (pleasant angel to wrestle with), this memory was with me. But the issues were different. I have noticed lately that I write in quatrains and couplets: a four-line structure lies disguised under my enjambed rush, in the same way that a regular iambic quatrameter (out of Isaac Watts) lies under my four-beat, accentual line. And if I look at "Making Love" from "Tomorrow" on, I see a quatrain, then a couplet, then a final *three* lines. There used to be a fourth. But I could not get the line right.

you will not remember, you will never know,
~~everything is as it should be.~~
~~this is how it was meant to be.~~
~~this is the way it should be.~~
~~all is as it should be.~~

All is as it, graceful in Aztec, is *awk!* in English. But when I thought of taking the last line off, the poem felt one line short, as if the resolving phrase in a hymn were not sung. The poem now ended on a *tercet. Eeeuw!* It felt all wrong. It felt almost morally dangerous, or dangerous even in some *physics* sense, as if the Protestant hymn-rhythm, that four-beat line in boxed quatrains, were the actual girder-system holding Berkeley, California (if not the universe), up.

But it was the only way to solve it. So I sent the poem out incomplete (*The Atlantic,* July 1985). Only this morning do I notice that its incompleteness may be right—to have an eerie sense of the unfinished is not inappropriate at a moment when you're thinking about not knowing.

MAKING LOVE

You can't ever remember it really.
You wake up and you do not know
where you are or who you are or
what you are, the last light of the evening is
coming up to the windows, not coming in, and it is
more like a cold mist than light,
greenish, standing there in the deep frames,
the bedpost a dark knob, not gleaming, the
heavy heavy body of the desk
between two windows—solid maple with its
curled resinous bird's-eyes shining inside the wood. And you
try to think back, you cannot remember it,
it stands in the back of your mind like a mountain,
at night, behind you, enormous, or a field of
snow at night, your pants are torn or
across the room or still dangling from one leg like a
heavy scarlet loop of the body, your
bra is half on or not on or you were naked to begin with,
you cannot remember, all you know is you feel
absolute, and everything is changed.
Tomorrow, maybe, taking a kid to school,
your foot half off the curb in the air you'll
see his mouth where it was and feel it and the
large dark double star of your two bodies
but for now you are like the one in the crib,
you are everyone right now,
the three milky greenish windows like
sentinels there saying Don't worry,
you will not remember, you will never know.

Barry Yourgrau

This was the original ending for "Pirates," a story of an elderly father's swashbuckling heroism. But I decided it made too tidy and soft a frame on things. So I left it off, leaving the story to end simply with the image of the old man's foolish but sweet-hearted posturing in the kitchen after battle. "Pirates" is from Wearing Dad's Head (Gibbs M. Smith, 1987 [USA]) *and* A Man Jumps out of an Airplane/Wearing Dad's Head (Grafton Books, 1988 [UK]).

. . . Two months after this episode he and my mother go on their annual vacation and that's when he develops a rare form of colic and, quite unexpectedly, succumbs. I have the slides he'd taken up to the point of their holiday, they're right here beside me as I write at my desk overlooking the mountains. Some of them are quite lovely indeed. They will always have a very special meaning for me.

Scott Sommer

Alternate ending to Still Lives (Viking, 1989)

The music stopped. Frankle recognized the woman to be Dakota Pomeroy. Blood was spreading down her blouse into the skirt. Her look of astonishment was directed over Frankle's left shoulder, and he turned to behold Stanley Starke still pointing a revolver. He was standing in a path of dusty sunlight that fell directly through the alleyway between the duplexes. His slack mouth was twitching slightly, as if he were suppressing laughter or tears.

"Stan?"

Starke held a hand up to shield his eyes from the sun and stared vacantly. Frankle noticed that his friend's leg had begun to tremble so ungovernably that he couldn't hold the pistol steady in his hand.

"You're scaring everyone, Stan." Frankle tried to find Nick and Constance in the blur of the crowd. "Put the gun down now."

Starke now aimed the gun at Frankle with both hands.

"Is she dead, Thomas? She looks dead."

"Please . . . the gun, Stan."

"Check if she's dead!"

Frankle put his hands up in a gesture to calm Starke and took a step forward, hoping to cover the exposure of people behind him. Cautiously, he reached out his hand for the silver pistol.

"Come on now, Stan. Steady down."

Starke's eyes seemed to clear and focus on Frankle.

"The gun . . . Stan."

Frankle thought he saw Starke begin to comply when footsteps sounded behind Frankle. At once Harry Chambers drew protectively in front of Frankle, brandishing an automatic weapon.

"What the fuck's going on!"

Starke began to laugh.

"That's one of your toys! It's a facsimile of what you used on the women and children."

"Don't bet."

"Stan," Frankle said. "Drop the gun. We want to get Dakota an ambulance."

Starke tried to step clear of the sunlight and, failing this, shielded his face with his arms.

"Are you siding with them, Thomas? Why?"

Frankle was about to answer when Gordon Busch came charging through the fire door behind Starke. Concurrently, Chambers himself charged forward, stepping first with the bad leg that would, a step later, collapse beneath the weight of his sudden surge for Starke, thereby preventing Chambers from ever reaching the gun. Still, more than likely, this fall spared Chambers his life, for when Busch slammed into Starke's back, the gun discharged, ending all light as it shattered forever the astonished heart of Thomas Frankle. And however stupefying this bad luck, it surely spared Frankle the horror of a berserk Harry Chambers bashing out Stanley Starke's brains with the butt end of a facsimile M16.

By the time the photographer for the homicide division had completed his shots of the dead, night had fallen and the party was over. It had happened so suddenly.

After that, at least as far as Thomas Frankle was concerned, all that remained of his earthly journey was to bury him in a grave less than thirty miles west of the city, at the right side of his father, where, it was widely hoped, he found peace at last.

As for the subsequent regret and wonder and disbelief, that would be reserved for those who went on living, in the various ways circumstances would let them live, in an ever-darkening world that Thomas Frankle would never again see.

Peter De Vries

Alternate ending of Let Me Count the Ways *(Little, Brown, 1965)*

The universe is like a safe to which there is a combination. But the combination is locked up in the safe.

John Updike

The original ending of Self-Consciousness *(Alfred A. Knopf 1989).*

. . . Even toward myself, as my own life's careful manager and promoter, I feel a touch of disdain. Precociously conscious of the precious, inexplicable burden of selfhood, I have steered my unique little craft carefully, at the same time doubting that carefulness is the most sublime virtue.

OPPOSITIONAL OTHER: *Pfauggggh!* Fearfulness and selfishness, that's all I've been hearing. What a little Fafner you are—"I have and I hold!" Clinging to a creed demolished everywhere you look, to a patriotism as obsolete as blood sacrifice, to a storybook small town that never existed, least of all in the dingy Thirties; toadying to any establishment that comes your way, from a high-school faculty to a Communist Writers' Union; so anxious to please and afraid of a little normal opposition your tongue and lungs can't get the words out; so afraid of losing a flake of your precious dragon's hoard of you-ness you resist every change from the condominium next door to the junking of the Electoral College and even think ending the Cold War may be a bad idea; in love with the status quo under the delusion that you've done well by it; obsessed with a painless harmless skin disease as if without it you'd be a raving male beauty; and now in this present chapter of egocentric rambling even slyly confessing to wanting, on the basis of medieval or at best eighteenth-century metaphysics, to preserve your miserable, spotty identity forever! What about the *big* picture!! Where in all these millions of words you boast about is there any serious consideration of the large issues that concern humanity in the mass?

Nuclear war! Holocaust! The industrial-military complex! Birth control! The rust belt! The national deficit! AIDS!

SELF: Well, I *have* written a play about a President and a novel about a coup. But morality and politics in general, it seems to me, were definitively handled in the works of George Bernard Shaw. All that a lively intelligence, generous spirit, and tireless style could do along these lines, he did. In any case the large ground is heavily trod. My own concern gravitates to the intimate, where the human intersects with something inhuman, something dark and involuntary and unsubmissive to man-created order. After all that Kierkegaard and Barth that I once consumed, it is hard for me to be reverential about the purely human. Nevertheless, I unfailingly vote; I contribute to charities, and even sometimes respond to especially shaming solicitations by mail; I recognize that the good and legal thing, in a well-policed society, is generally also the convenient thing—

O.O.: Scandalous! To put down—in limp parody of Fifties mandarinism—the core concerns of human society and enterprise as issues of convenience, and to find reality only in your chaos of intimate particulars, this babble of random and cagy candor sliding in slippery, unconscionable fashion from point to misremembered point—*aaargggh!* The title of this opus should be *Self-Serving. Self-Promotion.* One more slyly aggressive tome that the poor dear librarians think they have to buy. One more egotistical tax upon the stifling bookstores and groaning forests. You have your nerve, whining about the whale and the buffalo and how you and your alphabet blocks rose above dog eat dog.

No argument. I am weary of *Self-Consciousness.* What I have written here discomfits me: it is indiscreet and yet inaccurate, a greedy squandering of a life's minute-by-minute savings, a careless provisional raid upon the abyss of being. Fiction, which does not pretend to be true, is much truer. This stuff is embarrassing. The reviewers will jump all over it. I think I'll save myself a peck of trouble and not publish.

SELF: Oh, go ahead. It was written, after all, only by Updike; it has nothing to do with *me.*

About the Contributors

LEE K. ABBOTT has written four collections of short stories, most recently *Dreams of Distant Lives* (Putnam).

ANN ARENSBERG is the author of two novels—*Sister Wolf*, winner of the 1981 American Book Award for best first novel, and *Group Sex*, published in 1986 by Knopf. She lives with her husband in New York City and Salisbury, Connecticut.

NICHOLSON BAKER was born in 1957 and grew up in Rochester, New York. His work has appeared in *The Atlantic* and *The New Yorker*. He is the author of *The Mezzanine* (1988) and *Room Temperature* (1990), both novels. He lives in Mt. Morris, New York, with his wife and daughter.

JONATHAN BAUMBACH is the author of nine books of fiction, including, *Reruns*, *Babble*, *A Man to Conjure With*, and the recently published *Separate Hours*. His stories have been anthologized in *O. Henry Prize Stories*, *Best American Short Stories*, and *The Best of Tri-Quarterly*, among other collections.

MADISON SMARTT BELL is the author of five novels, most recently *Soldier's Joy*. Born and raised in Tennessee, he has lived in New York and in London and now lives in Baltimore, Maryland. He has taught in various creative writing programs, including the Iowa Writers' Workshop, and currently teaches at Goucher College, along with his wife, the poet Elizabeth Spires. His second collection of short stories, *Barking Man*, was published by Ticknor & Fields in 1990.

PETER BENCHLEY is the author of the novels *Jaws*, *The Deep*, *The Island*, *The Girl & The Sea of Cortez*, *Q Clearance*, and, most recently, *Rummers*. He has also been a speechwriter and a journalist, writing for *Newsweek* and *National Geographic*.

HAROLD BLOOM is the Sterling Professor of Humanities at Yale University and the Berg Professor of English at New York University. Among his recent works are: *Poetics of Influence: New and Selected Criticism*, *Ruin the Sacred Truths*, *The Book of J*, translated by David Rosenberg and interpreted by Harold Bloom, and *The American Religion*.

ROY BLOUNT, JR., is the author of ten books, including *Crackers*; *Now, Where Were We?*; and *First Hubby*. He is a contributing editor of *The Atlantic* and composes a monthly crossword puzzle-cum-essay in *Spy*.

ROBERT BLY is a poet, an editor, and a translator. He was awarded the National Book Award in 1968 for his volume of poetry *The Light Around the Body.* Recent publications include *Loving a Woman in Two Worlds* (Doubleday, 1985) and *Selected Poems* (Harper & Row, 1986). He was born in Minnesota where he currently resides.

JANE BOWLES was born in 1917 in New York City. In 1937 she met Paul Bowles and they were married in 1938. Her works include the novel *Two Serious Ladies,* published in 1942, a play, *In the Summer House,* published in 1954, and a collection of stories, *Plain Pleasures,* published in 1966. She suffered a stroke in Tangier in 1957 and was in ill health for much of the rest of her life until she died in Malaga, Spain, in 1973.

T. CORAGHESSAN BOYLE is the author of three story collections—*Descent of Man* (1979); *Greasy Lake* (1985); and *If the River Was Whiskey* (1989) and four novels—*Water Music* (1982); *Budding Prospects* (1984); *World's End* (1987) and *East Is East* (1990). He lives in Los Angeles.

KATE BRAVERMAN is a novelist and poet living in Los Angeles. She is the author of two novels, *Lithium for Media* and *Palm Latitudes,* and a collection of stories, *Squandering the Blue.*

HAROLD BRODKEY is a frequent contributor to *The New Yorker.* His stories have also appeared in *Esquire, MS.,* and *American Review.* His published collections include *First Love and Other Sorrows* and *Stories in an Almost Classical Mode.*

FREDERICK BUSCH's recent books are the story collection *Absent Friends* (Knopf, 1989), the novel *War Babies* (New Directions, 1989) and the novel from which his outtake comes, *Harry and Catherine,* published by Knopf in March, 1990.

ROBERT OLEN BUTLER has published six novels since 1981, most recently *The Deuce,* published in the fall of 1989 by Simon & Schuster. He was awarded a Tu Do Chinh Kien Award, in its inception year, by the Vietnam Veterans of America, an award given to a Vietnam veteran for "outstanding contributions to American culture." Mr. Butler teaches creative writing at McNeese State University, Lake Charles, Louisiana.

HAYDEN CARRUTH is a professor in the Graduate Creative Writing Program at Syracuse University. He has published twenty-six books, chiefly of poetry but including also a novel, three books of criticism, and two anthologies. His most recent books are *The Selected Poetry of Hayden Carruth* (1986) and *Tell Me Again How the White Heron Rises and Flies Across the Nacreous River at Twilight Toward the Distant Islands* (1989). He has been editor of *Poetry,* poetry editor of *Harper's,* and for twenty years an advisory editor of *The Hudson Review.* He has been appointed a Senior Fellow by the National Endowment for the Arts in Washington, D.C.

XAM CARTIER is the author of *Be-Bop, Re-Bop,* a novel. She is an Assistant Professor at San Francisco State University and writer-in-residence at the San Francisco Art Commission's Western Additional Cultural Center, where she leads the Black Words Workshop. She has also written for film, television, and the stage. Her second novel will be *A Void Dance.*

FRED CHAPPELL teaches English at the University of Greensboro, North Carolina. His new volume of poems is *First and Last Words* (L.S.U. Press) and *Brighten the Corner Where You Are*, a novel from St. Martin's Press.

AMY CLAMPITT was born and brought up in rural Iowa, graduated from Grinnell College, and has since lived mainly in New York City. Her poems began appearing in magazines in 1978, and her first full-length collection, *The Kingfisher*, in 1983, was followed by *What the Light Was Like*, *Archaic Figure*, and *Westward*. In February 1989 her play about the Wordsworth family, an outtake from which appears in this book, was given a staged reading by The Poets' Theatre at the Lyric Stage in Boston.

ROBERT COOVER's first novel, *The Origin of the Brunists*, won the William Faulkner Award in 1966. His subsequent novels include: *The Universal Baseball Association Inc., J. Henry Waugh, Prop.*; *The Public Burning, A Political Fable*; *Spanking the Maid*; *Gerald's Party*; and *Whatever Happened to Gloomy Gus of the Chicago Bears?* He is also the author of the *Pricksongs & Descants* and *A Night at the Movies*—both collections of short fiction. In 1987 Coover was awarded the Rea Prize for the Short Story. He lives with his wife in Providence, Rhode Island, and teaches at Brown University.

ALFRED CORN is the author of five books of poetry, the most recent *The West Door*, and a collection of essays, *The Metamorphoses of Metaphor*, all published by Viking Penguin. He has won several awards, including the NEA, the Guggenheim, an award in literature from the Academy and Institute of Arts and Letters, and a fellowship from the Academy of American Poets.

E. E. CUMMINGS was born in 1894 in Cambridge, Massachusetts, and educated at Harvard University. While in France during World War I as a member of a volunteer ambulance corps, he was imprisoned in a military concentration camp for three months on a false charge of treason. This experience was the basis of his novel, *The Enormous Room*, published in 1922. His first volume of poetry, *Tulips and Chimneys* was published in 1923, followed by fifteen other books of poetry over the course of his life. A book of autobiographical essays, *i: six nonlectures* was published in 1953. He died in 1962.

DEBBIE CYMBALISTA grew up in Milan and Geneva and is the author of *Danger*, a collection of short stories. She has studied experimental psychology at Princeton University and at N.Y.U. and has an M.B.A. from Columbia University. She lives in Manhattan where she is a consultant with a marketing and political research firm. She is currently at work on her first novel.

PETER DE VRIES is the author of over twenty novels, including, *Consenting Adults, Sauce for the Goose, Slouching Towards Kalamazoo*, and *The Prick of Noon*.

ANNIE DILLARD is the author of 8 books, including *Holy the Firm, An American Childhood, Teaching a Stone to Talk*, and most recently *The Writing Life*.

MICHAEL DRINKARD was educated at the University of California, Santa Cruz, where he studied Attic Greek, and at Columbia University, where he received a Transatlantic/Henfield award for fiction. *Green Bananas,* published in 1989 by Knopf, is his first novel.

JILL EISENSTADT was educated at Bennington College and Columbia University. She is the author of two novels, both published by Knopf, *From Rockaway* and *Kiss Out.*

LAWRENCE FERLINGHETTI is a poet, an editor, and the proprietor of the City Lights Bookshop in San Francisco and the publisher of City Lights Books.

EDWARD FIELD's most recent book is *New and Selected Poems* (Sheep Meadow Press, 1988). He has recently edited a selection of stories by the late Alfred Chester, *Head of a Sad Angel,* for Black Sparrow Press. He is the recipient of a Lamont Poetry Prize, the Shelley Memorial Award and a Prix de Rome from the Academy of Arts and Letters. Under the pseudonym Bruce Elliot, Mr. Field also collaborates with Neil Derrick in writing popular fiction for some of New York's largest paperback publishers.

F. SCOTT FITZGERALD was born in 1896 in St. Paul, Minnesota. He was educated at Princeton University, but left before graduating to join the army. While stationed in Montgomery, Alabama, he met and married Zelda Sayre. His first novel, *This Side of Paradise,* was published in 1920 when he was only twenty-four years old, to great critical and popular success. Among his collections of stories are *The Beautiful and the Damned* (1922) and *Tales of the Jazz Age* (1922). Among his novels are *The Great Gatsby* (1925), *Tender Is the Night* (1934), and the unfinished *The Last Tycoon* (1941), published after his death in 1940.

FRANK GANNON's pieces appear regularly in *The New Yorker, Gentleman's Quarterly,* and *Southern Magazine.* He is a graduate of the University of Georgia and lives in Demorest, Georgia. Among his humor collections are *Yo, Poe,* and *Vanna Karenina.*

VERONICA GENG is a regular contributor to *The New Yorker.* She is the author of *Partners* (1984) and *Love Trouble Is My Business* (1988), both published by Harper & Row.

ALLEN GINSBERG's signal poem, "Howl," overcame censorship to become one of the most widely read poems of the century. Crowned Prague May King in 1965, then expelled by Czech police and simultaneously placed on the FBI's Dangerous Security List, Ginsberg traveled to and taught in the People's Republic of China, the Soviet Union, Scandinavia, and Eastern Europe, where he received Yugoslavia's Struga Poetry Festival Golden Wreath in 1986. He is a member of the American Institute of Arts and Letters and cofounder of the Jack Kerouac School of Disembodied Poetics at the Naropa Institute, the first accredited Buddhist college in the Western world. He is currently Distinguished Professor at Brooklyn College. He is the author of *Collected Poems 1947–1980* (Harper & Row, 1984), *White Shroud Poems 1980–1985* (Harper & Row, 1985), *Howl, Annotated* (Harper & Row, 1986).

LOUISE GLÜCK's books include *Descending Figure, The House On Marshland, Firstborn,* and *Ararat,* all published by Ecco Press.

ALLAN GURGANUS's short fiction has appeared in *Harper's, The Atlantic, Granta, Antaeus, The Paris Review, The New Yorker,* and elsewhere. He has won many awards including two grants from the National Endowment. He is the author of *Oldest Living Confederate Widow Tells All,* published by Knopf in the fall of 1989. Mr. Gurganus has just completed, *White People,* a collection of stories and novellas that Knopf will present in January of 1991. He lives in Manhattan and in Chapel Hill, North Carolina.

MARILYN HACKER is the author of six books of poetry, most recently *Going Back to the River* (Random House, 1990) and *Love, Death and the Changing of the Seasons,* a verse novel (Arbor House, 1986). She received the National Book Award in poetry in 1975 for *Presentation Piece.*

PAMELA WHITE HADAS is the author of *Beside Herself: Pocahontas to Patty Hearst,* a collection of dramatic monologues, *Designing Women: Portraits and Poems,* and *In Light of Genesis.*

RACHEL HADAS's fifth and most recent book, *Living in Time,* which consists of essays/memoirs wrapped around a long poem, was published in the fall of 1990 by Rutgers University Press.

DANIEL HALPERN was born in Syracuse, New York, in 1945. He is the author of six collections of poetry, including *Tango, Seasonal Rights,* and *Life Among Others,* all published by Viking Penguin, and is editor of *Antaeus* and the Ecco Press. He has also edited *The American Poetry Anthology* (Avon, 1975), *The Art of the Tale: An International Anthology of Short Stories* (Viking Penguin, 1986), *Writers on Artists* and *On Nature,* both from North Point Press.

JIM HARRISON is the author of more than a half dozen collections of poetry, including *Returning to Earth* and *Selected Poems.* Among his books of fiction are the novels *Wolf: A False Memoir, A Good Day to Die, Farmer, Warlock, Sundog,* and *Dalva,* and two novella collections, *Legends of the Fall* and *Sunset Limited.* He has also written several screenplays.

SHELBY HEARON was born in Marion, Kentucky, lived for many years in Texas, and now makes her home in Westchester County, New York, with her husband, philosopher Bill Lucas. She was the recipient of an Ingram Merrill grant in 1987, a National Endowment for the Arts Creative Writing Fellowship in 1983, and the John Simon Guggenheim Memorial Fellowship for Fiction in 1982, and has five times won the NEA/PEN Syndication Short Story Prize and twice the Texas Institute of Letters best novel award. Her most recent book is *Owning Jolene,* a novel.

OSCAR HIJUELOS is the author of two novels, *Our House In the Last World* (1985) and *The Mambo Kings Play Songs of Love* (1989), winner of the 1990 Pulitzer Prize for Fiction. He lives in New York City.

EDWARD HOAGLAND is the author of four novels, two travel books and six collections of essays, most recently, *Heart's Desire.*

JOHN HOLLANDER's most recent book of poetry is *Harp Lake* (Knopf); *Melodi-*

ous Guile, a study of poetic language, appeared the same year, and a new and expanded edition of *Rhyme's Reason* has recently been published by Yale University Press. He has received the Bollingen Prize and the Levinson Award, and is currently A. Bartlett Giamatti Professor of English at Yale.

DAVID IGNATOW is the author of fourteen volumes of poetry and prose, including *New and Collected Poems: 1970–85* and *The One in the Many: A Poet's Memoirs* (1988). He was the recipient of the Bollingen Prize in 1977, two Guggenheim Foundation Grants, a Rockefeller Foundation Award, and numerous other prizes and awards. He is President Emeritus of the Poetry Society of America and a senior lecturer at Columbia University.

CHARLES JOHNSON is professor of English at the University of Washington (Seattle) and fiction editor of *The Seattle Review.* He is the author of two collections of drawings, *Black Humor* and *Half-Past-Nation-Time,* the PBS educational series "Charlie's Pad," and approximately a thousand drawings in publications such as *Ebony, Jet, Black World, Players,* and *The Chicago Tribune;* and two novels, *Faith and the Good Thing* and *Oxherding Tale.* His most recent works are *Being and Race: Black Writing Since 1970,* a critical study; and *Middle Passage,* a novel (Atheneum, 1990).

DONALD JUSTICE lives in Florida. His most recent book was *The Sunset Maker* (Atheneum, 1978). In 1980 his *Selected Poems* was awarded the Pulitzer Prize.

JAMES KAPLAN's stories, profiles, and other writings have appeared in numerous magazines, among them *The New Yorker, Esquire, Manhattan, Inc., The New York Times Magazine, Vogue, Premiere,* and *The Atlantic.* Mr. Kaplan lives in New York with his wife and son. He is the author of *Pearl's Progress,* a novel.

KENNETH KOCH's most recent books are *One Thousand Avant-Garde Plays* (Knopf, 1988), *Seasons on Earth* (Viking, 1988), *On the Edge* (Viking, 1986), and *Selected Poems* (Random House, 1985). His opera (music by Scott Wheeler) *The Construction of Boston* was produced in Boston in 1990. Among plays produced in New York are: *The Red Robins, The New Diana, A Change of Hearts, Bertha,* and *George Washington Crossing the Delaware.* Kenneth Koch lives in New York and teaches at Columbia University.

MAXINE KUMIN's outtake is from notes which gave rise to several of the poems in *The Long Approach* (Viking, 1985). Since then, Viking published another collection of poems, *Nurture* (Penguin paperback) and a collection of country essays, *In Deep* (Beacon Press paperback). She lives on a farm in New Hampshire where she and her husband raise horses.

ELMORE LEONARD is the author of over twenty novels, among them, *Mr. Majestyk, Fifty-Two Pick-Up, Stick, La Brava, Killshot,* and *Get Shorty,* and several screenplays, including adaptations of his own work. He lives with his wife in Birmingham, Michigan.

PHILIP LEVINE is preparing his fifteenth book of poetry for publication by Knopf; the working title is *What Work Is.* He lives in Fresno, California, and is currently teaching poetry writing at Fresno State. His awards include the National Book Critics Circle Award, the American Book Award, and the Ruth Lilly Poetry Prize awarded by *Poetry* and the American Council for the Arts "in recognition of outstanding poetic achievement."

GORDON LISH is an editor at Alfred A. Knopf. He was formerly the fiction editor at *Esquire* and is the founder and editor of *The Quarterly.* Among his novels are *Dear Mr. Capote* (1983), *Peru* (1985), and *Extravaganza: A Joke Book* (1989). Among his collections of stories are *What I Know So Far* (1984) and *Mourner at the Door* (1988).

PHILLIP LOPATE is the author of two collections of essays, *Bachelorhood* and *Against Joie de Vivre*; two novels, *Confessions of Summer*, and *The Rug Merchant*, two collections of poetry, and an account of his experiences teaching writing in the New York City Public Schools, *Being with Children.* He is a recipient of Guggenheim and National Endowment for the Arts fellowships. Mr. Lopate teaches in the graduate writing programs at the University of Houston and Columbia University.

THOMAS LUX's most recent book is *The Drowned River* (Houghton Mifflin). A recent Guggenheim Fellow, he teaches at Sarah Lawrence College.

CLEOPATRA MATHIS was born and raised in Ruston, Louisiana. She is the author of three books of poems, *Aerial View of Louisiana* (1980), *The Bottom Land* (1983), and *The Center for Cold Weather* (1989), all published by the Sheep Meadow Press. She lives in Hanover, New Hampshire, where she is an associate professor of English and the director of the Creative Writing Program at Dartmouth College.

WILLIAM MATTHEWS is the author of eight books of poems, most recently *Blues If You Want* (Houghton Mifflin, 1989); and one of essays, *Curiosities* (University of Michigan Press, 1989). He is Professor of English at City College in New York.

LEONARD MICHAELS was born in New York City in 1935. He is the author of *Going Places* (stories), *I Would Have Saved Them If I Could* (stories), *The Men's Club* (a novel), and *Shuffle* (fiction).

SUSAN MINOT is the author of a novel, *Monkeys* (1986), awarded the Prix Femina Etranger in 1987, and *Lust and Other Stories* (1989). Her stories have appeared in *The New Yorker, Harper's,* and other journals and have been included in *The Best American Short Stories* and the O. Henry Prize volumes.

HOWARD NEMEROV is the Poet Laureate of the United States. His publications include *Sentences* and *Inside the Onion* (University of Chicago, 1980, 1984), and *Figures of Thought* (Godine, 1978). His *Collected Poems* (1977) won both the Pulitzer Prize and the National Book Award. He has also published several novels and short stories and several books of criticism, most recently *New and Selected Essays* (1985).

HUGH NISSENSON has published two collections of short stories: *A Pile of Stones* and *In the Reign of Peace*. He has also published a nonfiction book and two novels, one of which, *The Tree 6F 35FEO* was nominated for the American Book Award. His most recent book is *The Elephant and My Jewish Problem: Selected Stories and Journals 1957–1987*.

JOYCE CAROL OATES is the author most recently of *The Time Traveller* (poems), and *Because It Is Bitter, and Because It Is My Heart* (novel).

SHARON OLDS's three collections of poetry are: *Satan Days, The Dead and the Living,* and *The Gold Cell.* She is the head of New York University's Graduate Writing Program and is a National Book Critics Circle Award Winner.

TOBY OLSON has published numerous books of poetry and five novels, the most recent of which, *Dorit in Lesbos,* appeared from Linden/Simon & Schuster in 1990. He received the PEN/Faulkner Award for his novel *Seaview* in 1983 and is the recipient of Guggenheim, Rockefeller, and NEA fellowships. He currently lives in Philadelphia and teaches English at Temple University.

LINDA PASTAN is the author of several collections of poetry, among them *A Perfect Circle of Sun, The Five Stages of Grief, PM/AM: New and Selected Poems, A Fraction of Darkness,* and *The Imperfect Paradise.*

MOLLY PEACOCK was born in Buffalo, New York, in 1947. She has published three collections of poetry, *And Live Apart* (University of Missouri Press, 1980), *Raw Heaven* (Random House, 1984), and *Take Heart* (Random House, 1989). Ms. Peacock has been the recipient of two Fellowships from the Ingram Merrill Foundation and two from the New York Foundation for the Arts. She lives in New York City, and serves as President of the Poetry Society of America.

STANLEY PLUMLY's most recent book of poetry is *Boy on the Step* (Ecco/ Norton, 1989). He has also written two other volumes of poetry, *Out-of-Body Travel,* and *Summer Celestial,* all published by Ecco Press.

ISHMAEL REED is a novelist, poet, and playwright. Among his novels are *The Free-Lance Pallbearers* (1967), *Mumbo Jumbo* (1972), *Flight to Canada* (1976), and *The Terrible Twos* (1982). His verse collections include *Conjure* (1972) and *Shrovetide in Old New Orleans* (1978).

MARY ELSIE ROBERTSON was born and raised in Charleston, Arkansas. She is the author of the novels *Family Life; Speak, Angel; The Clearing; After Freud;* and *What I Have to Tell You.* She teaches in the MFA program for writers at Warren Wilson College and at the University of Arizona and lives in upstate New York.

THEODORE ROETHKE was born in Saginaw, Michigan in 1908. His first volume of poetry, *Open House,* was published in 1941. He received the Pulitzer Prize in 1954 for his *Collected Poems* and a Bollingen Prize in 1958 for *Words for the Wind.* He died in 1963. Posthumously published, *The Far Field,* won the National Book Award in 1965.

MAY SARTON is the author of nineteen novels and numerous volumes of poetry and nonfiction. Her most recent novel is *The Education of Harriet*

Hatfield and her most recent book of poems is *The Silence Now*, both published by W. W. Norton. She lives in York, Maine.

DELMORE SCHWARTZ was born in 1913. He published his first book, *In Dreams Begin Responsibilities* to critical acclaim at the age of twenty-five. In 1959 he became the youngest poet to be awarded the Bollingen Prize in Poetry, for *Summer Knowledge: New and Selected Poems*. He died in 1966.

ANNE SEXTON was born in Newton, Massachusetts, in 1928. Her first volume of poetry, *To Bedlam and Part Way Back* was published in 1960. In 1966 she won the Pulitzer Prize for *Live or Die*. She died in 1974.

ALIX KATES SHULMAN has written four novels published by Knopf: *Memoirs of an Ex-Prom Queen, Burning Questions, On the Stroll,* and *In Every Woman's Life . . . ,* as well as two books on Emma Goldman, three books for children, and numerous stories and essays. She has been a visiting artist at the American Academy in Rome and has received a National Endowment for the Arts Fellowship in fiction. She has taught writing and literature at New York University, Yale, University of Southern Maine, and the University of Colorado, Boulder. Much of the year she lives on an island off the coast of Maine.

CHARLES SIMIC was born in Yugoslavia in 1938. Among his volumes of verse are: *What the Grass Says* (1967), *Somewhere Among Us a Stone Is Taking Notes* (1969), *Dismantling the Silence* (1971), *Return to a Place Lit by a Glass of Milk* (1974), *Charon's Cosmology* (1977), *Utopia and Vicinity: Poems 1967–1982* (1983), and *Unending Blues:* Poems (1986). He was awarded the 1990 Pulitzer Prize for *The World Doesn't End*.

MONA SIMPSON is the author of a novel, *Anywhere But Here,* and a past recipient of a National Endowment of the Arts Fellowship, a Kellogg National Fellowship, and a Whiting Writers' Award.

ISAAC BASHEVIS SINGER writes novels, short stories, children's books, and criticism in the Yiddish language. He was born in Poland in 1904 and emigrated to the United States in 1935. Among his novels are: *The Family Moskat* (1950), *Satan in Goray* (1955), *The Magician of Lublin* (1960), *The Slave* (1962), *Enemies, a Love Story* (1966, translated 1972), and *Shosha* (1978). Among his collections of stories are: *Gimpel the Fool* (1957), *The Spinoza of Market Street* (1961), *Old Love* (1979), and *The Image* (1985). Among the volumes of his memoirs are: *In My Father's Court* (1956, translated 1966), *Lost in America* (1981), *The Golem* (1982), and *Love and Exile* (1984). He was awarded the Nobel Prize for Literature in 1978.

DAVE SMITH is the author of several volumes of poetry, among them *The Roundhouse Voices: Selected and New Poems* and *Cuba Nights,* and two novels, *Onliness* and *Southern Delights.* He is also the editor of the *Morrow Anthology of Younger American Poets.*

W. D. SNODGRASS's first book of poetry, *Heart's Needle* (1959), was awarded a Pulitzer Prize. Other volumes of verse include *After Experience* (1970) and *Selected Poems 1957–1987* (1988).

SCOTT SOMMER is the author of the novels *Nearing's Grace*, *The Last Resort*, *Hazzard's Head*, and *Still Lives*, as well as *Lifetime*, a collection of stories and novellas. A graduate of Ohio Wesleyan and Cornell Universities, he lives in New York City.

GILBERT SORRENTINO was born in Brooklyn, New York, in 1929, and studied English Literature at Brooklyn College. The recipient of a Guggenheim Fellowship in 1973, he is the author of *Imaginative Qualities of Actual Things*, *Mulligan Stew*, *Odd Number*, *Something Said: Essays*, and *Blue Pastoral*, as well as numerous other works of fiction and poetry.

ELIZABETH SPIRES was born in Lancaster, Ohio, in 1952. She is the author of three collections of poetry: *Globe* (Wesleyan, 1981), *Swan's Island* (Holt, 1985), and *Annonciade* (Viking Penguin, 1989). She lives in Baltimore and teaches at Goucher College and in the Writing Seminars at Johns Hopkins. Her poems have been anthologized in *The Morrow Anthology of Younger American Poets*, *The Direction of Poetry*, and *Best American Poems, 1989*.

WILLIAM STAFFORD was born in Hutchinson, Kansas, in 1914. He has had numerous collections of poetry and prose books published over the years. His most recent work includes *Writing the World* (Alembic Press, 1988), *A Scripture of Leaves* (Brethren Press, 1989), and *Fin, Feather, Fur* (Honeybrook Press, 1989).

SHARON SHEEHE STARK is the author of a collection of stories, *The Dealer's Yard*, and a novel, *A Wrestling Season*, both from William Morrow. Her stories have twice been included in *Best American Short Stories* (1983 and 1985). A recent recipient of both NEA and Guggenheim fellowships, she makes her home in Lenhartsville, Pennsylvania.

DANIEL STERN is the author of nine novels, a play, and numerous essays and short stories. He has been, at various times in his career, a professional cellist, a professor at Wesleyan University, and the head of advertising for a television network and a major motion picture company. He is the Director of Humanities at the 92nd Street YMHA in New York, and his collection of short stories, *Twice Told Tales*, was published by Paris Review Editions in 1989.

RICHARD STERN is the author of many works of fiction, including *Other Men's Daughters*, *Natural Shocks*, *A Father's Words*, and *Noble Rot: Stories 1949–88*, published by the Grove Press in 1989. He is a professor of English at the University of Chicago.

MAY SWENSON's first volume of poetry, *A Cage of Spines*, was published in 1958. Later works include *New and Selected Things Taking Place* and *In Other Words*. She died in 1989.

ELIZABETH TALLENT's short stories have appeared recently in *The New Yorker*, *Grand Street*, and *The Mississippi Review*. Her books include *In Constant Flight* and *Time with Children* (stories), and the novel *Museum Pieces*. She spends time in northern California and in New Mexico.

AMY TAN was born in Oakland, California in 1952, two-and-a-half years after her parents immigrated to the United States. *The Joy Luck Club* is her first novel. She lives in San Francisco with her husband.

JAMES TATE was born and raised in Kansas City, Missouri. His first book of poetry, *The Lost Pilot*, won the Yale Series of Younger Poets Award in 1967. Since then he has published several other volumes of poetry, including: *The Oblivion Ha-Ha, Hints to Pilgrims, Absences, Hottentot Ossuary, Viper Jazz, Riven Doggeries,* and *Reckoner*. He has lived in Sweden, Ireland, and Spain, and has taught at the University of California, Berkley, Columbia University, and the University of Massachusetts.

DYLAN THOMAS published his first volume of poetry, *Eighteen Poems,* in 1934 at the age of twenty. Through public readings and work on radio plays such as *Under Milk Wood,* Thomas achieved a wide popularity in both the British Isles and the United States. His *Collected Poems* was published in 1952. He died in New York City in 1953 at the age of thirty-nine.

JOHN UPDIKE was born in 1932, in Shillington, Pennsylvania. He graduated from Harvard College, worked for *The New Yorker* as a reporter, and moved to Massachusetts in 1957. He is the father of four children and the author of over thirty books, including fourteen novels.

WILLIAM T. VOLLMANN's first book, *You Bright and Risen Angels,* is represented in this anthology. *The Rainbow Stories* deals with war heroes, lovers, and Nazi skinheads. *The Ice-Shiot* (Deutsch and Viking, 1990) is the first book in a septology recounting the history of our continent over the past thousand years. *Whores for Gloria* (Picador, 1991) describes the lives of street prostitutes in San Francisco. Three other books are in progress. Vollmann also builds his own books in collaboration with other artists and engineers, using such materials as steel, mirror-glass, snake bones, and whore-hair.

ANNE WALDMAN has published ten books of poetry, most recently *Helping the Dreamer: New and Selected Poems* (Coffee House Press, 1989), and edited several anthologies and is well-known for her readings and performances. She teaches full time at the Naropa Institute in Boulder, Colorado, where she is director of the writing program of the Jack Kerouac School of Disembodied Poetics.

PAUL WEST's most recent novels are *Rat Man of Paris, The Place in Flowers Where Pollen Rests,* and *Lord Byron's Doctor*. He received an Arts and Letters Award from the American Academy and Institute of Arts and Letters in 1985. His new novel, due from Random House in 1990, will be about Jack the Ripper.

RICHARD WILBUR received the Pulitzer Prize and *The Los Angeles Times* Book Award for his *New and Collected Poems,* 1988. The stanza here included was dropped from the poem "Castles and Distances," which first appeared in *Ceremony and Other Poems,* 1950.

NANCY WILLARD has published over twenty books: poetry, novels, plays, critical essays, and children's books. Titles include *A Visit to William*

Blake's Inn: Poems for Innocent and Experienced Travelers (winner of the Newberry Award), *Angel in the Parlor: Five Stories and Eight Essays,* the novel *Things Invisible to See, The Firebrat* (fantasy), *The Ballad of Biddy Early* (poetry), and a play, *East of the Sun, West of the Moon.* She has been awarded NEA fellowships in fiction and poetry.

LARRY WOIWODE's fiction has appeared in *The Atlantic, Esquire, Harper's, The New Yorker, Paris Review,* and many other publications, and has been translated into a dozen languages. His first novel received the William Faulkner Foundation Award and his second, *Beyond the Bedroom Wall,* was nominated for both the National Book Award and the National Book Critics Circle Award. In 1980 he received an Award in Literature from the American Academy and Institute of Arts and Letters. He has served as the director of the Creative Writing Program at SUNY-Binghamton, and currently lives in North Dakota with his wife and children.

THOMAS WOLFE was born in Asheville, North Carolina, in 1900. He was educated at the University of North Carolina and at Harvard. Two of his novels, *Look Homeward, Angel* and *Of Time and the River,* and a collection of stories, *From Death to Morning,* were published in his lifetime. His last two novels, *The Web and The Rock* and *You Can't Go Home Again,* were assembled from an eight-foot-high pile of manuscript pages he left behind after he died in 1938.

MEG WOLITZER is the author of three novels, *Sleepwalking, Hidden Pictures,* and *This Is Your Life.* She lives in New York City.

KIM WOZENCRAFT is a former undercover narcotics officer and the author of a novel, *Rush* (Random House, 1990). She is a graduate of Columbia University. Her work has been anthologized in *Best American Essays of 1988.* She lives in New York City.

BARRY YOURGRAU is the author of two collections of fiction, *Wearing Dad's Head* (1987) and *A Man Jumps Out of an Airplane* (1988).

Contributors